# SHADOW OF THE SENDING

## BOOK TWO OF THE NYXTERIA

### A.M. KAY

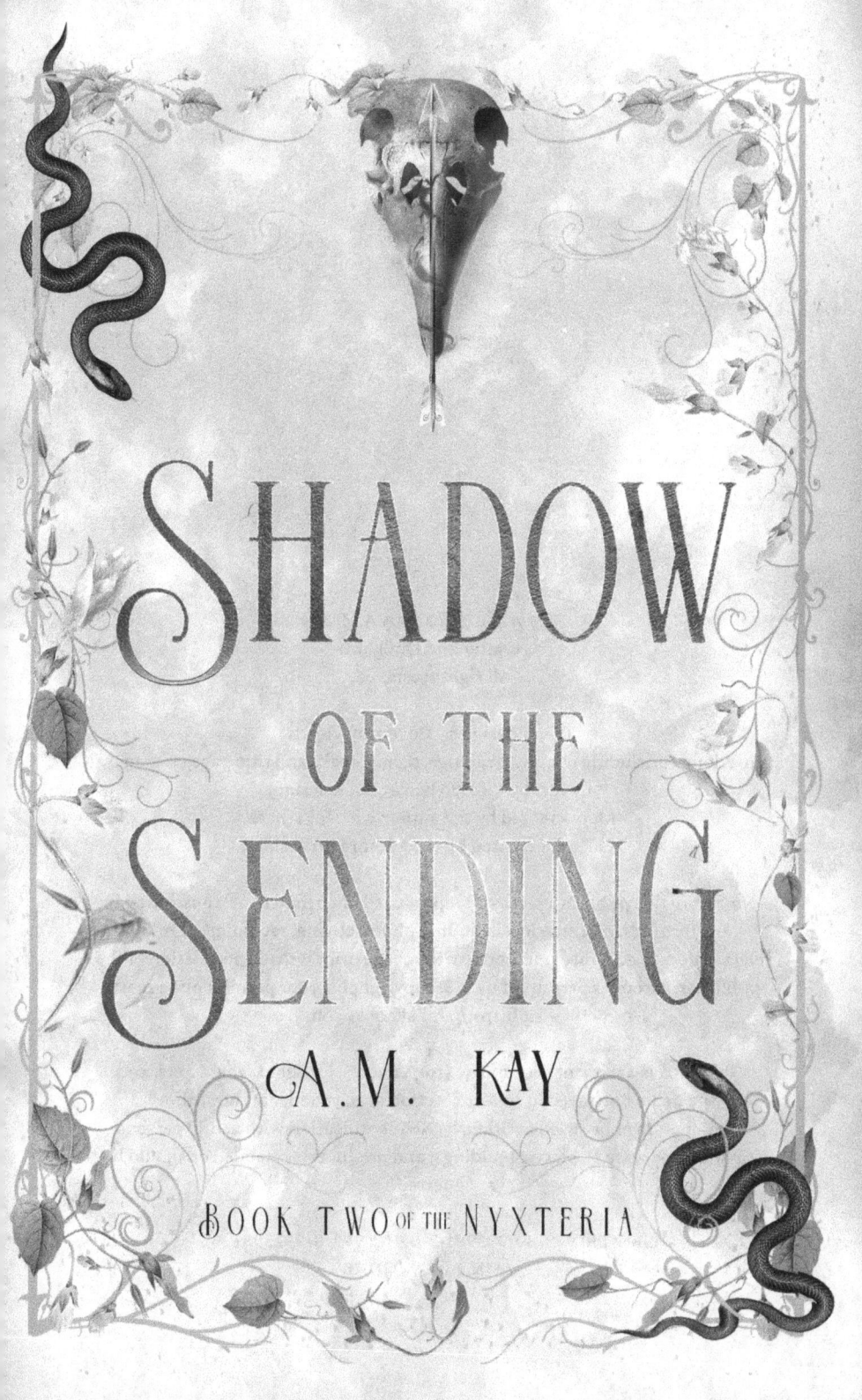

# SHADOW
## OF THE
## SENDING

### A.M. KAY

BOOK TWO OF THE NYXTERIA

Copyright © 2025 by A.M. Kay
Canter and Quill LLC
All rights reserved.

Cover design by Covers by Violet.
Interior art including chapter headings, scene breaks and title page created by
Covers by Violet @violet.book.design.
Maps created by the author with Inkarnate.
Calendar created by the author with Canva.

No part of this publication may be reproduced, distributed, or transmitted in
any form or by any means, including photocopying, recording, or other
electronic or mechanical methods, without the prior written permission of the
publisher, except as permitted by U.S. copyright law. For permission requests,
visit https://amkaybooks.com.

This book is a work of fiction. The story, names, locations, characters, and
incidents portrayed in this production are a product of the author's
imagination or are used fictitiously. No identification with actual persons
(living or deceased), places, buildings, and products is intended or should be
inferred.

ISBN: PB: 979-8-9923981-2-0; HC: 979-8-9923981-3-7
ASIN: B0FP5QJNNL

*To my sisters.*

*To anyone who has ever lowered themselves.*

*Rise up.*

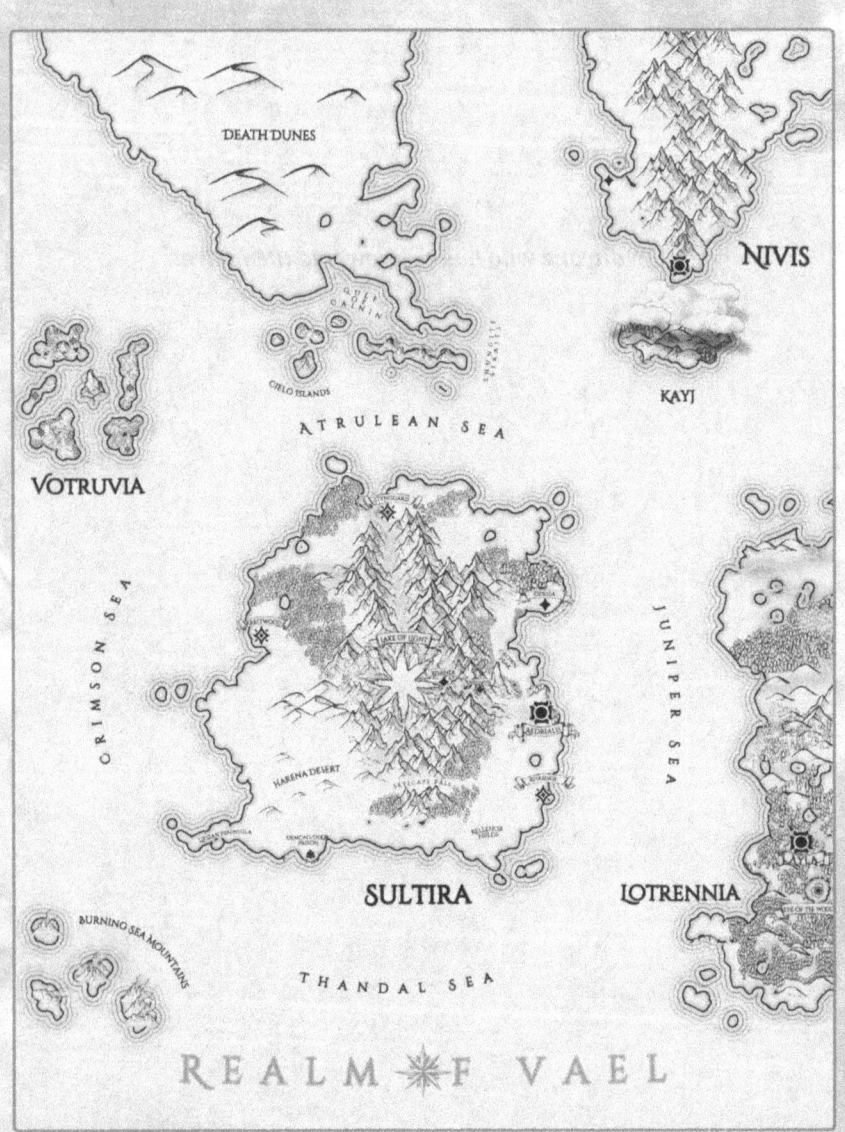

DEATH DUNES

NIVIS

KAYJ

CIELO ISLANDS

ATRULEAN SEA

VOTRUVIA

LAKE OF LIGHT

JUNIPER SEA

HARENA DESERT

SULTIRA

LOTRENNIA

BURNING SEA MOUNTAINS

THANDAL SEA

# REALM OF VAEL

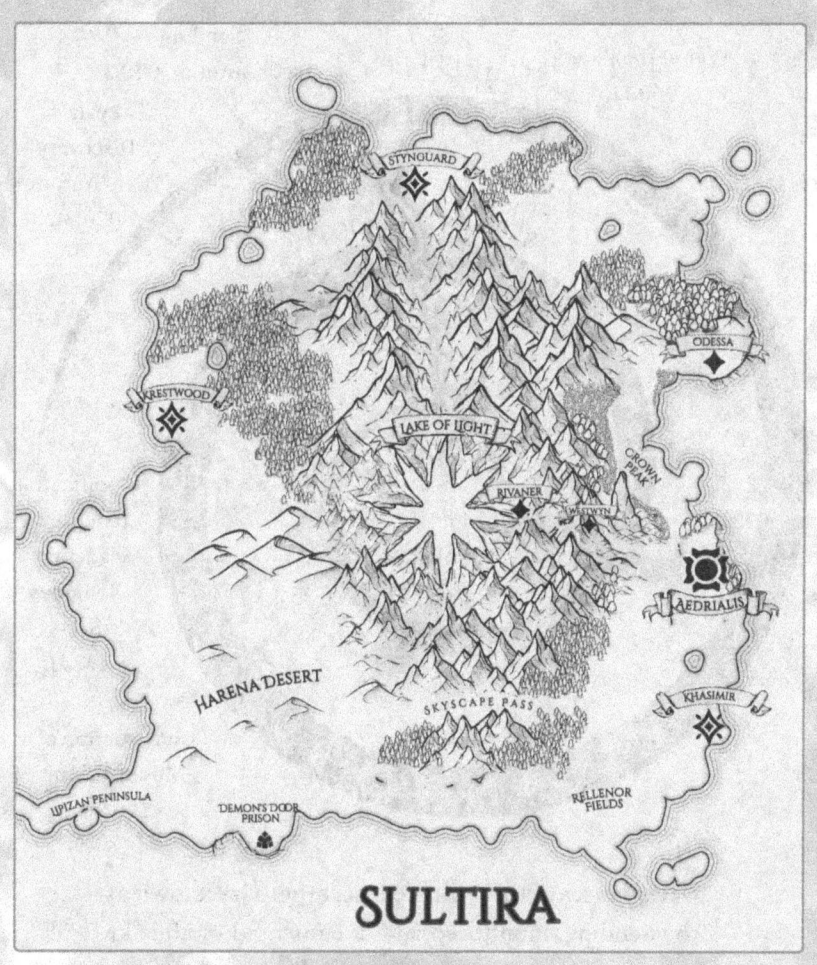

# SULTIRA

# SULTIRAN CALENDAR

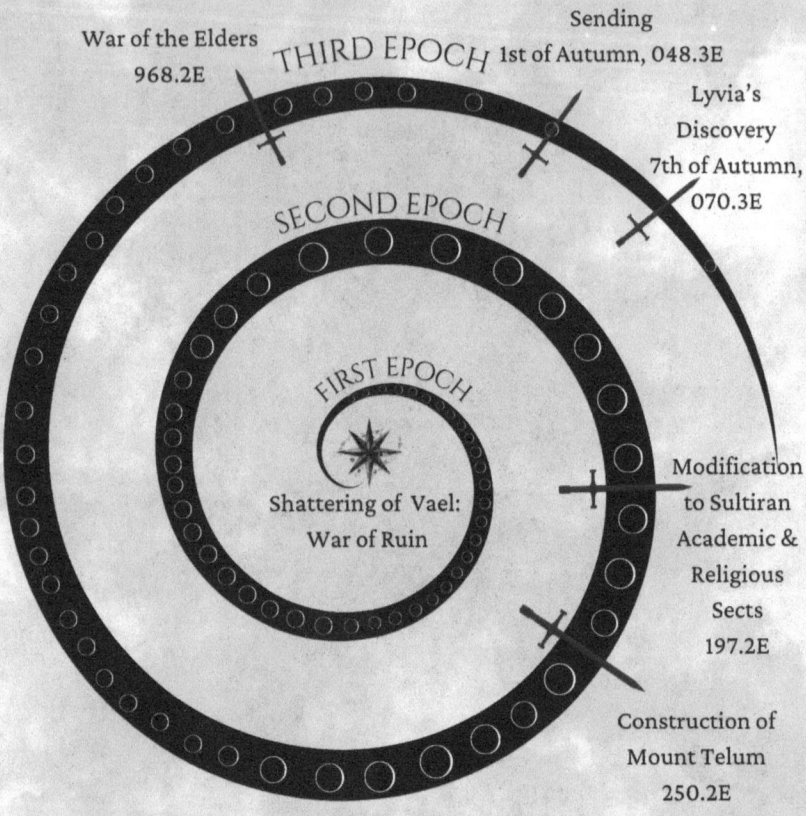

War of the Elders
968.2E

THIRD EPOCH

Sending
1st of Autumn, 048.3E

Lyvia's
Discovery
7th of Autumn,
070.3E

SECOND EPOCH

FIRST EPOCH

Shattering of Vael:
War of Ruin

Modification
to Sultiran
Academic &
Religious
Sects
197.2E

Construction of
Mount Telum
250.2E

Occurrences of the Twin Eclipse, otherwise known as
the Sending, monitored and documented by the Sky
Scholar order and marked by the following symbol:

# PRONUNCIATION GUIDE

## People:
Aeriden: AIR-rih-den
Antares: ant-AIR-eez
Astraeus: as-TRAY-us
Bayne: bane
Carina: cah-REE-nah
Daimos: DAY-mose
Drystan: DRISS-ten
Eira: EYE-rah
Enya: EN-yah
Evony: EH-vunn-ee
Ezrich: EHZ-rick
Galena: gah-LEE-nah
Isla: EYE-lah
Kellan: KELL-en
Khato: KAY-toh
Kresida: KRESS-ih-dah
Lelyth: LELL-ith
Lida: LEE-dah
Lyvia: LIV-ee-yah
Marian: MAR-ee-en
Nerissa: nerr-ISS-ah
Olienna: oh-lee-ENN-ah
Raek: RAYK
Ravindra: rah-VIN-druh
Ronan: ROE-nan
Saros: SAHR-ohss
Selvina: sell-VEE-nah
Vander: VAN-der
Vienah: vee-EHN-uh
Vulcan: VULL-can
Xenelpha: zen-ELF-uh

## Animals:
Aquila: ah-KEY-lah
Tempest: TEHM-pest
Tiberius: tie-BEER-ee-uss
Nishanth: nee-SHAHN-th

## Creatures:
Agrippa: ah-GRIH-pah
Amatohk: AH-mah-toke
Ashen: ASH-enn
Caeluma: kie-LOO-mah
Tauruk: tore-OOK

## Places:
Aedrialis: ay-dree-AL-iss
Ascendiel: ah-SEND-ee-el
Atrulean: ah-TRU-lee-en
Juniper: JOO-ni-per
Kayj: cage
Nivis: NEE-viss
Odessa: oh-DESS-ah
Pyracantha: pie-ruh-CAN-tha
Rhashtai: RAHsh-tie
Stynguard: STIN-gard
Sultira: sull-TEER-ah
Telum: tell-OOM
Thandal: THAN-dahl
Vael: vail
Votruvia: voe-TRU-vee-ah

## Bellator Powers:
Advetis: ad-VEE-tis
Aeterna: ay-TERN-ah
Celestyn: sell-ESS-tin
Obscura: obsk-YUR-ah
Palaega: pah-LAY-guh
Ramadiel: rah-MAH-dee-el
Soleia: soe-LAY-ah
Transcindiel: tran-SIN-dee-el

## Deities:
Aelius: AY-lee-us
Ganmira: gan-MEER-ah
Renova: renn-OH-vah
Tynan: TIE-nan
Sintarrak: sin-tah-ROCK

## Other:
Bellator: BELL-uh-tor
Bonscaíh: bone-SKY
Marisarma: mah-ree-SARM-ah
Maadon: MAY-don
Nyxteria: nicks-TAIR-ee-uh
Rubelline: ROO-bell-een
Sobraena: so-BRAY-nah

# A NOTE TO READERS:

*Shadow of the Sending* is an adult, high fantasy novel intended for mature readers and includes explicit content and certain dark elements that could be triggering for some readers. For a list of content warnings, please turn to the last page of this book.

# PROLOGUE
## BAYNE

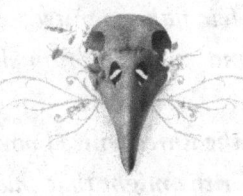

Waters of Ascendiel, Lotrennia.
Six weeks after the Battle of Odessa.

*D*eath lunged for me, its talons ripping at what remained of my jacket, the tatters hanging in long, bloody strips. A storm of black flames lashed against my shield as the creature of shadows twisted in the air, tucking its wings in tight before flaring them wide and bellowing a roar that shook what remained of the forest.

*Ash and smoke joined hands in the silent dance of death as they mingled in the air. The evidence of the battle draped across the land like a mourning veil. An angry desperation flooded my soul as Nerissa's cry ripped through the air in the distance. The grief in my sister's sob was almost enough for me to turn from the creature.*

*Pained moans and screams of terror echoed from all around, and I stole a glance up at the grating clap of a breaking branch. Heat lashed at my face, and my stomach weaved like the tree's twisting limbs as my eyes landed on the flames licking through the Living Library. I leaped as the massive branch crashed to the ground, the creature spinning out of its path and following me over a pile of charred, elven bodies.*

I had to stop this. *My eyes scanned the devastated land around me, my only companions lying lifeless in the surrounding ash and dirt.* I was the only one who could stop this.

*A bellowing rage surged forward, digging its way to the hollow of my chest where my Soleia flames ignited, an unimaginable power swelling in my palms and my vision funneling into the narrowed precision of a predator.*

*My chest heaved as the unrecognized power climbed within me, my body a mere vessel for the might that charged forward. I turned toward the creature of shadow and flame as it rose to the sky. A tightening in my chest built in pressure before the world disappeared from under me...*

My knees crashed to the stone floor of the Waters of Ascendiel, the warm water sloshing up my leathers and tunic as I heaved. I caught myself as I fell forward, staring at my reflection on the surface of the sacred pool.

My heart thundered in a panic, and my mind reeled from the vision of what awaited Lotrennia. *My kingdom.* A wave of concern drifted from where Aquila flew nearby, and I sent my own reassurance back to him as I caught my breath.

An unbending determination flooded me as I replayed the images gifted by the souls of the seers in the Waters of Ascendiel, at the feel of my own power. Where had the others been? Bodies had piled around me, and a savage dread clawed its way through my chest at not knowing who they were... I had to prepare... *I had to stop this.*

# CHAPTER ONE
## LYVIA

Pyracantha, Lotrennia.
Six weeks after the Battle of Odessa.

*Y*ou are not afraid of the dark, the shadow purred. *Let me out.*

Dulled gray irises darted between me and Ronan, unable to focus on either of us, as I reached my fingers to the milky white skin of the ashen restrained in a black web of vines. He bucked and thrashed as my hand clamped down on his gaunt, clammy shoulder.

Despite the mugginess of Lotrennia, his skin was frigid, like a sweaty body tossed into the winds of winter. The creature's stench clogged my throat, a mix of rotting meat, stale blood, and the dry, cold breath of death. My instincts screamed at me to run, but it was nothing compared to the dangerous new darkness swirling in my veins.

*Let me out.*

Strong hands gripped either side of the ashen's pallid face,

3

holding his head in place as he snapped his elongated teeth at my trembling hand.

It was Isla's idea to use contact. To touch the thing...the *man*...in front of me. She stayed behind today, often splitting her time between training me and Drystan, her protégé. I told myself it didn't bother me. Drystan needed her guidance to hone his powers and stand ready to face King Saros when we returned to Sultira. We'd need every human mage we could get.

Yet every attempt I'd made in reversing the transformation of the ashen, undoing what Dark King Daimos had done to them, had been a failure. My gut twisted under the pressure.

A company of Lotrennian soldiers had captured several of the creatures from a horde released on their shores after I'd shared my revelation with Queen Antares, Bayne, and Nerissa's aunt by marriage. I believed I could save them with the Transcindiel power hidden deep within me, though it was often lost under waves of darkness.

The Obscura roiled in my veins at the contact, bucking and thrashing as hard as the ashen in front of me, willing, *demanding* I release it. Isla had warned me about power of this magnitude, the strength it would take to control it. There had been eight Bellators. Eight powers, yet I wielded two.

I took a steadying breath, splitting my focus and strength between subduing the darkness and reaching for that thread of song-like power that allowed its Bellator to transform: *Transcindiel.*

My eyes closed as I searched, letting my mind's ear take over as I swam through a tunnel of consciousness, listening for the lilting tune.

A soft melody pricked my attention, and as I reached for it, a gut-curdling shriek pierced the air. My eyes shot open, hair standing on end. I stepped back, my hand clamping over my mouth as two freshly gnawed fingers dropped from the ashen's bloodstained lips.

"Call for a mender!" Ronan shouted as the elven guard held his bleeding hand against his chest. The elf's brown eyes were wide in dread and his mouth dropped in shock as he stared at me.

"NOW!" Ronan bellowed, moving toward the elf whose knees crashed to the dirt floor. The ex-queensguard ripped a shred of cloth off his dark blue tunic, tying a tourniquet around the elf's forearm as scenes from last year on board the *Evecta* edged into my mind.

Hand. We had to take his hand... The creatures Dark King Daimos created could spread the transforming curse with a single bite.

Ronan grunted as he pinned the guard to the ground, hollering once more for a mender. Steps shuffled from outside the room. I rushed to the guard's side, reaching for the other hand when the injured elf turned his face toward me, his brown irises lightening to a near-white as the blood drained from his face and his canines stretched into sharp fangs. His face tightened as animalistic violence surged into his being.

His pupils constricted as they landed on me, and shadows clouded my veins in preparation. His lips stretched over pale gums, and as he lurched toward me, Ronan plunged his dagger into the soft flesh beneath his chin. Guards rushed into the room as Ronan twisted the blade, with the last semblance of life drifting away from the elf's dulled eyes.

I pulled my gaze away in time to catch the glimmer of a blade slicing through the restrained ashen's neck so fast that its head sat there for a moment, balancing in place as the last bit of dull light left its once beautiful eyes. The head rolled forward, and I shuffled back as it fell to the ground with a thud.

Guilt raked at my chest. Another failure, two casualties.

The guards knelt next to their dead comrade, examining the eyes and mouth of the newly formed ashen. Their eyes slid to me in hostile accusation as they removed the body.

The guard behind me made a single, long sweep over his blade with a cloth after beheading the ashen. Purely out of habit, as the ashen had no blood circulating in their veins. Like so many, the elf avoided my eyes. Others, those who worshipped the Bellators of old, spat and cursed my name as they passed.

*Betrayer*, they hissed.

They believed Enya, the last Bellator to wield the Obscura, the power I felt so strongly, had nearly destroyed the world and the rest of the Bellators.

"I'm so sorry," I croaked. "I—"

"They know the risk, Lyvia," Ronan cut in, offering a curt nod to the guards before turning me toward the exit.

My shoulders sagged as I added another tick to the growing list of bodies that piled around me. Seven failed attempts since arriving in Lotrennia. On top of the thousands I had obliterated on the cliffs of Odessa six weeks ago.

Ronan's lips drew a hard line as he offered me a quick squeeze on the shoulder. Small, black vines slid out of the knot as the door swung open, shutting and relocking just as fast. The vines somehow knew who was allowed to pass and when.

The inescapable tangle of thorns made up Lotrennia's prison, Pyracantha. While the rest of the continent seemed all life and beauty, the prison was a thing of nightmares. Black and gray branches wound up and around the space so tightly that no light seeped its way into the maze of tunnels. Needle-like thorns covered every inch of the branches, making any misstep bloody, if not deadly.

Ronan had been wound tight since our arrival the month prior. He insisted on marching on Aedrialis by the end of spring for reasons he'd shared privately with me in Odessa. I understood the moment he told me. The need to get back, the fear, the worry. But he held it together, and the Rising forces still clung to his confidence, his calm determination.

And I'd kept his secret, from everyone except Tiberius, my winged miracle of a horse, who seemed to have almost unlimited access to myself. I could rarely keep him out without his cooperation.

And it had killed me to keep it from Bayne. He had been so busy playing a dangerous game of politics with the queen. I'd barely seen him, even before he left for the Waters of Ascendiel to search for answers on how to defeat the dark king and dethrone Saros.

If it hadn't been for the strange connection that linked us, I would have struggled to keep it together after everything that had happened in the last year. The loss, the death, the trauma...

I reached down that strange link to Bayne and slowly drew back the curtain, allowing the smallest bit of disappointment to seep through, letting him know the outcome of this most recent attempt. Was it simply a bond created from our link as Bellators? Or was there something more there? Moments later, warmth surged in response. *Comfort. Love. Forgiveness.* More than I deserved.

We were trapped here. All six hundred of us who arrived from Odessa. Negotiations with Queen Antares on the timing of our return, *how* we would even return, were constantly underway. The Juniper Sea was a death trap. Lotrennian mages had used so much power to get their forces and ours back safely to Lotrennia. The queen couldn't justify sending us back until the seas had settled.

The abrupt change in the pattern of Ganmira and Renova, our two blue moons, and the unexpected twin eclipse, left the seas in a wild, unruly state. Nobody knew how long it would take to return to normal, if ever.

And we *needed* to get back. Needed to remove King Saros from his tainted throne. Needed to stop the tribute, the vile sacrifice Saros made of his own people, sending them to the dark king, where they lived as slaves or were transformed into undead, mindless killers. We still didn't understand why he allowed it. Some deal struck long ago, the reason for which we had yet to unravel.

The terrified murmurs of the Sultirans on the tribute ship I boarded months ago often echoed in my mind as I stood before the ashen in Pyracantha. The snap of the soldiers' whips on Kayj, the dark king's forsaken island, rang in my ears as the ashen shrieked. And their faces... The slaves in the Crystal Castle, on the island of Kayj... They were there when I closed my eyes.

We had to get back.

I strode after Ronan through the dark tunnels, shuddering as I passed cell after cell. The moans of their occupants crept through the vines that imprisoned them.

The space behind my eyes ached as we stepped outside Pyracantha and were met with a blinding white light. I blinked, allowing them a moment to adjust to the bright, green forest. We were several miles southwest of Ayla, the capital of Lotrennia. Massive trees covered in mossy growth rose hundreds of feet into the air. The twitter of orange, native songbirds swelled and swooped above. My shoulders eased as we stepped away from the miles of black thorns.

A flash of bright open sky and hard air gripped my consciousness as Tiberius's view, his *senses*, merged with my own. *Casting.* That was what Bayne and Nerissa called it. Their giant seahawk, Aquila, could communicate the same way with the brother and sister Bellators. The icy breeze of Tiberius's altitude made me shiver, and the hot burn of muscles working his wings raced down my back, as if they were my own. I could see the forest in front of me, but also from above as he scanned the trees below, feeling for our bond. I cast my response, taking in my surroundings, every sense, every thought, every feeling, and sent them down the tight connection.

The bond between Bellator and caeluma was overwhelming. It was like splitting, or rather, *sharing* consciousness with another being. But Bayne had insisted Aquila wasn't a caeluma. Or if he was, he lacked some key elements.

Tiberius had become more than a mount. His soul had changed when I'd used the Transcindiel power to save us. I hadn't intended on turning him into my caeluma in those last, panicky moments as we hurtled off the cliffs of Odessa. It had been instinct, a last-ditch effort at self-preservation in the face of certain death. *And it worked.*

Ti landed nearby in a small clearing. Ebony, velvety wings tucked in tight as the massive horse made his way through the thick trees and ferns, twisting elegantly around the mossy boulders. The agrippa were enormous, but ever since Ti's transformation, he had eaten and grown and eaten some more. My thoughts drifted back to that burial chamber I'd discovered last year. Tiberius was now as large as Enya's steed.

I hopped on a boulder as I waited for Ti to approach, Ronan slowing and waiting next to me.

*You don't need a babysitter*, Ti grumbled in my mind. If he'd had a human face, it would have been drawn up in a sneer at the Rising commander. Instead, his ears flattened, and he bared his teeth as he approached. Ronan had the good sense to step back.

It had taken a month for Ti's voice to sound in my head. The shock of it sent my heart thundering as fast as his hooves. He sounded exactly as I would have imagined. Young, fearless.

Perhaps a tad reckless. The friend I'd always had, but one whose intelligence had been shut tight in a box that had slowly unlocked since his transformation. He was a different being entirely now. And the only one of his kind—a sad, lonely thought, but one that we shared.

*You'll be glad he was here after I fill you in*, I replied, my mind's voice defeated. His hooves clomped on the mossy ground as he placed his velvety nose on my cheek.

"Are you talking about me?" Ronan paused, turning toward us with pinched brows.

"No."

Tiberius huffed a snort and bobbed his head.

"Don't worry, I won't ask for another ride," Ronan muttered.

Tiberius sent a wave of amusement rolling down our bond as we recalled the one time he'd allowed Ronan atop his back. The ex-queensguard had vomited after our descent.

I made to leap on his broad, inky back when the thunder of horses rose from the forest to the north. I paused, waiting, as a party of elves atop gray Lotrennian steeds broke through the trees.

War Slayers, I realized, noting the fresh black paint that stretched across their faces from temple to temple and the matching inked wolf skulls on their shoulders.

The group split, and my heart stopped as I took in the bloody figure at the center of their party.

# CHAPTER TWO

*Bonds tethered with magic are unbreakable, unless by death.*
—*Bonded Magic, 18th level, Living Library.*

"Why is my soldier in the custody of Lotrennian War Slayers?" Ronan's voice held an edge of calm authority as he strode to where the group stopped. Darkness raced down my veins as I ran after him, and my stomach twisted as I scanned Vander's bloody face. He sat atop a mount, arms bound to his chest in a living web of vines. His light hair was matted with fresh blood, and his head bobbed as it lolled to the side.

Vander was like a brother to me, my own brother's dearest friend and one of the last anchors to my old life. Of Aedrialis, and the manor we'd spent years playing in the barn with my brother and Drystan. My brother Aeriden's face glimmered in my mind every time I looked at Van. Having him here in Lotrennia, so far away from home, was almost like having

Aeriden here with us. Still living. Still in this world, if only his memory...

"Vander Stryke has been accused of the murder of a Lady of Tomorrow in the Gulley and will be held in Pyracantha until his sentence has been decided," the War Slayer growled.

*Kresida*, Ti reminded me, *second in command.*

The Ladies and Lords of Tomorrow were the elves' equivalent to courtesans. And the Sultirans had wasted no time spending the money of the Rising on their services. The ladies and lords were breathtaking, chiseled, perfect specimens, ready to fulfill any and every fantasy.

Kresida slid brown, narrowed eyes to mine. Small daggers lined her cropped vest and belt that crisscrossed around her torso. Her dark skin was free from tattoos except for the wolf skull marking her position, identical to the ink on Nerissa and Vulcan. They had been War Slayers before they fled the queendom after the execution of Nerissa and Bayne's parents at the hands of their own aunt, the queen.

My face shot to Van. A vice gripped my chest at the idea of *any* of our men or women in that death trap of a prison, let alone *my friend*. Outrage sent the Obscura power racing wildly in my veins.

"We agreed the order and disciplinary actions of Rising soldiers would be handled by the Rising council in conjunction with the queen's court. Release him." Ronan's sapphire eyes sparked in the Lotrennian sunshine. Threat edged his words despite the practiced composure with which he spoke.

Kresida's lips twisted into a wide smile, her white teeth flashing as she stepped forward.

"The soldier in question has been accused of the brutal murder of an elf," she said, as Van began to slide forward off his mount.

Darkness bucked. I flinched as two War Slayers caught him before he slammed into the dirt ground.

"If the murder was committed in the Gulley, space occupied by the Rising forces, we have a right to question our own men," I snapped.

Kresida leveled a look that promised violence as she said, "This type of violence against *our* kind, on *our* soil, will be met with justice only determined by *our* queen."

"Do I need to use smaller words for you?" I continued, Tiberius's wrath mingling with my own, "If the crime happened—"

Kresida stepped forward with preternatural speed, her face inches from mine. "I don't give a *fuck* where it happened. And I don't give a fuck what atrocious power you have swimming in your foreign, human veins." She stood over me, eyes sliding down my body, searching for the darkness that lurked beneath.

It responded within an instant. Power rumbled in my chest as it raced to my palms, urging its release. Kresida glanced at the veins in my forearms, darkened by the shadows surging in my blood, and back at my eyes rimmed with a golden orange whenever the Obscura threatened to break free of its tether.

*Shut it down, Lyvia.* Tiberius's low warning sounded in my head.

*I have it under control*, I retorted.

I willed the power to cool and plastered a look of control on my face. I took a steadying breath before saying, "These were not the terms your queen agreed to upon granting us sanctuary in your lands. Release him."

Kresida's dark eyes didn't leave mine. "I don't take orders from lesser beings."

*Lesser beings.*

A strange mix of fury and hidden inferiority grappled

within me. *We are not the same...* Bayne's words from the Lake of Light all those months ago often rang in my head. The elves were so different from humans. Faster, more lethal. I'd seen it in Nerissa and Vulcan, and even Bayne in the past. But here, in their homeland, the differences between us seemed that much more evident. Humans were slower, weaker, and further removed from that primal part of us.

No, we were not the same. Even among the humans here, I wasn't the same. The Rising forces knew I was human, but our own soldiers feared me, and I couldn't blame them.

Not after those horrifying hours on the plains of Odessa when I'd let the Obscura power erupt. I may have saved us by obliterating thousands of ashen, but I'd killed nearly fifty humans. Many of them, our own forces. Including Oslo.

The pain of that realization haunted me. Of seeing that bit of bright metal peeking out from a mound of ash. That deadly weapon he'd been so excited to secure to his stumped arm.

Marian would never forgive me. She hadn't left the *Evecta* since our arrival two months ago, let alone look me in the eye. But it was nothing compared to my self-hatred.

My heart ached as I repeated the names of the people whose lives were lost because of me. *My list.* My mind chanted them, like a quiet, damning prayer keeping beat with my blackened heart.

Morwyn. Aeriden. Eira. Oslo. My father. The list continued to grow.

Lives I'd taken myself or was just as much to blame for. All among the countless ashen I'd slaughtered at the Battle of Odessa. The ones we didn't think *could* be saved. Their deaths were on my hands. Hatred clawed at the thought, and I let it sink into the shadow smothering my soul.

Ti nudged me from behind with his big head, but his voice remained quiet in my mind. He knew my grief. Could feel it himself. And unlike the others, he didn't try to justify it. He was part of me enough that he knew I deserved this guilt. To *feel* it. To let myself feel it because it kept me tied to that small bit of humanity I so desperately clung to.

I tensed as Ronan placed a hand on my shoulder and stepped forward. "I suppose we have more to investigate," he said calmly. "Where is the body?"

Kresida's smile was enough to curdle my breakfast. "In the Gulley. What's left of it," she replied, eyes flashing. "It's being prepared for the Beyond."

My stomach tensed. The elven menders stripped bodies of flesh as they prepared them for the Beyond. Life after death, as they believed. The bones were then burned to ash before a wind whisperer spun the ashes up to Aelius, god of the sun. The more I learned of the ritual, the more my heart broke for Bayne and Nerissa, whose father had been executed by drowning in the Juniper Sea. Whose bones would never be burned, never sent to Aelius, a fate bestowed on him by Queen Antares.

"How are we supposed to investigate a murder if the body's gone?" Ronan cut in, outrage threatening his composure.

My head whipped to the side as a grunt escaped Vander's lips. Two War Slayers had him by the arms, the tips of his boots dragging in the dirt as they hauled him toward the entrance of lethal vines.

"Not my problem." Kresida smirked, turning to follow her team.

"Vander didn't do this," I said, turning back to Ronan.

"I know," he replied, keeping his eyes on the backs of the War Slayers as the twisting thorns of Pyracantha snaked open, allowing them to haul the half-conscious Vander inside. "But if someone from the Rising *is* responsible for the elf's death, a shit storm is coming our way."

The Rising forces were anxious enough. The elves were distrusting enough. Centuries apart had cleaved a deep rift between the two races, and we were on their soil. If a Rising soldier had killed an elf, tensions would only grow.

"Bayne won't be back for another few days..." I murmured.

He'd gone north with Aquila. Queen Antares granted him leave to visit the Waters of Ascendiel, the sacred mountain spring that sat in the north of the continent. The waters were said to open the minds of the elves to a line of sight and possibility.

"We'll need Nerissa." Ronan nodded as he turned back to me.

"We need *evidence*," I stressed.

"Rising healers won't even get a chance to examine the body before all that's left are bones, and they're sent up in flames," Ronan muttered, shaking his head. He turned to where his Lotrennian mount stood waiting near the trees.

*Bones.*

The revelation hit me like a stone wall. Maybe I could fix this. Or at least stall it long enough to free Vander.

"What?" Ronan paused mid-stride and his gaze caught mine. "You have a look."

"What look?" I blinked.

"The look all you scholars get. You've figured something out."

"*Bones*, Ronan."

His brows pinched together, eyes brightening as he sorted it through. They darted between mine. Ronan's light curls bobbed as he nodded his head.

"You'll need to hurry."

# CHAPTER THREE

*Magic appears stronger in the presence of water. It acts like a*
*conduit, transferring power, along with life, in its tides.*
*—Journal of Khato, Master of Spells.*

I leaped atop Tiberius's broad back, and we shot into the
air, the movement natural, as if we'd trained this way all
along.

He leveled out two hundred feet over the treetops, and I
scanned the vast forest of green below, searching for the
sentries hidden among the canopies. The queen had many of
them waiting, always watching us.

Tiberius angled forward as the Gilded Fortress came into
view through the treetops, and the soothing rush of its falls
wound through the sound of the whipping wind. Castle wasn't
the right word for the massive stronghold sparkling through
the canopy. The buildings here were a conglomeration of stone

and various plants, the tree singers influencing their growth and movement with magic.

Thousands of birch and golden-barked trees wound together in beautiful twisting patterns, creating eight large towers and the hundreds of chambers that made up the massive fortress. Seated in the center of the city atop the three waterfalls that fed into the twining river running through its center, the fortress was alive. And some days, I swear I could feel it breathing.

The warm, late spring wind whipped through my loose black hair as our altitude dropped and Tiberius angled toward its gates.

My stomach threatened to drop through my ass as we made the plummet. I tightened my grip on his thick mane and clenched my legs around his warm body as I clamped my mouth shut, refusing to let the rush of air escape into a small scream. I released the breath as his hooves slammed into soft, fern-covered ground outside the Gilded Fortress.

My breath caught in my throat as it always did at the beauty of the castle's entry hall. The white and gold trees shot hundreds of feet into the air, creating a space that was somehow indoors but not. Light sparkled from the ceiling like sunlight glinting off dewdrops.

My thighs warmed as I raced as casually as possible up the winding staircase leading to the queen's hall. I slowed my breathing, mustering all the confidence I could manage as I strode through the domed, golden hallway.

Two guards stood outside a door made entirely of gold and silver twining vines. They crossed their long spears in front of the entryway, bits of sunlight glinting off the honed edges of the wide blades.

"I have urgent business with Queen Antares," I stated, shoving bravado into my voice.

The guards kept their eyes forward, as if I hadn't spoken a word.

A moment later, a beautiful, soft voice crooned from inside, "Come."

The hairs on the back of my neck stood. I knew Queen Antares couldn't be trusted. And after everything she'd done to Bayne's family—her *own* family, as she was his aunt by marriage—I hated her for it. But I had to take this chance. I had to try, had to free Van. Not only for his own sake, but to prevent chaos erupting in the face of already growing turmoil.

Spears hissed as guards whipped them back, clearing the way. The chain-like vines that wrapped around the hinges of the door to her chambers unwound in an elegant grace before it swung open. I stepped forward into the brightly lit chamber.

Flowering vines spiraled up columns along the edges of the space and hung from the ceiling in varying shades of greens, pinks, and whites. Queen Antares glanced up from behind a light wooden desk at the back of the hall. Her blonde curls fell below her bare shoulders in loose waves. She wore a billowy, soft blue dress that draped down her front and sides, pooling neatly on the smooth floor. A small ring of flowers wove around the top of her head, forming a casual crown.

Her eyes, the blue of summer sky, landed on me, and her pink lips curled into a welcoming grin. She looked exquisite, the picture of regal benevolence. Yet something about the way her eyes skittered along my arms left me edgy, as if something monstrous lurked beneath the beauty and grace.

Her smile bloomed into a grin, white teeth glinting as I dropped into a low bow, steadying myself.

"Your Grace, I'm here—"

"You're here," she cut in, eyes slowly drifting to my own, "to beg we release the murderer."

Her tone took on a soft, deadly lilt. I did my best not to shrink beneath her piercing gaze.

"No," I said, keeping my voice level.

"Then do enlighten me," she purred.

"I've come to ask," I began, taking a slow breath, "for permission to examine the remains of the dead. Before your menders commend her soul to the Beyond."

The air seemed to siphon from the room at what was clearly perceived as a vile request. Though her features remained unchanged, a flicker of threat danced in her eyes.

Before she could shut me down, I quickly added, "Before my discovery of the source of the Obscura power last year, I trained as a Death Scholar for four years. I have experience in examining skeletal remains and can determine a cause of death."

"Our menders have already determined the cause of death," she replied, her tone taking on a note of boredom. "She was brutalized. Beaten to death and stabbed. She died in terrible pain."

"And you've already arrested Vander Stryke," I cut in. "But you've no proof yet. He deserves a trial, at the very least. And an unbiased examination of the remains to provide as evidence."

"*Unbiased?*" she challenged, arching an eyebrow. "How could you possibly provide an unbiased examination?

"I am a scholar," I bit back, reining in my temper. "I work with the facts. And if we don't have a fair accounting of what happened to the Lady of Tomorrow, then our forces will have a difficult time accepting Vander's fate."

"Is that a threat, *Bonder*? What will happen if the young soldier is tossed into the Juniper? Will your forces react? Does the queensguard not have his hounds on their leashes?"

"It's a request for a peaceful resolution. If the evidence

implicates Vander, then we will support your authority to condemn him as you will."

The words tasted like ash on my tongue, and my gut sank. *There is truth in death*, I reminded myself. My heart hurt as I replayed Father Marcus's words. Was he still in the dungeons at Mount Telum? We never went back for him. *Was he even alive?*

The queen narrowed her bright eyes on me as she considered.

"I will make you a deal, Bonder."

My stomach twisted.

"I will allow you to examine the bones before their offering to the Beyond, in exchange for time with me to hone the Obscura and Transcindiel powers. Every day until the Rising forces depart."

I blinked. *Train me?* Queen Antares was a mystic. A very powerful one, if the stories from Isla and the others were true. I was still learning the basic commands of magic: water and wind whispering, spell work, and tree singing. Few mages were elevated to the status of mystic, often taking hundreds of years.

Unease stretched as she kept her cool gaze pinned on me, the temperature in the room sinking. The others would kill me for this.

"Not until our departure. We have yet to come to an agreement on that timing," I said as confidently as possible. "Five days. No more."

"Ten," she countered in a quiet command. "To be completed before the end of summer."

"Seven."

"Eight."

For fuck's sake. I reined in the scoff ready to escape. She didn't blink.

"Fine. Eight days," I conceded.

Her pink lips curled up in a conniving grin as she snapped her fingers. A young elven mage with dark skin and deep brown eyes approached. He bowed to the queen before offering me a polite nod.

"An air oath," Queen Antares purred to the young mage. "In the common tongue, if you please."

My stomach threatened to bottom out as color leached from my face.

"An air oath?" I stammered.

The queen raised a light brow at me. "Of course, Bonder. We don't take deals lightly in this land. It shouldn't be a problem unless you don't intend on holding up your end of the bargain."

*Fuck. Fuck. Fuck.*

"Come. We need to be closer," she crooned, motioning me forward with delicate, manicured hands.

My mind spun, searching for any possible solution to avoid being bound to the queen, coming up empty. We had to save Vander.

I stepped up to Queen Antares as she moved closer, stopping inches from my face. Her sickly-sweet scent shoved its way up my nostrils, and I opened my lips to breathe from my mouth. Her porcelain skin shimmered as she cocked her head.

A musty wind, spinning from the elven mage in her command, swirled around the room, clearing it, as he recited:

*"Wind becomes life, as air becomes breath,*
*and bound without it, so too it calls death.*
*With it, these words become law,*
*their binding set to rule all.*
*This thread, born of words, weaves with life when spoken.*
*Should words be stolen, tied life shall be broken."*

The wind stilled, as if hanging, suspended in the natural air of the queen's elaborate chamber. We then repeated the words of our deal.

"I, Queen Antares Ravindra, allow you to examine the Lady of Tomorrow's bones, in exchange for eight sessions of Obscura and Transcindiel guidance to be completed with me before the end of summer."

A gust of musty wind spun through the room, sending the queen's loose blonde curls flying in a crown of light around her head. I shuddered as the spell settled, and a wide grin stretched across the queen's face.

The shimmering doors behind us slid open in a soft hiss as a young, beautiful, light brown-haired elf timidly entered the hall. Bright green eyes, *Ravindra* eyes, hesitantly glanced up beneath her spectacles as she took in the sight before her.

*Carina.* Bayne and Nerissa's cousin, and the queen's sole heir.

She held a stack of books in her arms and donned a long, cotton dress, more modest than the rest of her elven kin. No crown donned her simple brown hair, wound back in a long, slender braid that ran down her back.

Carina's wary eyes skimmed over me and landed on her mother. She gave a soft nod and strode past without a word.

Queen Antares didn't acknowledge Carina, instead turning toward her desk and drawing up a correspondence before handing it to me.

"You have one hour, Bonder."

# CHAPTER FOUR

*The souls of departed seers linger in the Waters of Ascendiel,*
*their messages rare and obscure.*
—*Journal of Khato, Master of Spells.*

Twenty miles of sparsely wooded space spread below us. Small, cramped huts of brown rickety branches dotted the shaded greenery. The Rising soldiers shared the Gulley and its handful of amenities with some of the less-fortunate Lotrennians. A couple of taverns, shops, and sparring rings had been erected to keep them occupied. The space was dismal and crowded, shadowed under the magnificence of the queendom.

Ti's hooves slammed into the dirt as he cantered into the small town the Gulley had become. My mind drifted to the slums of Aedrialis as measly, gaunt-faced elven children darted in between the huts, chasing each other with sticks. A raven-haired boy paused a few feet from me, eyes wide with fear as he took in Ti's wings and large form before they darted to me, and he hissed.

*Foal,* Ti murmured, his ears pinned in the direction of the young boy, who bared his teeth before running off.

*He's half-starving,* I replied as I rushed to Van's hut. *Stop scaring him.*

All of the elves in the Gulley were starving. There was something wrong. Not just in the Gulley, but in Lotrennia. Bayne and Nerissa could feel it the moment we made landfall. Life was disappearing, the sacred Lotrennian wolves along with it. Harvests had dwindled in the past hundred years. It left the less-fortunate elven families hungry... and feral.

Kresida had returned to Van's hut. She drew her blade, crossing it in front of the entrance as Ti's massive black wings flung to the side to slow his momentum. I hopped off his back and shoved the queen's correspondence in her outstretched hand.

Her eyes narrowed on me as she sliced the seal open.

She bristled, reluctantly removing her blade, and I strode through the opening of Van's small hut. The dry scent of death met me as I stepped inside.

Unlike the shimmering, gold and silver art-like branches that made up the Gilded Fortress, the huts in the Gulley were drab. Brown and broken branches knotted together to form a small living space. Light peaked in from the gaps in the branches on the roof, casting streaks of shadows across the dirt floor.

Two menders stood at the center of Van's hut, hunched over a long, slender body that lay beneath a cream, silken shroud. The gaunt form revealed her flesh had already been removed—a spell I had no interest in learning. *From flesh to foliage.*

I cleared my throat. The elder of the two raised her gray,

withered eyebrows as I offered her the queen's correspondence. She must have been ancient. As best as I could determine, the elves aged roughly eight times slower than humans. Which made Bayne appear as if he were only in his late twenties, even though he'd been in this world for more than two centuries.

She pursed her lips and gave a silent command to the young elven mender at her side, who eyed me with distrust. They left the hut without a word, an eerie silence filling the space as the door scraped shut.

My eyes scanned the silken shroud covering the skeletal remains before me. As it always did, the weight of life pressed down on me. As if the soul of the departed hovered nearby, eyes narrowed and watching, waiting.

I tugged my leather gloves off and slowly approached the body. I had no tools. No journal.

Kneeling in the dirt, I lifted the silk off the Lady of Tomorrow. Her clean bones were bright in the dim light. So new. So fresh. So unlike Enya's remains I examined last year.

I closed my eyes for a heartbeat, granting her a moment of reverence, of respect, before allowing my scholar eyes to take over and begin my examination.

*Tynan's Hell.*

So much trauma.

A quick look-over revealed so much. A broken femur. Triangular nicks on her second and third left ribs, likely a stab wound. A fractured left wrist, matching fractured ankles. A broken jaw. A fractured left cheekbone.

Kresida was right. She had been brutalized.

My brows furrowed as I ran my fingers over her skull, where ringed divots adorned the top. I placed my thumb in a small ring. Illness could sometimes warp bone, leaving them deformed or showing changes in density, but this was different.

My mind drifted to the fire pox that ravaged Aedrialis years ago. That often left a small stamp of disease on bone, like it'd been struck with stones of fire. This was different, like the same stone had struck the bone multiple times. Something twisted in my stomach. I memorized the damage and moved on.

My lips pursed as the trauma became strange. Her left femur, the largest break, appeared to have been healed, and then *rebroken*. I shuddered, taking a step back and eyeing the entire body.

My gut sank. *All* of her breaks had been healed and rebroken. As if she'd been forced to suffer through each injury more than once. But the breaks were recent, fresh. This all happened in the last day.

But it didn't make sense. If Van *had* killed her, had done all this, how could he have known about these old injuries? We'd arrived in Lotrennia just recently. The first breaks... The first time she'd been stabbed... Based on its density and new bone growth, it happened years ago. She had years to heal before she was reinjured less than a day ago. Even if Vander was a psychotic sadist, intent on literally reopening old wounds, he couldn't have been this exact.

Frustrated, I stood and cracked my neck. While the elves may be biologically different from humans, the basic principles of Death Scholar analyses still applied. But this death made no sense. Maybe it was the disease? There'd been no word about illness in the Gulley or Ayla. And it didn't explain the brutality or the fact that none of the injuries seemed a likely cause of death.

My molars scraped against each other. *Shit.* Drystan should be here. He'd figure this out. My time was running out, and I had nothing to show for it.

My feet thudded on the dirt ground as I paced. I ran my eyes over the rest of the hut. My eyes snagged on the desk in the corner of the room. I stalked to where a stack of paper and an ink pen sat on the table alongside a deserted bottle of the sparkling wine the Lotrennians were partial to.

A strange sort of pressure shoved against my chest before coiling its way to my neck. I ran a hand over the thick scar that seemed to tingle and stretch. The constant reminder I shouldn't be alive. I'd cheated death when Dark King Daimos used the Ramadiel bone of power to heal me after Cyril had slit my throat. It hadn't bothered me in some time. Talon, the dagger that split it open, sat strapped to my ankle as it always did. I wasn't sure why I'd kept it.

I rifled through the papers, scanning anything for clues. Chore charts, ration requests, training exercises... I paused as my hand slipped over a note from one of our healers. *Vander's wrist.* His arm had been shattered at the Battle of Odessa, and his right wrist was still giving him trouble. So much so, he'd yet been able to wield a longsword with his dominant arm.

I had what I needed.

My heart leaped into my chest as the door swung open, casting a warm, bright afternoon light onto my back.

"Time's up," Kresida growled.

I rolled my shoulders as I turned, leaning over all that remained of the dead elf. I pressed two fingers to my lips and sent up a silent prayer to Ganmira and Renova, to light her way in the darkness of eternal night. The silk fell over her bones in a soft sigh.

NERISSA PACED like a caged beast at the steps leading to the Gilded Fortress, rage glittering in her bright green eyes as I swung off Tiberius's back and strode up the landing to speak with the queen.

I waited to *feel* something from her, a bond of some sort due to the connection of our powers, but none presented itself. And I didn't dare ask her about it. Either we had no link, making my connection with Bayne something wholly unknown, or her emotional wall was so thick nothing could pierce it.

Soleia, the power of the sun that she shared with Bayne, remained locked up just as tight. She'd decided on the journey here that she would hide her power as long as possible. Her power was a beacon, and we knew Queen Antares had been after it. Had plotted and married their widowed uncle in hopes the ancestral power would be passed to her heir, Carina.

It hadn't. And Bayne had a target on his back as much as I did. I glanced at her, waiting for her to combust from the pent-up emotion and power, but she simply schooled her face into a blank mask of control as she fell in line with me.

"Explain," she demanded through pursed lips.

"There was no time," I huffed as we jogged up the golden steps. "If Vander is executed, there will be chaos. I needed to buy us more time."

"At what cost?" she snapped.

My mouth clamped shut. She would find out soon enough.

Queen Antares lounged on the fur-covered chaise near the open balcony. Carina, looking small and mousy, peeked up from behind her book in the corner, her matching eyes shuddering as she shrank beneath her cousin's gaze.

"Niece," Queen Antares purred as she cocked her head to the side, examining Nerissa.

"Your Grace," Nerissa responded with perfect, feigned

submission as she dipped into a low bow that I sensed had her soul screaming in rage.

Nerissa was still as I reported my findings to the queen, who devoured the information with a keen fascination. I noted Carina's attention as I detailed the wounds and the inconclusiveness of the body. A nod from the queen when I finally finished.

"Curious. You're suggesting there's enough damage on the left side of her body that the soldier couldn't have committed her murder," she said at last.

I nodded once, my breath held.

"She's correct," a soft voice sounded from the corner of the room.

The queen's eyes snapped to her daughter, light eyebrows raising in question.

Carina cleared her throat, emerald eyes darting to her cousin for a moment before landing on me. "The menders mentioned something similar before they returned to prepare her for the Beyond. The damage to the left side of her body was extreme. And if the soldier can't even wield a longsword yet," she explained, turning a timid look to her mother, "it's unlikely he could have done this."

Queen Antares surveyed her daughter for a moment, and I'd never seen a starker contrast. The queen, bold and powerful, looked down her nose at her small, mousy daughter, even while she lounged on the chaise.

"Well, if a Sultiran Death Scholar apprentice and my own *daughter* agree the soldier couldn't have done this, then I suppose it's enough to release him from Pyracantha."

A soft sigh of relief escaped me, and I let my shoulders sag.

"But an investigation will follow, Bonder. I will share your findings with the Chamber of Mystics. I'd be endlessly grateful for any additional help you can provide." The queen flashed a sharp smile before flicking her eyes to Nerissa.

We turned to leave the queen's hall when she drawled, "I'll send word when it's time to begin your training. And don't forget, should words be stolen, tied life shall be broken."

As we strode down the glittering steps, Nerissa let out a string of curses so colorful I had to look twice at her. The fury that replaced the calm, collected mask straightened my spine as emotion poured from her.

"Stupid. So *fucking* stupid. You idiotic *human*," she spat.

My molars pressed against each other. It would be fine. I'd cleared Vander's name, for now. Eight days with the queen to prevent my dear friend's death... To prevent an uprising *in* the Rising...

*Nerissa looks like she's about to implode*, Ti snickered as we approached.

*Shush.*

"We didn't have time," I snapped back before Nerissa stormed off.

# CHAPTER FIVE

*Threadsight is a dangerous gift. I fear it more than what I've seen with it.*

*—Journal of Khato, Master of Spells.*

The salty teakwood of the *Evecta* filled my lungs as I heaved a sigh, letting the scent steady me. Tiberius and I had escorted Vander back to the Gulley from Pyracantha after the queen's orders had been relayed. He'd regained consciousness, and though he was sore from being bloodied up, he seemed in good spirits, as was typical with my old friend.

Vulcan and Nerissa paced where we met below deck to discuss my careless actions. Nerissa had chewed me up and spit me out for the better part of the hour. How I should have waited for her, waited for Isla, for Vulcan... For *any elf* to witness my conversation. But I knew it would have been too late. The menders were too close to burning those bones. I didn't point that out as a fire raged in Nerissa, ready to send the *Evecta* up in flames.

Vulcan grunted his agreement on several occasions, shaking his freshly shaved head. He'd sheared his blonde hair as soon as we'd arrived in the Land of Light and Life, with an elaborate design cut into the side of his head.

Isla was silent and pensive as her amber eyes stared into the distance during Nerissa's rant, giving my hand an encouraging squeeze.

"She saved Vander's life," Drystan cut in, his ebony brows narrowed at Nerissa as his hands made jerky movements, communicating the words. Drystan had known Van from our youth as well.

I shot him a grateful look as he crossed his arms.

Ronan sat in one of the chairs with his feet on the table, as at ease as he ever had been on board the *Evecta*. Back when he was truly a part of the crew. Though I sensed his apprehension about this deal with the queen, relief shone in his eyes.

"Drystan's right." Isla nodded, sliding her eyes to Nerissa.

"We have enough problems as it is," Nerissa interjected, cutting a glare at Ronan. "Figuring out how to get back to Sultira, dethroning King Saros, stopping the tribute, surviving while we're here." Her eyes sliced to mine. "Not to mention the ashen and Dark King Daimos."

"Exactly," Ronan cut in. "And Lyvia prevented a huge shit storm from landing in our lap."

Marian sat in the corner, listening, watching. She'd refused to make eye contact since Oslo's death. I had nightmares about that moment every night. The grief and guilt stormed inside of me during the day, mixing with my rage for King Saros and Dark King Daimos, swirling with the pressure of mastering these new powers, and finally colliding with that small bud of resentment toward Bayne, toward all of them, for concealing the truth from me for months, adding to the stack of betrayals that built up over the past year.

"Lyvia."

My head jerked up as Isla's elbow dug into my side. Nerissa gawked at me, eyes wide in disbelief at my inattentiveness. Ronan snorted from my other side.

"I'm sorry," I murmured, rubbing my eyes. "It's been a long day."

"I take it the attempt this morning on the ashen didn't go so well," Isla said softly.

Nerissa stormed from the small cabin, followed by Vulcan and Marian. I let loose a sigh.

"What are we going to do about the queen?" Drystan asked, his almond-shaped, blue eyes thoughtful.

I let my head fall into my hands and groaned. Drystan gave my shoulder a squeeze.

"An air oath with the queen was dangerous. Maybe a little reckless, but I agree it was necessary. She didn't give you much choice. And you *need* to figure out how to master the Transcindiel power. Here's the thing about Queen Antares," Isla murmured as she signed the words, "she's not innocent. She's spilled so much blood over the past three centuries, murdered many, many powerful elves. But..." she paused, voice becoming quieter. "She is incredibly powerful. She is a *gifted* mystic. If she weren't so horrible, I'd beg to train with her myself. You're stuck in this deal, but you may learn something. Maybe you need a different teacher, anyways." Her voice softened at the end.

My heart squeezed, and I gripped her hand as I shook my head. I'd gotten nowhere with the basic arts. The wind shuddered in response to my command, like a wall had been put up. The water stilled, as if a sheet of ice froze over a pond. Spells were a nightmare, repeating the old elven words with no result. And tree singing? Every attempt left me exhausted. Though it was one of the few times the Transcindiel power's song rose up and then stuttered, its voice caught.

My one redeeming quality had always been my ability to learn. My ability to be a student, to be honed into something new. Studying with the Death Scholars had given me identity, allowed me to funnel that desire to learn into the delusion that I'd one day escape my fate as a lady-in-waiting. And though my fate indeed changed course since my discovery of Enya's burial chamber, I still had no idea who I was. My identity had crumbled.

And I had utterly failed at learning the forgotten arts. It wasn't Isla's fault. She'd been the best instructor and had already taught Drystan so much. He'd mastered the basics in days aboard the *Evecta* before they'd come to rescue me on Kayj. I opened my mouth to voice as much, but she held up a hand.

"I'm simply saying, sometimes it helps to hear it from someone else. She's powerful. She's also crafty. You must be careful. Take in as much knowledge as you can and reveal as little as possible."

I nodded, chewing on her words.

"And she'll try to throw you off. Whatever she says, even if it seems irrelevant, everything is intentional with her. She is power hungry, and she'll do anything she can to grow her strength. She may be psychotic, but she's brilliant."

A weight settled in my stomach.

"I wish you could have examined the bones with me," I signed to Drystan, shaking my head. "The markings on her skull seemed *wrong*."

I'd explained my findings to the group. And something about her trauma, the breaking and rebreaking, the markings on her skull. It nagged at me.

"You couldn't have waited," he responded. "Do you think it's an illness?" He turned his head to Isla with the question.

She shook her head. "I'm really not sure."

"Would a mender know more? If a plague broke out in the Gulley... We can't lose these Rising soldiers. We need to get back to Sultira before anything of the sort spreads."

Isla narrowed her eyes in thought. "The Master of Spells would know. But getting him to talk..."

Her gaze found mine, and she raised a raven brow. "I think it's time we visited the Living Library."

SMOOTH, copper wood arched fifty feet high, marking the entrance to the Living Library. I gaped at the massive tree, the only structure that compared to the Gilded Fortress in size and presence.

But the organism I stood in front of wasn't a web of hundreds of trees spun together by the voices of elven tree singers. It was a single, solitary tree, sprouting thousands of iridescent golden leaves that hung in long drapes down its sides. One impossibly enormous tree that stretched over a thousand feet into the air. The radius of its massive circular trunk extended hundreds of feet and rainbows danced in the refracted light that bounced off the leaves.

I stopped walking.

"Impressive, huh?" Isla whispered next to me, as dozens of elves bustled past us.

I had no words. None to describe its beauty, its other-worldly glory. Drystan stayed behind as he'd taken on the role of training a handful of the Rising soldiers to wield the lost arts. Isla nudged me in the side.

"Come on. We have work to do."

She led me through the domed tunnel, lit with small, elaborate sconces lining the wall, containing a soft white glow, but no flame.

"How—" I began.

"Nobody knows," she answered before I could finish. "It's not fire. No flames exist here. It's always been this way. There are no records, and even our eldest storytellers have no explanation for the lights or the tree itself. It's always stood here in Lotrennia and held our most sacred treasures and deepest secrets, including its own."

Her amber eyes darted to the sides of the tunnel and narrowed, inspecting the organism around us.

"It's incredible," I murmured.

"Just you wait," she said, pulling her eyes back to mine with a wide grin.

Moments later, we stepped into a colossal rotunda that stretched higher than my eyes could see. Rings of balconies lined the outside walls that spiraled thousands of feet into the air. And beyond those balconies... My heart stuttered.

Stacks of books and scrolls spiraled farther into the trunk of the tree itself. My breath whooshed from my lips as I beheld the bowels of the Living Library. We were inside the tree. One that had been carved out to create a sanctuary for knowledge, yet still lived and created within.

Long, pulley-like vines lowered four wooden baskets to the ground and up again, transferring elves to various levels. Hundreds of them bustled around, going about their business, hardly noticing me. I sighed, feeling a long-forgotten, quiet peace. I could disappear in here.

Isla, noting the shift in my countenance, gripped my hand with a squeeze and flashed me a knowing smile.

"I should have brought you here weeks ago with Drystan. I'm sorry. Let's go."

She led me to a basket that had landed. Four elves shuffled out, arms full of books. I stepped into the basket, and Isla gripped the largest vine in the center.

"Forty-four, please," she said softly.

The door to the basket closed on its own, and she gave me a devilish grin.

My stomach dropped, and I clung to the sides as it ripped up in the air, slowing before it came to a smooth stop moments later.

A surge of unease wrapped around my belly as the basket opened on its own, and several thick vines braided together to create a wide walkway to the balcony. Without railings. I cast Isla a wary glance.

"Oh, come on, this can't possibly rattle you after soaring with Tiberius," she said, skipping across the bridge.

I loosed a breath.

"I trust Ti to hold me more than I trust myself to stay on his back. I'm not very coordinated," I mumbled, easing my way across the vines.

"So Vulcan says," she snickered.

I threw her a dirty gesture, and she stuck her tongue out in return as I reached the balcony. The wooden railing reappeared as the basket retracted its vines and raced down to the entry level.

She led me through levels of spiraling stacks, snagging a handful of books on the way, until we came to a small alcove in the center of the aisle where two chairs and a table sat below more of those mysterious glowing lights.

Isla plopped down and motioned me to follow.

Books. So many books. My heart glowed beneath the cloud of pressure smothering it in a relentless shadow.

"Start here," she said, opening a weathered tome with strange markings on its cover. "I think most of these will be in

Elvish, but these few are in the common tongue. Histories of maladies and ailments in Lotrennia, going back a few hundred years."

I nodded, gripped by a determination to figure out what had really happened to the Lady of Tomorrow. We pored over books and scrolls for hours, barely muttering a word to each other. Isla suddenly stopped, head snapping up as if she'd heard a silent alarm.

"I need to go for a few minutes. The master of spells has arrived," she said out of nowhere.

"How do you know that?"

"Wouldn't you like to know?" she said with a wink, and then she was gone.

I slumped in my chair and continued my search until a strange sensation washed over me. Almost like a tug. I cracked my neck, adjusting my posture when it tugged again. What the—

My eyes scanned the floor-to-ceiling shelves, searching for I didn't know what. I turned back to my current tome when I felt it once more.

*Tug.*

# CHAPTER SIX

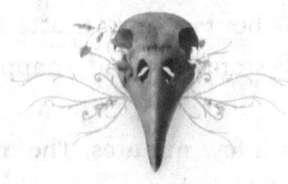

*Books have been known to disappear in the Living Library.
I'm asking, Ancient One, that you hide this when the queen
comes looking.*

—*Journal of Khato, Master of Spells.*

I whipped my head around, searching for some invisible force. My eyes snagged on a thin strip of white in the line of books down the hall. I plucked the book off the shelf and gently cracked it open. A soft sigh escaped the pages in a whiff of woody leather as they slipped through my fingers.

*Fabia's Fables*, the title read. I opened to the story of *The People of the Stars*. I pinched my brows, remembering the stories my father used to recite about the children of the gods.

What was a book of Sultiran fairy tales doing in the Living Library? I moved to flip through the small book when Isla's jasmine breeze floated through the stacks.

I slid the book back into its place before turning

toward her. She swaggered down the aisle, a look of triumph on her face as her black waves bounced in the soft light.

"Any luck?"

She smirked in reply. "Why would I need luck when I have this charm and this mind?" she said, an all-but-innocent look flashing across her face.

"He'll meet us on the fifth level. I've sent word to Drystan and Vienah to join us. They've both improved in manifesting their power, but any time we can get with the master of spells will be valuable, especially as we prepare for our return to Sultira."

"Good," I said, nodding. "Because I'm not finding anything in these." I gestured to the books.

"The menders commended her soul this morning," Isla murmured. "I saw the smoke."

A weight settled in my stomach. This whole thing seemed *wrong*. Isla was silent for a few moments, and she finally shuddered, shaking off the stillness of death.

"Hey," I murmured, glancing back at the stacks where the white tome seemed to have disappeared. "Have you ever heard of the People of the Stars?"

"Doesn't ring a bell," she replied, cocking her head to the side as if searching her memory.

She slapped her hands on the table before us, and I jumped. Her eyes pinned me with a mischievous gaze, and her lips tilted upward.

"We'll meet with the master of spells soon. But first, I have a surprise for you," she said, waggling her eyebrows.

She plucked out a large, crimson book she had tucked beneath her arm. She flipped through the pages, finally landing on the chapter she was looking for, and I choked as my eyes landed on the image before me.

She slid her amused gaze to me, delighting in my shock, and whispered, "The Slithering Serpent."

An hour later, we had pored over *Volume One* of the *Sensua*, the Lotrennian Book of Bodies. Laughter erupted from Isla, and she clamped her mouth shut as heavy steps padded around the corner.

My heart seemed to glow brighter from behind the shadow. Isla always knew when I needed this time with her, even if guilt accompanied every smile she pried from me.

"Okay, I'm sorry. But *these*?" I whispered, paging through the last few chapters of the volume. "Impossible. There is absolutely no way."

"These have all been tested and proven. These are not *theories*, you scholar." She laughed.

"So, you've tried them all?" I asked pointedly.

"Many of them, yes," she murmured, sliding her amber eyes toward me.

"I'm sorry, but there's no way. This one? *This one*?" I argued, stopping on a page and pointing to a couple in a ridiculous position.

"Get up, and I'll show you," she dared, raising her eyebrows in challenge. "Come on. I'll show you, and then you can give Bayne the surprise of his life when he gets back after the Awakening."

The Lotrennian celebration marked by the summer solstice would happen in a couple days. I barked out a laugh and stood.

"Okay, you be the man," she said, pointing to the stacks behind us.

"Why do I have to be the man?" I shot back. "If I'm doing this for Bayne, I need to play my part. You be the man."

"Fair."

She stood against the stacks and motioned to the floor in front of her. "Okay, so I think if you start with your back on the ground," she began as I lay down in front of her. "Yes, so now give me your feet and kind of walk—"

"Ow!" she yelped as I scooted my feet up the side of the stacks, knocking down books and shoving my heel in her gut. She grappled for my ankles and raised them above her shoulders. I grunted as I tried to hold my weight above myself, my shoulders and wrists barking under the strain.

"Yes." She struggled, holding my feet up in the air.

My back leaned against her knees and thighs, and she wiggled herself behind me, trying to line up.

"Yes, so I think if he is behind you like this..."

"There's no way," I grunted through ragged breath. "Look at the angle! He would break!"

A cackle burst from Isla's lips, and she dropped my feet. I tumbled over myself and onto the books I'd kicked down.

"Ow! You brat!" I yelled.

She doubled over. Laughter bubbled from my mouth as I shoved her to the side, trying to get up.

"I told you it was impossible." I laughed.

"Maybe this is supposed to be for two men?" she asked, craning her neck to look at the page in the book.

"Definitely still impossible!"

"You're right. Maybe we elves have devolved since writing this." She flipped to the front of the crimson tome, eyeing the date. "The elves that lived three thousand years ago must have had more flexible cocks."

Laughter cackled from my lips and tears formed in the corners of my eyes. Moments later, footsteps shuffled down the hall. Isla turned to me with wide eyes, and we scurried from the aisle to meet the master of spells.

VIENAH'S strawberry blonde waves bounced as the wooden basket soared through the center of the massive tree. I'd grown fond of the young woman I'd met in Odessa, one of the few magically gifted in the Rising. A spattering of freckles dotted the human water witch's light cheeks, making my heart ache as my thoughts drifted to Morwyn. Was it possible she had a little Votruvian in her blood?

A shudder ran through me as Lord Astraeus's face flashed through my mind's eye. After the Battle of Odessa, he'd sailed off on the *Hydra* with what remained of his crew to reconvene with the rest of his fleet of pirates from Votruvia. The Lord of Marisarma might have aided the Rising, but his motives were still unclear. I was glad to be far, far away from the pirate.

Vienah offered a small smile to Drystan, her brown eyes soft in the warm light of the rotunda. Drystan's tan cheeks deepened as a tinge of red rushed to them. He offered the water witch a close-mouthed smile before his almond eyes darted away. The gesture was not lost on Isla as her lips quirked to the side, eyes bright as she delighted in Drystan's awkwardness.

Isla led us through the stacks until we came upon a door off an alcove at the outer edge of the level. She knocked softly, and the vines twisting around the handle of the door unwound. We stepped into the brightly lit room, where a small man hunched over a table littered with scrolls.

Dark, slightly pointed ears poked out from beneath long, gray hair. His brown eyes raised up above his round spectacles and landed on me as he motioned for us to enter.

"Welcome." He motioned with his hand, and a warm breeze laced with cardamom and spice sent four chairs smoothly sliding over from the corner of the room.

"Thank you for seeing us," I said, leading our small group to the table.

"Khato, Master of Spells." Isla motioned to the mystic hunched over the table and offered a low bow before introducing the three of us.

"Isla said you had some questions for me," he began, his gray eyebrows raising as he motioned us to sit.

The fresh ache of loss swarmed my chest as Drystan found a seat across from me. He caught my gaze as he adjusted his glasses, a flash of pain sparking in his crystal eyes. We'd spent years in a similar place of learning together, looking to the older and wiser for guidance. This was familiar. It was as if we were back in the Temple of the Sky in Aedrialis, in Father Marcus's scholar room. Guilt raked at my chest. Was Father Marcus even still alive? We'd left him behind...

I blinked, finding the rest of the eyes in the room on my face, waiting.

"I'm most concerned about the rings on the bones," I said after divulging the details of my examination. "Have you ever come across this type of damage? Whether it be from injuries or illness?"

"I have not. Though there are scrolls here I've not had the time to examine," he replied.

My hands kept moving, translating for Drystan without thinking.

"What if she suffered the same illness years later?" I asked, finally voicing the ridiculous conclusion I'd come to. The other trauma to her bones...the breaks, the fractures, they'd all happened again. "Would that cause the circular wounds to appear in the same way?"

Khato frowned. "Unlikely," he murmured after a moment. "Ailments like the fire pox are more random than that. If she survived the first illness, it's unlikely she would have contracted it again. And if she did, it wouldn't have left its mark on the bone the exact same way."

Right. I knew this.

"But, it's always worth taking a closer look. Would you sketch them?" he asked, handing me a roll of parchment.

"Water Witch," Khato said, turning to Vienah. "I understand you've mastered the sky."

I glanced up from the skull I'd begun to sketch, and Isla froze. The *sky*? Vienah blinked.

"I'm not sure what you mean," Vienah murmured, cocking her head to the side.

I had to give her credit. She was a better liar than I was, but that didn't stop the slow smile that spread on the ancient elf's cracked lips.

"Come now," Khato huffed through his laugh. "I am Lotrennia's Master of Spells. I am seven hundred years old and have been a mystic for half that time. There is not much that goes on in this land I don't know about." He raised bristly eyebrows at her.

Vienah straightened, glancing at us.

"It is a rare gift," he continued, sitting back, "to influence the rain."

The rain. It *had* rained quite a bit since our arrival. I'd thought it was only because of the arrival of spring, or maybe my ignorance of the Lotrennian weather. And it had been *so* humid.

"Our forces need to eat," she said, shrugging her shoulders.

"Vienah's power is a welcome gift to those in Lotrennia," Isla said, pulling Khato's attention away from the water witch. "We are lucky to have her for the short while she is on our shores."

SOFT PAPER SLIPPED through my fingers as I shuffled my sketches, stepping to where Khato sat hunched in the corner of the room, reviewing a scroll that looked more ancient than him.

*Seven hundred years*, he'd said. To live that long... He raised his tawny eyes and nodded his head in thanks. I lingered for a moment, scanning the withered text in front of him.

"Why aren't there texts on the Bellators?"

Isla casually stepped to my side, and Drystan glanced up at the movement. The master's eyes softened as if he expected the question. As if he understood the desperate need for information about the foreign powers living within me.

"I'm sure your friends have already filled you in," he said softly, angling his head toward Isla.

"They were lost during the War of Ruin, after the demise of the Bellators. But how?" I motioned with my hands to the walls, the living structure that seemed sentient, protective, even.

A strange, glassy look coated his eyes for the briefest moment before he shook his head and shrugged his hunched shoulders. "It is a mystery we've spent hundreds of years digging for answers. Our best guess is that the texts were either lost or stolen during the war."

The corner of my lips hung in disappointment, and his gray eyebrows tilted up.

"These powers are new to you, Bonder. And having spent your entire life shadowed from the truth of the world, my guess is that they're overwhelming on a good day, suffocating on a bad one. But even if the Bellator texts remained, I am doubtful they would give you the answers you seek."

My brows pinched, and he offered a reassuring smile.

"What is transformation, but rebirth? Creation itself? It has pushed its way into a place clouded in darkness. There are two extremes now attempting to coexist in the walls of your inner being. Dark and light, death and life. They are to the other as oil is to water. And how do you mix the two?"

"Flour," Vienah piped in from her desk.

My lips twitched as Khato huffed a laugh.

"You need something to *bind* them," he explained, turning to me.

"I don't know what that is," I replied.

He gave me a sad smile. "The universe is cunning. It has a way of leading us to our fate on broken roads, over impassable mountains, and through treacherous waters. Trust it. Allow the universe to lead you to yours."

My heart stilled. He removed his spectacles, his penetrating eyes scanning the air around me as if tracing some invisible web.

"The gods certainly do have interesting ways of leading us to where we need to be," Isla added.

The master's eyes flicked to Isla. "It's not the gods, my dear. The threads of the universe..." he mused, eyes darting back to open air around my head. "Endless possibilities exist. Curious links and connections..."

I swallowed, the weight of my crumbled identity and crushing responsibility pressing down upon my shoulders, leading me blindly toward an unknown fate.

# CHAPTER SEVEN

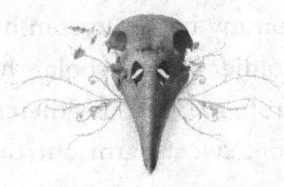

---

*I cannot unsee it. May Aelius forgive me for dooming his son*
*to a life tethered to the poisonous crown.*
*—Journal of Khato, Master of Spells.*

---

S weat poured from my temples after an hour of hand-
to-hand combat. Drystan dodged my uppercut and
swept to the side. Though he hated it, he'd conceded to
learning to fight. A cloud of night swept past as Tiberius
landed a few yards away to watch.

*It's time to fly.*

*You're bossy.*

*To the left.*

Drys threw a hook, and I dodged just in time.

"That's cheating." Drystan took a step back, signing the
words as he caught his breath.

Nerissa huffed her agreement from the edge of the ring.

Drys bounced on the balls of his feet, eyes darting between mine, before narrowing them at Ti.

I dodged the next blow and threw an elbow, barely missing his jaw. He took advantage of the opening and ducked, throwing his shoulder into my gut and scooping me up before plopping me down on my back. Drystan had gotten stronger, looking more like a soldier than a scholar these days. The move knocked the breath from me, and I lay there, coughing.

He reached a long, sweaty arm out to me. I grasped his hand, and he hauled me up.

"I've got to go. See you later, Drys," I murmured.

Drystan looked at Tiberius and nodded his farewell.

"Want a ride?" I asked Nerissa.

She scowled in return, not deigning to answer. I knew she would refuse, but it felt impolite not to ask. Though she'd never admit it, I had the suspicion the stalwart ex-War Slayer was afraid of heights.

She stalked toward a tie-up where a large, gray mare stood. The horses in Lotrennia weren't much smaller than the agrippa, but they were somehow more elegant. Their strong bodies were lean, with curved necks, thick manes, and feathery ears that tilted in toward each other.

They met us in a large valley full of targets. The field of green was draped in a lacey covering of white and pink blossoms that swayed in the slight breeze of late spring. We began a series of exercises on the ground and then in the air.

Riding Tiberius was entirely different from before he became my caeluma. His instincts were mine, and mine his. But my thighs... My damned thighs ached like never before.

Nerissa tossed me a bow and quiver, and all the confidence I'd racked up over the past hour was snuffed out in an instant.

*This is pointless*, I grumbled to Ti.

*You need practice. You're a piss-poor shot.*

"Whatever silent conversation you're having," Nerissa said, eyeing the two of us, "I agree with Tiberius."

Ti let out a low nicker of approval.

*Kiss ass.*

His ears tilted back, and he lifted his back leg, threatening a small buck, which I ignored.

Grabbing hold of the bow and nocking an arrow, we moved into a steady gallop. The muscles between my shoulder blades warmed as I drew back an arrow, holding the force of the bowstring between my fingers and breathing as Evony taught me. A warmth bloomed in my chest at the thought of her. I hoped she was alright and somewhere safe in Sultira. Hoped to the gods that Bear had been reunited with both her and Ezrich.

At the end of my breath, I let the arrow slip from my fingers where it found its mark on a target. Not exactly where I'd been aiming, but at least I hit it. My thighs tightened while Tiberius flared his wings wide and kicked off the ground, flapping strong gusts of wind beneath us. I nocked a second arrow, this time, taking aim from above. I held firm until I found my target, staying as steady and still as possible as we soared through the air. I released and...

"Are you kidding me?" Nerissa swore as she dove in time to avoid the arrow I'd aimed at the target twenty feet from her.

"I'm sorry!" I cried.

*You banked!* I accused Ti.

*I'm flying! What do you expect? There will be updrafts and other factors I can't control,* he retorted.

Nerissa took cover behind a large boulder and signaled me to continue. We banked, I loosed another arrow, and... Miss.

On it went for the better part of an hour before we finally called it a day. I opened a sliver of myself to that connection that tethered me to Bayne, allowing a bit of my day to pass through it...disappointment, laughter, hope, exhaustion. Just to feel a little of him. I received the faintest of emotions in return... *Longing, concern, love.* He was alive, and as far as I could tell, unharmed. I held on to that thought as I prepared to fulfill my oath to the queen.

IT DIDN'T TAKE LONG to reach the rocky strip along the northern curve of the Eye of the Wood. Queen Antares had chosen a location with a spectacular view of the lake.

Heavy clouds hung overhead, amplifying the muskiness of the humid summer that approached. They cast a dark net over the mysterious body of water. I stepped to the edge of the cliff, risking a glance over the thousand-foot drop. The lake was bordered by cliffs of varying heights, making it impossible to fish or traverse. The Awakening would bring a pilgrimage of elves from all over Lotrennia to these shores to celebrate the summer solstice.

Tiberius stalked to the edge of the pine forest that spread to the sea. A soft breeze blew from the north, and the smell of pine and sea mingled in the air for the briefest moment. I inhaled deeply, my heart squeezing at the thought of Bayne.

"I thought you might appreciate seeing the Eye of the Wood before the festivities," the queen crooned from behind, and I turned to face her.

Queen Antares was dressed in bone-white leggings and a vest. She wore a single, golden chain in place of her usual living crown of vines and flowers.

"The Awakening is a time of magic. A time of bounty and fertility," she preached. "It is the one day a year Aelius is high enough in the sky to illuminate the entire surface of the lake. Miracles have been known to happen." Her eyes narrowed as they ran along the length of the thick scar on my neck.

I waited for her to say whatever it was she wanted to say to me without the ears of the others. That was her condition. We came alone. But I wasn't unarmed. The Obscura power was quick to respond to my call these days. It took barely a thought before it surged forward, begging to be released.

"I don't need to tell you," she said, her voice taking on a charismatic lilt, "that there has been a plague upon these lands since Captain Ravindra abandoned us a century ago."

*Abandoned.* Such a deliberate word.

"What did you expect him to do?" I asked, unable to keep the accusation from my voice.

Light brows tilted up as her eyes bore into me. "If he'd been honest about his gift... If his parents hadn't hidden his powers, I never would have sentenced them. You are not a queen, Lyvia, but you are not stupid. If I'd let the seers continue their propaganda, our people would have suffered.

"Our land *has* suffered with his absence," she continued. "He had taken the essence of what is Lotrennia. The light and life of our soil, our land. His return is a blessing."

Everything she said was true. The land had slowly started to become greener, lusher, since Bayne's return, though it still wasn't back to its former glory. Many elves continued to struggle.

I'd seen firsthand how Bayne's power had evolved after the unexpected twin eclipse, the *Sending.* How he could literally give life to the leaves and the trees. It was more than tree singing... that took hours, days even, and sometimes several mages to influence the growth of saplings. Bayne could command the essence of the life that was already there.

"I thought we were here to train," I said, changing the subject.

Her eyes drifted between my own, as if searching for something.

"Indeed," she said, backing away from the edge of the cliff.

My molars scraped against each other in irritation. I wasn't here to play games with her. I took one last look at the sprawling lake before a hard hand hit the center of my back, and I was flung into open air.

# CHAPTER EIGHT

*He's poured all his power into a new shield surrounding the city. You must find another way to get through.*

*—Intercepted correspondence from Queen Galena intended for Sir Ronan Merik.*

T he too-familiar sensation of falling slammed into me as wind pummeled my body from every direction. I cast to Tiberius and was met with a panicked response. Two muffled reactions collided with my own from a great distance. Bayne and Aquila. My brain seemed to stop working as my body flailed against the wind.

The view of the overcast sky and the ominous lake somersaulted before my eyes. And that dark smudge... The lake was getting bigger. Closer.

*Where are you?!*

*I'm blocked! She's blocked me! I can't get to you!* Tiberius's voice shook with rage.

He cast to me, and I was suddenly in his body, thrashing against a different kind of wind that locked him in place. A shield that she'd thrown up at the edge of the woods.

I tumbled through the air, the words registering too slowly and the water below rushing up too quickly. The Obscura reacted to my panic and bucked against the eight-pointed stars on my palms, but I couldn't direct its power as we spun.

A woosh of warm, sickeningly sweet wind slammed into me, and my momentum was thrown upward. The jolt of the change in trajectory shoved my stomach into my throat, and I forced down the urge to vomit while falling upward.

I slammed to the ground, my face scratching against rock and pine needles as the wind pinned me into the ground. I tried to push up to my knees, and she sent another blast at my back, my face smacking into the stone. A gush of blood filled my nostrils.

The sweet scent vanished along with the force of wind at my back. The thunder of Ti's hooves filled my ears as he pounded up to me, nudging my shoulder with his wide, velvety nose. I gingerly rolled to my back and stared at the misty sky.

Those two muffled sensations of concern and panic continued to knock at my consciousness. I sent back my own relief and ease to quell the anxiety stretching from miles away before promptly shutting down the mental connection. Bayne and Aquila had work to do. They didn't need this distraction, and I could handle the queen.

*Are you sure about that?*

I put my hand on Ti's soft muzzle, not deigning to reply. She definitely *could* kill me. With that strength... I'd never seen magic used this way. Isla was powerful with the lost arts, as were Bayne and Nerissa. But *this*...

"It seems we have quite a bit of work to do," she sneered from several yards back. "Have you not mastered the basic arts? Any mage would have been able to throw up a shield of wind to at least slow their momentum."

I tried not to bristle at the criticism. A red smear stretched across the cream fabric of my tunic as I brushed my arm against my nose.

"I've been training," I growled, getting to my feet. "The basic arts have been challenging."

Her eyes narrowed on me, considering.

"Then let us not waste time with them. We'll focus on the Bellator powers. Though I'm surprised neither reacted to save you. That's what happened when both manifested for the first time, yes?"

I gave a reluctant nod. The Obscura manifested when Cyril prepared to slice me open in his tower on Kayj. And the Transcindiel transformed Tiberius into my caeluma, giving him wings as we flew off the cliffs of Odessa, pursued by Saros's soldiers.

"Curious. The Transcindiel... I suppose we don't know its limits yet. One would think it could transform anything. Turn a floating log into a boat. Or even turn the water itself into a cloud of cotton, protecting you from the impact... Transform the air itself..." she mused.

A strange sensation of protectiveness swept over me as her eyes took on a glassy effect. Greed. Desire. *She wanted this power.*

"I guess that explains why you've made no progress with the ashen."

The words hit like a ton of bricks. Guilt clawed at my chest. I glanced up, and her eyes held a cunning spark, waiting for my reaction. I relaxed my jaw, shoving down the emotions.

"The Obscura," she continued. "You could have sent that after me as well. Destroy the source of the attack, and the attack would cease." She uncrossed her arms and approached.

"Here's what we're going to do," she said, sizing me up. "We're going to explore the full potential of the Bellator powers. You may not like my methods, but by the end of this, you'll have better mastery over the powers you've dared to claim."

She turned and walked to the center of the clearing near the cliffs, motioning me to follow.

"Feet apart," she instructed, turning and standing in a battle-ready stance in front of me. "Use the Bellator powers to defend yourself. I won't kill you." Her eyes were hard, determined, as she lifted her hands and sent a blast of wind, raising several small broken sticks up into the air. Her mouth twitched to the side, and she flicked her wrists, sending them flying toward me like airborne blades.

I was ready this time. I opened my palms to the projectiles and let the build-up of emotion swell in my chest, offering it to the Obscura. It greedily grabbed hold of it and burst through my palms, streaming toward the projectiles, swallowing them up and leaving trails of ash floating to the ground.

Queen Antares wasted no time. Her eyes narrowed, and she threw her arms into the air, her honeysuckle wind roaring in turn. I stepped back as several small boulders rose into the air and hurtled toward me.

I reacted, sending the darkness reaching for the boulders when I realized too late, I'd never successfully destroyed anything other than organic material. A spasm of panic sent me diving for the ground as the boulders flew through the darkness, past me, and over the edge of the cliff.

Disappointment escaped the queen's lips in a click as I got to my feet.

"No stones. I assume no steel then, either?"

I pulled my gaze away.

"Pity."

58

Another volley of boulders burst forward, hurtling toward Tiberius. My heart leaped in my throat, and a wild hysteria grew as I released the Obscura. This time, I sent it right for the queen's smug face.

The boulders faltered in the air and dropped, rolling to where Tiberius had previously stood. He circled overhead, waves of rage rippling off him. The queen threw up a shield of her own as her eyes locked on mine, narrowing in focus. Icy rage raced through my veins, feeding the Obscura. The darkness swarmed as I released it in ribbons of black mist. They bucked as they hit her shield, and I pushed. How *dare* she come after Ti?

I loosened my control over the darkness, allowing it to search the shield for weakness.

*Harder*, I demanded.

It obeyed, thrilled with my rage.

The queen's eyes locked on mine, triumph glimmering in their depths. I blinked and closed my hands, choking off the darkness. The power recoiled as the black streaks along my forearms slowly receded. Tiberius landed in the distance and snorted as his massive hooves stomped on the ground.

*That was a test,* he grumbled.

*I realize that now,* I snapped.

The queen looked between the two of us as she let her shield drop.

"I suspected there was more to the bond than magic wings. You can speak, can't you?" she asked, arching a delicate eyebrow.

Her smile widened when I didn't respond, and my stomach dropped. I was exceedingly outmatched by this woman.

The queen's sweet wind whipped up from the ground, flipping my feet above my head in a vice grip. Tiberius let out a snort as he cast to me from behind another cage of wind. I sent the Obscura after her, attempting to distract her enough to drop the force of air. She threw up a pile of logs into the shadows, forcing it to obliterate the wood instead of herself.

I strained to block out Tiberius's rage and panic, trying like hell to concentrate on breaking the hold she had on me. I slowed my breathing, pushing past that sickly smell, allowing my mind to empty as it did during my centering exercises with Vulcan.

A tiny, prickling sensation snagged my attention. It was foreign, curious. I opened my eyes and glanced into the forest around us. My gaze snagged on the smallest glimmers of silver, flickering in and out of the dense pocket of leaves.

The queen snarled in irritation, and she hurled a group of stones at the silver, which disappeared, along with the tingling sensation.

Her wind shifted, and I began to spin. The world around me tilted and blurred. I swallowed the nausea that rose and reached desperately for that connection with the wind. My brain rattled in my skull as she picked up speed. I opened my mouth to beg when I thumped on the damp forest floor with a hard thud.

I stood on the wobbling knees of a foal and blinked against the still-turning world when my heart stopped. A crazed look of delight danced in the queen's eyes. She held a new shield against Tiberius, whose black wings pumped wildly as he reared before her. Rivers of black mist streamed from the tips of his soft feathers as he blew a cloud of raw darkness and power in her direction.

A look of wild triumph crossed the queen's features, and my stomach plummeted.

*STOP!*

His anger was the only response.

My lips parted as Tiberius's massive hooves cut through

the air, shadows of death rippling from his wings and chest, a mighty and formidable sight. My knees crashed to the ground in shock.

Tiberius's dark eyes flashed to mine, and he galloped to where I knelt, the shadows siphoning back into his raven body as he snorted and huffed, frothy sweat dripping from his withers.

*How did you... When did—*

*I don't know,* he replied, his voice wavering in my head. *I thought she was going to kill you—*

"You've been keeping things from me, Bonder," Queen Antares purred, her tone deathly sweet.

My stomach dropped. We hadn't even known...

"As you both wield the power," she continued, "Tiberius is bound to our air oath. He'll train with us." Her gaze greedily snaked over him, and he pinned his ears in response, lifting his head high.

My stomach dipped as I repeated the words of our air oath... *To hone the Obscura and Transcindiel powers...* She'd said nothing of training me, just the powers...

*I'm sorry,* he repeated.

*You have nothing to apologize for,* I replied. *She's a manipulative bitch—*

My mind's voice caught before I hurled into a nearby bush, my stomach still reeling from the queen's attack.

"What was that?" I asked, more to myself, as I wiped my mouth on my arm and glanced at the bush where the silver disappeared.

A sound of disgust escaped the queen's lips.

"Pixies," she murmured, pursing her lips. "Bad luck. Death follows their flight." She plucked a small leaf from her shoulder before pulling her eyes away from the bush.

"We're done for today," she said, a satisfied smile tugging at her lips.

I resisted the urge to claw her face off as she waved a hand in dismissal. I made to turn when she raised an expectant brow.

*She's waiting for us to bow*, Ti said.

*Don't you dare lower yourself to her*, I replied before leaping onto his back.

# CHAPTER NINE

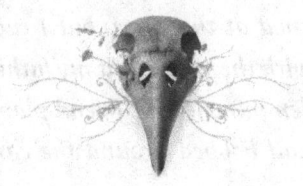

*The High Priest is safe, and none of your concern.*
—*Correspondence from General Calvus to Lord Pavel.*

The twelve-year-old version of my brother winked as he trotted past on his gelding, my father clomping alongside me on his black stallion. I squeezed my old mare into a trot, heading toward the summer solstice celebration along the streets of Aedrialis.

"Stay with Aeriden, Badger," my father called.

A look at his guard and I knew I'd have an unwanted escort, but even at elven years old, I could outmaneuver them.

I launched the mare into a lope, weaving between carriages and wagons until I caught sight of Aeriden sneaking into an alley. I hopped off my mount and slunk into the side of the building, where he thrust an oversized shirt and a pair of trousers into my hands.

"Hurry up. Van and Drys will be here soon," he whispered, ushering me behind an unused cart.

63

*I swiftly changed clothes and pulled my hair into a little cap. Aeriden smirked when he turned around.*

*A tall, lanky form rounded the corner and skidded to a stop, his mouth spreading into a wide grin. "Tynan's Hell, you look like a boy!" Vander exclaimed.*

*My cheeks reddened at the curse, but I tucked it away for use during my training with the young colt my father had gifted me.*

*"Shut up." Aeriden punched his friend playfully in the shoulder as Drystan's dark head bobbed around the cart. His lips stretched into a broad smile.*

*"I didn't offend her. Right, Lyvi? You're tough." Vander's bony elbow caught me in the ribs.*

*I suppressed a giggle.*

*The four of us snuck through the winding avenue of carts that led to the sectioned-off avenue housing the traveling festival. A large man with a bristly beard stepped in front of us, raising a brow.*

*"We're 'ere ta muck the stalls," Aeriden said, pinching his words with a dialect of the slums of Aedrialis.*

*"Nag master din't say nothin' 'bout a buncha urchins comin' this way." The man's mustache twitched as he looked us over, eyes narrowing on the stray strands of long black hair poking out of my cap.*

*"Who else is gon' shovel their shit?" Aeriden clapped back as he took a step forward, shoving me to the side.*

*The man took a long drag of his pipe before jerking his head behind him. "Three streets down," he growled. "And if I catch your snoopin' eyes or sticky paws anywhere else, I'll box yer ears."*

*"Yes'sir," Van mumbled as the four of us scooted past the barrier.*

*Festival workers lined the street, all dressed in an array of costumes and painted faces. Drystan and I chased after Aeriden and Vander, who shot past the horse stables and ducked into an alley. Aeriden paused and placed a finger to his lips, lifting the flap to a large tent.*

*I stifled a gasp as we stepped inside. Rows of elaborate wagons and cages lined the great tent. Bleating, roaring, and hissing sounded from all around, the potent scent of shit, piss, and loamy musk surging into my nostrils.*

*We crouched behind a water trough, and Aeriden's sapphire eyes darted between the various cages, searching for the infamous bear. He pointed to a set of cages in the corner draped with long black curtains.*

*"One of those," he signed to the three of us.*

*A spike of excitement buzzed in my veins as we crept along the tent's edges. Aeriden stopped before the first cage, pulling the back of the curtain to peer inside.*

*"Let us see!" I whispered, doing my best to shove between the two older boys.*

*Aeriden elbowed Van to make room for me and Drys.*

*"It's just a box," I murmured.*

*My heart leaped into my chest as mumbled talking reached us. I whipped my head around to spy three workers rounding the corner.*

*"Dammit!" Aeriden whispered. "Quick!" He fumbled with the latch on the cage for several long seconds as Van shoved him aside.*

*"Let me do it!" Van grumbled. A small pick appeared in his hands, and he slid it into the large lock, wiggling it around enough until there was a solid click.*

*"Hurry!" Aeriden whispered, urging us into the darkness of the cage.*

*We stumbled over each other as Van swung the door shut and whipped the curtain down as the door latched in place.*

*We crouched low in the darkness as the footsteps grew louder. My breath caught in my lungs as the festival workers passed, keeping my hand on Drystan's arm. Aeriden let out a sigh of relief as the sound of their footsteps disappeared into blended animal bleats.*

*"That was close," Aeriden whispered as he laughed, "Come on, let's—"*

A soft clatter bit through his words, the rattle echoing through the darkness, and I tightened my grip on Drystan.

"What was that?" Van breathed, still as death.

A soft hiss slipped through the space, and something thudded from the center of the wagon.

"It's a snake," I said in a shaky whisper, not needing to see Aeriden's face to know it had paled.

"Shit," Van whispered as he backed away from the center of the cage and bumped into the bars lined with a lattice of wires.

I signed to Drystan in the limited light, and his body went rigid.

Aeriden's hand gripped my gangly arm as a soft swishing whispered from the box, followed by a light thump as the snake slithered out.

"Van, get the pick," Aeriden ordered, pulling me behind him.

"I don't—" Van's boots scuffed as he scrambled around the back of the cage, feeling along the floor. "I must have dropped it!"

Aeriden cursed and scooted along the edge of the cage, putting space between himself and the rest of us. "Spread out," he murmured, eyes wide enough I could see the whites of them in the darkness.

The spiraling form of the snake shifted as we moved, its heart-shaped head swiveling to watch us. It stopped as it landed on Aeriden, and the little forked tongue that escaped its mouth flicked twice as if it could taste my brother. The snake's head lifted off the ground, coiling the center of its body in toward itself as it did so, poised to attack.

"I found it!" Van whisper-yelled from opposite the cage, where he fiddled with the lock pick. Metal scraped as rattling and hissing built into a threatening crescendo.

Van swung the door wide as the snake lunged for Aeriden. He dodged to the side the same moment the heel of my riding boot slammed on its rattling tail. Aeriden surged toward me as the snake retracted, coiling in on the pain before it whirled to face us. Aeriden's hands were on my back, shoving me out of the cage. We tumbled out, tripping over the steps, and landed in a heap.

I stared at the gold and white topped tent as we lay on the ground for a heartbeat before the booming voice of Lord Pavel, my father's confidant, reverberated through the small space.

"I thought I'd find you here. You're in for it, Aeriden. Your father's not happy. Your sister is missing—"

"You don't have to tell him," Aeriden pleaded as he jumped to his feet.

Lord Pavel opened his mouth and paused as his eyes landed on mine, recognition and a speck of amusement dancing in them.

"Sisters spare me," he muttered beneath his breath. "Come on."

Lord Pavel slipped a few gold coins into the hands of the beast master as he turned around. We trudged out of the tents, heads hung low, knowing we'd return to Cantor Manor and straight to the stables for chores instead of the Sun Dance.

AELIUS'S SHATTERED morning rays shifted, bouncing off the diamond-shaped mirror hanging in Isla's guest room and landing directly on my sleeping eyes. I cursed and threw the downy pillow over my face as Isla sprang the door open.

"Happiest Awakenings, Lyv!" she sang as she bounded across the room.

I groaned and rolled over.

"Get up! We have *minutes* to get ready for the celebration."

I tugged the blankets over myself. "This is the *one* day I get to sleep. Leave me alone."

She ripped the blankets off, and I reached blindly, swatting at the air.

"We are headed back to war soon. Who knows where we'll

be for next year's Awakening, or when we'll be back here. I am not letting you miss this."

She dodged the pillow I chucked at her face and crossed her legs beneath her as she plopped onto my bed. "Wake up. We have twenty-four hours to get utterly smashed. And drunk Lyvi is my favorite." She winked.

I rolled my eyes and flipped her a vulgar gesture, murmuring, "Happy Awakening to you, too, Isles."

"We leave all our worries behind today. Celebrating only." She waggled her eyebrows. I let out a tight chuckle, nodding before reluctantly climbing out of bed.

"Oh! And something came for you. Maybe a surprise from Bayne?" She led me through the twining halls of her tree and stone house.

A large red box with white ribbon gleamed in the sun on the table in the kitchen. Butterflies danced in my stomach. I opened that channel to him to send a little sprinkle of feeling his way. *Love. Longing. Happiness.*

That familiar sense of him returned, faster than expected. *Anticipation. Determination.*

I loosened the velvety ribbon and lifted the lid to the box. A small square paper lay in the center, and my stomach dipped as I glanced at the signature.

"This isn't from Bayne," I murmured.

Isla peered over my shoulder and let out a sound of disgust.

*Happy Awakening, Bonder.*
*We all must look our best on the brightest day.*
*—Queen Antares*

I crumpled the paper and tossed it aside. My fingers slid over the slippery material as I held up two pieces. The top was a skimpy, corset-like vest with lacy sleeves that hung over the shoulders. The billowy pants came together at my ankles in thick cuffs with golden thread.

Isla let out a low whistle.

It *was* beautiful. And in the appropriate fashion for the Awakening, according to Isla. But this was from the queen. And black as night. I knew from conversations with the others that everyone would be in bright colors for this event. This was a beacon for me, a way to distinguish myself from the others, to make me easily identifiable. As if Tiberius's presence wasn't enough to do that already.

Isla pinched the fabric between her fingers.

"Agh, slippery. It's meant to keep the *nebulis* off you." I raised my eyebrows in question. She returned it with a grin. "Nothing to worry about. We can work around that," she added, her grin turning wicked.

# CHAPTER TEN

*Find her family. It won't take long to draw the witch out if she sees the smoke.*

*—Correspondence from King Saros to General Calvus. 19th of Summer, 070.3E.*

We strode down the main road of Ayla, where hundreds of elves had gathered in the frenzy of celebration. While all of them dressed in bright colors, with ribbons and flowers in their hair, Isla stood out in her bright pink top and bottoms that glittered with white jewels and silver thread, a stark contrast to the stunning bronze of her skin. Her black hair was curly and loose, framing her face.

Sea glass and gems were hung in woven vines draped from the crossing bridges above the city. The streets were lined with vendors, and bouncy music rose in the air, floating in from various alcoves along the side streets.

We ducked into a large wagon where a petite elf scanned my long, olive arms and torso. Isla tossed her a coin, and she began her work.

Golden swirls of various designs covered my bare skin by the time we left, each curve reflecting the sun's bright mid-morning light. The twisting silver ferns on Isla's dark skin shimmered as she hooked her arm in mine, and we joined the celebration, falling in line with others making the pilgrimage to the Eye of the Wood.

Isla scooted into a tavern, and Tiberius sauntered up behind me as I waited outside. The crowd split for him, a hush running through it. I gave his velvety coat a pat on the shoulder, hot from the sun.

I reveled in the glee and activity of the festival. The brightness of dawn and ensuing festivities could almost make me forget about the ashen. About the dark king and the tribute and the civil war happening in my own home. Even Tiberius looked on curiously. Performers of all kinds lined the roads from musicians to theater troupes, to elves that swung on vines and branches, flipping across the road, wearing little more than undergarments.

I blinked as Vulcan stalked up to us.

"Surprised to see me?" he grumbled, giving a nod of respect to Ti. He was dressed in his usual leathers, not bothering to don the billowing pants of the other male elves and going shirtless altogether. He scanned the activity around us, eyes snagging on the musicians a street ahead.

My mind drifted to those first few nights on the *Evecta* last year when he'd filled the deck with his soul-wrenching voice, nearly bringing me to tears with words I didn't understand in his tenor vibrato.

"Can I expect you to bless us with that voice of yours today?" I murmured.

71

"You utter a word about that to anyone on this continent, I'll make your morning training a living nightmare," he warned.

Tiberius tensed, and I sent my reassurance along our connection.

"You sang on the *Evecta* after you rescued me from Mount Telum," I countered, still not looking at him.

"I didn't *rescue* you."

I resisted the upward tug of my lips. "Still. You sang for me."

He bristled. "I didn't sing *for* you. I sang *in front* of you. And if we're being honest, I didn't think you'd survive this long to be able to tell anyone."

"That sounds dangerously close to a compliment," I said, unable to keep the smile hidden.

I glanced at him and could have sworn his lips twitched upward before he schooled his features. "Wasn't meant to be."

Isla skipped up to us, handing me a cold glass of some fruity drink along with a handful of decadent, buttery sweets. "Vulcan! What a surprise. You may join us, only if you promise not to be a killjoy. I assume that's why Nerissa isn't here?"

Vulcan raised his blonde eyebrows at her.

"Kidding! Gods above, I'm kidding. Where is she, anyway?" she asked, looking around.

"She's decided to stay with Marian," Vulcan muttered.

It was enough to suck the joy right out of me. Guilt churned my stomach. She still hadn't left the *Evecta*. I'd tried to talk to her so many times since Odessa. Since I'd killed Oslo. I was nauseous from the thought of it, and the shadow over my soul answered back, *You deserve to be.*

As if sensing it, Isla put her arm around me and murmured, "Whatever you are thinking, *stop*. Today is a day to celebrate." She gave my shoulder a squeeze.

Liquid burned along the ridge of my eyes. I certainly didn't deserve her.

We continued our trek with hundreds of elves, all heading into the forest where the road was wide and worn after years of elves traversing the sacred path to the Eye of the Wood. The trek would take most of the morning, and we would arrive at the large lake before noon, when the sun was highest, to illuminate the entire Eye.

An hour and a couple of drinks into our trek, a wide river opened through the thick branches of the forest. Isla glanced up at the sun and then pulled me aside, Vulcan following closely behind.

Isla led us through a thicket to the edge of the cool, rushing river. The aqua blue of the water reflected brightly against the beaming sun. I leaned into the soft, floral breeze that followed, savoring the coolness in the stifling heat that had arrived midmorning. I closed my eyes for a moment, listening to the trickle of the clear water and the whisper of the trees as the wind rushed through them.

I opened them, smiling for a moment before Isla slammed her hands into the center of my back, sending me flying into the calm waters at the river's edge.

The chill water sent a shock through my system. My feet scrambled against the stony bottom, my hands slipping on the slick green algae coating the larger rocks I used to push myself up.

"What the hell!?" I snapped, leaping up.

"You looked hot!" She laughed. "And I'm sick of seeing you in all black."

Vulcan rolled his eyes before turning back to the main road.

Isla stepped forward into the water.

"Trust me," she said, holding out a hand and winking.

I shook the water off myself, glancing at the golden paint still intact along my arms.

I grabbed her hand, holding her in place as I splashed her with my other.

"You brat!" She laughed, shoving me back into the water and hurrying up the bank. Laughter escaped my lips as I got to my feet.

I paused as the familiar tingling sensation crept over my shoulders. I whipped my head around, scanning the rocky banks across the river, looking for the silver flash of pixies.

I waited a moment, eyes scanning the thick green and brown brush across the river, searching the dark shadows that separated them. They snagged on a set of glowing, golden orbs.

They disappeared a second later and then reappeared a few feet away. Eyes. They blinked again, and another set blinked open. I craned my neck to see better as more blinked open. I counted six sets, that tingling sensation growing stronger.

"Let's go, Lyv!" Isla called from the top of the embankment.

Like a snuffed candle, the eyes disappeared in an instant, along with that curious tingling. We were back on the main road a moment later when Drystan found us.

"Why are you soaked?" he asked, amusement dancing in his eyes as he took in my sopping form. He donned billowy, blue pants to match his striking eyes.

I threw a look at Isla, who snickered, wrapping her arm around Drystan's shoulder and tugging him into the crowd.

I suppressed a laugh as Tiberius stalked to a cart of fruits of vegetables, waiting in line for the carrots at the bottom. The vendor eyed him warily, looking between the massive, winged horse and the rest of his patrons. They merely shrugged, and he continued helping those in line ahead of Tiberius.

A thunderous boom echoed ahead, followed by the vibrant

cheers of the elves around me and the joyous laughter of children. A boisterous beat of drums and a chorus of voices followed. I whipped my head around and stared in awe as plumes of fine, brightly colored powder exploded into the air, raining down on the elves below. *Nebulis.*

I side-eyed Isla, who stared at my soaked black clothes, smirking as her plan unfolded. We hurried forward into the ensuing chaos of another boom. Golden powder exploded overhead, and I leaped through the shimmering power, arms wide, coating me from head to toe. The gold shimmered overhead and clung to my garments, brightening my attire and blocking out the black entirely.

Tiberius stalked through the next explosion of powder, emerging on the other side covered in bright pink. Vulcan choked before turning away.

*What's wrong with him?* he asked, turning his head toward Vulcan.

*You look great,* I said with a wink.

He snorted in reply, ruffling his feathers and spraying me with pink.

We continued our meandering through the forest, stopping alongside various entertainers and vendors, until finally we arrived at the Eye of the Wood. Tents of various colors surrounded the cliff-lined lake and the tens of thousands of elves that gathered along its edges.

Queen Antares stood atop a large dais in front of a newly sung throne of vines and bright flowers. She scanned the throng of elves with a benevolent look plastered on her face. Isla caught my eye and smirked. We both knew if the queen wanted me found, it wouldn't be hard. Not with her soldiers or the countless spies in the crowd. But I was no longer a beacon in black.

I spied Tiberius out of the corner of my eye as two elven

children eyed him curiously. He lifted his big head toward them, wings tucked in tight. The elder of the two elven children stopped only a few feet away before dipping into a deep bow.

*Good gods.*

I rolled my eyes as the second quickly followed suit. Tiberius held himself higher and flared his wings in acknowledgment.

They said something, and he bowed his head. The older one pulled out a sack of orange powder, and Tiberius stretched out his wing. The elf tossed the nebulis into the air, the shimmering dust floating down over his long, dark feathers. A laugh escaped my lips, and Ti whipped his big head to mine and leered.

*Have fun with the foals.* I winked.

We edged our way through the throng as eight mystics, identifiable by the large wreaths of berries on their heads, stood at the edge of the cliff with arms raised high.

"I wouldn't bother getting close enough to hear," Isla murmured next to me. "It's the same every year... 'Prayers and thanks to Aelius, Brother of the Sun, yada yada,'" she mimed.

We continued inching our way closer to the mystic ahead of us. A man, older than Bayne and the rest of the crew but not as ancient as the master of spells.

The crowd shifted as we grew near, those around us moving aside as Tiberius sidled up to me. The mystic's gray-blue eyes caught on mine, and something flashed in his eyes as his lips tilted up in a deadly grin.

My stomach dropped as a familiar swirling liquid silver flashed in his eyes.

# CHAPTER ELEVEN

---

*There is an orb in the council room of Mount Telum. He says
it is a trick of the light, but I swear I've seen faces.*

*—Intercepted correspondence from Queen Galena,
intended for Sir Ronan Merik.*

---

My heart leaped into my chest before beginning a
steady gallop, and I staggered back. I'd seen those
eyes twice before. First, in Mount Telum, the night
I'd been taken by the kingsguards and then again in Stynguard,
when High Priest Helmar had strapped me to that chair.

Dread coiled in my gut. That soldier was *dead*. The kingsguard with the unnerving, silver eyes was dead. Dead by the
hands of Cyril's soldiers. I blinked, and the mystic's eyes had
returned to their gray-blue hue, continuing his scan of the
crowd.

"The past hundred years, we've suffered after the loss of

one of our own. The *Son* of our *Sun*. The one that brings life and light to all Lotrennia."

I shifted on my feet, catching Vulcan and Isla's wary eyes. The mystic scanned the crowd, whose murmurs filled the space.

"Aelius has blessed us this spring with his return. And with it, the return of the prosperous fruit that once thrived on these lands."

My stomach churned.

"Bayne Ravindra, Forgotten Prince, Bellator Reborn, has at last come home. And in his journey across the Juniper Sea, he has delivered the Bonder of Bellators."

A deep shade of pink flooded my cheeks, and I shrank between Drystan and Isla, grateful for the glitter that concealed the black clothes. Still, the elves around us glanced in our direction.

Hushed murmurs spread throughout the crowd, and I resisted the urge to sink back into the expansive forest behind us. Instead, I kept my gaze firmly on the mystic ahead, grateful Bayne wasn't here for whatever agenda this mystic had planned.

The mystic began a series of prayers, all in elven, the crowd joining in murmured repetition. Soon, the humming of thousands of elves lining the Eye of the Wood rose up in beautiful song.

The Transcindiel stirred within me for the briefest moment, a soft, thin tendril of magic tiptoeing through my entire being. I didn't manifest it, but I reached a strand of consciousness toward it in acknowledgment. The power had slumbered for so long, and the voices of the elves of Lotrennia acted like a little signal, calling it awake.

Room was made for the elderly and the youngest elves at

the edge of the cliffs. Those who had never seen the Awakening, or those who might have limited years to witness it.

Isla nudged Drystan and me toward the edge so that we might be able to see the entire lake, but I shook my head as Tiberius and I shared a look. He sauntered away, the crowd parting for him as he made his way back to the forest.

I pulled my attention back to the expansive, glittering lake. The mystics extended their hands in front of them, murmuring under their breaths as little bits of tiny lights danced along their fingertips.

I scanned the crowd for Vienah, curious to see if she'd made the trek to witness their water whispering. As one, the mystics moved their arms in swooping circles as the blazing sun rose directly above the lake.

Gasps of awe filled the air as the whooshing of the water below grew louder. The lake water spun, as though the mystics lining its edge wielded massive oars.

The spinning water rose up the cliffs, a tapestry of white, sapphire, and aqua blue stripes and swirls dancing along the ivory stone. It rose until the mist from the spray kissed our faces, thousands of feet above the water's surface. The elves along the edges didn't balk. In fact, they reached their hands out before touching their fingers to their brows and kneeling in prayer.

Like a wave of its own, all of those surrounding the Eye of the Wood were on their knees, myself included. I reached for the bond that tethered me to Tiberius, opening the connection, and found myself hundreds of feet above the lake, wings beating strongly, looking down into the swirling tempest.

I gasped as I took in the sight below where Tiberius flew, the lake so deep that the squall didn't even lighten the water in the center. It spun down hundreds of feet, where black-blue water swirled quietly in its center, lightening as it ascended.

I held onto Tiberius's cast, not wanting to miss this as he hovered in place.

We stared at that spot for several moments, captivated by that dark, calm water. Like a starless night before the rising of our two moons, Renova and Ganmira. That place between the stars that held everything, yet nothing at all. Tiberius's wonder mingled with my own.

A long, black line rose at the center of the darkness, sucking in that black-blue. Lightning fast, it split down its center, like a giant eye opening.

A sea blue circle filled the center of the lake with a black oval constricting against the blazing sun overhead.

*An eye.*

Tiberius hovered mid-air, and we marveled at the creature staring at him from the depths of the lake, when a torrent of wind and water crushed down from every direction. My heart dropped.

*The mystics have stopped the water whispering!* I screamed into our bond as water flooded Tiberius's vision. I struggled to maintain the cast and shoved my way through the crowd to find the long line of mystics lowering their fatigued arms.

Tiberius's wings beat wildly as he tried to ascend through the wall of water crashing down on all sides. The lake water soaked his sleek body, his velvety wings sopping wet, dragging him down.

*YOU WILL FLY!* I screamed down the bond.

I threw my strength into his wings, the muscles between my shoulder blades burning, my neck aching, my eyes watering, and my lungs stinging as water shoved up my nostrils.

Blackness and then...

The brightest light slammed into us as Tiberius broke through the crashing waves of the lake and into the blazing sun. Gasps echoed along the edges of the cliffs as Tiberius's dark form emerged from the center of the Eye of the Wood.

He spun midair, spraying water around him that glinted in the sunlight, the thin arc of a rainbow trailing around him. He was magnificent. A spectacle that had thousands of elves gaping in silent awe, before erupting in a chorus of cheers.

I HUGGED Ti's giant neck and rubbed the inside of his fuzzy ears with my thumbs an hour later. He finally dismissed me as a mother hen and stalked into the forest on his own.

"Ronan and Vander brought a handful of Rising soldiers." Vulcan approached the small table where my friends sat with plates full of food. "They're at the south end of the lake."

Smart. Steering clear of the queen and her quarry was a good idea. Especially Vander. Even with his release, there was enough for us to worry about.

Yet thousands of us danced and celebrated. Saros still reigned in Sultira. The dark king still haunted the world from the north. Countless remained enslaved as ashen on his godsforsaken island.

I glanced around, taking in the jubilant Lotrennians, celebrating and dancing without a care in the world. Isla's warm arm brushed against mine as she leaned in.

"They've suffered too," she murmured, as if reading my thoughts.

"How can we sit here and..." I looked around. Kegs of ale were tapped, and a jaunty chorus began in the distance, where pairs began a bouncy, choreographed dance.

"And celebrate? And *live*?" Isla's dark brows lifted.

I ground my teeth and shook my head, unable to meet her amber eyes.

"Lotrennia suffered for hundreds of years after the War of Ruin. Most of the ashen turned early on were elves. And you must remember, we live a long time. We've lost so many. And after Bayne and Nerissa left these shores... The mystic wasn't lying. Lotrennia suffered then, too."

I shot her a look.

"I'm not blaming them," she replied, holding her hands up. "I joined them, for gods' sakes. I'm saying that this..." She gestured to the celebration around us. "It's a miracle they still have the ability to *do* this. To *be* this. *They* are the unbroken ones."

My shoulders sagged. She was right, of course. She nudged my side.

"We deserve to live a little, too," she said, a spark lighting her eyes. "Come on. We're dancing. And finding those Rising soldiers."

# CHAPTER TWELVE

---

*Soulbinding remains the most mysterious and powerful of magical oaths. Mages have been known to elevate to mystic, and non-magic wielders have been granted otherworldly gifts.*
—Bonded Magic, 18^th level, Living Library.

---

We made our way to the southern end of the lake and found Ronan, Vander, and a horde of men and women by early evening. The Rising soldiers were at ease, loose and laughing. Van scooped me up into a one-armed back-cracking embrace before slapping his hand against Drystan's in greeting.

Ronan's eyes scanned our group, his brows dipping slightly.

"She's not here," I murmured as I stood next to him.

He shrugged his shoulders in that why-should-I-care way,

and I raised my brows. His breath hissed through his teeth as he shook his head.

"You need to tell her," I began. "You need to tell all of them."

I glanced at the tall soldier, and he kept his eyes forward, scanning clusters of Rising soldiers as they shrugged off their burdens for the evening.

"I will. When the time is right," he mumbled, glancing sidelong at me.

"They'll understand. You could have told them about the Rising before Crown Peak, you know. You should have been open with them from the start. Trust is harder to win the second time around."

He raised a light eyebrow. "Speaking from experience? Can I assume Bayne is getting the same lecture?"

I rolled my eyes as my molars pressed against each other. "Bayne has paid for his dishonesty. And things are... different between us now."

Ronan barked a bitter laugh. "So, now that you have access to his *feelings*, you trust him? That's not trust, Lyvia. That's a crutch."

A slow, burning sensation coiled its way into my chest. In a way, he was right. And it made me angry.

"He came clean. And he explained why—"

"Why he lied to you for months about who he was?" Ronan cut in. "Why he stayed so close to you in Sultira? Doesn't it bother you that he kept all that hidden, even after Kayj? Even in Odessa?"

A dryness formed in my throat. I had forgiven Bayne for hiding so many things, including his true identity. The power of the Bellators that he'd inherited from his ancestor. For his initial intentions of getting close to me. He had *feared* me. Feared what I would do with this power.

He never intended to let me leave after the crew of the *Evecta* took me from my cell in Mount Telum. In fact, he might have tried to kill me if things had gone differently.

But then he'd fallen for me as much as I had fallen for him. If I didn't feel the truth in those emotions coming down the connection we had now, would I have this trust in him? Would I have forgiven him? Would he still fear *me*?

"We're not talking about my love life."

Ronan opened his mouth, and I held up a hand.

"I don't completely trust *you* yet, either, Ronan."

He smirked. *Smirked.*

"You're an ass."

"I like keeping you on your toes, *Bonder*," he added with a wink.

I rolled my eyes.

"Tiberius put on an impressive spectacle." Ronan changed the subject, nudging me in the side. "Think the queen is okay with him showing her up?"

"I'm afraid to even think about it," I admitted.

He slid his gaze along my bare shoulders and torso, the golden script still shining bright in the low, orange sun.

"You'd make a good elf," he said, that familiar swagger entering his voice.

I elbowed him in the ribs, but a part of me eased at hearing that carefree tone return. His back was straight and his shoulders tense, but he seemed more relaxed tonight.

"Quite the contrast to that white and pink lacey thing you wore at the Sun Dance last summer." He pulled his sapphire eyes from mine and looked out at the men and women of the Rising, now joining in the dancing.

I blinked. "How do you know that?"

He glanced back, narrowing his light brows. "I was there, obviously."

I elbowed him again. "I know *that*. I saw you," I said, raising my eyebrows as I remembered the queensguard draped in his finest armor, white cape and all, shining like a black beacon next to the queen. "There were hundreds of people at that ball. You knew who I was a year ago?"

He turned to face me, eyebrows shooting up. "You really don't know?"

"Know what?"

He chuckled and shook his head, turning back to the celebration. "You were a highly sought-after lady-in-waiting. The men at court, those young lords. You were talked about ever since your entry into society four years ago... Wait, five? When was your birthday?"

Pink stained my cheeks. "End of summer."

"Noted." He tapped a finger to his temple and gave me a wink. "Anyways, you were an enigma. Beautiful, powerful, and yet all you wanted was to wear those damn black robes. Don't you remember Lord Pavel's nephew approaching you that night?"

I blushed as his words sank in. "He asked for some pointers about a couple of his mares. He seemed nervous. I thought maybe he was going to see if I could come work with them myself, but..."

I glanced up at Ronan, whose eyebrows rose to the dimming sky.

He barked out a laugh as he threw his head back, curls bouncing. "Oh, you *really* had no idea. I couldn't blame him. At least he was brave enough to approach you. Half of them gawked."

I chuckled and shook my head. Ronan gave me a roguish grin.

"Can you blame them? You looked..." His eyes took on a

glassy quality he searched his mind for memory. "Regal. Even Galena commented."

The red in my cheeks deepened. I glanced up at Ronan, whose countenance had shifted since his mention of the queen. I bit down on my lip as worry and an overall seriousness seeped back into his face.

"We'll get back, Ronan," I said quietly. "Soon. We'll find a way. Even if Tiberius has to fly us all the way there."

Ronan snorted. "Not sure that proud horse of yours would allow me on his back again." He nudged me, eyes softening.

*Definitely would not,* Ti's brazen voice sounded in my head.

*Get out!* I snapped back, severing our connection.

"You need to tell the crew the whole story," I said, returning my attention to Ronan. He eyed me warily as the internal conflict brewed. "The risk of not getting back in time *has* to outweigh the importance of the secret. Think about it."

The music paused for a moment as a new group of musicians replaced the exhausted, jubilant elves who had been playing. They pulled out wooden instruments and picked up a fast, jaunty tune.

Ronan heaved a sigh, as if shaking off the weight of his secret. "Since my duties prevented me from asking you last year"—he turned toward me, holding out a calloused hand—"dance with me?"

I grinned and gripped his hand, grateful that we had opened that door of communication those months ago in Odessa. Grateful for his friendship.

He pulled me into the throng of winding bodies, and we skipped along to the bouncy beat, twirling and laughing as we danced.

Torches lined the edge of the lake and lights hung stretched between branches, creating a web of dazzling flames as Aelius finally dipped beyond the horizon. The melody shifted as the night wore on. It picked up in beat and intensity, as if the music itself danced to the flames that swayed and skipped in the night wind.

The dancing turned sultry, with limbs and hips making smooth movements as bodies moved closer. Something deep stirred inside, and my thoughts drifted to Bayne. I pulled my eyes away from the elves pairing off.

Isla grasped my hand and pulled me into a throng of people. She spun me around, and we danced with each other. I let the music take me as I flung my arms into the air, spinning and closing my eyes as I took in the freedom of this moment, allowing myself to participate in this joy, in this ongoing cele-bration with the elves of light and life—with the mystical queendom I hadn't known existed a year ago.

I spun, losing track of time and my friends after several songs. Another blast of nebulis powder, this time silver and sparkling and smelling like cedar and something else, some-thing familiar. It filled the space between the torches, and I reached a hand into the glowing shine that floated through the air, my eyes catching on the stars blinking open in the midnight sky.

I ran my fingers through my hair, marveling at what the silver did to the black strands. I let the wild waves tangle together as I spun, eyes drifting closed once again. I opened them moments later as the air stirred around me, the elves moving aside, giving me space. I slowed my spinning and turned to the billowing cloud of gold nebulis exploding in the distance.

My feet stopped moving along with my heart. I sensed him

before I saw his tall, dark form stalk through the shimmering powder that rained from above. A brilliant, green gaze caught mine across the distance as Bayne prowled through the night.

# CHAPTER THIRTEEN

*With the rare occurrence of soulbinding, some couples have taken to air oaths, binding themselves to their choice of mate by breath, rather than soul.*
 *—Bonded Magic, 18<sup>th</sup> level, Living Library.*

I t took all my strength to keep from sprinting into his arms. He stalked toward me, closing the distance between predator and prey. A role I loved to play with him. He let a bit of that brilliant light out as he moved through the distracted crowd, easily disguised among the flashes of colored powder and bodies writhing around us.

I scanned his body as I searched for injuries or changes, my heart easing after finding none. His scent hit me like a bucket of water as I took a deep breath of cool pine and salty sea. My heart galloped against my ribs as his eyes roved from my bare feet up to my face and back down, filthy with dirt, sweat, and six different types of nebulis powder.

He crossed the distance in an instant and had my face in his warm hands a heartbeat later. His nostrils flared, scenting everything happening to me in an instant. I opened my connection to him and let it pour from me. The love, the *need*, the happiness.

"I didn't feel you coming," I murmured.

His mouth, inches from mine, quirked up into a wicked smile. "Surprise. Happy Awakening, Angel."

He brought his lips to my forehead, planting a soft, tender kiss in its center. My mouth found his in an instant as he pulled back to look at me. His lips... *Gods*, I missed his lips. They were soft and hard, burning and cooling, smooth and claiming all at once. I opened my mouth to his, and his tongue slipped against mine, smooth and practiced. I devoured him as my hands slid through his dark hair, gripping him harder against me. I pressed my body against his, and the shimmering powder smeared against my chest.

Home. This was home.

As if sensing it, he pulled his lips away from mine and murmured, "I'll always come back to you."

"Bayne!" A drunken Isla skipped through the crowd and danced around our forms.

"Happy Awakening, Isles," he said, flashing her a smile and sliding his hands to my waist.

She continued her skipping, now drawing the attention of the elves surrounding us. Their eyes widened as they took in Bayne. Several of them bowed or placed their fingers to their brows.

Bayne frowned, taking it in. He was used to the elves' respect, but he wasn't seen as nobility. He looked back at me, a question forming on his lips.

"I'll fill you in later," I murmured, eyeing the elves near us. I let out a sigh. "I have a lot to fill you in on, actually." My thoughts drifted to my air oath with the queen, the failed attempts with the ashen...

His fingers found my chin, and he gripped it with his thumb and forefinger, bringing my face an inch from his.

"Me too, but not tonight," he whispered, shaking his head. "Tonight is about life. Dance with me."

His fingers snaked down my arms and twined with my own as he twisted me around, crossing my arms in front and pressing me into him. He leaned in close, head tucked above my shoulder. I sagged into him, breathing in his scent and falling into the rhythm he set with his hips against my back.

I'd never danced with someone like this. The frenzied beat of the music had subdued, pressing the bodies of those matching its notes closer together. His fingers released mine, and my hands slid along the back of his neck as he moved behind me. His hands found my hips and torso, still slick with sweat from the muggy day.

"Gods, I missed you," I breathed, the words barely audible over the heavy beat of drums.

"I missed everything about you. Your scent," he murmured into my ear as he sucked in a deep breath.

The hard length of him pushed behind me, and a rush of familiar longing skirted down my abdomen.

"Your taste." He bent his head, his tongue sliding along the line between my shoulder and neck. I shuddered, my skin pebbling in its wake. He let out a chuckle that reverberated through my bones.

He spun me to face him, and his eyes shuddered, a darkness I'd grown to love dancing within his forest green irises.

"Let me show you how much I've missed you," he whispered, the plea on his breath brushing softly against my lips.

*Please*, I mouthed.

A soft growl escaped his lips. His hand slid down my arm,

and he laced his fingers with mine, turning and leading us through the writhing bodies and boisterous celebration.

A network of small caves and underground rivers flowed south of the Eye of the Wood, connecting to a labyrinth of sinkholes dotting the southern end of the forest. The sound of distant celebration disappeared in the rushing of waterfalls as we entered a cave a mile away. Soft moonlight slithered in from the various openings in the stone ceiling, rippling along the shallow, clear waters.

Bayne dropped my hand and dove into the spring. The water stripped the glittering nebulis from him and fanned out in a cloud of silver and gold. He kicked, aiming for the opposite wall, where his dark head breached the surface, and he shook his hair, white droplets of water spraying off the chiseled body his wet clothes clung to. He turned to me, lips tilting up into a mischievous, beckoning grin as those piercing green eyes devoured me where I stood.

I stepped to the edge of the small pool, sucking in a breath before I leaped from its edge. The crisp water cleared the fog brought on by the fruity alcoholic drinks. I poked my head through the surface, keeping half my face in the water as Bayne stalked toward me. He knelt in the pool, lowering himself to where I crouched.

Unable to resist the urge, I spat the water at his face. Maybe the cool dip hadn't completely cleared my mind. He blinked, face quiet with shock, before he threw his head back and let out a laugh that danced along my limbs.

His predatory gaze returned, and I jumped, ready to escape his grasp as he leaped on me. I let out an uncontrollable giggle as his forearm wrapped around my waist, and he pulled me to him. I half-heartedly attempted to wriggle free, earning me a nip on my shoulder. I twisted toward him, melting into his warmth in the chilled pool as I wrapped my limbs around him.

My blood thundered over the rippling water. Need pulsed through every part of my body, as if a part of my soul had been missing this past month and made whole again in a split second.

Bayne opened himself to me, and his matching emotions slammed into me.

Need. Love. And something darker, something I couldn't place...

I frowned, opening my mouth to question him when his mouth crashed into mine, smooth and wet. An overwhelming, intoxicating wave of need washed over me. I threw my own emotions down our connection, and he moaned, the sound setting me on fire in the cool water.

The wet fabric of his loose shirt clung to his body as I tugged it off. His hands slipped into the laces on my back, freeing the silky wet top. My damp breasts peaked against the midnight air. Hard hands slid down my back as he continued to claim my lips, moving for my pants. My fingers grappled at the laces on his leathers as I at last kicked my pants free, the billowing black fabric floating away.

*Gods,* those leathers. The snug fabric hugged his muscled legs and ass... I never wanted him to wear anything else, but now I needed them off. My fingers fumbled as I tried to get the wet laces loose.

Had it really only been a week? Too long. A fucking life-time. His hungry mouth slammed against mine, teeth sliding along my tongue. I yanked, finally freeing that long length of perfection that seemed to be made just for me. A low growl rumbled up his chest and through the breath that escaped into my lips.

"Lyv..."

Gods, the way he said my name lit me on fucking fire. *His* fire. The fire of the sun itself, an exhilarating burn. My power swirled in response to the storm of feeling that flew through me.

I sucked in a breath, diving below before he could stop me. I wrapped my lips around him, taking him in fully. The moan that escaped my lips reached my ears in a ripple of vibration underwater. It danced along my bones and sent my tongue moving in those ways I knew drove him crazy.

My movement was quick and eager, and the air in my lungs quickly urged me back to the surface. My hand replaced my mouth as I shot up, drinking in the muggy night air. Feral desire danced in his bright green eyes as they landed on me. Taking my time, I lazily drew a line from his hip to his neck with my tongue as I worked him below the surface.

I sucked in a breath, ready to dive again, when a growl escaped his lips, and he gripped my ass, hauling me out of the water and onto a nearby ledge under a light, trickling waterfall.

"I said *I* would show you how much I missed you," he purred.

I could sense the pressure building in him, the control it took to stop me.

Firm hands braced my hips against the cool stone, and his lips hovered inches above mine as he purred, "I have time to make up for. Let me."

His mouth found its way to that spot beneath my ear, and he uttered a low whisper, "I missed the way you come alive when I do *this*." His lips grazed my heated skin, sending a ripple of little bumps rising along my neck and down my arm.

I focused on my breathing, already prepared to combust. He peppered small kisses down my neck and over my chest. I arched into him, my back scraping slightly against the stone, unable to keep still. A soft chuckle escaped his lips.

"I missed those little sounds you make when I do this." His

fingers drew torturous lines from the inside of my knee to the apex of my thighs.

A tiny sound escaped my lips, and I bit down to keep from making more. He smiled against my skin as he continued his slow trek down the line of my abdomen.

"And I missed the way your leg twitches when I do this," he said against my skin as his tongue drew a trail down the center of me to that space between my legs, pounding with desperate need.

My leg twitched in response, and I didn't care. All I cared about was him. I needed this. More of this. I needed more of that tongue, more of him, *all* of him.

As if in response, his tongue roved over me in agonizing, smooth circles. I arched again, sliding my hands above my head to a divot in the cave, water slowly trickling onto my face and breasts, desperate for this. Two fingers replaced his mouth as he pumped them in smooth movements.

"I missed this, most of all," he whispered, sending all his feelings and emotions down the link that connected us.

A claiming storm of love and need and overwhelming desire curled itself around my own, our souls practically touching. The pounding between my legs intensified, and blood rushed to that spot in the center as his tongue returned to the peak. I let out a cry, the pleasure racking through me as I shuddered against his touch.

A satisfied groan escaped his lips as he kissed the space between my legs all the way up to my neck. I locked my lips on his, the taste of myself now mingling with *his*, still on my tongue. A perfect pairing. He nuzzled his face into my shoulder, nibbling the space at the base of my neck, sending sparks dancing once again between my legs. He inhaled against my neck, scenting my recovery, and I reached for the length of him between us.

He let out a guttural groan as I focused my attention back on the thick, pulsing length that hung between his legs. I pressed my hand against his tanned shoulder, wrapping my legs around his torso.

I eased him into me, savoring that burning stretch of pleasure, settling him deep inside. A perfect fit. Like we were made for this. I smiled against his lips in the darkness of the cave. The moons' soft blue light peeked in, highlighting the raised scar on his temple. So beautiful.

His hands found my hips, and I allowed him to move me how he wanted. The drums from earlier in the night banged in my mind as he moved faster, matching their writhing rhythm. He kept a hand on my hip as he moved against me, as the other drifted to my breast. He squeezed and rubbed his thumb against my nipple, the sensitive peak hardening against his touch.

He reached both hands to meet my own above my head as the space between us shrank, his chest crushing against my own as the pulsing intensified. Our mouths met, his tongue rough and claiming. I sucked it into my mouth, urging him faster. Thunder shuddered in my core as Bayne began to shake.

Pinned to the wall, I let my hands slide down his muscles. The eight-pointed stars on my palms met his in the center of his chest. As fireworks danced behind my eyes, we burned and froze and created as our powers released on their own accord, dancing as we crashed into ecstasy together. A flash of black and white and brilliant gold escaped the cracks between our skin and lit up the cave around us. It was gone as soon as it appeared, and I sagged against him, letting the trickle of water cool our steaming bodies.

We stayed there, panting into each other's mouths, until finally, I let out a shiver that racked my body. Bayne's arms wrapped around me as he slid out, lifting me off the ledge and out of the shallow pool. He pulled a large fur from a pack concealed in the corner of the cave. I looked at him quizzically.

He shrugged. "Surprise."

Tossing the fur around our shoulders, he found a dry space for us deep in the cave, where I wrapped myself around him, soaking in the warmth of his body and drifting off into peaceful oblivion, whole at last.

# CHAPTER FOURTEEN

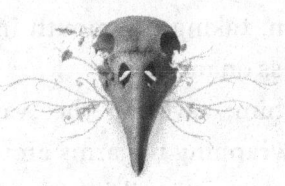

---

*Threads can be strengthened, or even created, through bonded magic.*

—*Bonded Magic, 18th level, Living Library.*

---

Fractured, coral light smeared in streaks across the rough cave wall as dawn broke. I glanced around the softly illuminated cave, eyeing the vines of blue flowers that ran along the stone walls. I didn't remember seeing them last night, though perhaps this was Bayne's new power manifesting in its own way.

I ran my fingers over Bayne's chest as it rose and fell. His features were still a mask of deep sleep. I traced the whorls of black ink that covered his chest, hiding the eight-pointed star that marked him as a Bellator.

After sailing to Lotrennia, I'd realized quickly the center of his inked sun was the coastline of his home. And spinning out from its center, ferns and vines unfurled wildly, looking so much like the rays of the brilliant power he harnessed. The power of the sun itself. *Soleia*.

He stirred under my touch, grumbling sleepily. I nipped his chin in reply, his long stubble scratching against my teeth. His brilliant eyes fluttered open as he ran his fingers along my cheek. He leaned in, taking my mouth in his and planting a luxurious, sleepy kiss on me.

I melted into him, savoring the warm hardness of his smooth body and wrapping my arms around his perfect form. He pulled away, his lips tilting up in a grin of true contentment.

"I have something for you," he said, sudden eagerness pulsing through the connection.

Pink rushed to my cheeks as he pulled out a rough gray rock, the size of my palm, wrapped in a bow of green ribbon.

I tugged the ribbon loose, and the rough rock fell open to reveal an orange and white crystal center. Inside the geode sat a folded piece of white silk. I flipped the folds over and plucked up the amber oval resting in its center.

My thumb smoothed over the hard, translucent resin, carved into an oval that connected to a thin, braided chain.

"It's beautiful," I breathed, marveling at the amber glowing in the dimness of dawn.

"Open it," he murmured into my ear.

I flickered my eyes to his as my fingers slipped along the edge of the pendant, finding a barely perceptible clasp. I flipped it open, and the oval split, revealing flat, tightly curling spirals of what looked to be some type of shell. Fossilized remains of a creature, I realized. I marveled at the fossil that looked so much like the ferns draping the land of Lotrennia.

"We call them tendrilytes. No one has ever seen one living, but they're all over Lotrennia, if you know where to dig for them." The corner of his mouth tilted up as he threw me a wink.

Warmth flooded my chest as the thoughtfulness hit me. The remains inside, a little bit of me, and the likeness of the ferns, a little bit of him. I blinked away a small drop of liquid forming in the corner of my eye.

"It's an amplifier," Bayne said softly.

I raised my eyes to him in question. All of the amplifiers, even the Bones of the Bellators, were destroyed when used properly.

"You won't destroy it," he said with an air of confidence. "I promise."

My lips parted, the question already forming, and he shook his head.

"Trust me."

And I did. I closed the pendant and held it against my chest. "Thank you," I whispered as he pulled it over my head. The amber glowed against my olive skin in the early morning light.

We sat there for a few minutes before I finally took a deep breath and divulged the maelstrom of shit that had unfolded during his absence. Bayne, Aelius bless him, met it with calm confidence. Even when I confessed to the bargain with the queen, despite the alarm that soared down our connection, he simply ran his rough hands down my arm, squeezing me closer.

"Nis was right in that this was dangerous. But I agree, you didn't have much of a choice," he murmured. "Even if Vander had killed her, *his* death sentence would have meant the Rising's..."

Relief swelled in my chest at his understanding. He shifted, so he faced me. "And Antares... We'll find a way to deal with her."

"Your turn," I murmured against his lips. "What did you see at the Waters of Ascendiel? Or is it a secret?" I teased.

He kissed me slowly, as if not wanting to rush this quiet, rare time we had together, before we returned to Ayla, where the weight of our burdens awaited.

He pulled away, smoothing a strand of loose hair away from my face. His face tightened, his brows narrowing slightly, as if in deliberation.

"I saw a vision of a battle, here in Lotrennia." His eyes drifted to my forehead briefly as he paused.

"The ashen? Daimos?" I asked, sitting up onto my elbow.

Bayne shook his head, his forehead creased.

"Something worse. Something I don't fully understand," he murmured.

I opened my mouth to probe further.

"We all need to prepare. We need to be at our strongest." Bayne's eyes had taken on a glassy effect as he stared at the ceiling of the cave.

My stomach twisted.

"I know you've struggled with the Transcindiel..." The words dripped with hesitation as they left his lips.

A weight pressed against my chest, and an unspoken strain pushed against our connection.

"You think I should focus my efforts on the transformation," I said quietly for him. "Forget about the death of the Lady of Tomorrow for now."

He murmured his confirmation.

Unease settled in my stomach. Something about her death reeked of evil. Could I let this go?

And the ashen transformations... I'd been trying. The question of why I'd been failing continued to nag at me, an accusatory finger pointing at my own insecurities, at my own selfish fear of losing the man I loved.

I knew so deeply in my heart that Bayne loved me. My failures had nothing to do with saving Lida and turning her back into an elf. I knew that when I finally transformed Lida, Bayne's last love, the *reason* he'd gone to Kayj in the first place, that he'd stay with me. He might still love Lida, always love her in some way, but there was something deeper between Bayne and I. Wasn't there? Wasn't that what this connection was between us?

Yet that same, shameful thought crouched at the back of my consciousness. That maybe I didn't *want* to change her. That I was so selfish, I couldn't allow someone else near his light.

Bayne's palm flipped up as little bits of fire and light danced above his hand. Beautiful, white flames dipped and swirled together. We lay there, watching the light ebb and flow in fascinating patterns.

"Try it," he murmured into my hair as my mind drifted to my own powers.

My body tensed. I didn't have this level of control. I could summon the Obscura easily now, but it was a blast of raw power. Directing a small bit of concentrated power like this...

Bayne's reassuring warmth slipped into that connection of ours, and my heart calmed.

"*Try*," he said again, brushing soothing strokes of his hand through my hair.

I flipped my hand over, summoning a small bit of Obscura to rise above the luminous star at the center of my palm. The blue of my veins turned midnight black as I let darkness pool at the surface. It flowed to my palm, slow and steady. I released a breath as I allowed a bit of it to escape.

A small, steady black tendril of power winked into existence above my hand. It hovered, unmoving, like a teardrop of black sky suspended in midair. Bayne slid a cautious curiosity down our connection, enough for me to release more.

Darkness exploded in the small space. I let out a cry, terror seizing my chest at the loss of control, uncertain if it was Bayne's fear or my own, when white light swept through the cave, smothering the shadows.

He let out a low whistle as I clamped my fist shut.

"Too much," I said, shakily.

"Maybe a bit," he murmured with a breathy chuckle.

I let out a low, shaky laugh. But that one bit of power... We'd have to find more time to train together in the coming days. I opened my mouth to say as much when Kresida's demanding voice barked from outside the cave.

"Her Majesty requires an audience, Captain," the War Slayer called.

My stomach twisted at her undetected approach as her words hauled us back to our weighted reality.

# CHAPTER FIFTEEN

*The key has been stolen. Rumor has it Nyxteria landed in the*
*Land of Light and Life.*
*—Correspondence from Sea Spear to White Hawk.*

Anxiety snaked its way through my chest as I was ushered into the Gilded Fortress. Hours after Kresida escorted Bayne to the castle, I'd received the same summons.

A long, round table glimmered like a mirror in the middle of the room, cut from the center of a massive tree, hundreds of rings spiraling into its center. Ronan and his two commanding officers sat across from Isla and Bayne, whose eyes found mine immediately. I scanned the room for Vulcan and Drystan, but no sign. I slid into a chair next to Nerissa.

Bayne's gaze held mine for a mere moment, his face tight as he let a glimmer of feeling slip past the wall he'd thrown up.

*Warning.*

He threw it back up as he pulled his gaze to the golden-haired queen seated at the head of the table. Ronan and Isla met my eyes, and though I didn't share that intimate conscious connection with them, wariness hung in their gazes.

Across the hall, three mystics entered, one I recognized from the Eye of the Wood. I scanned his eyes, searching for that unsettling bit of living silver, but found none as he took his seat. Behind him, Khato, the master of spells, shuffled in, giving me a soft smile. I returned it as best I could, despite the unease pitting in my stomach.

A moment later, Carina quietly entered from a door in the back and scurried into the waiting chair. She kept her brilliant Ravindra gaze down, not daring a look at the others. It was hard to believe Carina came from the same family as *any* of the commanding elves in the room. The petite elf glanced at me beneath her round spectacles before they darted to her mother.

"I've gathered you all here, as I have important news to share for the future of the Rising," Queen Antares began, her eyes sliding to Ronan.

"My scouts report that the waters of the Juniper Sea have finally begun to calm after the unprecedented Sending. They may not yet be safe for the Sultiran ships that carried you here from Odessa, but we've made a few successful passes with Lotrennian ships to the southern coast."

The crew of the *Evecta* straightened in their seats, and my heart quickened in my chest at the information. If Lotrennian ships could make it, the *Evecta* would have no trouble at all. I glanced at Ronan, noting the flare of hope in his eyes.

"That being said, I'm unable to spare the ships needed to carry all of the Rising forces back to Sultira."

"Why?" Isla blurted out.

"The dark king sails for Northern Lotrennia," the queen responded, leveling a hard gaze at Bayne.

"We must send enough forces to prevent him from moving troops inland," Queen Antares continued, "Ashen and ground troops alike. I will not risk the lives of Lotrennians to simply transport your forces back."

The mystics nodded to each other, glancing briefly at the commanders.

"My scouts also report Rising forces gather in Southern Sultira," she continued, nodding to Ronan.

I blinked. How had she gathered this information? Ronan searched her eyes, as if wondering the same thing.

"I sent aid to the Rising at Odessa, as requested by Commander Merik, and offered you sanctuary here in my home. We saved *all of you*." She stressed the last words, eyes snapping to mine before pulling back to the rest of the group. "I've gathered you here to call in the debt that is owed."

My stomach churned. I hadn't thought about this... That she would demand something in return. I glanced at Ronan from across the table, his face lightening a shade as his azure eyes met mine. Though Bayne still held the curtain tight against our connection, I could sense a quiet wrath rising in him.

"Before I go into details about what I require, I have news to share that I think will be of some value to this group. Rumor has spread through Aedrialis that Queen Galena is with child."

Dread unfurled in my chest. If rumor had already spread in Aedrialis... The queen's eyes slid to my own, before looking at Ronan.

Color leached from the ex-queensguard's face, horror rippling off his shoulders. Nerissa stiffened next to me, though she didn't let a wink of emotion shatter her disinterested countenance. He should have told them. *Gods*, I tried to tell him.

Ronan's commanders shifted, angling themselves toward their leader. They both knew Ronan's true connection to the queen, the reason he'd tried to rush the attack on Aedrialis last spring.

"And as you all know," the queen continued, smiling at the tension she'd spun through the room, "wives and children of King Saros typically don't last long."

Ronan clasped his hands together, trying his best to keep them from shaking. Isla's movement was barely perceptible as her arm slid closer to his. She knew he needed contact, needed someone to keep him grounded and remind him our salvation lay in the enemy's hands.

"Saros will be distracted in the coming months. All the more reason for the Rising to attack soon." She nodded toward the Rising commanders.

"Based on the numbers reported, we feel confident we can beat Daimos back in the coming months. I am willing to send Lotrennian ships to escort the Rising troops back to Sultira, to reconvene with the rest of the Rising as soon as the Bonder retrieves the next Bellator Bone."

Silence rippled as all eyes in the room slid to where I sat. I stared at the queen, letting the debt I was to pay settle in my bones. I glanced at Ronan, his brows angling upward in a pinched apology.

"Dark King Daimos has the Ramadiel Bone," Isla cut through the silence. "Are you suggesting we try to sail to Nivis while he attacks our shores?"

The queen's eyes didn't leave my own as she shook her head, the soft curls bouncing at her shoulders. "That's not the bone I'm talking about."

The others stirred. She nodded to Carina from across the table. The petite elf stood and hurried to the corner of the room, where she picked up a handful of scrolls.

My stomach dropped as I took in their caramel hue, my mind spinning back to Enya's burial chamber. She placed the scrolls on the table, reverently unrolling the first to reveal the map, the *original* map from the excavation.

My palms pressed against the smooth table as I leaned forward. How did they get these? Carina's eyes flitted to my own as she pulled out a second scroll, one I hadn't seen before, and laid it next to the map.

"A key to the map," she began, her voice small and meager compared to the commanding presence of her mother, "to the location of the burial chambers of the other Bellators."

Silence cleaved the room. No one dared a breath as they gaped at the small elf who adjusted her spectacles. A *key*. I hadn't even considered what else the map might be showing. I shrank as the magnitude of this missing piece hit me.

Queen Antares's pink lips twisted, delighting in the unease settling among the group. "We believe there is a burial site marked here, in the Death Dunes," she said, motioning to the ancient scroll.

Hushed murmurs spread through the table as I eyed the Death Dunes, the land north of Sultira, uninhabitable due to the frigid temperatures and unforgiving land. Miles of tundra and snow stretched across the continent, even during the heart of summer. No plants were known to grow in the area, and the only beasts ever seen were the terrifying dune runners—reptilian-looking wolves that devoured anything landing on their shores. The perfect hiding place.

"Commander Merik," the queen said at last, turning to Ronan. "You promised me access to Bellatorian powers to at last put an end to Dark King Daimos if aid came to the Rising."

Ronan grimaced as he nodded. "Access...yes. But that was before the return of the Bellators. Before Lyvia claimed the power and it became a part of her. Lyvia is not under my command."

The queen's eyes narrowed as she glanced at me. "We may

not be bound by an air oath, Commander, but a promise sworn to an ally in a time of war is as binding as one. I require *access* to the Bonder's powers. When Lyvia returns with the bone of power that's hidden in the Death Dunes, I will escort your forces back to continue the fight."

I shifted in my seat, mind racing. Bayne said we needed to prepare, that we needed more power. I could do this. I could find the bone... I'd always had a way of finding the dead. And with the vast nothingness of the Death Dunes, I had no doubt I'd be able to pick up the pulse of power.

"You will leave at dawn, while the Juniper Sea is trekkable, as we don't know how long that will last. We'll spare one ship to retrieve the bone for Lotrennia, while our others will sail north to defend against Daimos."

My throat bobbed. Nausea churned as I thought of a bone of power in the hands of the queen, but what choice did I have? She remained standing, awaiting my response. I eyed Bayne, waiting for his easy confidence I'd become so used to, but was met with a blank look.

"If I'm to locate this burial site and find the bone," I finally said, meeting the queen's stare without flinching, "then I choose the crew I'm to sail with."

The edges of the queen's lips tilted. "Of course," she purred. "You may choose a handful of companions."

"Okay," I conceded, an uneasy bitterness sweeping over me. I would do this one thing to get the Rising forces back to Sultira. To end King Saros. To save Queen Galena and her unborn child. To stop the tribute and turn our forces back to the true enemy in the north.

"There is the matter of your agreement, however." The queen's lips spread into a wide smile as her gaze bore into me. "My requirement with the Transcindiel and Obscura powers. You agreed to eight training sessions before the end of summer. With your departure, Tiberius will need to remain behind."

I blinked. *Leave Tiberius here?* My head shook in denial and my stomach pitched as the words settled in.

"An oath is an oath, Bonder," the queen crooned. "You're bound by your breath. And you don't have much of a choice unless you're ready to forfeit the Rising's alliance with the elves. Think about what's most important. Think about those you left behind in Sultira, in Kayj. Rising forces need to return home. We need the next bone of power or elves and humans will continue to suffer under the cruelty of the kings. Surely, the two of you can spend a few months apart and reunite stronger than ever."

Fuck. We needed to discuss this in private. I stood, darkness clouding my veins, ready to leave. The others followed suit and began to shuffle out. Bayne's steadying hand slid to my lower back as we reached the back of the room.

"One more thing to note," the queen purred from behind, still standing at the head of the table. "Assuming Khato's most recent revelation proves true, should Bayne accept my offer, not only will we ferry the Rising forces to Sultiran shores upon Lyvia's return, but fifteen thousand Lotrennian soldiers will accompany them in an alliance to aid in dethroning Saros."

Bayne's hand froze on my back.

# CHAPTER SIXTEEN

*Death arrives in the dunes when the darkness meets the light.*
*— Correspondence from White Hawk to Silver Dragon.*
*73rd of Summer. 071.3E.*

The *Evecta* rocked softly against the waves pouring into the sheltered bay from the Juniper Sea, yet I heard nothing beyond the thundering of blood in my ears.

Marriage. The queen had *proposed* to Bayne. A brilliant, wicked move on her part. And the words of the mystics that day at the Awakening ceremony, all to build off the fervor of the elves to see Bayne as their savior.

The queen was only related to him through marriage to his uncle. It wasn't unheard of. And their union, the union of a powerful mystic queen and a Bellator, "Aelius's son" himself... They would be unstoppable.

In return, the Lotrennians would escort the Rising forces

back to Sultira, *and* they would send fifteen thousand fighters along to crush Saros. We could end this in months if he said yes. She'd set him up for this, to spring the offer on him, and then throw it in his face before he had a chance to talk to us, to talk to *me* about it. And with the presence of the other elves and mystics in that meeting, word would spread quickly through Lotrennia.

Repulsion settled in my gut. What choice did he have? We'd all sacrificed for this. And the Lotrennians were his people. He *deserved* to be king, would thrive as king. The land, the people, the *world* would thrive. But could anyone keep the ill intent of Queen Antares leashed?

I was going to be sick. I couldn't meet Bayne's eyes as we all gathered below deck. His gaze burned against my face, along with the gentle caress of his consciousness as he searched for a way to reach me. I had thrown the curtain up the second I pieced together what Queen Antares had said. The second I realized he hadn't immediately rejected her offer, that he still considered it.

My stomach pitched. What did I even want from him? I'd avoided the Match, the marriage protocol for the Court of Two Moons, for as long as I'd been in society, clinging to the hope I might be accepted as a Death Scholar one day. I didn't want to be married. I *hadn't* wanted to be married. But with Bayne...

Shame snaked its way into my heart as the selfish feelings ripped through me. I pinned my eyes on Ronan, and he glanced at me before sliding his gaze to the others. Marian, Drystan, and Vulcan eyed the group warily, uncertain what events had transpired.

"Well *fuck*," Isla sighed the words. "She has you by the balls, Captain."

Bayne pulled his stare from my own and raised a dark brow at her.

"Can someone fill us in?" Vulcan growled from the corner.

"Queen Antares proposed marriage to Bayne," I murmured.

"That's nothing compared to what Khato claims," Isla interjected, her words sharp yet wary as she slid her gaze to Bayne. His face paled as I searched it for meaning.

"It's not true," Nerissa cut in quietly, her voice dripping with accusation and devastation. Her face was as pale as Bayne's, repulsion lining her wan lips. "Tell me it's a lie."

"What claim?" Ronan asked, straightening in his chair.

All eyes landed on Bayne as he uncrossed his arms and rubbed his face. Silence stretched. I counted my heartbeats as we waited.

"The master of spells has elevated his powers enough to unlock the ability of threadsight. Khato can see the threads of the universe, connecting everyone and everything, living or otherwise. See them and *identify* them..."

I looked to the others, still not understanding what this meant.

"Get on with it," Nerissa growled, pinning Bayne to the spot with her matching eyes. Bayne's throat bobbed as he caught my eye.

"He's identified a soulbinding thread linking the queen and me."

An inexplicable laugh escaped my lips, and the eyes in the room turned toward me. I couldn't pull my gaze from Bayne's as I slowly shook my head.

"That is," I began, my lips curving up. "I mean, come on. There is no way, right? There's no possible way." My head continued to shake.

Isla leaned forward, grasping my hand, and leveled a serious look at me.

"Bayne—" I began, my voice foreign and far away.

"Have you felt it?" Nerissa's words were quiet with accusing outrage.

The dark lashes above Bayne's green eyes shuddered as his gaze drifted away from mine at last.

I barely processed the filthy string of curses leaving Vulcan's mouth as the world seemed to drop out from beneath me. *Soulbound*. Or rather, the potential to be. The universe, sick and twisted as it was, sought to bind him to someone who had done such horrific deeds to his parents.

Nerissa stood frozen in her outrage, eyes not leaving Bayne.

"Queen Antares is power-obsessed. We know that soul-binding amplifies the powers of those bound. It's no surprise she's fixated on this," Isla began. "But just because you've felt it, doesn't mean you have to act on it. Soulbinding must be *consensual*. You have a choice, Bayne." Her voice bent with urge.

I choked as I tried to swallow the dryness in my throat. "What does it feel like?" I rasped out.

Bayne shook his head, and my chest caved inward.

Tension rippled through the small room as several moments passed in silence. This couldn't be happening. Drystan's crystal eyes found mine, and I bristled at the pity in them. Isla at last broke the silence with a frustrated groan.

"And there's the matter of you going after the bone in the Death Dunes," she murmured, turning toward me.

Vulcan snapped his head toward me, and I scowled.

"I didn't have much of a choice in that," I retorted, glancing at Ronan. "And I'm sure I can find it."

Isla held up her hand. "I've no doubt you can find it. I'm worried what your separation will do," she said, rubbing her thumb and forefinger in the space between her eyes.

My brows pinched.

"This is all a part of her scheme. Separate you, distance you from Bayne, from Tiberius, position you as the enemy. The

Lotrennians might not like you, but they don't see you as a real threat yet because of us." She motioned to herself and those left in the room. "Because we are family."

"But Bayne will come with," I interjected, looking to him for confirmation. My stomach plummeted as his eyes dipped.

"They are starting to trust you," Isla continued. "And after Tiberius's little performance at the Awakening..."

Pointed stomping began above deck as Tiberius listened in on our conversation.

"Yes, you," Isla snapped back, looking up at the smooth teak ceiling. "With that little rainbow display at the Eye of the Wood, they see you both as gods. Antares needs to weaken us. And the first step in doing that is separating you two. And then to dangle the alliance in front of us like that..."

Bayne's dark lashes shuddered a moment before he blinked and finally sat down at the table across from me, reaching for my hands. I let him take them, as the realization filled my chest with a painful ache.

"You don't have much of a choice in going to the Death Dunes," Bayne murmured. "And with the marriage, with the soulbinding, she's promised a way to fight for the freedom of my love's homeland. To protect her in a way I can't without her."

I frowned, small buds of liquid forming in the corners of my eyes.

"No," I said, resisting the urge to scream.

Bayne's hard gaze found mine.

"No, we'll find another way. Come with me... You could..."

"I can't leave," Bayne murmured, dropping my hands as he stood and began to pace in the small space.

"Why?"

"Because Lotrennia is dying," Vulcan answered, words cutting through the silence.

I snapped my gaze to his. "What do you mean it's *dying*?"

Vulcan's hazel eyes surveyed Bayne. "I'm right, aren't I?" he asked, blonde eyebrows raised high. "The land has been dying for years. It got worse when we fled, decades ago, because Aelius's essence left the continent. And since our return, the land has recovered slowly, but only in Bayne's presence. Tell us what you saw on the way to the Waters of Ascendiel."

Bayne's dark gaze flickered as they met Vulcan's across the room.

"Death. Ground that will not yield crops. Animals have fled. Even the fish seem to have abandoned the rivers and lakes. And the wolves are indeed gone. I need to protect Lotrennia," Bayne answered in a hoarse voice.

"That's why she allowed you to go," I said quietly, color leaching from my face as the others looked at me. "She wanted you to see what leaving did to your kingdom. What will happen if you leave again. Already, she's chained you here." The last words escaped my lips in a whisper.

Bayne's shoulders heaved as his breath quickened, the rage storming inside him barely constrained against the wall he'd thrown between us. Nerissa hadn't moved a muscle, and I briefly searched her face for any sign of the power raging beneath her skin.

I weighed my next words carefully, knowing I treaded dangerous water as my mind drifted to what Isla had shared with me months ago. About the cause of the strain in Bayne and Lida's relationship.

"We could fight..." I murmured cautiously. "*You* could take the throne."

The power of the sun exploded in front of me. Terrifying white flames, flaring without heat, ripped into the small room below deck in a cascade of waves, blinding us. They were gone within an instant. Isla's hand reached for mine as the Obscura surged to my palms in a quick, reflexive response.

"*I CAN'T!*" he bellowed, throwing his arms to either side. "Because if I take back the throne, I throw our entire fucking land into a civil war, all while Dark King Daimos attacks from the north and Sultira is too busy fighting their own war to send aid!"

My voice caught in my throat as I blanched. The crew stilled, Bayne's break in control freezing everyone in place.

Nerissa took a quiet step forward and seethed, "Get it together, Bayne." She shot a quick look at Ronan, disgust, betrayal, and pain shining in her eyes before stalking to the exit.

Ronan rose, knocking his chair to the ground as he surged toward her. "Nis—" he began and was cut off by a sharp hiss as he reached for her hand. "*Please.*" Ronan looked as if he was about to vomit as the plea broke his voice. He licked his lips, face pale as he gripped her arm.

Nerissa turned to face him, eyes heavy with betrayal. He slid his hand down her arm, grasping hers. She yanked back, but he held firm. Her lips wobbled, and Ronan's light brows pinched up. He kept his gaze on Nerissa's forest green eyes and the arrival of a shallow pool of tears, enough to brighten her irises without falling.

It was to her that he finally told his story, Ronan's secret I promised to keep when he'd divulged so much in Odessa. The only reaction Nerissa let show was a slow blink, allowing one tear to trickle down her cheek as she processed Ronan's last words.

*Sister.*

Galena, Queen of Sultira, was Ronan's sister... and a fraud. The two of them grew up in the streets of Krestwood, clawing and whoring themselves through their early lives.

The brother and sister pair had witnessed the horrors of the tribute, losing both their parents early on, barely escaping the grasp of Dark King Daimos in the process. They'd eventually found work and refuge with the Lord and Lady of Krestwood, a quiet nobility rarely seen in the Court of the Two Moons. And when the family had taken ill, the fire pox ravaging the western cities, the brother and sister seized their opportunity.

They'd been teenagers then, reckless and desperate. They'd bribed and silenced using money stolen from the manor, with Galena posing as the daughter who had died. The two of them slowly found their way to Aedrialis through masterful lies and manipulation. Ronan rose quickly in the ranks of Saros's army with his own vicious tenacity. They arrived in the capital as a soldier with shining reviews and a young lady-in-waiting who had stolen the heart of the old king, willing to sacrifice everything to end him.

Stunned silence followed.

"She's pregnant," Ronan breathed, his throat bobbing. "Whatever spell that allows Saros to live so long... It doesn't keep *all* of him working." His eyes finally left Nerissa's and darted between the crew members.

"Her consort is dead. He was spiked to the walls of Aedrialis before we left. She is *alone*. He will kill her and the child."

"That's why you pushed for an attack before the end of spring," Bayne finally murmured, that mask of control once again plastered onto his face. "Before Saros would learn of her pregnancy."

A defeated nod was the only response from Ronan.

"I always thought *you* were fucking her," Isla blurted out.

Ronan bared his teeth, cutting her a disgusted glare.

She shrugged. "Didn't everyone else?"

Drystan raised his ebony brows at me before shaking his

head. Ronan *was* always close to her. They were both beautiful, the queen and the queensguard. And as he stood on her other side, opposite Saros, it was easy to assume the queen would favor him, but Ronan had never looked at Galena the way he looked at Nerissa.

"I'm sorry," he finally rasped, looking back at Nerissa. "I'm sorry I let you believe the rumors. I'm sorry I didn't tell you the truth before... Before all of this."

There were unspoken words between them, some story I didn't know. Whatever their turbulent history, this truth played into it...was a missing piece in whatever storm ripped through their relationship.

A tiny breath escaped Nerissa's mouth as her lips parted. She pulled her eyes away and left the room, her brown hair rippling in a cascade of waves. Ronan blinked once before hurrying after her.

"I'm sorry," Bayne murmured finally, his face dark in defeat. His throat bobbed as his eyes landed on me.

I suddenly felt small, insignificant in the vast network of threads of the universe. Isla ushered the others out, leaving us alone.

"I'm sorry I suggested it. I shouldn't have," I whispered, unable to keep tears from pooling in the corners of my eyes.

Bayne shot across the room and wrapped his arms around me.

"Don't," he whispered into my hair. "Don't apologize. We'll deal with it all. Even the trip to the Death Dunes... My fearless angel. It's why I fell in love with you in the first place."

My heart cracked, and a soft sob escaped my lips.

He rocked me, pulling me onto his lap. I closed my eyes, the agony of the events of the last two hours ripping into my heart. The scent of salty sea and pine wrapped around me, and my lungs greedily gulped it down. I couldn't lose this, couldn't lose him.

"I can't do it, Lyv, and you wouldn't want me to," he murmured against my head.

I pulled back, meeting his unwavering, piercing gaze.

"I can't let the world burn."

I blinked through the tears streaming down my face. He was right, of course. Bayne was many, many things. And despite being an unbroken, rogue captain, Bayne's integrity was second to none.

But for a fleeting moment all those months ago, I thought I'd seen it in his eyes. In Cyril's tower on Kayj, a *fury* hot enough the melt the world.

That was not who he was, though, and a small piece of me hardened at the realization. He wouldn't burn the world down for something as simple as love. He did what was *right*. He always would.

# CHAPTER SEVENTEEN

*"I give willingly the essence of my being, the essence of my soul."*

—*Ode to Aurora, Lyrics for Soulbinding. Sir Ronan Merik's private quarters, Mount Telum.*

A rumbling vibrated through the floor, as if the massive tree took a deep breath while I searched for any literature that might explain the death of the Lady of Tomorrow. I didn't know why I was back at the Living Library, but something still nagged at me, and I couldn't push it from my mind, even with the unsettling revelations over the past day.

My stomach churned at the task ahead. Isla, Nerissa, Ronan, Vienah, and Vulcan would join me with whatever crew Queen Antares selected. And though we spent over an hour trying to figure out how we might wiggle our way free of our deal with the queen, there was no way around my separation from Tiberius.

My chest caved in worry as I thought about the sentries stationed throughout Lotrennia, always watching.

*Quit hovering*, he murmured. *We'll be fine. I'm an agrippa turned caeluma.* His voice hardened with a pride echoed in my heart. *It will take more than a few iron bolts to bring me down.*

*You're not making me feel better*, I replied, my stomach churning.

*We'll still be able to communicate. Bayne and Aquila were able to cast when you were separated last winter. And you'll be back in a few months.*

If I could find it. And if we survive the deadly environment.

*You will.*

Tiberius's unwavering faith did little to ease my worry about what awaited him while I was gone.

Arms full of books and scrolls, I strode through the winding shelves, making my way back to the center of the massive tree. Mind still spinning, I barely registered the soft scuffle of boots against the stacks as Khato, the old master of spells, stepped in front of me, blocking my way.

I balked at his sudden appearance, nearly dropping my haul.

"My apologies. I didn't mean to startle you."

Wisdom swirled in the tawny eyes that surveyed me. My stomach clenched at what had been revealed in our meeting. As if reading my thoughts, he gave me a soft, sad smile, his cloudy gray brows tilting up.

"I found something that may be of use to you in your search for information." He nodded his head toward the books in my arms.

He extended a tightly curled scroll from the collection he carried. I made to take it from him.

He held firm and murmured, "You may find what you're looking for on the eighth level." I eyed him warily, and his gaze deepened. "Water shows us the way. I'd better get going. The winds of the west bring a blanket of clouds this evening. The stars tell us stories, you see, and I'd rather not miss their tale tonight."

I cocked my head as he swiftly stepped past me. Eighth level. I could swing by on my way out, though, I was supposed to be meeting the crew soon for last-minute planning...

But the body... Those markings... I hurried through the stacks, peeking at the tightly wound scroll Khato had given me. I slowed my gait, unfurling the scroll as rivers, valleys, and mountains spread before me. My brows pinched in confusion as I stared at a map of Lotrennia.

I stopped walking as I scanned the terrain. My eyes snagged on black ink etched near a cluster of rivers that met in the north. The elven symbol for the number eight. My eyes scanned the intricate letters, and I slowly sounded out the Elvish words they spelled.

*The Waters of Ascendiel.*

A three-hour flight from here, if I had to guess. I replayed the words in my head to my caeluma, who was quiet for a moment.

*Bayne said the Waters gifted those who visited with the rare power of sight. The Master of Spells wants you to see something. Something he couldn't tell you, even in the privacy of the stacks at the Living Library,* Ti's voice sounded eager in my head.

*A blanket of clouds,* I mused.

*Under cover of darkness,* Ti continued my own thought. *We'd be able to slip out and return before dawn, before you have to leave.*

*And maybe we could find a clue to the battle Bayne saw, as well as the Lady of Tomorrow's death. We'd need to leave soon.*

*I'll meet you outside.*

WE FLEW over the trees of Ayla straight into a thick blanket of clouds, aiming for the small bay where the *Evecta* sat docked, making sure the sentries saw us flying west before we caught an updrift and soared north.

Isla was stoic as I'd relayed what transpired with Khato. She listened, then shoved a pair of fur-lined leathers at me before forcing a loaf of bread in my pack, stating that even with the cloud cover, we should fly higher to be sure none of the queen's sentries could spy us. Isla would relay everything to Bayne.

We soared in silence as the world below shifted from a thick smudge of gray clouds to smaller, sporadic wisps that gave way to the dark green ground below. The hours ticked by, and we slowly descended when the winding rivers came into view from the treetops.

Ti's thunderous landing echoed in the mossy clearing. We'd passed the dying ground Bayne eluded to. The trees this far north were dense, the forest more overgrown and unruly, compared to the trees bordering Ayla.

We trudged through the thickness of the brush, which mottled out the distant moonlight, picking our way through ferns and lichen-covered trees and rocks. Orange crystals lined the rocky walls forming around us, a small trail appearing in its center. I peeled off the thick, fur-lined jacket and tied it off at my waist, as sweat trickled down my neck and between my breasts. Tiberius's inky coat was slick with it, white foam gathering on his chest.

*This place is old,* I whispered.

*Nobody can hear us in here, you know,* he said back, though I caught a hint of wariness in his voice.

Water showed us the way...

I kept an eye on the black river rushing east, the same direction we walked, until we finally came upon a looming dark ruin. Stone and trees rose hundreds of feet in the air, wound together, arching over a tunnel where the rushing river flowed.

*I guess this is where I leave you.* I couldn't help the trepidation that had seeped into those words.

*If it were a trap, he wouldn't have spoken to you in code. This is where we should be. I feel it.*

I repeated Ti's words in my head, willing my heart to calm as I tugged off my riding boots and leathers, stepping into the edge of the river that flowed into the heart of the Waters of Ascendiel.

*Cast to me.*

I gave him a nod, kicking off the edge of the bank and letting the river pull me into the dark, cavernous entrance of the ruins.

MY LEGS and arms pushed and pulled against the swell of water floating me toward the darkness, keeping my head above water. I passed under the arch of the ruins and blinked as the darkness dissipated, replaced with a soft, foggy blue glow, as if Ganmira and Renova's essence lived in this space. I rode the river into a massive cavern that opened to a large, round stone structure in its center. A narrow staircase spiraled around the stone, leading to the edge of its towering lip.

I could barely make out the arch to my right, where another river converged. The water swelled rapidly as it met with the one I floated in on. I kicked against the surf, aiming for the edge of the stone path that bordered the massive structure. My hands dug in, slipping on the algae coating the smooth stones. I pulled myself out, grateful for the vacancy of the ruin as I only bothered keeping my undergarments on.

I circled the stone structure, eyeing at least four more river entrances, when at last I found the base of the stairs. Slick with the water rushing in, I steadied myself with a hand on the wall of the stone as I began to climb.

Minutes passed, and my thighs burned, sweat mixing with the river water dripping from my body. My feet were still soaked. I glanced down at the slippery stone and paused. Water flowed upward, over my feet, and up the sides of the massive stone structure. I cast to Tiberius and was met with a wave of awe and wonder.

I climbed until I finally stepped into a thick fog as I reached the top of the stone structure. There was no lip to its edge. I counted my steps as I made my way inward, toward the center of the space, following the flow of water. It began to deepen, slowly covering my feet, eventually reaching my knees, always flowing to the center of the circle.

The fog began to clear, that curious blue light illuminating the space before me. I stopped, the water reaching above my knees, as I took in the scene before me.

Calm waters swirled to the center of the stone landing, where it stopped and ascended into the sky above, as if it were a waterfall, its strong current hurtling upward to form a ring of solid water. A water*rise*.

I kept my cast to Tiberius open as I cautiously made my way into the Waters of Ascendiel. My hand reached for the solid stream of water, sliding in. Sucking in a deep breath, I stepped into the ring of rising water.

# CHAPTER EIGHTEEN

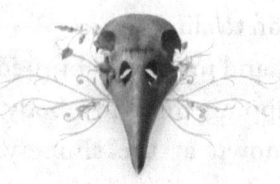

*The Marisarma Lords remain focused on Sultira. The path is clear.*

*—Correspondence from Anonymous to Queen Antares. Date unknown.*

D arkness enveloped me. I'd been here before. Months ago, on the streets of Stynguard, when Cyril sliced through my neck with Talon. That dream-like state, somewhere between life and death, floating along through my not-consciousness. Where I saw that young man on the ship. Where I witnessed Enya's last moments. But this was different, somehow, and I could still feel Tiberius with me, knew he still held the cast.

Warm water swelled around my legs. I was distantly aware of the sound the strange water made as it whooshed upward, but I couldn't see where it went with the darkness that loomed, familiar yet uncharted. It was the darkness before sleep bids farewell, like the quiet space between the stars. And then a shimmering light peeked through the black night, sparkling and lovely.

Small, barely perceptible lights, like gemstones in the depths of the ocean, suddenly linked, forming glittering, ribbon-like whorls that swirled and danced to some unknown ballad above.

Threads.

*My* threads.

A dark, twisting ribbon spun with a brighter golden one, weaving together in a living knot of beauty. All I could do was stare as it continued to twist over itself. My powers—the Obscura and Transcindiel.

My fingers grazed the edge of spinning powers above my head, and the shimmering lights stopped, suspended in midair, before an explosion of color and lights lit up the darkness. Threads of all sizes and colors erupted from its center, stretching for miles in every direction, creating a brilliant web of light, like never-ending constellations.

Six ribbons shot from the center of the twisting knot of powers, stretching in different directions. Five were identical, looping and twisting in a glistening mixture of blues and greens, like underwater plants tethered to the bottom of the sea, swaying in its tides. Six ribbons connected to my powers... Bellators?

My eyes snagged on the sixth, the same, yet brighter and taut, like the cable that connects the ship to its anchor. I looked closer, noting a second, braided thread wrapped itself tightly around the first, as if to strengthen it.

The tips of my fingers neared that taught thread, and a pulse of warmth beat through the air as it brightened. It sparked as I neared, sending a wild white flame dancing down the thread toward a brilliant white knot at the other end. A warmth filled my chest. I wanted to follow it. My heart leaped. *Bayne?*

I reached up to grab hold of it when I spied other braided threads in the distance. Two or three, giving off a gentle pull, calling me to whatever lay at their ends. Silver flashed, and my eyes locked onto one in particular. The silver pulsed, as if whispering to me. *Soon*, it seemed to say, *soon.* Shadowed silver glimmered off that thread. Powerful. Dangerous. *Unyielding.* And yet...

My hand hesitated, and I stared as the braided threads called to me. I dropped my hand and heaved a breath. Why was I here again?

*Can you hear me?* Tiberius's voice was a distant thing.

*Yes.*

*Are you alright? The cast broke an hour ago.*

An hour. Shit. I came here to get answers about those bodies. About the great battle in Bayne's vision. I looked up into the tapestry of dancing ribbons of light and formed the question in my mind.

*What happened to the Lady of Tomorrow?*

I scanned the undulating threads that made up this mini universe. A brightening of one of the Bellator threads was the only answer I received.

*Was it an illness?*

Again, that same thread brightened for a moment before returning to its quiet sway. I didn't understand.

*We need to go,* came Ti's voice.

My gut twisted.

*How can we win the great battle in Lotrennia?* I asked the waters.

My powers flared to life in response, a line to the silver braided thread igniting, sparks zapping down it in quick bursts from my knot of powers. *What does this mean?*

*Lyvia...* Ti's voice held an edge of warning that sent my heart on a steady beat in my chest. How was I supposed to get out of here? I scanned the expanse of the darkness and light, my eyes catching once again on that taught, silvery thread leading far away.

*Ti, I don't know how to get out.*

Nothing.

*Ti?*

*Find me in the threads,* his voice was quiet, distant.

There were so many... Gods, there had to be hundreds of them swirling in different patterns and connecting in different places...

The golden thread in the magnificent knot glowed brighter as a bit of onyx slipped loose from the knot and shot down, as if it were diving in an endless ocean. It sank, farther and farther, until a bang sounded from below.

*Bang.* Louder this time, a fist pounding against a locked door.

*Bang.* Louder, more fists pounding.

*Bang.* Louder, as hundreds, thousands... Perhaps *millions* of fists beat in unity against the door in the deep, creating a chorus of drum-like thunder echoing in this universe of threads.

What in *Tynan's Hell?* I had to get out of here.

I forced my attention back to the gold, and I reached for it. My fingers seemed far away, as if I wasn't wholly in control of them. The gold began to glow, and I strained, trying with all my might to get my fingertips on it. As soon as my skin slipped into the light, the threads went out.

Darkness swallowed me, the smooth stone floor of the pool pressed against my feet, and warm water lapped at my legs. The cool mist from the ascending water tickled my arms, and I blinked. Dim blue light returned, illuminating the ring of rising water around me. Above, a soft gray and blue cloud loomed where it met the ring of water.

I sloshed out of the ring of water, heading back to the winding staircase and through the arches where the rivers flowed in.

*Where are you?* I probed into the thread that connected me to Tiberius. It now seemed so obvious. This bond with him. My mind bounced between feeling as if I'd learned all I ever needed to know, yet walking away with unclear answers. Bayne's thread...

Ti's reply reached me as I toweled off.

*We need to get back. It's been two hours.*

Blacker than the night that had spread through the mighty forest, Tiberius's hulking form wound through the wide leaves and snaking vines that hung across the trees, wings tucked in tight.

*Shit.* I yanked my pants on as fast as I could, the fur-lined leather sticking against my sweaty legs in the muggy night. I mounted Tiberius, and he made his way to the clearing we'd arrived in. I could barely keep my mind leashed to my body as I unloaded everything I'd seen to Tiberius.

The temperature plummeted as we surged higher, and I hastily laced up my jacket, pulling the extra leather flap across and buttoning it down my side. We leveled out above the silky clouds drifting down from the north, bringing with them a smattering of rain.

*The death of the Lady of Tomorrow had something to do with a Bellator,* Ti said as we talked through what I'd seen, tiny bits of ice biting at my cheeks as we flew through the thick clouds.

*Or simply a Bellator power,* I said. *But how? And which one?*

*Not Bayne's, if the one with the braided thread didn't illuminate,* Ti murmured.

I shook my head in agreement. That braided thread...

"Oh, my gods," I said aloud, my heart swelling in realization. "I know what his thread is."

# CHAPTER NINETEEN

*The vision was as clear as day. I need your help. I'll do anything.*

*—Hidden correspondence from Bayne to Khato. 5th of Summer, 071.3E.*

A sliver of morning sun crested over the horizon like an orange rind as we approached Ayla. I peeled my cheek off Tiberius's warm neck as he banked and blinked against the frigid air. I suppressed a shudder and leaned into Ti's warmth. Gods, he had to be exhausted.

The peel of orange gradually cast a net of coral and gold along the powdery clouds that met us on our descent.

*I'm going to miss this,* Ti murmured.

My stomach dipped at his words and the impending separation we faced. I'd be leaving in a couple hours.

*I'm going to miss you, too.*

A blossom of warmth spread down the bond that echoed

the unsaid words in Ti's responding nicker. We dipped into the clouds, a warm fog enveloping us in the dim light of morning.

*Maybe we could just follow the clouds*, I murmured, closing my eyes and breathing in the sweet mist that floated up from the Juniper Sea. *How long do you think we could stay hidden?*

Ti's head stretched out in front, and he heaved a breath, as if tasting the air.

*We'd get bored. Saving the realm is a more exciting existence, don't you think? I also won't mind fucking with the queen.*

I choked out a laugh, playfully landing a smack on his neck. *I'm serious! You need to be careful. Stick close to Bayne.*

Warmth bloomed in my chest in anticipation of telling Bayne what I saw. Ti snorted and tucked his wings, hovering midair for a moment, before he dove. My heart leaped from my chest, and I clung to his neck as his body went vertical and began a tight spiral.

*Level out, asshole!*

We broke through the clouds, and a blanket of green yawned open in front of us.

Great black wings flared to the side with a gust of wind as we soared over the canopy, barely clearing its uppermost branches.

In the distance, an emerald bay stretched, slowly morphing to turquoise as the morning sun finally ripped through the sheet of clouds. A dark ship stood out among the golden Lotrennian fleet.

Hope snuffed out the lurking dread that had arrived with the revelations of the last day. It would all be alright.

My heart hammered as we crossed the *Evecta's* shield, and the smell of sickly-sweet honeysuckle shoved into my nostrils. I swung off Ti's back into a running dismount as his hooves thundered down the main deck.

Marian aimed for me as I hurtled toward the captain's quarters. Without thinking, I probed at the thread tethering me to Bayne and was met with a solid wall. I bristled as I swung open the cabin door and stopped mid-stride.

In nothing but a thin night shift that left little to the imagination, Queen Antares stood in front of Bayne's desk, bent over a map of Lotrennia. Bayne straightened as I entered, shock replacing a look of concern.

"What's going on?" I asked, stepping up to the desk, becoming keenly aware of how thin the queen's nightgown was.

A muscle in his jaw feathered, and I caught his eyes drifting to the thick scar on my neck before snapping back to my face.

"You were right, Lyv. A plague is spreading."

My stomach pitched.

"I came here as soon as news reached my doors," Queen Antares continued. "The Awakening is a sacred celebration of light and life, and nearly eighty elves ended up dead."

"From a plague?" I asked, turning to Bayne.

"Not all of them bore signs of an illness, but most of them did. The fire pox, as you suggested. But there were unexplained injuries as well, similar to your findings on the remains of the Lady of Tomorrow," Bayne answered.

"But what could cause that? Did a fight break out?" I shook my head as I turned to the queen, whose eyes narrowed in annoyance.

"We don't know. The menders are conducting a detailed examination now."

The pink hue of morning light crept in through the far window beyond the curtain, where I noticed Bayne's bed sat undisturbed. He hadn't slept. A twinge of guilt raked at my chest. The queen's eyes followed mine.

"Your ship departs soon, Bonder. I'll see you at the top of the hour."

That twisting scent followed Queen Antares as she sauntered from the room, slivers of skin peeking out as her hips swayed beneath her shift. Marian followed her out, closing the door behind her. I turned back to Bayne and gripped his hand, my lips kicking up in a smile despite the unease this news brought.

"I saw the threads, Bayne. My threads. *Our threads*," I finally said, leaning in close after I relayed everything that transpired, my heart beating rapidly in hopeful triumph. "We are bound by more than Bellator powers. A soulbinding thread was there. *I saw it*."

I squeezed his hands as my heart threatened to combust. Bayne quietly listened, his emerald eyes never leaving mine. His calloused thumb brushed strokes over the top of my hand as his brows pinched upward.

"Lyv," he began, eyes softening. "Only mystics have ever had threadsight. You have yet to whisper with the wind or water," he continued gently, eyes drifting to my lips as he cupped my face with his other hand.

I reined in the twisting in my gut, my own inadequacy sinking into the darkness that smothered my soul. *He didn't believe me.* Bayne's brows tilted ever so slightly in regret, an apology forming on his lips. I quickly shook my head, squashing the self-pity.

"I'm so sorry," he continued, a pained look crossing his features. "But it's impossible. Elves and humans cannot be soulbound. They say the Waters of Ascendiel show you what you *need* to see, not what you *want* to see."

Blood rushed from my face as I wilted before him, devastated at his disbelief. I was so certain what I'd seen... Had I imagined it? Had I simply seen what I wanted to see?

"But—" I began, as I tried tapping against our connection once more, running into a solid wall. "Why won't you let me in?" I whispered, the minutes suddenly turning into seconds.

He held my gaze for a moment before he swallowed.

"I can't," he said, voice cracking. His throat bobbed as he shook his head.

The air sucked from my lungs as his next words sank in.

"There is a thread linking the queen and me. I can *feel* it. And I'm sorry, Lyv, but it is different from what I feel with you. I must keep myself cut off from my connection with you all, or I fear she will use this bond with me to get to you. I'm so sorry." His thumb brushed against my lips as he planted a kiss on my forehead.

I blinked away tears. "But you won't do it, right? You won't bind yourself. You can't."

Bayne dropped his hand to mine, his eyes again shooting to my neck before he began shaking his head.

"You are my anchor, Lyv. My home. The night that brings the stars."

He reached toward the door, and I grabbed his hand.

"Bayne—"

"Say you'll remember this," he murmured, lips inches from my ears.

"I'll remember," I breathed.

"I would do anything for my kingdom. I would do anything for you," he said, thumb and forefinger gripping my chin as he leaned in. "Anything."

The kiss he planted on my lips was hard but brief, bringing an air of finality with it. My heart cracked as he pulled away, a strange mixture of grief and self-doubt colliding in my chest and replacing the spark of hope that had ignited at the Waters of Ascendiel.

# CHAPTER TWENTY

*I must caution you on your interpretation of your vision in the Waters of Ascendiel. Your mother used to say the souls of the seers were cryptic.*

*—Hidden correspondence from Khato to Bayne. 7th of Summer, 071.3E.*

The *Centurion* rose from the turquoise bay like a golden monument in its sparkling waters. At twice the size of the *Evecta*, the waves pushing their way into the sheltered bay did little to rock the massive vessel. A wooden carving of an elven female, with a crown of flowers atop her windblown curls, and nothing more than a smattering of vines crossing over her breasts and bare stomach jutted out from the front of the ship. My stomach twisted as I gazed at Queen Antares's figurehead.

Golden in the bright morning sunshine that had chased the last of the lingering clouds away, the ship floated steadily.

Elves bustled on and off the gangplank as they finished loading the supplies for the trip that would take the next few months.

My mouth hung open as they'd loaded large, cylindrical iron weapons onto the ship—air canons, they called them. I'd only seen them once before in that strange, dream-like state when Cyril had slit my throat. They'd been on board the ship with that young man with the dark eyes, surrounded by men ready to hurt him. My heart squeezed for some strange reason.

I'd been told wind whisperers could use the weapons to fire balls of iron at enemy ships if needed. My stomach churned at the sight, but it was nothing compared to the waves of dread and loss that pushed into my heart as I said my goodbyes to Bayne and Tiberius.

Bayne watched from a distance, apology written across his face. Vulcan gripped his hand, his hazel eyes hard on the captain. They stared at each other for a heartbeat, the air seeming to still, before Vulcan finally gave him a curt nod and stalked past me onto the ship.

Queen Antares stood before her court in a soft pink gown that wrapped around her curves, adorned with the living crown of flowers. A goddess of life and light.

Nerissa prowled past the group, the ex-War Slayer hauling a pack of her own.

The queen said, "Safe journey, niece. May we only grow closer upon your return."

My connection to Nerissa quivered for a moment. Her face, bland yet white with rage, softened as she turned to the queen and sketched a low bow before she boarded the *Centurion*.

Ronan clapped Bayne on the shoulder as he made his way to the ship. He met my eye and gave a nod as his gaze shifted to where Nerissa stood next to Vienah.

A warm hand clapped onto my shoulder, and I turned to find Drystan. His lips were drawn back in a half-smile. He wrapped his long arms around my shoulders in a tight hug. He'd be staying here. Drystan's training with Isla had paid off, and he was one of the few magic-wielding humans who had joined us from Odessa. He'd already trained a handful of Rising soldiers in the lost arts and would stay to see it through. I squeezed back for a long heartbeat before he pulled away, ruffling my hair.

"I'll miss you," I signed to him. "Keep an eye on Ti for me?"

"I'll make sure he doesn't get into any trouble," he responded with a chuckle.

*I'll do as I please*, Ti retorted.

*I should probably offer to pay Drystan...*

A bristle of irritation raced down the connection with my caeluma, and my lips tugged upward.

"Try not to let curiosity get the best of you," Drystan continued with a wink.

I landed a soft punch on his arm as he jogged back to where Bayne stood.

Behind the queen, the group parted to allow Carina through. My mouth hung open as the small, mousy elf, dressed in a conservative, cotton travel dress, shuffled through the crowd with a pack on her back and made her way to the ship.

I blinked and shifted to the side, giving her a wide berth as Kresida brought up the rear. Kresida's dark brown eyes slashed to mine, and her mouth curved up in a sinister grin before she paused.

The queen's War Slayer loomed over me, nose crinkling in a sneer as she said quietly, "I may be leaving Lotrennian shores, *Bonder*," her last word dripping in condescension, "but I have eyes on both of you." Her gaze drifted up, scanning the sparse, cottony clouds for Tiberius.

I bared my teeth at the threat toward my caeluma.

"Fuck off, Kresida," Isla's clear voice cut in, curbing my anger.

Kresida straightened and turned toward Isla. Though she towered over her small frame, Isla somehow looked down at her over the bridge of her nose.

"Shoo," she said, flicking her hands in the War Slayer's direction before Kresida stalked off.

My gaze returned to Isla, who I now realized was wearing a soft green dress that wrapped around her feminine figure.

"What—" I began.

"I have to stay, Lyv. I'm sorry. Bayne thinks he can get me time to train with Khato."

I opened my mouth to protest.

She cut me off with a swift shake of her head. "Just trust me, okay?"

I swallowed and bit back the tears I knew would start to form if I let her goodbye sink in.

"Come back soon." She gripped my hand before pulling away.

With a quick look at Bayne, I climbed aboard the *Centurion*.

TIBERIUS FLEW alongside Aquila for the first hour of our departure before returning west. My chest hollowed out as his dark figure disappeared along the gray horizon, a piece of my heart soaring away.

It was odd, being on a ship that wasn't the *Evecta*. Even with the massive size of the *Centurion*, waves rocked the ship as we entered the wild of the Juniper Sea.

Vienah plopped on the bench next to me. "Surprised they felt it necessary to bring me along," she murmured, eyeing the fifty sailors bustling about the main deck. "I counted at least three mages." Her strawberry blonde hair had been braided tightly against her head. Little wisps of curls poked out of the hood she pulled up against the wind.

"I think your power is pretty coveted, Vienah. Mastering the weather is no small thing. I feel safer with you on board if that makes you feel any better."

Vienah scoffed but offered a small smile.

"Let's find where we'll be sleeping tonight. I'm already exhausted," I murmured.

The weight of the revelations over the past days settled in my chest like lead, doubt plaguing my thoughts as I replayed what I'd seen in the waters over and over again. Had I imagined that thread?

With Aelius now high in the sky, we meandered through the bustling deck, heading toward the stairs when Kresida's clear voice cut through the activity.

"Sparring deck is open, deserter."

I tensed. Nerissa and Bayne had fled with Vulcan and Isla after Queen Antares had killed their parents. Though the sailors continued their duties, many paused, glancing at the dark War Slayer standing in the center of the prow, the black paint against her face illuminating the whites of her eyes as they cast daggers at Nerissa in close discussion with Vulcan.

The deck quieted as the former War Slayer commander turned her Ravindra gaze on Kresida.

"Bold words for a number two," Ronan drawled, appearing at Nerissa's side. His gaze was filled with threat as he scanned Kresida.

Nerissa's shoulders tensed at his sudden appearance. Kresida's lips curved into an amusing grin as her stare hopped between the two of them.

"Trouble in paradise?" she taunted, lips turning down into a pout.

Vulcan murmured something inaudible to them both, leading them the other direction. Nerissa looked as if she was about to follow, pulling her lethal stare away from the War Slayer.

"Pathetic. No wonder you ran away," Kresida said.

A tremor shot down my connection with Nerissa. She was barely containing her power. The only people on this ship who knew her true identity, that she shared the Bellator power with Bayne, were the three of us from the *Evecta*.

Nerissa stopped, schooling her features into cool challenge as she turned back to Kresida. "Up for a sparring match, sweetie?"

"Deck's open, old-timer."

Ronan cut a glance across the deck at me, eyebrows high.

We followed them to the sparring deck at the stern, where Kresida made a show of removing the lethal daggers from her vest, boots, and pants. Ronan choked as she unsheathed two, thinly curved blades she'd somehow kept beneath her breasts, and a final, small dagger that she slipped from a small pocket between her thighs, dangerously close to the space at the center.

Nerissa watched, a mask of boredom plastered over her face until Kresida finished. She unstrapped the leather sleeve that held her twin blades behind her back before tossing aside four daggers of her own.

I waited for the silent salute that precluded any sparring session, but Kresida leaped on her before I could blink. The War Slayer was airborne as a black boot flew at Nerissa's face. She ducked, swiping out with her own leg as Kresida came down, deftly hopping over Nerissa's leg. Fists flew faster than my eyes could register as the pair jabbed and parried for endless minutes.

Vulcan leaned against the edge of the ship, crossing his

arms as he watched the two fly through the air. Ronan's body was taught in a battle-ready stance I'd seen so often. The corners of his eyes creased as he watched the lethal pair throw everything they had at the other.

Ten minutes. Twenty. Forty. An hour.

The sun moved across the sky, a warm golden glow shining off the bright ship. Nerissa and Kresida didn't stop. Sweat coated the deck, adding a level of slickness the two easily adjusted their fighting styles to.

"The nerve to come back," Kresida breathed at her, the first words spoken. "To return after you scampered away," she continued. "Pathetic. *Coward*."

She spat the last word as Nerissa landed the first blow, an uppercut that hurled Kresida backward, slamming into the side of the ship. Kresida snarled as she bounced off and launched herself at Nerissa, knocking her off balance and wrapping her limbs around her. Nerissa slipped her hold, sending an elbow careening into her nose.

Kresida's yelp was quickly replaced with a roar as she swung her leg out as Nerissa got to her feet. Nerissa hit the deck with a thud. Kresida leaped, a wounded wolf, utterly out of control. As she reached her, Nerissa twisted on the ground, slipping beneath her and wrapping her forearm around her neck.

I waited for the move I knew would come to slip the choke hold. But as Kresida's hands moved to where I expected, Nerissa's legs wrapped around the War Slayer's trunk, pinning her strong arms to her side. Kresida's face darkened with pressure as Nerissa moved her lips to her ear.

"Call me coward one more time."

I shuddered, remembering what it felt like to be on the receiving end of one of Nerissa's threats, with the icy bite of her dagger against my neck last year...

Kresida bared her teeth as she strained to slip Nerissa's grasp, her hands seizing and her legs flaying in an attempt to wrap around Nerissa.

Kresida's boots thumped against the deck as a cool calm settled over Nerissa, and she waited for the inevitable tap out. Shaking fingers tapped twice against her calf, and Nerissa released the War Slayer, who sagged to the ground.

# CHAPTER TWENTY-ONE

*Lotrennia burning. Charred elven bodies. A dying library. And a creature of nightmares.*

*—Hidden correspondence from Bayne to Khato. 13ᵗʰ of Summer, 071.3E.*

The next few hours were blessedly uneventful, yet being aboard the *Centurion* sent me yearning for those days on the *Evecta*. Even the days that were shrouded in grief after my escape from Kayj. I'd done so much healing on that ship, with my friends, my family. And while some of my friends were here, I left so much of my heart back in Lotrennia.

I slumped between Ronan and Vienah as we settled into our cots and hammocks in one of the various crew cabins below deck. Nerissa was quiet since her loss of control. Ronan eyed her as she sat down nearby.

"You should get some water on that," he said, nodding at the bruise forming beneath Nerissa's eye.

Her eyes cut to Ronan. "You should learn to mind your own business," she spat. "I don't need you to defend me."

Ronan's lips formed a thin line as he glared right back at her. "You want to have this conversation now?" he asked, raising his light eyebrows.

Nerissa's lashes shuddered. "It doesn't change anything. You still left."

Ronan gaped. "It changes everything!" he bellowed.

I blew out a breath, catching Vulcan's eye as he gave me a nod. Vienah and I shuffled out as he moved to the door, leaving Ronan and Nerissa to whatever conversation they still hadn't had.

I MEANDERED through the halls below deck, hands braced against the wall as the ship rocked, following the soft lights that illuminated the cramped space. A slew of curses came from a nearby room, and I paused, angling my head to peer into the dimly lit space. Carina was on all fours on the ground, gathering up various books and scrolls that had tumbled down from the bookshelves built into the side of the cabin.

Carina's Ravindra eyes shot up as I stepped in and knelt next to her. She paused, wariness returning to her gaze as she scanned me. I offered her a soft smile and helped her gather the books and scrolls.

"They need to add a belt of sorts to that shelf now that the seas are so unruly after the Sending," I murmured, feeling the stretching effects of the twin eclipse.

She blinked before returning to roll up the scrolls. "It should be temporary," she murmured. "The seas. At the rate of change we've seen over the past couple months, they should return to normal by the end of the year."

"That's good," I said, handing her the last book as I stood.

Carina's cautious eyes narrowed, and I stilled, keenly aware of whose daughter I spoke with. She folded up the scroll and placed it neatly among several others. I glanced at the names of the books stacked next to them, and my stomach pitched as my eyes landed on one.

"Where did you get this?" I breathed, my brows furrowing as I reached for the first edition of *The Horseman's Duty*. My eyes settled on my father's name before they shot back to her. My *father's* book.

Carina's lashes fluttered, and she swallowed before saying, "Vander Stryke. I asked Ronan if there was any literature regarding the agrippa. The herd. Where they came from, originally, and he said Vander knew your father and might know more..."

My hackles rose, the Obscura slithering down my arms in response. I blinked through golden embers in my eyes as I stared at Carina.

"Why do you want to know about the agrippa?" My voice sounded distant in my head, as the potential threat to Tiberius settled in my bones.

As if reading my thoughts, Carina's small hands shot up, palms facing me, as she shook her head. "I meant no ill will, I swear it." Her head continued to shake as her eyes flicked between my own. "The agrippa are renowned for their fearlessness, even in Lotrennia. And with the return of the Bellators, with your *own* agrippa becoming your caeluma..."

My heart began a steady gallop in my chest. The queen was curious about Tiberius, too... I cast to him, allowing him access to my conversation with the queen's daughter.

A gasp escaped my chest as my cast stretched into space,

taking longer to reach him. My heart stuttered at the distance, a deep ache forming. A moment later, the connection formed, and Ti's eyes opened behind my own.

"You're misunderstanding me. I'm not looking for ways to bring Tiberius, or even other agrippa, under my control, or that of my mother's." Her last words curved with a pinch of distaste. "But should all Bellator powers be found and unlocked, where do they find their caeluma? Tiberius is the only one of his kind. Isn't he lonely?"

A flicker of emotion drifted from Tiberius before he severed the connection, either by choice or because of the distance. The brief cast set me on edge, uneasy that it took so much effort to hold it in place. Bayne had coached us on how to cast to each other at great distances, but he'd had years of practice with Aquila.

I blinked, vaguely aware that Carina had said something else and now watched me for a response.

"What?"

She tilted her head, a keenness entering her eyes that reminded me too much of her mother.

"Any information about the Bellators has been lost for a very long time," she said. "I found a scroll in the Living Library that spoke of an army. I was very young at the time. But once word got out about what you found, I went back to search for it, unable to find it. I can't help but feel that the return of the Bellators has meaning that we don't yet understand. And if the Living Library doesn't want you to find something, you won't."

Carina pulled my father's book out of the stack and handed it to me. "I meant no harm by reading this."

I stared at my father's name on the cover. My chest burned with lingering guilt, still clouding my grieving soul. I tucked the book under my arm and nodded my farewell to Carina before making my way back to the shared crew cabin, where a thin hammock awaited me.

AFTER A MONTH AT SEA, the snaking, finger-like islands stretching south of the Death Dunes rose on the horizon. Barren, snowy cliffs jutted from the dark Atrulean Sea. The mouth of the strait waited in the shadow of the towering cliffs. Only a few miles wide, the straits stretched along the southern side of the Death Dunes, leading into the gulf.

Our ship crossed into the strait as a looming darkness materialized at our rear. The mage's shield held firm as the massive shadow announced the arrival of the Mortis Shroud. My heart hammered as memories of our encounter with this evil rushed forward. We'd been on our way to Kayj when the sentient fog engulfed the *Evecta*.

Now, the cloud of shadows closed in on us, snaking up the center of the ship in a big arc over our sails and spider-webbing down the sides. The elven sailors kept to their posts as they watched the ribbons of death spread, choking out the light.

My breath became shallow. A tingling sensation pricked the back of my neck, and the darkness turned its attention to me. The shroud ripped back from its probe of the *Centurion*, and its massive form floated a few feet away from where I stood, white knuckling the rail. The Mortis Shroud speared into a living arrowhead as it floated with its tip pointing directly at me.

I waited for the roiling reaction of the Obscura power and found it sitting lazily in the center of my chest, unperturbed.

I stood there, facing the Mortis Shroud, aware all eyes on deck were pinned on me. That prickling sensation continued to nag at me. The Mortis Shroud slowly rotated in midair before it dissolved into its natural, cloud-like form, turning north as if searching for something. I blew out a breath as its attention released me.

My gaze remained pinned on the retreating darkness until Nerissa stepped to my side.

"That was something," she murmured, eyes following my own on the horizon.

I didn't respond, unsure of what had happened. I glanced to my right, where Vienah's face had taken on the hue of the ashen.

"I'd better talk to her," I murmured and stepped over to the young water witch.

Vienah did her best to hide the flinch that shook her shoulders as I stepped beside her. My heart winced at the fear in her eyes as she beheld me.

"I'd heard of it, of course," she said quietly. "But seeing it. *Feeling* it." She shuddered.

"I know."

Vienah's brown eyes turned back to me, assessing and curious. "It seemed like it could see you. Even with the shield in place."

My swallow caught in my throat, and I kept my eyes pinned on Aquila, who sat perched at the quarterdeck. His gold and green eyes were hard on me, and he sent a wave of reassurance down our connection. I leaned into it.

A wave of storm clouds crouched on the horizon, and a shout from the captain reached us. We straightened at his approach.

"Vienah, may I ask your assistance with these?" He jerked his head toward the gray clouds forming on the horizon. "It would be best if we could make it through the strait with more visibility."

Vienah scanned the sky, and her brows pinched in concern. "I'll do what I can."

The captain nodded his thanks.

The water witch placed her hands in front of her, palms up, and murmured a spell under her breath as she closed her eyes. The spattering of rain fizzled off into a light mist, and a massive blast of wind sent the storm clouds hurtling north. I glanced behind me to find the three elven mages with steepled hands, sending the *Centurion* chasing the retreating clouds.

It took two days to clear the strait, and I couldn't stop myself from gazing southward. Despite the lingering tingling sensation, there was no sign of the Mortis Shroud.

AS THE EARLY morning rays of the sun eclipsed the horizon behind us, I sighed through my nose. My morning routine with Vulcan was considerably more enjoyable inside the sheltered gulf.

Vulcan leaned against the foremast, staring past the bowsprit. His hazel eyes grew distant as he watched the mouth of the gulf approach. Vulcan was most at peace after our sessions. And I was content enough with his silence to come close to enjoying his company. I stood beside him and followed his line of sight.

Vulcan's eyes narrowed, and he rushed to the edge of the prow, searching the horizon.

"Marisarma ship incoming!" he bellowed.

I flew to the rail and followed his gaze, straining to see the ship in the distance. Aquila's screech filled the air in confirmation as he soared north. My stomach plummeted as sailors rushed across the deck, arming themselves for attacking pirates.

# CHAPTER TWENTY-TWO

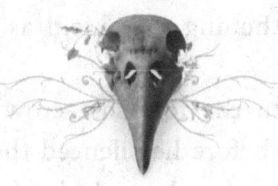

*Tell me more about the creature. All may not be as it seems.*
    *—Hidden correspondence from Khato to Bayne. 20th of*
    *Summer, 071.3E.*

I sprinted to the small cabin below deck, strapping on the double leather scabbard and gathering my bow and quiver. My hands shook as bloody images of Odessa flooded my mind. I squeezed my palms shut as the Obscura raced through my veins, pounding for its release. My stomach dipped at the thought of letting it loose in a battle once again, putting our own soldiers at risk as I remembered the piles of ash and unintended lives I took. I wouldn't allow that to happen again. I'd fight without this power as long as I could.

Elven sailors took up positions above deck with lethal efficiency. Vienah found me a moment later, and I ushered her and Carina below deck.

Carina wholly ignored me and moved across the deck to

converse with the captain at the quarterdeck. The three crow's nests held two archers each, and twenty more lined the prow rails of the deck. The remaining crew members took up positions below deck, taking aim with the dozens of air cannons on board. Elven mages spaced themselves out in the center deck, strengthening the shield as we hurtled toward the ship.

Vulcan moved to the foremast crow's nest, earning an earful of rumblings before he silenced them with a look. He took aim, two arrows already nocked. I found Ronan and the others near the stern, armed and ready for whichever Lord of Marisarma sailed toward us in the approaching ship.

I squinted, trying as best I could to make out the ship. A carved, wooden female broke through the fog, framed by six hideous serpentine creatures that sprang from where her legs should have been. The *Scylla*.

The monstrous figurehead ripped through the waves as the captain shouted, "Hold!"

Nerissa loosed a breath beside me, glancing to Ronan. He nodded, his mouth forming a thin line.

"We need to play this carefully," Ronan muttered a warning. "If Lord Astraeus has been in touch with the captain of the *Scylla*, he'll know."

His eyebrows raised at Nerissa as she pursed her lips. *Shit.* My stomach sank at the thought. Lord Astraeus knew exactly what power Nerissa wielded.

The *Scylla* cleared the fog, and the looming Marisarma flag flapped into the misty light. The crimson *M* rippled like blood against the black fabric as the mages' blasts of wind careened into its shield.

A deafening boom echoed as the *Scylla* fired three air canons at our ship. We rocked as they bounced off the shield, our mages standing with legs braced and brows furrowed in concentration. A volley of arrows followed, their metal tips bouncing off the complex elven shield.

"Fire!" the elven captain commanded from the helm.

Canons erupted from below, shaking the deck. I widened my stance as Ronan caught my elbow, steadying me. A volley of arrows followed the cannons, aimed at the precise location where the cannonballs met the *Scylla's* shield to weaken it.

My thoughts scattered as Vulcan shouted, *"FIRESHIP! Starboard!"*

My gaze shot to the right, where a raging fire blazed through the waves. A foreign wind pushed the burning ship toward us. The center mage flung his hands up toward the sails, sending us flying the other direction.

I lost my balance at the maneuver, scuffing my knees against the smooth wooden deck and scrambling to get upright as the *Centurion* barely skirted past the approaching *Scylla*. The burning ship careened into the shield behind the stern, sending a ripple of damage up the invisible defense. A barrage of cannons and arrows rained down from both ships.

"Fix that!" the captain shouted at the rear mage, but the elf had been knocked unconscious.

The remaining mages were red in the face as they poured energy into repairing the shield that had been damaged by the flames.

Shouts erupted from the starboard side of the deck as I struggled to my feet. I staggered, thumping back on my knees, as all attention moved to the *Scylla*, now a mere twenty feet from our ship.

Another volley of cannonballs rocked our ship, and a second mage fell limp, passing out from the power needed to sustain the shield against the attack.

"Your Highness!" the captain shouted in warning.

Carina strode past the unconscious mage in the center of

the deck and steepled her hands. A massive shudder of wind ripped through the *Centurion* as the young princess locked her own shield into place. Nerissa's eyes widened as she took in her cousin, power rippling from her small frame. The third mage, still standing, shook his hands out in relief as he moved to the rail, sending blasts of wind against the *Scylla*.

I reached the port side of the deck, clinging to the rail as the two ships continued to pummel the others' shields. I scrambled up the side of the rail, ready to brace for the inevitable impact.

My eyes briefly scanned the small islands in the distance before my stomach sank, and I bellowed, "*Hydra* incoming!"

There was no doubt in my mind it was Lord Astraeus's blue coat that flashed at the prow of another ship approaching from the west. Vulcan echoed my cry, and then quickly corrected it.

"Marisarma ships! *Kraken* and *Cetus* from the south. *Hydra* from the west!"

My heart lodged in my throat. *Three more ships.* I threw a glance to the south, where two more ships stalked us in the distance.

Trap. *This was a trap.*

The attacking *Scylla's* shield finally cracked with a deafening *rip*. The elven mages below deck wasted no time firing cannonballs into the side of the ship.

The elven captain of the *Centurion* turned his attention to the three approaching ships closing in, forcing us to stand and fight or attempt to flee.

"Port cannons!" he called to the mages below deck.

Flames erupted from the sails on the *Scylla* as the elves peppered them with blazing arrows. The pirates scrambled to put out the fires as the ship slowly retreated from us.

Attention turned to the three approaching ships as they

rocked their own cannons at us, but Carina's shield held, unwavering.

Astraeus's ship, the *Hydra*, cut across the path ahead of us as the remaining two Marisarma ships approached from the right, forcing us to sail directly to the coast of the Death Dunes. Carina jerked her head to the side as the crew of the *Scylla* shouted their pleas and dove overboard as flames engulfed the ship. Screams echoed over the water as she flung a hand behind her and sent a current of lilac-scented wind to the shattering *Scylla*.

Her wind snaked around the crumbling ship and snatched up the main mast as it snapped. The blazing mast and sails soared through the air and crashed into the Marisarma ship nearest us. The *Cetus's* shield shuttered before a following blast of cannons ripped through it.

Nerissa glanced at her cousin. Carina's wind slammed more flaming debris at the defenseless ship. The second Marisarma ship went up in flames.

Two down.

Ahead of us, the *Hydra* turned sharply, angling its bowsprit at us.

"What in gods' names—" Ronan yelled, motioning to the monstrous figurehead of the *Hydra*.

The jaws of one of the *Hydra's* scaled, serpent-like beasts opened, and a wide, iron tube extended from its throat.

"Get down!" Vulcan screamed as a glowing red cannonball soared toward our ship.

Carina flew backward, body cracking against the main mast as the strange cannonball ripped through her magic, shattering her shield as it smashed through the chest of Queen Antares's figurehead and into the hull. A blast of icy cold air filled the space left behind by the shield as chaos erupted.

The *Hydra* and *Kraken* flanked us. Their crews readied grappling hooks as they neared our ship through icy waves, their eyes dancing with wild murder. Kresida paced like a wolf behind the front line of elves, flipping her blade between her hands, eager for bloodshed. Nerissa and Ronan rushed to the starboard side, positioning themselves beside her.

Flaming arrows hit our sails, and I ran to the stairs, shouting for Vienah. She sprinted with me above deck, where she sent small streams of water into our blazing sails. A mast cracked overhead as fire ripped through it. I spied Carina's body through the chaos and scooted past the soldiers running about.

Carina was pale. I lifted her head and slapped her cheek to wake her.

"Get up, Carina," I urged, still reeling at the display of magic she'd shown. It came close to her mother's. A *mystic*...

Carina groaned.

"Get up," I yelled, shaking her shoulders.

Another crack overhead, this time from directly above. My heart thundered in panic, and I gripped her under the arms and heaved. My boots slipped on the deck, slick from the water Vienah desperately spread throughout the sails.

I scrambled, lifting Carina by the torso and throwing us both to the side as the crow's nest crashed down in flames. I slid Carina against a stack of crates before Vulcan's shout drew my attention back to the fight.

He signaled to Aquila, picking off the remaining soldiers clinging to floating debris from the destroyed ships. Aquila banked, angling toward us when he let out a panicked shriek of warning.

A spine-tingling bay sounded from deep beneath the waves as grappling hooks flew from both sides of the ship. Soldiers from the two remaining Marisarma ships boarded ours as their lethal-looking hooks latched onto the ledge and remaining masts. Only two, I realized, as our Lotrennian ship began to shatter.

The metallic scent of blood filled the air as battle broke out on board the *Centurion*, hurling me back to those horrendous hours in Odessa. Adrenaline, driven by self-preservation, curbed the dread, and I unsheathed two blades, ready to launch into an attack, not trusting the small bit of aim I'd gained with the Obscura power. Too many lives here... I shook my head. I wouldn't let this be Odessa.

I launched into the chaos as that deep baying groaned once more, this time closer. I reached Vienah, ready to guard her back as she put out the flames, when the milky white jaws of a massive sea beast yawned out of the dark sea. They closed around the *Centurion's* hull, sending elves screaming.

My jaw dropped at the monstrosity emerging from the depths, but as I prepared to summon my own darkness, I was in Lotrennia.

# CHAPTER TWENTY-THREE

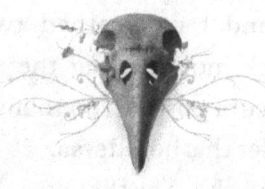

*A winged creature made of shadows and onyx flames. Its essence, destruction, its power unmatched. I was the only one left standing against it. We need to prepare. We need more power, all of us.*

*—Hidden correspondence from Bayne to Khato. 24th of Summer, 071.3E.*

A bright clearing opened before my eyes as muggy Lotrennian air filled my lungs. Trees and boulders sat uprooted, their previous resting places dark and damp. Splintered branches made way for a view of the Eye of the Wood in the distance.

Tiberius's left hock ached, and a steady stream of blood trickled from his shoulder. A vicious smile stretched across Queen Antares's petal pink lips as she raised her arms, locking an invisible shield into place. Her palms flipped to the bright sky, small shards of sharp rock lifting from the ground to follow the movement.

*Ti!* I screamed into the cast. *I can't stay! We're being attacked!* Somewhere, fire and pain and death beckoned, but the queen's words locked me into this shared cage of consciousness.

"Speak to me, Tiberius. Let me in," the queen purred.

*Lyvia.* Ti pleaded, exhaustion and panic making his mind's voice weak. His ears pinned against his head as he readied a blast of shadows.

Dread sliced through me. What had she done? We never should have parted...

The queen's light brows narrowed, and her lips curved upward. As her porcelain hands twitched, a volley of shards sped toward Tiberius. He bolted, sending his own wave of Obscura hurtling toward the rocks and bucking against the queen's shield.

Pain lanced through his flank, warm wetness dripping down his side.

"You're strong, Tiberius. Too strong for a human. Lyvia does not have what it takes," she urged, dropping her hands and turning to a small pack settled in the nearby bushes. "You need an elf to bond with. A mystic. A *queen*." She knelt as she removed something. A flash of silver drew Ti's eye as he caught his breath.

She turned and stood.

"And if you do not bend, you shall break," she declared in soft threat, as she let the object unravel from her hands. A thick, leather whip loosened itself from the handle. Thinly braided fortissa chain wrapped around the whip from its handle to its tip, where it met with a sharp iron point.

A stillness came over me as rage pounded through my

body, wherever it was. Tiberius sent a blast of Obscura, obliterating the leather base of the whip, but the fortissa remained.

*FLY!* I screamed at Ti as the queen's toned arm lifted the whip above her head and slashed at a diagonal for my caeluma's withers. White-hot pain lanced through his shoulder as the sharpened tip cut through his smooth coat. Muscles strained as he spread his wings.

"*BEND!*" the queen bellowed as her arm raised once more. "Or you will bleed!"

Ti faltered as pain seared across his wing. My heart pounded, my hysteria rising as my mind frantically searched for a way to help Tiberius. Far. I was too far to protect him...

*Shield, Ti! We need a shield!* I screamed as his wave of darkness reached for the queen and bucked against her wall of wind.

*Darkness is all I have*, he heaved. *Death is all I have.*

His wings were injured. He flapped again and staggered. I clung to our connection with desperation, my mind racing as fast as Ti's breaths.

*It's not!* I called back as that small tune of transformation pricked my consciousness.

"Come to me, Tiberius," Queen Antares commanded as she lifted the fortissa whip once more.

*I love you.*

*CHANGE IT!* I screamed. *TRANSFORM THE DARKNESS!*

Tiberius's mind raced against my own as he processed the words, the iron tip of the whip arching in a long, silver line against the blue sky. I shoved that song-like power down our bond from miles away, sending every bit of love I had for my caeluma—my horse, my shared soul—with it.

A surge of energy buzzed out of my being and into his, colliding with a strange, powerful force. He gathered it in his chest, and I sent an image of a ship's sail sliding down our casting connection.

Dark power erupted from him in a blast of black, tiny sparks of golden energy hovering at its edge as he *stretched* that darkness into an impenetrable sail, separating himself from the queen.

The iron whip clanged against the dark shield, its tip bouncing back and ripping across the queen's cheek. She staggered back, her delicate hand flying to the blood dripping down her face and the whites of her eyes flashing.

Tiberius funneled the darkness into the shield of death, and I poured my love down our connection. The two of us shared a fleeting moment of triumph.

The queen's shocked wrath morphed into curious greed as her eyes slid from the blood on her hand to Ti's shield.

"*Transcindiel*," she murmured, as she stood. "You can transform...death?"

Her lips spread into a wide smile, insidious delight dancing in her eyes.

Death... A distant memory pricked my mind.

"The magnitude of this power," she mused, snapping her own shield back into place. "Death and transformation... *Creation*. Used together... *Let me see*, Tiberius. An oath binds us, whether you wish it or not."

Queen Antares stalked toward Tiberius.

"It's tied to our last breath, *caeluma*, until fulfilled. Or until death."

*Air oaths can only be broken by death...* Tiberius whispered.

A question formed in my mind, but my thoughts scattered as Tiberius blew a snort and bared his teeth. The queen stepped closer, eyeing the shield of darkness, her wind testing its defenses.

The queen's hand on the iron whip twitched, Ti's eyes

narrowing in on the movement. She raised the weapon once more, and the fingers of her free hand contorted and twisted as her wind spun the shards of rock back into the air.

Ti's massive hooves shot into the air as he reared, and I bellowed a war cry down our connection as the force of our bond morphed back into that strange energy. He shoved the Transcindiel power alongside the darkness, and as his shield dropped, the darkness shifted.

Ti's long, crimped tail merged into a whip of his own as his hooves crashed into the dirt. He spun, the tip of the death whip sharper than any iron blade, and it snapped through the space between them.

Silence stretched for an invisible moment before a blast shook the clearing and sent Tiberius and the queen flying away from each other. Ti's ears hollowed out as air whipped from his lungs, searing pain slicing a line down the center of his chest.

*My chest.*

What?

Dread squeezed me like a vice, and nausea rose as my cast with Tiberius shattered, dragging me away from my caeluma and back into my body. My lungs gasped in the frigid air surrounding me, and I let out a scream as I looked into Vulcan's panicked eyes.

They held firm, as did his hands, and he growled through breaths, *"Do not let go."*

Vulcan's hands gripped my wrists as I hung over the edge of the upturned *Centurion*. Fifty feet below, icy waves crashed against floating debris. The screams of men were drowned out by the baying of the ancient beast, and I caught a glimpse of a white fin as it surged toward a group of men huddled on a stack of crates floating in the surf.

I snapped my attention back to Vulcan, covered in blood, and I twisted my hands to grip his wrists. He narrowed his blonde eyebrows at me. I clung to Vulcan, trying my best to squirm my way up the sinking ship, but the golden hull was smooth and slippery. If the beast patrolling the waters didn't feast on us, we'd fall to hypothermia unless we got out of the water and into the shelter of a shield.

The *Kraken* sailed north in the distance, retreating to a shallow cove on the shores of the Death Dunes. An explosion blasted from behind, rocking what remained of our ship and tipping the upturned hull. Vulcan swore as the momentum shoved him over the edge, and I lost my grip on his left hand. I swung outwards, still clinging one-handed to his other arm as I slammed into the rudder. A scream ripped from my lips as my back hit its sharp edge. Vulcan scrambled, reaching for me as I swung back and forth, a blazing pain ripping through my arm. He caught hold of my other as the warm wind propelling the *Hydra* engulfed us.

The ship cut through the burning wreckage and slowed fifty yards from where we hung. Lord Astraeus rushed to the ship's edge and waved his arms.

"He's signaling us to swim," Vulcan called to me over the chaos.

I glanced back at the *Hydra*, shield still intact.

Vulcan read the wariness in my face, and he said, "We don't have a choice. Don't let go."

I squeezed his wrist in response as he released his legs from the rail he clung to, and we fell into the icy surf.

The shock of the glacial water sucked the air from my lungs. I floated below the surface for a moment, the icy water soothing the sharp line of pain on my chest. My lungs screamed before my brain finally commanded my legs to kick. My head broke through the surface. The icy wind against my face was worse than the frigid waves.

Flames and smoke clouded the air above the surface. Vulcan kicked, and I followed.

We surged forward, swimming as fast as we could, putting distance between our upturned ship and nearing the *Hydra* when Aquila called to us in warning. My stomach turned to liquid as the current of the approaching sea beast rushed beneath our legs.

# CHAPTER TWENTY-FOUR

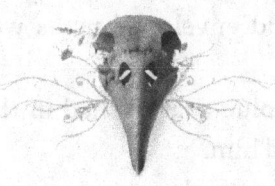

*I will train Isla myself. The Mystic Magnum remains closed to her. Be careful what you trade for the power you seek. Not all sacrifices are worth it.*

—*Hidden correspondence from the Khato to Bayne. 33$^{rd}$ of Summer, 071.3E.*

The beast surged past us, heading straight toward the *Hydra*. Its massive head burst through the waves. Jaws opened, and my stomach churned as bits of bodies and blood clung to its long, jagged teeth. I reached inward, readying the Obscura, as a looming black fog swept in from behind a burning ship.

The Mortis Shroud swarmed, and the sea beast let out a bone-chilling cry. The pale white creature sank below the water in retreat, and the snaking, black fog settled on the surface of the sea before it shot high into the air. The Mortis

Shroud hung above the surface and then flew west, in chase of its prey.

"Swim!" Vulcan commanded.

My body obeyed, and we surged toward the *Hydra*.

We climbed the ladders thrown overboard, and the warmth of the shield enveloped us as we were swarmed by pirates.

Lord Astraeus's blue coat flashed in the corner of my eye, and I whirled toward him.

"You bastard," I seethed.

Tanned, tattooed skin peeked from under his unbuttoned shirt beneath the long, flapping coat.

"I am that." He chuckled as he swaggered to us, removing his black hat. His dark, auburn hair was braided along the sides of his head, with half of it tied tightly back. A neatly trimmed, dark beard cut over his sharp jawline, and the pirate lord flashed a too-white smile. His voice was smooth, the Votruvian accent sliding over his tongue like silk. My heart squeezed as I thought of Morwyn, and he raised a dark eyebrow at me.

"You've looked better, *Bonscath*." His striking eyes slid over my soaked leathers and ripped vest as his lips tilted in a grin, and he winked. "I've been looking for you. Though I rather expected to run into Captain Ravindra and the *Evecta*." Lord Astraeus looked casually back at what remained of the *Centurion*, aflame and sinking beneath the waves, along with my father's book.

"How did you find us?" Vulcan demanded from behind.

Lord Astraeus slid his eyes to Vulcan.

"It turns out," he said, "that crafty queen of yours thinks she can buy loyalty from my spies." He shook his head, beads from his braids clinking against each other as he did. "Little does she know that loyalty to the Lords of Marisarma cannot be bought. Though it did offer us a little insight into her plans."

His eyes slid to mine. "It didn't take long to convince the others of what we might gain, should we reacquaint ourselves with this little bloodhound of yours." Astraeus lifted a leather and cedar-scented hand to flick my nose.

I blinked at the movement before slapping his hand away.

Vulcan stiffened, and I caught movement at the stern of the ship. A small group shuffled to the center of the deck. A flash of strawberry blonde hair caught my eye, and Vienah opened her mouth in warning when Lord Astraeus's warm hand slid around my forearm. He clamped something cool onto my wrist.

The blazing red cuff seemed cut from the same stone that had hurtled into the *Centurion*, and though it glowed as if it were a living flame, the stone bit into my wrist like ice. I hissed as I tried to pull it free, whipping my hand back at its sting. I tugged on the Obscura, summoning enough to set my eyes on fire when I was met with a solid black wall. I blinked, and Lord Astraeus's grin widened into an unnerving, handsome smile, teeth flashing.

"What—"

Lord Astraeus wagged a ringed finger at me as he chided, "I thought perhaps I might need a leash for my bloodhound."

*A leash.* My gut churned as memories from Kayj swept into my mind's eye, the phantom weight of that heavy collar pressed upon my neck, the chain, the *leash*, hanging down my front...

His dark eyes softened as he scanned my face, and I willed steel into my veins. He had somehow suppressed my powers. I reached down, searching for that tether of Transcindiel, and ran into a wall, but there was a pounding on the other side, as if my powers searched for a way out.

The cuff on my wrist chafed, the red glow of it pulsing, as if it were a living thing. And the cannonball... It had to have been made from the same material. It was the only thing that could break through Carina's shield. My mind whirred at the implications of such a weapon.

My stomach pitched as a sound escaped Vulcan's lips. Four men had his arms pinned to his side as a fifth held him in a chokehold, all attempting to wrangle him to the ground to get his hands bound.

I glanced at Vienah heading past us toward the stern, where they lined up prisoners from the *Centurion*. I scanned the group, searching for the others. Vienah's brown eyes caught mine, and she gave me a soft shake of her head. From a distance, her soaked traveling dress was torn, and she had a small cut on her cheek. My heart began a panicked gallop as the unknown fate of the others sank into my chest. I eyed the *Hydra's* men, keenly aware I hadn't been bound yet.

Pulling my gaze back to Lord Astraeus, I asked, "And what is it you think this bloodhound can do for you, Astraeus?"

The pirate's eyes darkened, a look of predatory enjoyment crossing his striking face, as he stepped closer. The lines of black ink flexed on his neck as he leaned in.

"*Lord* Astraeus, Bonscaíh. One of the five of Marisarma. Though I suppose I could be one of three, thanks to the mystic on board. We weren't expecting that, were we, lads?"

He grinned as his eyes swept over his hardened crew. A few of them spat and cursed as they walked past. The ship lurched in the direction of the Death Dunes.

Mystic. Carina was a *mystic*. Was? Oh gods, where was she?

As if reading my thoughts, Lord Astraeus shrugged his shoulders. "Fear not. She and the queensguard are on the *Kraken*, heading to shore. Along with the feisty Ravindra."

Nerissa. Thank the gods.

Lord Astraeus strode past me to the rail and surveyed the burning waters, with his back to me.

I surveyed my weapons as best as possible. My blades were gone. I couldn't feel the leather straps against my chest, and the cumbersome weight of my bow and quiver had disappeared.

Freezing in the waterlogged boots, I wiggled my feet against the solid length of my dagger. Talon's smooth hilt was in my palm an instant later, and my arms were around Lord Astraeus's broad frame as I reached for his neck. *I would kill him.* His rough hand wrapped around mine, and he twisted.

I screamed as my tendons strained against the movement, refusing to drop my dagger. My nails raked against his neck with my other hand. He snarled and the world flipped as he twisted and hurled me over his head, slamming my back into the sodden deck of the *Hydra*.

Pain blazed through the back of my head as I blinked back stars. Body braced against mine, he shoved his forearm against my neck, my chest screaming as he forced the air from my throat. His dark eyes shuddered at the reaction, his forearm loosening its touch. He opened his mouth to speak when a heavily tattooed arm wrapped around his throat.

Astraeus grunted as Vulcan's fist connected with his side, the elf attacking with unrivaled viciousness. Lord Astraeus slipped Vulcan's hold, landing a blow beneath the elf's chin.

Fast. The pirate lord was *fast* to keep up with Vulcan's attack. Perhaps not quite like the elves, but for a human, he moved like a mountain cat. Head pounding, I scrambled for my dagger. My hand reached for its hilt as a boot slammed down on top of its golden gem. I jerked my gaze up and came face-to-face with the sea green eyes of Astraeus's first mate. I'd seen him in the tents at Odessa. He sneered at me, placing my dagger at my own throat. The move sent my heart leaping into my chest, and the Obscura thundered against the endless wall.

Astraeus barked a curse over the chaos. The edge of Talon brushed against my skin as I whipped my head around. Astraeus, livid and nose bleeding, lurched toward Vulcan. The ex-War Slayer feigned left but leaped right, swinging his leg to the side to catch Astraeus in the ribs, but Astraeus anticipated the move, spinning to the side and slamming his own muscled leg into Vulcan's core. A grunt escaped Vulcan's lips as he went down. Six of Astraeus's men leaped atop him.

"Stop!" I screamed, jerking against the first mate as his men pinned Vulcan down, Astraeus cracking his neck and swiping his dark hair back in a casual movement.

His eyes whipped to mine, widening as they landed on the dagger at my throat. His mouth parted for a moment, his face going slack, before he schooled his features.

"Raek," he said, holding a hand out, unspoken command in his voice. He blinked once, his eyes focusing on the golden gem at the hilt of Talon.

"Attack Lord Astraeus again," Raek seethed into my ear, "and we'll send the rest of your pointy-eared friends swimming." He slowly lowered Talon, flipped it in his palm, and handed it to his captain.

Astraeus's dark eyes bore into me as he wiped the blood from his nose and slid a hand over the thick scratches that stretched across the side of his neck and over his tattoos. His lips twitched briefly as he pulled his fingers back to look at the smear of blood I'd left for him.

"Get your men off him," I growled.

Arms pinned, Vulcan's head slammed back as a fist crashed against his nose. Another across his cheek, aiming for the twining fern that adorned the side of his face. Fresh blood coated his already soaked shirt.

"*Stop!*" I screamed, unable to keep the plea from my voice, ready to launch out of Raek's grip. I yelped as his hand twisted my own, the same Astraeus had injured. "*Please, stop.*"

"Take *this* below deck," Astraeus snarled, jerking his chin at the men who'd lost their hold on Vulcan, the ones beating the living shit out of him.

"And bind her," he added, nodding to me. "The Death Dunes await."

# CHAPTER TWENTY-FIVE

*Any sacrifice is worth saving this kingdom.*
—*Hidden Correspondence from Bayne to Khato. 37th of
Summer, O71.3E.*

Vienah's wet hair hung in matted ripples ahead of me as we marched down the gangplank and onto the icy shores of the Death Dunes. My chest had been sliced, blood seeping through the front of my shirt, but I had no idea when or how that had happened.

A small group stood in the snow, hands bound to the long line of rope connecting them. Ronan, bloodied and bruised, hung his head. Nerissa held him upright, eyes tight with worry as she found mine across the snow.

Carina was there, cuffed and frightened. Kresida stood in the center, covered in blood, but it was hard to tell whose it was from. I scanned the group. The captain...and six more from the *Centurion*. No sign of the elven mages.

Lord Astraeus and the captain of the *Kraken* stood at the front of the group. I glanced behind me, searching for Vulcan.

The captain of the *Kraken* turned his scarred face to me as we stepped into the icy snow. The pirate lord was an older man, maybe twenty years Astraeus's senior, and wore a jet-black coat. Its hem was lined with rows of small finger bones. He grinned at me, and a silver tooth shone in the afternoon sun that managed to cut through the clouds. The Marisarma mages stood at the edge of the two ships, extending their shields onto shore. The warm air melted the upper layer of snow, creating a cold, wet slush.

Lord Astraeus pointed his curved blade toward me and inclined his head. Movement from Ronan caught my eye, and he glanced at me through the blood that streaked across his face.

"You are all alive because of this woman," Astraeus called to the group, jabbing his curved blade in my direction.

The line of prisoners slid their eyes to where I stood at the end of the chain.

"For how much longer," he continued, surveying the small group, "that remains to be seen."

"We're here for one thing," the captain of the *Kraken* cut in with a craggy voice, as he stalked along the line of prisoners, angling his head at me. He slowed as he approached. "A bone of power. That whore of a queen, *Antares*, sorely underestimated the power and influence of the Lords of Marisarma when she sent you sailing so close to the Crimson Sea."

The *Kraken's* captain approached me and smirked as he grabbed my chin with his thumb and forefinger. I bristled, as smoke and old ale wafted off his lips. He held firm, pinching the small amount of skin.

"Find the bone. The rest of you may go free."

I jerked my chin away and spat in his face. A growl escaped

his lips, and I braced myself as his fist slammed into my stomach. Once. Twice. Three times. I doubled over, forcing down the cry and sea water that threatened to escape.

He stood and stalked back to the front of the line, where the elven captain of the *Centurion* stood, a look of disdain and disgust written across his proud face.

The captain of the *Centurion* straightened as the pirate approached and said, "You make no such commands of my—"

The *Kraken's* pirate lord plunged his blade through the elf's chest as screams echoed down the line of prisoners. He ripped his curved blade free, and the snow below his feet quickly turned to a pool of crimson slush.

Carina wept as the captain of the *Centurion* choked out a gasp and shuddered as he lay dying at the end of the line.

"A captain should always go down with his ship," the Lord of Marisarma murmured as he shook the blood from his blade. He turned his attention back to me at the end of the line.

"Refuse," he said, raising his eyebrows, "and I can do this all day, sweetheart."

He moved down the line, pointing his blade at the various prisoners. I kept still, willing myself to make no reaction, though bile rose in my throat. I was here before, only months ago. The brightness of the surrounding snow suddenly mirrored the shimmering walls of the great hall in the Crystal Castle, and I was back there, with my father broken and bleeding on its floor as the dark king tried to force me to use my powers....

A gasp from Vienah pulled me back to the snowy shore, and I jerked my gaze to the *Hydra* where two men hauled Vulcan down the gangplank and shoved him into the slush. His body slid, leaving a bloody trail.

My stomach pitched as he moaned, struggling to stand. He turned his face to the side, and I gasped.

Bloody strips of ravaged skin hung where the twining vines of inked black ferns once were. Vulcan's arms shook as he pushed against the ground, and one of the men kicked him down.

"I'll do it," I breathed, as I watched the warrior who'd always seemed so indestructible be beaten bloody in the snow.

The *Kraken's* captain stalked to me, and he slid a greedy gaze down my torn leathers, still cold and dripping from the trip through the frigid waters. His tongue slipped over cracked lips.

"You'll do that and more, I reckon."

My stomach twisted as his eyes darkened. He sucked on the silver tooth shining from beneath his lips as a dagger ripped through the front of his neck.

Chaos erupted.

Warm droplets of blood splattered across my face as the Marisarma Lord lurched forward. I pulled back, yanking Vienah along with me, and we tumbled into the snow. Shouts erupted from all directions as swords were drawn, and the pirates of the *Hydra* and *Kraken* crashed against each other.

Ronan, somehow free of his bounds, palmed a dagger and sliced through the long rope that connected the prisoners. I scrambled in the snow back to where the *Kraken's* captain lay, a spark of gold catching my eye amidst the blood coating the back of his head and neck.

*Talon.* I ripped the dagger from the back of his neck, the sickening squelch of the blade pulling free loud in my ears despite the chaos of the fight. I sliced through my own bounds before freeing Vienah. I reached for my cuff and was met with the sharp bite of ice. The dagger would have to do.

Nerissa and Kresida met the blades of the pirates with swift kicks and dodges of their own, disarming them quickly. Men flew down from the *Kraken*, but didn't make it far as archers, hidden on board Lord Astraeus's ship, fired arrows at their backs. One ripped through the *Kraken's* mage, his shield dropping and shuddering against the air.

Lord Astraeus's blue cloak flapped as he threw a spare blade to Ronan, who caught the handle and whirled on the *Kraken's* men. I blinked at the sudden alliance. I rushed to where Carina stood, tearing at the cuff on her wrist.

I grabbed the back of her dress and pulled her with Vienah to where Vulcan lay in the snow. He groaned as Vienah tilted him over and lifted his head. Angling myself between the three of them and the bloody fight, I flipped the dagger in my hand as I split my stance, diving into that darkened part of me.

A man broke free of the fight and surged toward us with curved blades. I ran at him, flinging Talon at his face, where he batted it away with his left blade. I ducked, sliding in the slush as a blade slashed at me and kicked my leg out. My shin barked in pain as it met his ankle, but he went down.

He flipped, blades ready and swiping for me, but I was already up, diving to the side as my friends had taught me. On his feet now, he reached for me, but his legs went flying from behind him. Vulcan, somehow alert and upright now, towered over him as he disarmed him, wasting no time slicing through his neck and silencing the pirate.

The crashing of blades quieted, and the moans of the dying echoed against the waves. I scanned the wreckage. Bodies lay strewn across the red snow. Stripes of blood cut across Lord Astraeus's blue coat as he stepped over sobbing forms, silencing them. Ronan pinned his sapphire gaze on mine. Nerissa moved to his side, moving swiftly across the space to where Vulcan still stood in front of me.

Her brilliant green gaze dimmed as she took in his shattered face, the destroyed tattoo, and his eye barely saved. I blinked, having never witnessed Nerissa show emotion for her second. I flinched as Kresida stepped to my side. The warrior was bloody but seemingly unfazed by the rapid turn of events. She picked up Talon, examining the elaborate hilt before handing it to me.

Lord Astraeus approached Ronan in the distance.

"What in gods' names just happened?" Vienah murmured behind me.

Lord Astraeus muttered something to Raek, who began barking orders to the crew of the *Hydra*. They swiftly boarded the *Kraken*, killing anyone who remained. He held out his hand to Ronan, motioning to the last of us from the elven ship. The two of them approached our small group.

"What the hell is this, Astraeus? We made a deal in Odessa," Ronan simmered.

"A deal that *ended* in Odessa." Lord Astraeus smirked, winking at me as he swaggered by.

"*Fuck you.* Our captain is dead. *Fifty elves* are dead," Kresida spat.

My stomach sank. We'd lost almost the entire crew of the *Centurion*.

"Were you in on this?" Kresida seethed at Ronan, teeth bared.

"He wasn't," Lord Astraeus cut in. "I freed him right after that little incident."

"Traitor," I snapped.

The pirate lord paused and turned toward me, his eyes darkening.

"You think I have an *ounce* of goodness in me, *Lady*? I had one reason to join the Rising's cause. You think I give a fuck what happens to the people of Sultira? The people who so easily abandoned their neighbors to the west? There's a reason we call it the Crimson Sea. A reason the waters of Votruvia run red. Our islands float in *blood*."

"What do you want?" Ronan cut in.

"He wants the bone," I spat.

Nerissa shook her head. "When you learned of Queen Antares's plan to send us here, you baited the other Lords of Marisarma to join you and claim the bone. And then you took them out. Am I right?"

Her green eyes narrowed at the lord, and he met them with a calculating confidence.

"Mmm." His throat rumbled, the sound deep, primal. "Ever the thinker, aren't you, Nerissa? Indeed. The others weren't particularly pleased that I'd allied with the queensguard." A jerk of his chin toward Ronan. "And eliminating them was part of the plan, yes."

"But not Lord Haro, the *Siren's* captain. Where is he?" Carina's shaky voice sounded from behind me.

Lord Astraeus bristled at the mention of the lord's name and shook his head.

"Lord Haro is none of your concern. Though I am very curious how *you* stayed hidden for so long on the *Centurion*. My mages didn't detect a *mystic* on board until your wind whispering."

The group's gaze narrowed at Carina as she sank back. Kresida tensed, casually stepping to the side of the now powerless mystic princess.

"Youngest ever, I would guess?"

Carina shrank against the praise that rang through in Lord Astraeus's voice, but she remained quiet. Movement to the left caught my eye as Vulcan swayed. Ronan's arm was around his waist in an instant, steadying him.

"What the fuck happened here?" Ronan snapped at Lord Astraeus, drawing his attention from Carina to Vulcan.

Lord Astraeus bared his teeth at Vulcan. "That," he seethed, "was entirely due to his actions on board *my* ship." A sharp glance at me, and he moved to stalk away.

"Dry clothes await you on board the *Hydra*. Don't try anything stupid. I won't hesitate to kill you. I only need one of you to get what I need."

# CHAPTER TWENTY-SIX

---

*Once upon a time, a young maiden fell in love with a god. A lowly deity, the ruling gods paid him little heed, relying on his limited power to convey messages via the mind to the outer reaches of their world.*
*—Fabia's Fables, "People of the Stars."*

---

I stared at the roof of the small, cedar cabin I shared with Nerissa, unable to stop the torrent of thoughts flooding my brain. My fingers cautiously rubbed at my chest. A long, crimson line ran from the hollow of my throat to the base of my sternum. Nerissa deemed the slice shallow enough I didn't need stitches, but tender bruising shadowed the long line. My lungs ached with each breath.

"What are these?" I finally asked, dreading what another hour of silence would do to my psyche. I held my wrist in the air, and the red stone glowed in the dimness of the *Hydra's* cabin.

A disgusted sound escaped Nerissa's lips. "I have no idea. Something that can subdue magic. Stop it completely, apparently."

Carina and Kresida hadn't said anything about the matching cuff on Nerissa's wrist. If they noticed it, they didn't show it, though we didn't have more than a couple minutes before we were hauled onto the *Hydra* and locked up.

I opened my mouth to reply when the warm summer breeze of Lotrennia filled my lungs.

Tiberius soared over the lush green canopy of Ayla. He banked and angled down, fixing his focus on the bright spires of the Gilded Fortress jutting out of the vast expanse of greenery.

*You're okay*, I gasped as the casting connection formed, swift relief flooding my senses.

*Yes, I'll explain soon.* His response came a moment later. *But watch.*

Tiberius circled high above the white stone rotunda that hung over the waterfalls surrounding the castle. A large gathering of elves stood on the border of the giant balcony, more lining the living bridges and streets below the castle.

He swooped lower, close enough to see who stood at the center of the glimmering stone, and my heart plummeted.

Three forms took shape as he descended. Queen Antares, dressed in a tight-fitting gown of shimmering gold that stretched into a ten-foot train, stood at the center, a veil of sheer white with glittering golden embroidery attached to a delicate golden crown wrapped in living vines. She held her hands to the sides, palms forward, as Bayne stepped toward her.

He was dressed in a dark golden tunic and formal, fitted pants. He looked resplendent, with a golden crown upon his dark head and a vine snaking around its edges.

Palms forward, he placed them upon the queen's. Numbness spread throughout my body, or maybe it was Ti's. We watched them move their joined hands to the side and over their heads before sliding to the opposite hands and bringing them down the center, clasping them between their chests.

Khato, Master of Spells, slowly approached, murmuring words we couldn't hear. Tiberius hovered for a moment before the vines entwined on their crowns burst with white flowers, Bayne's power activating, and they made their way to the edge of the platform overlooking the elves of Ayla.

My heart pounded against my ribs as they clasped their hands once more, raising their joined fist above their heads to a resounding chorus of cheers echoing through the trees. Their fists lowered, and the queen's face tilted up to meet Bayne's...

"What's happened?" Nerissa's voice cracked in the silence of the small room on board the *Hydra*.

My breath escaped in small, panicked huffs as the cast broke, and Tiberius's consciousness ripped away from my own.

I was quiet for a moment, unsure I'd be able to keep my voice from shaking. My heart thumped in my chest, and Nerissa turned to me, her elven ears no doubt picking up its beat.

"Lyvia?"

A shuddering breath escaped my lips. "I think..." I began, my voice unbearably small. "I think your brother is married."

Saying it out loud...a small piece of my heart cracked as I relayed everything I'd seen, barely able to keep the flood of shock and devastation at bay. Nerissa's stillness turned preternatural.

"Was there music?" she breathed.

I shook my head. "I don't know. I..."

Nerissa stilled further, if that was possible, before lifting a hand and hesitantly patting the top of mine. Once. Twice. I glanced at her stony expression and noted the slight pinch of her brows before she looked away, and my heart squeezed in response.

"Bayne is doing what he thinks he needs to. He will resist."

"Aquila hasn't indicated any change?" I took a shuddering breath. "What if it wasn't a marriage ceremony... What if he's soulbound to her now?"

"Aquila has heard nothing. But Bayne wouldn't. He can't." Despite the consistent shaking of her head, doubt plagued her words.

"How do you know?" I whispered into the darkness, feeling the world slipping out from beneath me.

"I don't. If he has..." She paused, her throat bobbing. "If he has, then he's forgotten. What she is, what she's done, who *he* is..."

I choked on the small sob forming in the back of my throat and wiped the incessant tears rising in the corners of my eyes. Nerissa sat up and perched her elbow beneath her as she looked at me through the darkness.

"*If* he's soulbound, we return. We will remind him who *he* is. And you will remind him who *you* are." She slumped down on the scratchy mattress and turned to face the wall, saying nothing more the rest of the night.

FED AND DRESSED in thickly lined furs and waterproof boots, the seven of us trudged through the dense snow of the Death Dunes with Lord Astraeus and half of his crew. Despite the clear summer skies, the surrounding landscape was a vast tundra of ice and snow, painted in swaths of blush and orange in the early morning light. Little clouds of breath puffed from my lips as the movement warmed my body. Thank the gods we were here in the middle of summer and not the dead of winter.

*A generous offer,* Lord Astraeus had crooned as we accepted the tools and clothes needed to join his crew on the hunt for the bone. He agreed to spare our lives after we found the bone, but made no offer to get us back to Lotrennia. We were sorely outnumbered. I recognized a handful of his crew from the Battle of Odessa. Aquila had kept his distance, knowing we couldn't trust Astraeus and his men.

Vienah patched up Vulcan's face as best she could, but streaks of blood soaked through the bandages she'd used. I slowed my pacing to match Vulcan's sluggish steps.

"I'm sorry for what happened," I murmured, well-aware he despised the pity. I braced myself for the quick snarl that would come.

He merely grunted in reply. "The men of the *Hydra* lack imagination."

I glanced up, and he slid his hazel eyes to me. A blotch of bright red blocked out half the white of his eye near the slice that had taken off his tattoo. My eyes watered at the sight of it.

"Can you see alright?"

He rolled his eyes in response. I nodded. *Okay then.* We trudged through the open tundra for the rest of the day, only stopping when the setting sun cast a bright, violet shadow across the expansive terrain.

"No sign of dune runners," Kresida murmured as we crowded around the small fire.

"I've got scouts out," Lord Astraeus said as he approached our small group. "Bonscaíh, a word." He motioned me to his tent.

"Not alone," Nerissa cut in, a hard grip on my arm.

Lord Astraeus kept his gaze on me but nodded. "Have you felt it?" he asked, gesturing to the seats in front of him.

We remained standing.

"She's not a fucking dog," Nerissa snapped. "And why do you call her that? What is *Bonscath*?"

Lord Astraeus ignored her as he raised his dark, auburn eyebrows at me. I lifted my wrist at him, the cuff still glowing red in the dimness of his tent.

"Not a chance." I shrugged and crossed my arms. He let out a breathy chuckle.

"There are ways to heighten your connection to the Bellator Bones," he said softly, eyes slicing to a small teapot resting on a crate.

I tensed as those harrowing memories from Stynguard hurtled into view, when I was forced to consume an elixir to heighten my connection to the Obscura Bone. High Priest Helmar's cruel smile. The kingsguards' viciousness. Those swirling silver eyes...

Nerissa angled herself toward Lord Astraeus and bared her teeth.

"I'd prefer not to force it down your throat," he said, as if aware of my history with the elixir. His eyes traced the scar on my neck. "We could start with a small amount."

"You're not starting with anything," Nerissa snapped, stepping closer to me. "Take these cuffs off."

"You are in no position to make demands," he clapped back. "You either use whatever connection you have to these bones, and catch its scent, or I will force it down your throat. You are outnumbered here." Lord Astraeus let out a soft whistle, and six guards stepped into the small tent.

Nerissa hissed as they closed the space between us.

I shifted closer to Nerissa. We *were* outnumbered... And it was why we'd come.

"Give me until tomorrow," I said, holding up my hands. We

didn't need any more bloodshed. Not tonight. Not after we'd lost so much.

Lord Astraeus narrowed his eyes, the promise of death lingering in their depths. My heart galloped as I waited for the arms at my side. *The hands on my face as they shoved the liquid down my throat...* But he held my gaze for a moment before nodding.

We returned to our small camp, where the remainder of those on the *Centurion* huddled around the fire. I found a spot between Vienah and Ronan, the former leaned forward, deep in discussion with Carina.

Carina paled as the attention turned to her.

"Youngest mystic ever?" Vienah asked in hushed tones. "Amazing. That's incredible. What you did..."

Nerissa stilled, ready to find her seat, but remained standing, her gaze frosty against Carina's matching green eyes. "That title should belong to Isla Jasira," she seethed, voice barely audible over the crackling of the embers.

I snapped my head to her. "What?"

"She was rejected by the Council of the Elders, despite getting a letter of recommendation from the master of spells himself. I always wondered why that was," she continued, eyes casting daggers at Carina. "I think I know now."

"I had nothing to do with that," Carina said, frustration building in her words.

"Unlikely," Nerissa spat as she moved to walk away.

"Please, *Sobraen*," Carina pleaded.

Nerissa stopped and cut an accusatory gaze at her cousin. Her voice was quiet and lethal as she said, "Cousin? Is that still what it is? Or is it *aunt*?"

Any color left had completely drained from Carina's face. "What are you talking about?" she whispered.

"Congratulations are due to your mother and my dear

brother, it appears," she sneered at the group before stalking off.

I shrank as Ronan let out a soft swear and shot a sympathetic look at me.

"I'm not sure what you're so upset about," Kresida murmured across the fire. "Kings and queens take mistresses all the time."

Kresida raised a brow in challenge at the glare Vulcan threw her, and my stomach pitched as all eyes landed on me. *The mistress.*

HOURS LATER, I sat alone on a small pack near the dying fire, the flames settling into a soft waltz and forcing my thoughts to Bayne.

I tugged the gloves off my hands and waved them through the flickering flames. The fire bit the pads of my fingers, but I held them there as the icy air nipped at the tops of my hands. I frowned as my eyes drifted closed.

Bayne had become as unpredictable as the flames jumping at my fingers. Warm and comforting, but not without risk. I reached into my jacket and pulled out the amber pendant, the amplifier Bayne had given me. The smooth resin was warm against my touch as I ran my thumb and forefinger over it.

A wave of emotions slammed through me as his absence hit. Wetness pooled between my shut eyelids, cooling as they hit the night air. *I missed him.* But I was also angry and uncertain. Uncertain of what I had seen at the Waters of Ascendiel. Angry that he doubted me. Angry at him for marrying the queen. Angry at myself for not finding another way.

*You will remind him who* you *are.* Nerissa's words echoed in my mind as the night wore on, but who was I *to him?*

I had to get back. Find the bone, get back to Lotrennia, return to Sultira. As quiet as I could manage, I snuck from our little camp and tiptoed through the icy slush to Lord Astraeus's tent.

The pirate sat with his arms crossed, his boot on the small table, one foot crossed over the other. His lips tugged upward, still holding the blunt of rolled enderleaf he smoked. My eyes settled on him.

"The smallest bit," I said quietly. "And only when I say so."

He inhaled through the smoke, his eyes sparking against the light from its burning end.

My gaze scanned the few crates scattered around the small tent. "I don't suppose you brought any sugar or cream."

Lord Astraeus's lips widened into a grin.

# CHAPTER TWENTY-SEVEN

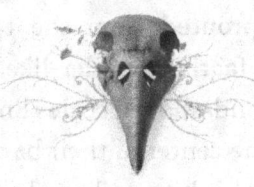

> *The young maiden was a slave in the palace but became a queen in her dreams.*
>
> —Fabia's Fables, "People of the Stars."

The buzzing that slithered into my veins was a foreign, dreadful thing. Somewhere, far beneath the nullifying power of the cuff on my wrist, the Obscura and Transcindiel bucked at its trespassing.

The bone was here. And as we trekked in the coming days, its intensity would fade, as if we took a wrong turn. We'd adjust, testing out various directions until I picked up its scent again. We continued this game of hot and cold until a painful, spine-tingling howl stopped our pursuit.

I slapped my hands over my ears at the blaring roar and rushed from my tent to find the pirates forming a semi-circle around the camp. The bit of afternoon light that slithered through the fog sparkled off the ice-like scales of the dune runners that surrounded us.

Ten... Fifteen...

I stopped counting after twenty massive, reptilian-looking silver wolves with black eyes pinned hungry gazes on us. Two large white horns sprouted from the tops of their heads, bordered by smaller, feathery antler-like bones. Their silver, white, and blue diamond-shaped scales lined up in an intricate pattern, pointing to the center of their backs where the largest met in a sharp line of white spikes along their spine. They clinked together as they stalked back and forth.

"Astraeus," Ronan's hiss cut through the silence that stretched through the camp. "Arm us."

Lord Astraeus angled his curved blade at the dune runner closest to him. He bristled as if weighing the risk. The dune runner crouched, turning its head toward the pirate before launching off its hind legs.

"Second crate from the left!" he shouted as he dodged the dune runner's attack and slashed with his curved blade.

The remaining dune runners crashed into the line of pirates. Screams echoed across the tundra as the ice wolves ripped into several of his men, including the mage in his crew. I followed Ronan as he sprinted to Lord Astraeus's tent.

He tossed me two bows and a quiver with not nearly enough arrows, and I checked that Talon remained strapped to my ankle inside my boot. Lord Astraeus had forgotten to check me for the dagger.

Kresida caught the blade Ronan tossed to her and swiftly fell into a defensive position in front of Carina. Nerissa armed Vienah, though I knew she had no training with weapons, and stood in front of her as a dune runner eyed the two of them, stalking back and forth. Ronan stepped to her side, their movements a perfect mirror to each other.

Vulcan found himself at my side. He motioned to a small ridge after I tossed him the bow. "Get to the higher ground!" he commanded.

We scurried up the slippery ridge. He spun, taking aim at the dune runners, immediately releasing three arrows. I slipped, the ice slicing through the side of my hand. I caught myself, ready to turn and release an arrow of my own, when a line of black caught my eye in the distance. I squinted at a row of dark trees lining a large sheet of ice that began over the ridge. A frozen lake.

The buzzing surged. *There*. The bone was there. The surety of it ran through my veins.

"Lyvia!" Vulcan's snarl drew my attention back.

He released two arrows in the amount of time it took me to draw my own and scan the chaos for my target. The dune runner nearest Ronan and Nerissa dropped dead as Vulcan's arrows caught him in the mouth.

Kresida stood between a circling dune runner and Carina, angling her blade as she feinted left, and the dune runner lurched after her. She sliced into his side, her blade bouncing off its scales. I let my arrow fly, aiming for the soft spot under its throat. I missed, hitting it in the shoulder, but the momentary distraction was enough for Kresida to catch a glimpse of the fur beneath its coat and sink her blade into the soft spot.

Five...only five left, but as I scanned the bodies below, I counted only twelve dead dune runners. I eyed our shared quiver, and my gut sank. Empty. Vulcan grimaced as he scanned the slaughter below before he whipped his attention to the one stalking up the ridge.

"Dagger," Vulcan commanded, holding out his hand to me.

I pulled Talon from my boot and slid the hilt into his hand. Vulcan's bandage had come loose, and his freshly slashed face only added to his lethal appearance. He crept down the slope, as lithe as the dune runner in front of him, mirroring his steps in the thick, freshly fallen snow. The dune runner's dark eyes flicked to mine for a moment before turning back to his prey that stalked him down the slope.

I mimicked Vulcan's movements, getting low and creeping in the opposite direction, as if to attack from the side. The dune runner flicked his eyes again to mine. He launched off his hind legs, aiming for my throat as Vulcan moved and plunged Talon into its chest. The massive form collapsed into the snow as he ripped the dagger free.

A scream echoed from below, and we whipped our attention to the camp. Blood dripped from the maw of the ice wolf that had ripped through a pirate. Lord Astraeus leaped to the side as it lunged, swinging his curved blade beneath the arm before skewering him in the chest. Silence rode the tangy scent of iron as it crawled over the wreckage.

I surveyed the damage. The blood of the dune runners glistened against their ice-like scales, sparkling in the sun that crept through the fog. Human bodies littered the ground.

Carina knelt beside Kresida, applying pressure to a wound in her shoulder. Nerissa allowed Ronan to brace her as she limped back to where Vienah tended to one of Astraeus's men. Of the twenty-two that we joined from the *Hydra*, only twelve of Lord Astraeus's crew members remained.

We made our way down the slope as Carina wrapped a bandage on Kresida's blood-soaked shoulder, looking as if she might be sick. "She'll need to rest," she called to Lord Astraeus, who stood staring at the bodies his men dragged into a pile, his mouth set in a hard line.

"Did you hear me?" Carina called to the captain.

He turned a hard gaze on her. "We do not rest."

As if remembering we were now armed, Astraeus's men moved with slow precision, flanking our group.

"We don't need to go anywhere," I called as I approached the pirate lord. "It's here. In the lake."

Lord Astraeus's dark eyes sparked for a moment, eyes slipping to the ridge behind me, before ordering his men to disarm our group.

THE CONSTANT BUZZING created a dull pulsing behind my eyes. A headache that wouldn't go away. We'd burned Lord Astraeus's fallen men and now sat huddled by the fire.

Lord Astraeus crunched through the crimson snow to our group and leveled a stare at Nerissa as he said, "You're getting us below that ice."

Carina pinched her brows, looking at her cousin curiously.

"How could I possibly get us below that ice?" Nerissa asked coolly, eyes sliding to her fingernails.

Lord Astraeus raised his brow, glancing at Carina and Kresida. A grin slowly spread on his face, whitening the scar on his lower lip.

"Have you been hiding it?" he mused, cocking his head.

Ronan tensed as he watched the captain and Nerissa.

"Is that why I didn't see that magnificent light display during our attack in the gulf?"

Carina's mouth fell open as she processed the captain's words, and Kresida's dark eyes widened. The black paint of her rank had been wiped free since the attack on the *Centurion*.

"Nerissa?" Carina asked quietly, eyes sliding to Nerissa's wrists where she'd tugged her jacket over the glowing cuff.

Lord Astraeus didn't balk from the daggers in Nerissa's gaze. His grin widened as he shook his head and chuckled. "Not my business, I suppose. You'll melt it and keep it melted while we go in."

The muscle in Nerissa's jaw twitched at the command.

"And you, as a mystic," he continued, turning toward Carina, "should be strong enough to send a wind tunnel through that lake, splitting its water so we can look for the bone."

Carina blinked. She opened her mouth to protest, and Lord Astraeus cut her off.

"You will come with me and my men," he said, pointing to me with his white dagger. "As will the three of you." He motioned to Ronan, Vienah, and Kresida. "As a little extra protection. Wouldn't want you dropping a lake of water down on top of us." He winked at Carina before stalking off.

Vulcan opened his mouth as three of Lord Astraeus's men slammed into him. Lord Astraeus turned slowly.

"You," he said, jamming a finger in Vulcan's direction, "are more trouble than you're worth. You stay behind. Under guard."

Vulcan bared his teeth, struggling under the grip of the captain's men, still weak from his beating and the trek here.

THE AFTERNOON SUN hung in the bright blue sky, taunting us with distant heat. Lord Astraeus gripped Nerissa's wrist, murmuring something beneath his breath as he twisted the cuff ever so slightly, doing the same to Carina's. The glowing red light dimmed, as if whatever nullifying power the cuff used had lessened.

"This won't be enough," Carina said, looking at her hands as if they belonged to someone else.

"It's all you get," Lord Astraeus said, turning toward the lake, "I won't dial it back any further. You drop the wind tunnel, we all die." He motioned to Kresida, Vienah, me, and Ronan.

Nerissa flexed her hands, stretching her fingers. She slid her eyes to Lord Astraeus.

He met them with cool resolve. "Same goes for you." Lord Astraeus glanced pointedly at Ronan, whose lips formed a thin line.

Carina and Nerissa stepped to the edge of the frozen lake, and my eyes cut to the line of dark trees watching in the distance. Nerissa's head fell back, and she closed her eyes. The rays of the sun were golden against her tan skin, as if she allowed them to awaken the Soleia power within her that she'd shoved down all these months. She held her hands in front of her, flipping her palms up. A brilliant white light materialized above her hands, and the sun itself shone brighter above. Nerissa opened her eyes and rotated her palms, directing the power of the sun to the ice before us.

I blinked, shading my eyes with my hand as a beam of blinding white light shot from Nerissa's hands straight into the ice. Carina gaped at her cousin's powers, and Lord Astraeus bristled, wary of Nerissa's strength.

A crack sounded in the center of the ice. Then another. Soon, hundreds of tiny cracks spiderwebbed from the center of the lake where Nerissa directed her power. Dark waves sent thick chunks of ice bouncing to the edges of the lake.

Nerissa shut her fists, closing off the power of the sun, and gave her hands a shake. She rubbed her wrist against her leathers before nodding at Carina.

Her cousin, still wide-eyed from Nerissa's display of power, stepped forward and steepled her hands as bits of little light shot from the center. Lilac-scented wind snaked through the camp behind our ridge, gathering strength. She widened her stance and grimaced as she sent a massive blast of it racing toward the edge of the lake, knocking against my knees.

Her brows pinched as she narrowed her concentration into a small spot in front of where our group stood. Her hands shook as she closed them against each other and pointed the tips of her fingers to the edge of the lake. The wind tunneled into a concentrated blast as it ripped into the lake, sending a massive blast splitting the water down the center and creating a dark path of wet sand leading to its depths.

"You have two hours, at best," she said through shaky breaths.

# CHAPTER TWENTY-EIGHT

*Keen of mind, with sharp eyes and wit, the Messenger plotted
as he watched the ruling gods.*
—Fabia's Fables, "People of the Stars."

---

Walls of navy water stretched to the bright sky,
shadowing the soaked, sandy floor of the lake
from the afternoon sun. The damp scent of eggs
and decay wafted from its depths despite the continuous wind
Carina tunneled through the water. Shorter strands of hair
ripped free of the tight braids Vienah and I wore. Though the
cuff suppressed her powers, the water seemed to react to
Vienah as we walked through the tunnel, waiting for that
whisper of command.

Lord Astraeus and Raek flanked me as we trudged down-
hill. Carina's wind continued to push a wall of water ahead of
us, and I let that incessant buzzing lead us in an insufferable

zigzagging pattern through the lake. Six of the pirate's men joined us in our scouting mission at the bottom of the lake.

"What do you plan to do with it?" I asked him as we stepped over a row of algae-covered, ragged rocks and into a slimy blanket of limp, rancid weeds. *Life*. So much more life than we'd ever imagined in the Death Dunes...

Lord Astraeus cut a quick glance at me as he pondered his answer. After a moment, he said, "I'll use it to protect my people."

An exasperated scoff escaped my lips. "Really?" I said, turning to him as we walked. "*'There isn't an ounce of good in me.'* That's what you said. You expect me to believe a Lord of Marisarma is going to use the power of the Bellators to protect his people? *What* people?"

His dark eyes narrowed as he said, "Votruvians, of course. We've been outcasts for hundreds of years. Saros's protection for humans ends at the borders of Sultira. And with the islands constantly fought over by the sea lords, the people have suffered from more than just the ashen."

"Then you admit the Lords of Marisarma are a part of the problem. Are you going to kill off the other one and make yourself king?" I asked, remembering the stories Morwyn told me about her homeland.

"There's much you don't know, Bonscaíh," he said, smirking as he patted the top of my head.

I leaned back, smacking his hand away. "Did you just *pat* me?"

Another smirk. "Bloodhound, right?"

"Fuck you," I snapped.

He held his hands up in defeat as I put distance between us.

"The bones don't *hand* the power over," I said after a moment. "Daimos could only wield the two he acquired because he is an incredibly powerful mystic who has lived hundreds of years. And as far as Bellators go..." I glanced at him sidelong.

He placed a hand to his heart. "What? You don't think *I* could be a noble Bellator? I'm hurt."

I bristled at the sarcasm. "You're reckless and cruel," I spat, thinking of Vulcan's ruined face. "I could never trust you."

I opened my mouth once more, and he abruptly stopped, gripping above my elbow and spinning me toward him. I tensed as he leaned in, close enough I could see tiny flecks of gray in his dark irises. A wave of cedar and leather snaked into my lungs.

"I don't need your trust," he murmured. "I need you to do your job."

My molars scraped against each other, and I envisioned my forehead crashing into Lord Astraeus's nose, but my brain promptly took control. I shoved out of his hold and continued walking, following that miserable buzzing.

"How long has it been?" Ronan asked from behind after a few moments of tense silence.

"Fifty minutes, give or take," Raek answered. He shifted next to me, eyeing his captain.

"We'll need time to make it back out, *Bonscaíh*," Astraeus murmured.

Something tugged on my braid. I snapped my gaze to Astraeus, and he cocked an eyebrow, the seriousness from moments before gone.

"Don't touch my hair. And stop calling me that," I snapped, irritation cutting through the words.

Raek let out a low chuckle next to me.

I whipped my head toward him, "What? What does it mean?"

Raek's lips twitched to the side, and he opened his mouth to answer.

"Shadow," Astraeus cut in.

I followed Raek's eyes as they darted to the pirate lord.

"It means 'shadow,' in Old Votruvian. Appropriate for you, I think?" Astraeus explained, eyes sliding to my hands and then to my chest, as if he could see the shadow that smothered my soul. His brows pinched for a moment. "We could try another dose."

I turned back, my gut reeling at the suggestion. The buzzing inched toward unbearable.

"No. We're close," I muttered.

Carina's wind followed my movement and pushed forward, the water falling away and revealing a steep hill.

"There."

The sandy trench merged into a set of stone steps, leading to a small, round gate at the bottom. An eight-pointed star sat at its center, marked with the various symbols of the Bellators.

Vienah approached as I knelt in the sand, running my fingers over the markings. My dual powers stirred at our proximity to the bone below.

"This is Elvish," Vienah said, noting two sets of script. "Do you know what it says?" she asked, turning toward Kresida.

The War Slayer knelt beside me, and her brown hands stretched across the snow-white stone. Her dark eyes slid to mine, and she pinched her brows before reciting:

*"Life is nothing without it.*

*As small as a thought; as strong as the tides.*

*As quiet as whispers; as loud as thunder.*

*It exists in the light and the dark."*

"What in Tynan's Hell is that supposed to mean?" Ronan blurted out.

"And what about this?" I asked, motioning to the smaller script at the base.

Kresida squinted and leaned forward. "*Cast your weapons down. Honor opens more than doors.*"

I frowned, running my fingers along the edge of the wide gate, feeling for any type of handle or lock. Tiny, round divots lined the outer edge of the circular door. No, not exactly round, but *pointed*, as if something sharp were to fit inside. My hands drifted inward, eyes scanning the various Bellator symbols circling the center of the door. Larger divots, like wide slices, were dispersed in a random pattern around the symbols. And in the center of the eight-pointed star, a shallow, round indent.

Astraeus's men began to slide their blades along the edges of the door, attempting to pry the stone free.

"I don't think that's going to work," I murmured.

"We don't have time to solve a riddle," Lord Astraeus replied, motioning for his men to continue.

They began to hack away at the stone. I cringed as small bits of white stone chips flew into the air, destroying the delicate filigree etched into the edges of the circle.

Wrong. This seemed wrong. I eyed their swords as they continued to hack away. The tips of their blades were too thick for the edges of the door. But...

"Stop," I said, stepping forward, holding my hands up. "Stop! You're not getting in that way. I know how to open it."

Astraeus snapped his head toward me, dark eyes narrowing. "Explain."

"Give me your arrows," I said, nodding to his man in the back wielding a bow. He eyed the pirate lord warily, who gave him a cautious nod.

"It's a puzzle," I murmured, mind drifting back to Enya's tomb. My heart squeezed for Drystan.

I eyed the small divots, looking strangely like stars. Could it be a constellation? I recited in my head as I counted out eight arrows, doing my best to recall the exact constellation alignment of the eight brightest stars on the day of the twin eclipse, each *Sending*.

"If the center is the sun," I said, kneeling at the center of the door. I aligned myself facing the text, fingers sliding up to the top of the eight-pointed star. My finger slid into the uppermost divot above the star and over, before sliding one of the arrowheads into the divot. And then another, counting and aligning them in the exact position. *Gods*, I wished Drystan was here.

"What are you doing?" Astraeus demanded, yet his voice held a soft sort of awe.

"It's the Sending," I said, standing and turning toward him. "I need your sword now." I held my hand out, waiting.

Raek scoffed, chuckling, but the pirate lord held my gaze.

"*Cast your weapons down*," Astraeus repeated the strange verse. "Not aside. *Down*."

His dark eyes slid to the stone door and the slices I'd examined. He stepped forward, unsheathing his curved blade. Kneeling before the eight-pointed star, his fingers slid over the little cluster of five stars, the symbol of the Celestyn power. He plunged his curved blade into the slice next to it. A perfect fit.

A wry smile formed on his lips as he glanced at his men, jerking his head toward the door and ordering them to insert their blades in the door.

The fletching of the arrows and hilts of the blades stuck straight up in the air, and nothing happened. I cocked my head.

"There's no handle," Vienah murmured. "Even if it's unlocked, how do we open it?"

That was it.

"*Handles*," I clarified to Vienah, feeling smug, and gripped the top of Astraeus's blade and one of the opposite arrows. I pulled and pushed, attempting to twist the door counter-clockwise.

I grunted as I pushed. Ronan reached around me, adding his strength. Nothing. *Dammit.*

Astraeus edged around the blades, his finger grazing the shallow center of the star. He let out a soft chuckle.

"We're missing a piece, Bonscaíh," he said quietly. "*Honor.*"

"Well, there's not much of that in this group," I snapped.

He turned toward me, a wry smile on his face. "Your dagger," he said, jerking his chin toward my boot where I'd concealed Talon. So, he hadn't forgotten I still had the blade.

"What do you mean?" I asked.

"The name of your blade is *Honor.*"

I pinched my brows, shaking my head, and he leaned down and snatched it from the inside of my boot, his hand gripping the back of my calf.

He held the dagger, almost reverently, between his hands, as if weighing the perfectly balanced blade.

"*Onoiren,*" Astraeus murmured, his finger sliding over the barely perceptible script on the length of the dagger. "*Honor,* in old Votruvian."

I blinked. This was a *Votruvian* dagger that had somehow ended up in the Crystal Castle, in Cyril's hands. My mind didn't have time to process what that could mean as Astraeus took the blade and placed the hilt, its golden gem a soft glow against the white stone, at the center of the eight-pointed star. A soft *click* sounded.

"*Honor* opens more than doors," Astraeus murmured, turning back to me, his eyes soft. He motioned toward the door.

We gripped the blade and arrow once more and barely nudged the door before it twisted smoothly in a full circle. Air whooshed, followed by the squelch of sandy lake bottom as the door lifted open.

Lord Astraeus let out a low whistle, eyeing the dark staircase spiraling into a deep chamber beneath the lake. "After you, Bonscaíh," he motioned me forward with a wink.

Vienah threw an encouraging nod in my direction, and I stepped into the darkness.

MY HAND SLID along the dry, chilled stone wall as we spiraled below the lake through a vertical tunnel. A dry, loamy breeze floated from its depths. Astraeus's men lit two torches that they'd brought along. I held one in front of me as I slid Talon, or rather *Honor*, back into my boot. Astraeus noted the movement, curiously keeping his mouth shut. The other blades and arrows above were stuck, the price of this tomb.

Lord Astraeus ordered his men to seal the gate above us should Carina's powers falter, insisting the creators of this tomb would have built a second exit. Her sweet, lilac wind vanished as the stone gate thudded against the top of the tunnel, sealing us in.

The constant buzzing in my ears drowned out the bickering that had begun several steps behind me. Beneath the wall of whatever magic this cuff wielded on my wrist, my powers seethed.

My foot finally met the hard, frozen stone of the base of the stairs. My eyes went wide as I took in the bare, circular white chamber.

In its center, a large round sarcophagus rested. Its cover was adorned with images of a fierce battle. Elves, evident by the pointed ears, and humans, fought side by side on various winged animals.

Fire and ice clashed in the skies above. Creatures of death and pain, the likes of which I'd never seen before, snaked across the tomb. Scales and talons tore apart the winged warriors. And at the bottom of the tomb, an ocean of nightmares stalked the ships. I glanced at Astraeus, whose eyes were narrowed on a particularly vivid depiction of a hydra, the same creature carved on the front of his ship.

My eyes snagged on a simple round symbol in the center. A circle with two lines cutting across the center. So strange and simple, yet something about it reminded me of Enya's tomb.

I stepped forward, vaguely aware of the others shuffling off the staircase behind me and inching around the large casket. There was little more than a few feet of space between it and the walls. I ran my fingers over the etchings as I studied the lid.

"How are we going to get the top off?" Kresida asked as she hopped off the final step of the staircase. Her movements were quick and energetic despite her injured shoulder.

I eyed Astraeus, opposite of where I stood. He'd grown quiet since entering the chamber, not taking his dark eyes off the constellations that lined the outermost edge of the sarcophagus. He lifted his torch, leaning over the lid, pupils dilated, as he reached for that simple symbol in the center.

"You won't."

# CHAPTER TWENTY-NINE

> *At night, the Messenger took the maiden's form, the only*
> *sliver of his race shining in his eyes like stars. Love took root,*
> *its vines wrapping around the young maiden's heart and*
> *mind in the sweeping, savage way only love can.*
> —*Fabia's Fables, "People of the Stars."*

Lord Astraeus's wide eyes shot to mine. The slight whistle of several bowstrings whined, and I stiffened, waiting for their release.

I blinked as I spotted at least ten warriors, eerily hidden against the walls of the small chamber, camouflaged in white leathers, with matching paint adorning their hands and faces.

"Remove your hand from the resting place," an accented voice commanded.

I picked up my hands from the lid, bringing them to my sides as I slid my gaze back to Lord Astraeus. A cold calmness had come over him as he carefully removed his hand.

Footsteps padded from far beyond as the white stone on the far side of the chamber smoothly slid away, revealing a hidden hall. I flinched as a short figure stepped into the chamber, bones clacking as their steps slowed. A massive skull of some great horned beast sat atop their face, obscuring it from view. Rows of bones hung draped across a white, furred tunic and pants.

The skull rotated slowly, scanning our group, one by one. A white spear, its blade hewn from bone, lifted its point at Vienah. I caught Ronan's eye before he moved in front of the water witch, and a blade appeared at his throat.

The ivory point of the spear slowly shifted, and I pulled my gaze back to the strange leader as they leveled it at me. The Obscura power bucked at the wall in place and the sudden arrival of a threat.

The skull tilted, as if the giant beast cocked its head, curious about its prey, and the figure slowly stepped closer to me. I willed my pounding heart to settle.

I blew a slow breath through my lips as the figure placed the ivory tip at the center of my chest. They stopped, the dark eyes somehow bright beneath the mask, and lifted a gloved hand, covered in long, curved claws, which clicked together in some unspoken command. A sudden push of air whispered across my cheek, and my stomach turned.

"Your Holiness," Lord Astraeus crooned from across the sarcophagus, hands still in the air, head angled down. "May I present to you Tynan's Accepted, Lyvia of Sultira, Bonder of the Bellators, here to claim the bone of power."

Lord Astraeus lifted his eyes to me, and a small grin appeared on his lips. I blinked, processing his words as the room stiffened. He held my gaze for a heartbeat before I pulled it away and settled it on the form of bones and claws in front of me. Willing my heart to calm, I rotated my wrists, palms flipping to the low ceiling, and showcased the luminous eight-pointed matching stars on my hands.

The arrowhead poised at my neck dipped. Despite the feeling of dread it invited, I plastered a look of subservience on my face and purred, "I am at your service, Your Holiness."

The figure before me waited several agonizing heartbeats before responding. "No."

The word rang through the chamber in a clear, damning female voice from the small form before me. The stone ceiling let out a soft hiss, and my powers pounded wildly against the thick wall in response.

*"Languidus smoke!"* Kresida warned in a panic.

Ivory smog floated from the ceiling. I clamped my mouth shut and held my breath as my pulse banged against my neck.

A white, ashy substance clouded the chamber, stealing my sight. I whipped my head back, creating a small amount of distance between my neck and that ivory spear, as I shoved the base of my palm up the shaft. I ducked into a crouch and swiped my leg out, clipping the armed ankle of the small woman. My shin barked in pain at contact with the sharpened bone, and the woman staggered.

Grunts and thuds echoed from across the chamber as we engaged the hidden warriors. A shout from my right, and Ronan backed into me as he sliced through the archer behind me. The woman in front recovered her stance and blindly thrust into the white haze. I kept low and barreled into her, the force of my tackle knocking the wind from my chest. She toppled over, barking a curse. I took a damning breath as instinct took over and the languid smoke snaked its way into my lungs.

My fingertips tingled as I struggled to get to my feet. The white staff of the woman's spear shoved against my chest, and

I flipped onto my back as nausea clawed its way into my gut. I attempted to shove her off with waterlogged limbs.

Fuzzy darkness encroached on my vision. I blinked rapidly, resisting the urge to succumb to the smoke. The woman shoved again, pinning me to the ground, knocking the air out of my chest, and forcing me to take one more fateful breath before darkness took me.

A HALL *of sparkling jewels spread before me as I put one foot in front of the other, crystals of varying blues creating a swirling stream of stones beneath my feet that led me down the center aisle. A different view of the Crystal Castle, my semi-conscious mind realized, as once again I watched through Enya's eyes.*

*A group of warriors stood at the front of the dais, many eyeing me with distrust, others, fear. A grin formed on my lips, and I snapped my teeth at them. The woman in the center tsked her tongue.*

Such manners, *the foreign voice chided in my head.* Ordell promised you'd behave.

*I resisted the urge to rake my darkness down her face, seething at her intrusion.*

Ordell has a soft heart, *I murmured before slamming my mental wall down, cutting off the queen who stood at the center of the dais.*

*Olienna.*

*There was something strangely familiar about her, my half-conscious self noted, as I gazed at the beautiful queen. A loud crack clapped from behind, and I whipped around to find a warrior's dark, almond eyes glaring at me as he strode past and joined the group at the front.*

Faron, *Enya's mind said. The copper of his skin gleamed with* the melted snow that shook off the thick white fur slung from his shoulders.

Enya snapped my attention back as Olienna's lips tilted into a soft grin as she stood. The fabric of her black gown rippled down the front.

Watch, Enya seemed to say. Listen.

"Welcome, Sister," the queen said. "Thank you for coming." She gestured to the oval table between them as the Bellators shuffled around, finding their places.

I stopped walking a few feet before my seat.

"Ordell said there would be snacks," I said, crossing my arms before the group.

A scoff left the sensuous lips of the man to my right. His bright green eyes flared as he glanced at me before softly shaking his head.

"What a sneer to wear on the face of a gentleman, Kyson," I crooned, clucking my tongue. "One might think I wasn't welcome."

Kyson watched as I placed a hand on my heart, noting the darkness slithering in my veins. It rarely left these days, its strength growing to a level I scarcely imagined. A flicker of apprehension crossed his features before he schooled them into cool confidence. That look, my half-conscious self thought. The Ravindra eyes, the Ravindra look.

"One might think you were working with them, given your destructive history, Enya," Kyson said, his clear voice ringing through the vast, crystal chamber.

The others shifted in their seats at the tone of the king of Lotrennia.

Fury lit the fuse hitched to my powers, and I let a small shadow spin into my palms, where it hovered above my skin.

Kyson's gaze transformed from green to white flames as he took in the blatant threat. His hands curled into fists.

"Seems you've lost your kingdom and your wits if you think I'd ally with them," I snapped.

Olienna opened her mouth to interject when the door to the great hall opened, and the warm scent of cinnamon drifted in with the cool breeze from the surrounding mountains. My heart skipped a beat, but I didn't let myself turn around.

"I brought snacks," Ordell proclaimed as he strode down the hall, tossing a bag of sweets onto the round table.

Do not smile.

I chanted the command in my mind as the handsome, tawny-eyed elf shot a quick look in my direction before finding his seat among his brothers and sisters. He ruffled his short, sandy brown hair in that I-don't-give-a-shit way before pulling a round, sugary piece of taffy from the bag and popping it into his mouth.

"Caramel?" His lips kicked up into a smirk as he lifted an eyebrow and nodded to me.

My eyes lingered briefly on the perfect curve of his lips. "I prefer chocolate."

A quick, barely perceptible twist of his wrist ignited a sprinkling of golden power, and the caramel in his hand took on a dark, creamy hue. He extended his palm toward me, which I ignored. I scanned the rest of the group watching me with wary interest.

Brothers and sisters in bond, not in blood.

The Band of the Bellators.

The final seven. Eight, I realized, if I were to join them.

"We don't have much time," Olienna said from the head of the table, her violet eyes sparkling. "By coming here, Enya, you've answered the call. The call to protect the innocent from all threats to this world."

"One thousand, four hundred and fifty years," the woman to my left said, her heavily accented voice ringing through the room. "According to the constellations."

Her hair, as dark and deep as red wine, hung in tight curls, draping past her shoulders. I lifted a brow at the young woman.

"Lelyth has never been wrong. And we are the last," the man

*nearest me said, pinning his soft brown eyes on me. He lifted a dark hand and scratched at the thick beard covering his chin. "Fifteen hundred years is a long time. Even for the elves, it is too long. We start now or never."*

*I blinked at the powerful man sitting before me. My mind whirred as I began reading between the lines. Was he suggesting...*

*"They are coming for all of us. They want what was taken. We must decide..."*

MY CONSCIOUSNESS GRAPPLED at the memory in a panic. I *needed* this memory. Enya reached for me as I slipped away. But I wasn't slipping back into consciousness... I was slipping further from it...

MY HEART EASED *as I swam in eternal darkness, following the glimmering ribbons of light. I was back in that strange in-between, back with the threads binding me to the universe. But being in this place, gliding through it, instead of looking up into it as I did at the Waters of Ascendiel, was vast bliss.*

*The web was a complex, intricate thing of beauty. Threads danced, one tugging lovingly as I passed. I tugged back and poured my love into the thread bonding me with Tiberius, not knowing exactly how I knew it was him, and not caring.*

*I continued swimming, oblivious and indifferent to where my human body was, forgetting what Enya had been trying to tell me.*

*A flash of silver, and that daring, braided thread materialized in the distance, pulsing, beckoning, as if it were nearby. I stared at it, curiosity getting the better of me, and extended my not-hand toward it. The silver light of it, like the light of a star, shone brighter.*

*Was I smiling? Could I smile in this place? I thought I might be. Somewhere, the heart inside my human body picked up a steady beat in response. I wanted to swim inside this thread, explore it in every way, never leave it.*

*But my eye caught on those lovely Bellator ribbons that swayed in the water-like darkness. I leaned into the current that pulled me toward them and ran my fingers through the six. Had I been in my human body, I would have shuddered against their touch. And there it was.*

*That one bright one, similar to the rest, but not the same. Bayne. My fingertips grazed that connection, a wave of sunlight shuddering in response, confirming what I'd tried to tell him. It gave a sad, gentle pulse.*

*Somewhere far away, a resigned sigh escaped my physical lips. I knew all along this was here, hidden. Ignored. Even if Bayne thought it impossible. I reached out, and the thread brightened, as if coming fully awake for the first time.*

*And then it snapped.*

*A terrible rip cracked in my head as I was torn from that blissful state of connection and hurtled back into my physical body.*

# CHAPTER THIRTY

*Time passed differently for the young maiden. Days disappeared, memories were lost, and she began to have strange thoughts, unable to distinguish the voices in her head from her own.*

—Fabia's Fables, "People of the Stars."

P ain blazed in my chest. Was it physical, or was it from that terrible rip in the connection? Had something happened to that soulbinding thread? A wave of hysteria washed over me, and my heart pounded in panic.

Another icy hot blast slammed into my chest, cracking bone.

A voice in the darkness, a command. Hands gripped my arms, hauling me up. My arm barked in pain as it was wrenched behind me. I was being bound. *Wake up.*

My consciousness drifted between that state of darkness and the light that accompanied the pain. A flash of light before icy air filled my lungs as I gasped into the night. I blinked rapidly, trying to take in my surroundings. My elbow ached, and I tugged against the rope binding me to a post. Or a tree?

A dark room. Small and fucking cold. I blew out a breath that clouded in the pale blue light seeping in from a tiny window in the ceiling. A groan rumbled behind me, and I jumped, fiery pain ripping through my elbow and ribs.

Something wiggled at my lower back, and I yelped, trying to squirm away from it. I craned my neck, trying to see who was tied behind me, feeling long arms resting beside my own.

"Wake up," I croaked, my voice hoarse from ingesting the languidus smoke, whatever the hell that was.

Another moan. I wiggled my arms against whoever sat behind me.

"Wake up!" I hissed.

The person stiffened and jerked their arms forward, sending an unbearable sharpness through my elbow. I let out a soft whimper, biting my lip to keep from screaming.

"Fuck. *Fuck*," he growled. "Bonscaíh?"

Godsdamnit.

"Where are the others?" I whispered. "Did you pass out?"

"Obviously," he murmured. "If you can shift your elbows to the sides, I can probably get us out."

Bracing myself, I sucked in a breath and attempted to move my elbows as pain ripped through my arm. "I can't," I breathed. "I think my elbow is dislocated."

Lord Astraeus let out a low swear.

"And I think my ribs may be cracked," I added, noting the sharp ache accompanying each breath.

Lord Astraeus's head turned. "Sounds like you did more than pass out."

I frowned. "You think they tried to revive me?"

"I'd say they did, seeing as you're awake and talking to me now."

I gritted my teeth as an insufferable edge of sarcasm rode his voice.

"Well, what do you plan to do about this?" I snapped. "You got us into this mess. Fucking disaster."

A deep, throaty chuckle reverberated through his arms that made me want to claw his face off.

"You're seriously laughing at this? Fuck you," I hissed.

"Mmm, maybe another time," he crooned.

Heat rushed to my face despite the frigid room, and I scoffed, the movement sending an ache rippling through my chest.

"Why not? You've got a thing for pirates," he mused. "Though I'd hardly qualify the honorable Captain Ravindra as a pirate."

Blood leached from my face. *Bayne.*

Oh gods, had something happened to Bayne? My heart hammered. That tether, that thread was my link to Bayne. *Why hadn't he believed me?* A weight crushed onto my chest. Khato had to have suspected our link, sending me to the Waters of Ascendiel to show me my own threads, to show me possibilities. My stomach pitched. I could have tied myself to him before all of this...

"Despite running away from his throne," Astraeus continued, his voice cutting through my thoughts, "he's rather righteous, isn't he? Though I suppose he has dabbled in theft enough to warrant the title of pirate, noble as he may be."

My blood raged. "Stop talking," I hissed.

"Or what? Does the pup bite?"

His words curved, and I could hear the grin forming on his lips.

My blood boiled. "Fuck you."

"Oh, I'd fuck you silly, love. But now is not the time."

My jaw ached. I blew out a short breath, willing my temper to calm. "You know nothing of what Bayne has been through. Do us both a favor and shut your piece of shit mouth."

Another throaty chuckle, and my nails sliced into my palms.

"I know more than you realize, Bonscaíh. Bayne is a liar," he countered, the damning word forcing the recent ache of betrayal back into my heart. *Liar*.

"He's a liar and a thief," he continued. "And a damn good one at it, I'll give him that. He uses his charm...that *charisma*, to get what he wants."

A vice wrapped around my chest, as if the pirate lord were speaking aloud the intrusive thoughts I couldn't shake from my mind since Ronan revealed Bayne's dishonesty. His charm... his charisma... But things had changed between us, hadn't they?

"And he's stolen much from the Lords of Marisarma. We've lost great value thanks to him," Astraeus said, scattering my thoughts.

"Seems like you care more about your treasure than your people," I bit out, wishing I could slap the smile right off his godsdamned face.

"I *am* talking about people," he murmured, voice going deathly quiet.

"What do you mean?"

"I think that's enough for now," he said, forcing his voice back into that casual tone. "We don't know who is listening. Stealthy fucking creeps."

I stilled, squinting against the darkness and searching for any sign of an outline or whites of an eye, but we'd missed them so easily in the burial chamber. Where were the others? How long had we been down here? Carina couldn't have held the water much longer if we'd been out for more than an hour. Did they think we were dead? I swallowed a dry breath, shut my mouth, and waited for our captors to return.

Minutes, maybe hours later, I blinked my eyes open. Soft light peeked in from the corner of the room, indicating the rise of Ganmira and Renova, illuminating the icy chamber in swaths of blue and white.

Astraeus hummed a soft melody, the smoothness of his voice reverberating into the trunk that bound us, sending small vibrations into my back. I twisted, my best attempt at avoiding the movement, irritated at its calming effect.

"Do you think they could be the People of the Stars?" I finally asked, thinking of the fairytales in the book that had shown itself to me at the Living Library. I'd lived my entire life not knowing there were other beings besides humans. Elves... Would it be that preposterous that the children of the gods would be real? Demi-gods living in hiding?

Astraeus stilled behind me. "No."

"How do you know?"

I winced against his shrug, and my elbow barked in pain. "Then who are they? Why did you call her *'your holiness?'*" I whispered after a few heartbeats of silence.

Lord Astraeus was quiet for several moments before he responded. "In Votruvia, there are tales we are told as children about the People of the Dead. Wraiths, with nothing left of their human form but bones, led by their holy mother, defending the souls of the deceased."

An eerie awareness snaked through my gut. "Defending them from what?" I whispered.

"*'Impostors,'* my mother would say. An enemy never here

but never gone. More riddles. A cautionary tale, of course. 'Affront your elders, the People of the Dead will take you from your beds.' But there's always a bit of truth in them, isn't there?"

Lord Astraeus shifted behind me, as if scanning the room. "I wouldn't be surprised if hundreds of years ago, Votruvians encountered the locals here in the Death Dunes and some made it out alive. History belongs to the survivors."

"We need to get out of here," I murmured. "Take this off me."

The irritating cuff chafed against my wrist. I considered casting to Tiberius... But would it be worth the energy required? And what good would it do? He couldn't do anything for us while he was in Lotrennia. No, I'd save that for when I had something more practical for him to respond to.

"Can't. Need my hands for it or I would have already," he said as he opened his bound hands and waggled his fingers against my lower back.

"Stop that," I hissed.

"Ticklish?"

Before I could respond, my heart leaped from my chest as a horn blared in the distance and the smooth slide of ice on ice groaned from behind me. Soft, orange light floated into the small room, outlined by two large shadows that split. The first knelt in front of Lord Astraeus and the second stalked before me.

The warrior, clad in white and bedecked in hundreds of bones strung together like armor, eyed me from behind the human skull he wore as a mask. He held a spear in one hand and the long, thick humerus of some large beast in the other.

I flinched as he lifted the bone and prodded my elbow with the rounded head. I bit back the scream that tried to escape as pain ripped through the joint. He murmured something in another language to the other, who gruffed in response.

My body stilled as he knelt, removing the binds from my wrists before hauling me to my feet with a dagger poised at my lower back.

I stumbled as he shoved me from behind, glancing back at Lord Astraeus, whose face was haggard. Blood had frozen on his short, cropped beard, and his dark eyes glanced at me as the man standing before him raised the thick bone into the air. A sickening grunt ripped from Lord Astraeus's lips as it crashed into his thigh.

The dagger pressed dangerously against my spine as my captor gave another shove. My stomach churned as the door slid shut behind us. I didn't care for Lord Astraeus. In fact, I think I hated the man, but I couldn't help the growing nausea as his pained growls chased us down the hall.

I scanned the walls of ice as we walked, taking mental note of every turn we made until a second door slid open and a vast rotunda stretched before us.

My breath caught as I took in the massive arena, entirely made of ice and as grand as any castle. Hundreds of rings lined the space that spiraled down into the center of the icy amphitheater. Glowing blues and whites mixed in a frozen, twirling tapestry. White and silver etchings of a bloody battle with fearsome warriors and winged monstrosities covered the flat space at the bottom, an elaborate portrait of a battle.

At the center stood the short woman from the tomb, draped in a cloak made of bones and white feathers. Her arms spread to the side as she gazed at the domed ceiling, where the carvings continued. The markings on the ceiling mimicked the pattern of stars as they appeared on each Sending, each twin eclipse. She turned toward us, still wearing the massive skull of the strange beast. She peered through its large nasal cavity and motioned for us to descend.

All too aware of the dagger at my back, I scanned the rest of the rotunda, slowly making my way down the rings. Several guards posted throughout the upper ring, arrows nocked in my direction.

When we reached the bottom of the vast chamber, my bonds were cut. I staggered back a step as the tall form, hidden among his own set of bones, reached for me.

"Your arm," the small woman before me explained, her voice clear and commanding with that strange accent.

My eyes snapped to the man slowly reaching for my left wrist.

"I can do it," I said in a shaky voice. I stepped back, reaching for my wrist and biting my tongue to keep from crying as I twisted and snapped it back to my shoulder, sliding the joint back into place. Unbound, I turned to the woman, reaching for any type of connection to my powers.

She stepped forward until she was a mere foot in front of me.

"Bonder... Tynan's Accepted... Death Digger... Daughter of Darkness..." she mused, scanning me with dark eyes shadowed beneath the mask.

My stomach churned at the names. How could she possibly know what the Stone Witch and Dark King Daimos had called me? She made slow circles around me.

"What names they have given you. But who are you, Lyvia? Who will you *be*? Death Scholar, no more. Lady... I think not. Daughter..." She threw me a knowing look as she paused her pacing.

My heart sank.

"Chosen by the gods," she continued. "But *were* you? A twin eclipse... That was no doing of Ganmira and Renova's, which means someone is to blame for manipulating it. And how does that tie into Olienna's prophecy? Fate? Or was it even a prophecy to begin with?"

*Manipulate* it? What in gods' names could possibly do that? My brows pinched as she made a large, sweeping motion with her staff in the air above us. Her opposite hand stretched between us, as if counting something invisible.

"Intriguing," she murmured. "Bound, yet wholly unbound."

"What is that supposed to mean? How do you know all of this? Who are you?" The questions tumbled from my lips as I adjusted my stance.

Her body relaxed, and she tossed her long staff into the air, catching it gently in the palm of her two hands, extending it for me to see.

I took a tentative step forward, eyeing the staff. Tiny carvings of skeletons were etched onto it, bowing to a man with his arms stretched out before him...

The woman snatched back the staff, clanking it on the ground three times, to which the guards shuffled from the chamber.

"The stars whisper to me about a great many things. I am Xenelpha, Matron of the Rhashtai. We are the Guardians of the Dead. Soldiers of Tynan, at least in this realm."

I swallowed, and a dead weight pressed on my chest. "And what commands does the god of death give?"

Her lips tilted up in a small smile, the white powder on her skin cracking, revealing a small line of deep, dark copper.

"Protect."

# CHAPTER THIRTY-ONE

*Soon, the young maiden was a maiden no more, and the lowly messenger god who had stolen her heart had also stolen her mind.*

—*Fabia's Fables, "People of the Stars."*

A twisting formed a knot in my stomach, and my throat bobbed. "Protect what?"

"Many things," Xenelpha replied, "What you came for, of course. The bone of the Bellator whose sacred resting place you entered." I took a sharp inhale, my ribs aching at the movement, the incessant buzzing from the bone flaring as if in confirmation of her words.

"And where are the rest of my friends?" I asked, changing the subject.

"*Friends*," she mused, tilting her head as her eyes drifted to the glowing cuff around my wrist. "Is the one who put the rubelline on your wrist a friend?"

*Astraeus.*

"Do you know how to get it off?"

The massive ivory skull tilted down as Xenelpha responded, "I do. Would you like me to retrieve your *friend's* hand for you?"

My stomach churned. She meant to bring it to me without the rest of him, but I'd had enough of severed hands.

"The magic is tied to his skin, and his alone. He's been quiet, that mage, with his magic."

I blinked. Mage? I hadn't realized Lord Astraeus possessed any magic. He hadn't let a bit of it show, even in Odessa. Had Astraeus intentionally hidden his magic?

"What is it? And where are the people I came here with?"

"So many questions, yet you have not answered mine. Who will you *be*, Lyvia? Will you bring *demin*, destruction, or *m'ando*, hope? Until you can answer that, Faron's Advetis will not yield. Even to you, *Bonder*."

*Advetis.* The word rang through my memory like a thousand bells chiming in the wind, settling within me. *Advetis*, the bone seemed to whisper from behind a wall, *Show me where you will take me.*

"May I see the marks?" Xenelpha asked after another moment, eyes flicking to my hands.

I held them out and flipped my palms up, the luminous eight-pointed stars glowing in the blue light of the massive ice chamber. Xenelpha peered at them for several moments, unmoving.

"Twice blessed or twice cursed, I wonder," she mused, "Either way, you must find the balance. What is it that bound them in the first place?"

I snapped my hands closed at that, sick of the riddles and tired of being a captive. I'd had enough. We were here for the bone. We would leave with the bone. I'd figure out how to harness the damned Transcindiel power if it killed me. I'd save the ashen.

"I'll tell you who I am," I said, straightening my spine and letting my hands fall to my sides, "I am Lyvia. The gods have hurled daggers at me, and I am sick and tired of being on the receiving end of whatever shit they've concocted. I've come for the Advetis Bone. And I'll be leaving here with it, along with my friends. I will return to my caeluma and the other Bellators. I will keep it safe until I find its master, or they find me. We will retake Sultira. We will end Dark King Daimos."

Xenelpha's eyes flashed in the shadows of the skull, and I held a breath, a sudden certainty spreading over me. The command in my voice was relieved, as if it had been subdued for too long.

A line of bright white spread beneath the mask as Xenelpha's lips tilted into a wide grin. I braced myself as she reached into her thickly furred coat and pulled out my long, sharp dagger. Talon... Or rather, *Honor's* golden gem shone in the icy chamber like an ember in the snow.

"This," she began, as she took the blade in her gloved hand before offering me the hilt, "does not belong to you."

I gripped the dagger, tucking it safely in my boot.

"It didn't belong to the elf, either," she continued, and my stomach churned at the image of Cyril's sneering face, danger and bloodlust dripping from the tongue that flicked over his lips.

"I don't care who it belonged to." I straightened. "It's mine now."

"You may someday." Xenelpha's smile grew beneath her mask, and a small chuckle escaped her lips. "You and your... *friends,*" she continued, "may stay here for a short time. But the fate of Advetis rests on you. I will take you to the bone. Should you unlock it, you may leave with it."

I blinked. Just like that? *Why?*

Xenelpha's staff clanked four times on the ice beneath us, the sound reverberating across the vast chamber. My knees buckled as the ice beneath us shuddered and the blaring groan of ice on ice boomed through the chamber as eight massive sections of the ceiling spun counterclockwise, lifting away from the center like a blooming flower. The same way Enya's tomb had opened.

Darkness flooded in its absence as it opened to the night sky. A sigh escaped my lips as thousands of stars, all varying colors, like none I'd ever seen, dotted the sky like a blanket of sparks. The sun had set long ago, as I followed her gaze and eyed Ganmira early in her trek above, giving chase to the brilliant blue orb of Renova, already high in the sky.

"Come," Xenelpha beckoned as she walked up the frozen steps of the amphitheater.

TOWERING, conical trees came into view as we ascended the steps, their large shadows like giant guards posted along the Rhashtai village. Hundreds of small buildings, most erected straight from the ice and some as tall as their neighboring trees, spread in a zigzagging pattern. The village was small, yet somehow grand, as I traced my eyes over the intricate designs carved on each building and the sophisticated light system connecting the street lanterns.

I followed Xenelpha through the sleeping village, catching the eye of several warriors, clad in the same bone armor, their gazes following us as we trailed the winding road in its center until we came to a domed ice structure.

Though our bond was stifled by the rubelline cuff on my wrist, I pushed against the thick wall and sent my emotions screaming toward Aquila. *Caution. Safety.* The best I could manage, giving him some indication of our location and status. A veiled sort of response hit me a few moments later. *Reassurance.* My heart warmed at the faint connection.

"The rest of your party is inside," she said, placing a small pouch of something in my hand. "This should wake them. They are your responsibility. *Maadon* is in one week. You may stay until its celebration. And then you must move on, with or without the bone."

"What is Maadon?"

"A day of balance, a turning point. When darkness meets light."

My swallow was dry. "The equinox? The autumnal equinox is in one week?" I asked, my voice hollow. Had we truly been gone almost three months? My stomach twisted.

Xenelpha nodded and turned to leave, and I asked, "What about Lord Astraeus?"

The small form stilled before turning back toward me. "The lord..." the matron mused, rubbing her chin with her thumb and forefinger. "He's not the threat I suspected he was..."

I opened my mouth to question what the hell that meant when she paused and surveyed me. "A word of advice. Life is but a frieze, a carving of the series of choices we make. Each etch of the chisel, each choice, a creation of who we are to become," she said, her voice as clear and crisp as the nearing snowy morning. My mind drifted to the elaborate etching at the base of the icy amphitheater.

"Choices shape us," she continued, "They can transform the engraving into something of true beauty or destroy it entirely. I will leave his fate in your hands."

The weight of her words settled as an internal conflict began to brew. My hatred for the man seemed at odds with the urge to free him. I'd see him to get this cuff off either way and decide what to do with him later.

A LARGE, unlit fireplace sat in the center of the chilled chamber, surrounded by thick, twirling, beautiful structures of ice that spun up through the middle, opening to the ceiling to allow smoke its escape. The remaining nine members of the party we'd entered the lake with sat bound together around the hearth, unconscious.

I knelt beside Ronan and lifted his chin. Dried blood caked on the side of his head, his usual light curls, dark and crusty. A nasty bruise formed beneath his left eye. Water filled my eyes as I sniffed the small bag Xenelpha gave me. Celosia powder, I realized, as the phantom sting snaked its way up my nose, accompanied by images of High Priest Helmar's face. I placed a small amount on my finger and rubbed a tiny amount on Ronan's upper lip with the tip of my pinky.

A ragged cough filled the chamber, followed by a sneeze. Ronan's groan was deep and sleepy.

"Wake up, lazy," I whispered.

"Lyvia," he murmured as I cut his bounds loose. "Where are we?" Sapphire eyes blinked as he took in our surroundings and rubbed his wrists.

"Welcome to Rhashtai, home of the Guardians of the Dead," I murmured, moving to rouse Vienah, who was blessedly in better shape.

I kept Kresida, Raek, and the rest of Lord Astraeus's men bound as I woke them, one by one. Ronan and Vienah cleaned up and stood on either side of me as they all regained consciousness, tugging on their bounds. The soft, orange gleam of morning light crept its way into the round, thin

SHADOW OF THE SENDING

sheets of ice lining the chamber, providing window-like openings as clear as glass.

"Good morning," I said, circling the group bound around the hearth.

"Here is how this is going to go," I continued, looking each of them in the eye, "I am done taking orders from any of you. *We* are done taking orders from you. From Antares. From Astraeus."

I stopped as I neared Ronan and Vienah.

"Where is Lord Astraeus?" Raek demanded, his sea green eyes sharp.

"Being held elsewhere," I answered. "And the first thing I'll be doing after our little discussion will be getting the rubelline cuffs removed from myself and Vienah."

Raek's eyes widened before a sneer slapped across his face.

"The Rhashtai have offered us shelter for the next week. I will decide what that looks like for the seven of you."

"Why am I still tied up?" Kresida's voice dripped with fury as her dark eyes found mine. I slowly made my way around the hearth and squatted before her.

"Where does your allegiance lie, War Slayer?" I asked, quietly placing the sharp tip of Honor against her chest in the dimness of dawn.

"It lies with Princess Carina Ravindra. It always has, it always will," she said, straightening as best she could with the restraints still in place.

"Are you a liar, Kresida?" I whispered. "Have you sworn an air oath to Queen Antares?" My eyes scanned hers as they widened. Nerissa had told me she expected as much. And according to Ronan, it was why Nerissa had received such backlash when she promoted Vulcan to her second, years ago, as he claimed he would never swear an air oath. Nerissa had

233

served her uncle, and the air oath that she'd sworn as a War Slayer had ended with his death.

"While I believe your loyalty to Carina is true, I can't be certain you're not bound to her mother. I cannot trust you. At least not entirely."

"Untie me," Kresida shook with rage. "Untie me or—"

"I am *done*," I snapped. "I am done being ordered around. I am done bowing to your queen. I am done being held captive."

Ronan chuckled, earning a hiss from Kresida. I spun on my heel and stalked from the small chamber, Vienah and Ronan closely behind.

I led Ronan and Vienah through the village as people shuffled about in the early morning. Men, women, and children of all ages set to work, many of them forgoing the bones and white paint, appearing far more friendly. They casually observed us, curiously glancing in our direction as we walked by.

We stopped dead in our tracks as the tree line shook, a boom rumbling through the needles. My jaw dropped as two ivory tusks, each longer than I was tall, crushed through the trees. The massive creature that emerged was covered in shaggy, brown fur with one long snout that swung along the snowy ground as it stomped through the forest. A Bone Warrior sat atop its back, spear resting casually against her shoulder. A line of downed tree trunks dragged behind the massive beast.

Ronan let out a low whistle as we watched the beast enter the village.

"Good heavens," Vienah whispered beside me.

"I don't think they answer to the heavens," I murmured, though I smiled and couldn't help but share in her awe.

"I like this new Lyvia," Ronan muttered as we made our

way to the center of the village. "Sounds like this matron gave you more than a pep talk."

I glanced sidelong at him.

"I was being honest," I said, eyeing the guards that trailed us despite our freedom. "I'm tired of all of it."

"I know," he said, voice softening. Vienah remained quiet. She didn't know everything that had unfolded in the last year. Ronan placed a hand on my shoulder, halting me. I turned toward him, and he settled his gaze on mine. "We'll get back. We'll do it all."

Something in my heart melted at the truth in his words, at the softness in his expression. "We need to find the others we left at the lake. Contact them somehow."

My mouth quirked to the side. "Already ahead of you, Commander," I said, throwing him a wink. Ronan's returning smile would have sent butterflies dancing in my stomach a year ago. Now, it flooded me with the steady warmth of friendship. I turned to Vienah.

"Let's get these taken off," I said, holding up my wrist. While her brown eyes still held deep shadows beneath them, the smile she offered me was full of light and determination.

# CHAPTER THIRTY-TWO

*A child was born, one gifted with godlike abilities.*
—*Fabia's Fables, "People of the Stars."*

A wave of nausea washed over me as I entered Lord Astraeus's holding cell. Xenelpha said he wasn't the threat she thought he was. Who did she think he was? Blood stained the icy floor. The tang of iron mingled with the rancid stench of piss and vomit covering Lord Astraeus's pants and the front of his blue coat. Guilt swept through me as I took in his injuries, my mind flying to the brutal death of the Lady of Tomorrow in Lotrennia.

Cold blood soaked into my leathers as I knelt beside him and rubbed the celosia powder beneath his bloodied nose. His long lashes fluttered for a moment, the curved shadow hovering above deep bruising beneath his eyes. I wiped his blood on my leathers as he wheezed, rising to consciousness.

"Bonscaíh," he murmured, eyes blinking open. "I see you fared better than I."

"Take this off and I will cut you loose," I urged, doing my best to avoid looking at the terrible gash in his leg. I moved behind him, examining his hands, when he said, "How did you get loose? Did you find the bone?"

"Hurry, we don't have much time," I lied, "If we move quickly, we might be able to escape before the sun comes up."

His hand opened around my wrist for the cuff. Rough, calloused fingers slid around my palm, brushing against the star, until they stilled.

"You're lying, Bonscaíh," he said quietly, letting his head fall back against the post he was tied to.

"Hurry," I urged him, "I cannot get us out with this on."

A wet chuckle gurgled from his lips. "Lies," he breathed. "I can see you have your Honor back. I could tell from the way you moved just now."

My fingers stilled against his hand.

"They freed you."

My mouth clamped shut, and I listened to his ragged breathing for a few moments before saying, "Take the rubelline off, Astraeus."

A bitter laugh reverberated through the chamber.

"Learned a thing or two while I was being tortured, did you?" My stomach churned. "What else did they tell you?"

"Take it off."

"I'll take it off on one condition. The bone is mine."

"You can't *decide* who can harness the bone. It needs to stay with the Bellators."

"And you're the one to determine that? I have more right to that bone than any of you."

"What are you talking about?"

Silence.

"*Astraeus.*"

"It's not yours."

"It's not yours either."

"It's not *for* me."

"Then who—"

"I'm not taking it off unless the bone leaves with me," he snapped, cutting me off. "Keep me here, let me rot, if you wish."

Fuck. *Fuck.*

The Obscura thrashed beneath the thick wall of the rubelline at his words. I wasn't going to cut off his damned hand. As much as I hated the man, seeing him like this...

I made to stand when Ronan stormed in through the sliding ice door and slammed his fist into Astraeus's face. The pirate lord's head cracked against the trunk, and he slumped over.

"What are you doing?" I snapped, "Look at him! He probably already has a concussion!"

Ronan rolled his shoulders, "He'll be fine. He obviously doesn't need to be conscious to get the rubelline off if Xenelpha suggested taking his entire hand."

I blinked. He was right, I realized, feeling utterly stupid for waking him with the celosia powder when I could have tried his hands on my own.

"Try," he said, nodding to Vienah as she timidly stepped in, her hand flying to her nose at the stench.

"Oh gods," she murmured as her eyes scanned the pirate. She knelt behind him, her hands going to his. "When he loosened the hold on Carina and Nerissa, I saw him slide his forefinger and thumb like this."

She slid my coat up over the cuff, still glowing bright red, and placed Astraeus's hands around it, sliding his finger and thumb along its edge. As she did, the phantom grip within me loosened. A flash of shimmering black and gold exploded behind my eyes as she completed the twist. The cuff clanked off, the brilliant glowing red winking out.

I gasped, sucking in the frigid air, as the Obscura and Transcindiel surged through my veins, savoring their freedom. The darkness danced against my palms to the song that floated from the transformational power. They were *back*.

Vienah's smile was bright as she scanned my eyes. I helped with hers, and she sighed as the cuff fell off. I tucked one away in the pocket of my coat and clamped the other on Astraeus's wrist.

"He's a mage?" Vienah asked, eyes wide.

"Full of secrets, apparently," Ronan murmured, eyeing the unconscious pirate. "What do we do with him?"

I sighed, scanning his injuries. "Clean him up. Keep him with the others."

"I'll help," Vienah said, her voice edged with pity.

A WARM PUSH of relief reached me as I walked toward Xenelpha's dwelling. I scanned the break in trees above the village, searching for any sign of Aquila, knowing he was smart enough not to be seen. My heart warmed as his emotions reached me, and I smiled, allowing myself a small bit of hope that the others were fine.

Xenelpha stepped from her chamber. I balked, startled by her change in appearance. Gone were the white paint and bone armor. Dark, copper skin shone in the midday sun, and a lovely smile spread across her face. Wrinkles crinkled in the corners of her dark eyes, years of wisdom lounging in their depths.

"Freedom feels good, does it not?"

I nodded. "Indeed." A soft growl rumbled behind her, and I

jumped as the large, reptilian head snaked around Xenelpha and peered at me with intelligent eyes. The wolf-like body inched around her, its scaled tail snapping back and forth. I paled at the sight of the dune runner.

"My *amatohk*," the matron murmured. "She doesn't trust you after your encounter at the lake."

The beast growled, and I took a step back, hands up, though the Obscura leaped down my veins. The dune runner, the *amatohk*, glanced between my palms and softened its gaze, tilting its head, almost dog-like.

"We've collected the bodies of those you killed," Xenelpha said, her voice softening. The creature's fangs glinted in the sunlight, and I had a hard time feeling guilty. "Their deaths will be honored. And we will wear their bones as armor."

"And the others at the camp?" I asked.

The sides of Xenelpha's lips tilted, "There was an encounter, of course. An elf and three humans are being held at a neighboring village. We'll bring them here if you wish."

I nodded, my stomach twisting with nerves. "Please. What state are they in?"

"A human is still healing from our amatohk, and the small mystic has been unconscious. It seems she tried to use more power than she was capable of with the rubelline on her wrist."

I averted my eyes and gave her a nod, hiding my relief. Vulcan and Nerissa had to have escaped.

"This way to the bone," Xenelpha murmured after a moment.

She led me to an elaborately carved tunnel where she placed a torch in a shallow pool of liquid that sat in a raised line in the center of the hall. Fire flew down in a thin stream, illuminating the shadows of the walls that shifted from ice to stone.

Xenelpha slid a small key to the center of an eight-pointed star carved in the rock at the end of the tunnel. She murmured beneath her breath, and as she pressed her hand into the rock, she rotated it, the circular carving following in its direction. The rock smoothly slid open to Faron's burial chamber.

The familiar scent of dry, dusty air filled my nostrils as we stepped into the ancient room. Xenelpha bowed as we entered, and I followed suit, my mind drifting to the last set of remains I examined, the brutal damage to the elf in Lotrennia pricking against my mind.

"Lord Astraeus is mistaken," Xenelpha said in hushed tones as she approached the stone sarcophagus. "A line of Bellators runs in his blood, but he has no connection to this bone."

I balked. Astraeus's bloodline? I squinted at her through the darkness. "Do the bones only answer to those within the original Bellators' bloodlines?" I asked, already knowing the answer.

Xenelpha shook her head, the straight salt and pepper hair swaying like shadows in the darkness as she murmured, "We do not know how the bones choose."

"You think the bones *choose* their warriors? Like they are sentient?"

Xenelpha's mouth curved as she said, "You tell me."

I bristled under the weight of her gaze and looked toward Faron's sarcophagus.

"How do you know all of this?"

"Death tells us a story. You know this already."

"The god of death? Did Tynan tell you this?" Was it possible she somehow communicated with the god of death, or was this another riddle?

I ran my fingers over the carvings of the sarcophagus, tracing the bloody battle. Waves of magic blasted apart castles, and winged beasts rained fire from above.

"Your human eyes see the physical markings on bones," Xenelpha continued, her eyes bright, "What was left behind, the tales of the being whose body they held. How old they were, what type of life they led. Imagine what you could see if you could read the *non-physical* markings on the bones."

"You mean use magic to examine bones? Does that have something to do with why you wear them?" I asked, brows pinched.

A small dip in her chin as she reverently ran her fingers over the stone, following the path in the smooth divots.

"One of them. They also symbolize our victories. Bones are added to our warriors' armor only when they earn it. Bone is what remains long after our passing," she explained, "Bones are the keepers of our stories. The keepers of our truths. What is it your Death Scholars say? There is truth in death?"

I nodded, churning her words over in my mind.

"How do you know all this?" I asked, eyeing her across the tomb.

"There are many ways to see—" she began, her eyes again searching the air around my head, as realization hit.

"You see them," I cut her off, eyes widening. "You can see the threads. The magic, the connections binding us." I stepped around the sarcophagus and eyed her pleased expression.

"Can you—"

"I cannot tell you what happened to the person at the end of that soulbinding thread," she murmured, "I am only blessed enough to discern the types of threads holding you to another. That is the only reason you are here, alive," she said, her words edged in steel.

*I fucking knew it.* My heart stuttered in grief. I should have pushed Bayne... I opened my mouth, and she held a small hand up. "We are not here to discuss my threadsight," she declared with an air of finality.

Xenelpha's dark hand slid down the side of the sarcophagus and up to the very top of the lid, where a small bird had been carved. She pressed her finger on its head, the small bit of stone sinking beneath the rest. The center of the sarcophagus hissed, and a round stone, small enough to fit in both hands, rose from the lid.

Xenelpha motioned to me, and I gently took the stone from the center of the lid. The buzz off the stone wasn't as abhorrent as it had been with the elixir. Without the cuff, my senses clear, it was more of a flutter, I realized. The small wings of a hummingbird, rather than an irritating insect.

As I leaned over the sarcophagus, I spied the darkness of the inside of the tomb below. My eyes lingered on the ivory bones that gleamed at its center, and I couldn't help the curiosity that bubbled up.

"Do not linger," Xenelpha murmured, eyeing me as I let my gaze search the bones beneath the lid. "I will grant you limited access to this room each day to attempt to open it. And then you must return it to its place."

I nodded as my eyes scanned the round stone in my hand. Etchings of strange, membranous wings stretched from the center of the stone to its edges around a spiral design. I ran my fingers over them as if I could feel Tiberius's velvety feathers beneath. My heart squeezed in response.

"What do you know of his caeluma?" I asked as Xenelpha watched me.

"Her last form was as an amatohk."

*A dune runner caeluma*, I mused, glancing up at Xenelpha as I processed her words. "*Last* form?"

A slight dip in the matron's chin as she eyed me and murmured, "We all change, Lyvia. I'll wait outside."

Alone with the block of stone, I let myself sink into the beat of the bone's fluttering. Though the amatohk had no wings.

243

The stone container holding Enya's bone of power was a puzzle. I tried twisting the sides of it, but the etching wasn't mismatched. This wasn't a puzzle. Gods, I wished Drystan was here.

I blew out a breath as I turned over Xenelpha's words and recited the riddle we'd seen on the lid of the tunnel leading to the tomb. Did I need to speak to it for it to open?

*Who will you be?* Xenelpha had asked. Maybe I could try answering that? A list of ridiculous names cycled through my head.

"I am Lyvia. I am a Bellator." *I think*, I added silently, in my head. "I am a scholar..."

This was fucking stupid. Icy anger slithered into my growing frustration, and I let the words flow.

"I am afraid. I am changed. I am... a murderer..."

My breath came out in a soft, gray cloud. I was fucking afraid. And I deserved to be. What awaited me in Tynan's Hell after the lives I'd taken?

The round stone sat in my hands, utterly unchanged. I stuck my tongue out at it, some feeble attempt to quell the realization that had hit me.

I searched inward for that unbreakable bond, that thread of steel that connected me to Tiberius. As I grabbed hold of it, throwing myself into its connection, a brief, salt-filled whiff of wind hit me before Tiberius's consciousness twined with my own. I let out a soft sigh.

*Are you alright?*

His answer came several moments later.

*Yes. Are you? What happened? I tried to hold your cast to show you Bayne, but... Did you find the bone?*

I had the strange, yet familiar sensation of Tiberius gazing through my eyes, but fatigue ripped at my mind. And his voice was strained, stressed. We were too far for this.

*Yes,* I replied, *We're with the Rhashtai. Safe for now, I think. They are the Guardians of the Dead, the people of the Death Dunes.*

*Fitting, they found themselves a death digger.* Tiberius's tone returned to his usual light-heartedness. I responded with a chuckle, sending a wave of warmth down the bond to him. I recited the riddle on the entrance to the tomb. Ti was silent, and I looked up, scanning the rest of the burial chamber for him.

*Any ideas?* I urged, already feeling him slip.

Several moments passed.

*Ti?*

*I'm coming to you.*

*What? You're flying this far, alone?*

*I'm not alo—*

# CHAPTER THIRTY-THREE

One maiden turned to ten, turned to hundreds. And in secret,
the lowly messenger god fathered an army of half-breeds.
—Fabia's Fables, "People of the Stars."

B reath whooshed from my chest as the casting severed,
cutting off Tiberius's last words. I eased myself to the
ground, the energy from casting at this distance
hitting me like a stone wall. Unease twisted its way into my
gut. What else had happened? And who was he with? Could it
be Bayne?

Conflicting emotions warred at the thought. A desperate
need to see him, to make sure he was alright... Grief at the
death of a future he deemed impossible... Anger at his
disbelief...

His marriage to the queen...

My eyelids fell shut as I refocused on the stone, and I
slowed my breathing. *Think*. What would matter the most? I

tapped the rock, knocking with my knuckle in various places as I twisted and pulled on its edges, searching for any opening.

"I am—" I began again as the stone door slid open.

"Out of time," Xenelpha finished from across the room. "You may return tomorrow."

RAYS OF MIDDAY sunshine gilded the tops of the conical trees surrounding the ice village. Children chased after one another while men and women returned from hunts with massive stags and plump, aquatic creatures I'd never seen before. There was so much life among the Guardians of the Dead.

I had one week to figure out how to open the damn stone container before we needed to leave after their celebration of the equinox, *Maadon*.

Two massive, tusked beasts stomped through the center avenue, one with a basket-like saddle on its back, where a handful of warriors sat, many waving to the gathering crowd. The second was flanked by four amatohk riders on either side and pulled a caged sled behind it.

I rushed through the crowd, coming face-to-face with the massive, shaggy creature, blocking its path in the road. A young man stood atop the first beast, staring down beneath his mask of bones and nodding in respect to Xenelpha as she approached. Ronan appeared at my side a moment later.

The warrior gently tapped the side of the beast's head with the base of his spear. The creature slowly got to its knees, lowering its head and swinging its long trunk, and the young man slid down its outstretched leg. He stepped forward to Xenelpha and dropped to his knees, placing his armored head against the frozen ground.

"Thank you for your journey," Xenelpha said, taking the

clawed hand of the warrior and lifting him to his feet. "Our visitors," she motioned toward me, and I bowed my head toward the young man as I stepped forward. "Lyvia, Ronan, and Vienah of Sultira. My nephew, Kai, Guardian of the Rhashtai in the east. He's brought the rest of your party."

"With your permission, I'll take responsibility for the group now." My eyes darted to the bodies in the cage behind the second beast. Bound and unmoving.

"Your responsibility," she confirmed. I moved to step past Kai, and he held an arm out.

"Two others," he said, voice thickly accented, tilting his head as he examined me beneath the large skull on his head, "escaped in our initial encounter. We've sent scouts into the woods and have been unable to locate their tracks."

"Nor will you," I replied, keeping my voice respectful, yet firm. His dark eyes blinked behind his mask, and I stepped past him to what remained of our group from the lake, bound and bloody.

"I would like to request a separate lodging, one safe and comfortable, for Carina Ravindra, Princess of Lotrennia."

The men and women within earshot peered curiously in the cage, eyeing the female.

Xenelpha surveyed the unconscious princess for a heart-beat and gave me a knowing look. She nodded to me, the massive skull dipping as she did so.

"Only the best for a *free* princess," she murmured.

A *FREE* PRINCESS. The debt I racked up with Xenelpha began to feel heavy, as she fulfilled yet another favor I had asked. Carina was not bound by an air oath.

The elven princess blinked as the celosia powder drew her

from her slumber, and she took in the icy, yet warm, chamber Xenelpha procured for her. White furs draped the wooden cot she lay on, and her Ravindra eyes held a thousand questions as they scanned me.

She eyed my wrist, no doubt taking note of the absence of the rubelline cuff. I glanced down at the red glow peeking beneath her torn sleeve. She opened her mouth, and I held up my hand, "We found the bone."

Her emerald eyes widened as I relayed all that had transpired, and I straightened as I held her gaze.

"I need you to listen very closely to this next part. I will get this cuff taken off," I said, motioning to her wrist, "And we will return to Lotrennia with the Advetis Bone. But I am done playing your queen's games. My allegiance is not to her, or even to Lotrennia. But an *alliance* with Lotrennia, an alliance with *you*..."

Carina straightened in her cot, swallowing the uncertainty building in her gaze.

"I will ally with you, Carina."

She straightened her cracked spectacles, whisps of disarrayed hair floating down as she shook her head, "To stand against my mother..."

"You are not bound to her. Not with an air oath," I countered. If Carina was surprised that I knew she was tied to no oath, she didn't show it.

"No. She leaves that for more important people in the court," she murmured.

"*You* are important, Carina. And you are worthy of your title."

Carina blinked twice, as if seeing me for the first time.

"Think about it," I continued, giving her a nod. "For now, I have a favor to ask."

"GOOD AFTERNOON, MILORD." I sketched a bow to the man lying on a cot in the corner of the small ice structure, hands bound with rope and cuff glowing from beneath his coat.

"Solitary confinement..." Lord Astraeus mused as he sat upright. "Who knew a pretty thing like you could be so cruel? Where is my crew?" The pirate lord's dark eyes flashed, and I returned the look with an innocent smile.

"With the others I have little trust in," I said as I neared the edge of his bed. "I brought you lunch."

Astraeus kept his eyes on mine as I dropped the plate of roasted venison and bread on his lap, a sudden stretch of silence crawling through the small ice structure as I waited for him to acknowledge the meal.

"Are you going to eat this or not?" I asked, jerking my finger to the roast. He dragged his gaze from mine and edged his way up the back of the bed with a groan.

"What do you want, Lyvia?"

I blinked, realizing it was the first time he'd said my name. Unease followed by something warmer twisted in my gut at the way it rolled off his tongue.

"I came to negotiate our departure from Rhashtai."

Lord Astraeus scoffed as he shoveled the deer into his mouth. A small groan escaped his lips, and I shifted on my feet.

"Then negotiate," he murmured.

"In exchange for an alliance with you and safe passage to Lotrennia, I will lend my service in the hunt for the bone connected to your family bloodline."

A deep, throaty chuckle filled the small chamber.

"No."

I bristled at the tone, the Obscura responding in kind. The

corner of his lips twitched, and he glanced up, his gaze softening in curiosity.

"Those eyes..." he mused, "Like embers in the night."

"Stop looking at my eyes," I snapped.

Lord Astraeus sat back as he smirked, resting his head against the icy wall as he lifted his bound hands to take another bite. My eyes shot to his lips as he sucked the fatty juice off his thumb, before darting up to find his dark eyes searching mine.

"The Advetis Bone does not belong to you," I continued, "and you will not leave with it. But another might."

"It does not belong to *you*," he retorted. "What do you know?"

A demand, not a question.

"The matron of the Rhashtai knows of your connection to one of the Bellators. If there is a bone you think you can harness—"

"I told you already, it's not for *me*," he cut in.

"What do you mean?"

The pirate lord's lips drew a hard line before he ripped back into the venison.

"*Astraeus*."

He raised his dark auburn eyebrows at me and *winked*. These fucking *men* and their inability to have a conversation without throwing a gesture like that into it... Fine. Just fucking fine.

"Now that I think of it, I only need what's left of your crew to sail the *Hydra* to Lotrennia." I crooned, leaning in close. "This was a courtesy, as it is your ship after all. But I have no more patience for your games. You may stay here if you wish."

I turned on my heel to leave.

"*Wait*, Bonscaíh," he groaned, and I moved for the door.

"Wait!" Astraeus called, his voice echoing off the icy walls. "For fuck's sake, it's a deal."

"Swear it," I said, turning around slowly.

"Fine," Lord Astraeus dropped the venison in his bound hands and held them up, grungy palms facing me. "I swear it."

"Swear an air oath to me."

Lord Astraeus's hands lowered as he raised an eyebrow. "An air oath?" he asked quietly. I nodded at him.

"You know what that means, right?" he said softly, "We'll be bound in our own way. Until our last breath."

I held his gaze in confirmation, refusing to balk beneath the weight of his dark eyes, but a pang of guilt slipped its claw into my chest.

"You'll need a wind whisperer."

"Way ahead of you."

SNOW CRUNCHED as I slid the icy door open, and Carina's small silhouette darkened the entryway in the dimness of the evening. Lord Astraeus kept his dark eyes on me as I led Carina to the hearth. Orange flames danced along the blue ice of its watery walls, and for a fleeting moment, I marveled at the meeting of the two extremes, at the unexpected balance. My eyes slid to Astraeus, the skipping light casting a golden glow against the pirate lord's sharp features.

Carina eyed the captain with disgust as he stepped next to her and held out his hands. I pulled Honor from my boot and cut Astraeus's bounds, the blade slicing through them like water.

Lord Astraeus pulled his gaze from me and settled it on Carina. He sketched a low bow, murmuring "Princess," as he straightened. Her lips formed a thin line as she held her wrist out.

He slid his fingers around the rubelline cuff, and Carina let out a sigh as the red glow vanished and the white cuff clanked to the floor. I tucked it inside my coat before turning to Lord Astraeus.

"Are you sure about this, Lyvia?" Carina asked, voice low in warning.

"Aren't you going to ask me?" Lord Astraeus took a step closer to me. Carina narrowed her eyes at him and backed up a step.

"I'm sure," I said, nodding at Carina. Her eyes searched mine for a moment before finally shaking her head. I stepped up to Lord Astraeus, bristling at the memory of my proximity to the queen, and craned my neck to look up at the man. His beard, overgrown and crusted with old blood, hung just above my head.

"You'll need a stool," Carina murmured.

"What?"

"It's an intimate ceremony," Lord Astraeus purred as he gazed down at me. "We need shared air, shared *breath*, for the magic to work."

"I know that. I've done this before," I snapped.

"Eye level."

I slid my gaze to Carina, and she nodded her confirmation. She dragged over a log meant for the hearth, and I hopped on.

Little flecks of gray danced in Lord Astraeus's dark irises as I met him at eye level for the first time. And something in them brushed against my mind. Why did they look so familiar...

Carina cleared her throat and steepled her hands before murmuring the spell beneath her breath. Her lilac wind spun through the small space for a moment before it stilled, as if suspended in the natural air of the ice chamber.

The flames in the hearth quieted, listening carefully to the next words. She nodded her head toward Lord Astraeus. I turned back to peer into his dark eyes as he said clearly into the dimness of the chamber, "I, Lord Astraeus..."

Carina, hands still steepled, cleared her throat and murmured, "Full name."

Astraeus's dark eyes flashed at her once, and he began again, "I, Kellan Astraeus..."

*Kellan.* A distant memory blinked an eye open.

"I, Kellan Astraeus, swear on my last breath to assist you, Lyvia Cantor, in your call to protect the innocent from all threats to this world. My oath to you shall not break until the air of death escapes your lips, or my own."

Something primal stirred. The puffs of air off Astraeus's lips kissed my own as he spoke his oath. From the corner of my eye, Carina's head bobbed, nodding to me. I'd chosen the words carefully, for both of us, ensuring Tiberius would not be tied to this oath.

"I, Lyvia Cantor, in return for your air oath, swear upon my last breath to assist you, Kellan Astraeus, in the search for the bone of power tied to your bloodline and restore it to its chosen owner. My oath to you shall not break until the air of death escapes your lips, or my own."

A gust of lilac wind spun around the room, sending strands flying wildly from my braid. Lord Astraeus's loose hair whipped around, shadowing my face from both sides. Kellan's gaze was hard on mine as air siphoned from our lungs, where it mingled for a moment in the small space between us and shot into our mouths as we gasped. An exchange of breath.

Lord Astraeus's eyes darted between mine as he caught his breath, *our breath*, his chest rapidly expanding, the wind tunnel around us settling. My eyes reluctantly traced the striking lines of his face. I slowed my breathing as my heart raced and noticed a small tug of air laced with notes of cedar and leather drifting from the man before me.

# CHAPTER THIRTY-FOUR

---

*The messenger god watched as the demigods discovered their power in the centuries to come. They aided the humans in a war, striking a devastating blow to the ruling gods, taking a kernel of their magic as they fled in the aftermath.*

*—Fabia's Fables, "People of the Stars."*

---

"Where did you find those words?" Carina whispered from across the room. I glanced back at Lord Astraeus, still a breath away.

"Her heart," he answered, voice rough.

I rolled my eyes as I gripped his wrist and slid the rubelline cuff off. He let out a soft sigh through his nose. He kept his eyes on me and ran a hand over his wrist, rubbing away the phantom grip of magic.

"You're free," I breathed, voice quieter than intended.

"Am I?" He raised an eyebrow, eyes darting to my lips. I

cleared my throat as I stepped away, releasing myself from whatever trance-like state the air oath had put us in.

"Sorry we're late to the party," Nerissa crooned as she strutted into the small tent.

Astraeus's hand gripped my elbow, and my heart leaped into my chest as I turned to find Nerissa and Vulcan standing in the doorway. I whipped my head back to Astraeus, and he blinked before dropping his hand from my arm.

I scanned my friends, searching for additional injuries. The spattering of black tattoos cut across the irregular, raised scars that littered the side of Vulcan's half-ruined face. A pang of guilt slithered through my gut, realizing I just bound myself to the man who had done this to him. Who had ordered him beaten, his crew so intentionally destroying the artful ink on his face. I heaved a sigh and stepped away from Astraeus.

I gave Vulcan a soft smile and nod, relieved to be reunited with the elf. The permanent scowl remained on his face, but I thought I caught the softening of his eyes.

Nerissa stilled as Ronan appeared in the doorway, his sapphire eyes flashing against the dancing flames. Her eyes shuddered, and Ronan's shoulders sagged in relief. Neither moved.

Lord Astraeus cleared his throat as he rubbed his wrist, that insufferable smirk forming on his lips.

"Took you long enough," he drawled, stepping into the soft glow. Vulcan's eyes held the promise of violence as they swept between us.

The air oath left me shaken. While I'd felt a connection form with Queen Antares, this was different. It was like a small strip of air in my lungs that could cause me to sigh or cough if pulled too hard.

I held my hands up between the two of them, briefly explaining what had transpired in the last few days, earning myself more than a few glares from Vulcan and looks of disbelief from Nerissa.

"An alliance once again," Astraeus said through a grin, clapping his hands together once, nodding to Ronan. "Seems like we'll be spending more time together."

"Don't you have somewhere to be?" I snapped.

"Wait," Nerissa said, holding her arm out, the soft red glow of the cuff shining dimly through her jacket, "Take this off."

"I don't answer to you, sweetie," Astraeus murmured, his swagger sharpening into steel.

Nerissa's lips curled over her teeth as she let out a soft snarl, Ronan gripping her arm.

"Astraeus," Ronan warned, his own voice dipping an octave.

"You answer to me," I cut in, my eyes shooting between the two of them. "Take it off."

The pirate's dark eyes slid to mine, amused.

"I do not *answer* to you," he said, "That is not what this is between you and I."

I opened my mouth to interrupt, but he said to Nerissa, "But, seeing as we could use some of your special sun power in what's to come, I'll throw you a bone."

Astraeus slid his hand over Nerissa's cuff, dismantling it. I held out a hand for it, waiting.

"Not a chance," Astraeus chuckled, tucking the cuff into his pocket and offering a curt nod to the others.

"Bonscaíh," he winked at me, sketching a mock bow as he left our small group. Nerissa bristled as he strode away, his blue coat flapping in the icy breeze that blew through the trees.

Aquila's massive form dove from the midnight sky outside the hut. An unobstructed wave of warmth and happiness crashed into me from the sea hawk as he blew a great gust of wind, sending waves of fresh powder into the small room. I returned it with my own, never more grateful for this reunion.

LELYTH'S *dark wine curls bounced as she strode through a long wooden hall, a stable of sorts, with long iron bars lining the walls. Massive, white bears peered out, many of them offering low growls or slashing with their curved black claws at the bars as we passed. The Obscura thrummed beneath my skin at the presence of the threat. Nivis's mounted bears, a cavalry of sorts.*

*"Where are we going?" I asked, irritated at the young human's cryptic comments in the weeks that had passed since Olienna's Bellator gathering.*

*"Out," she replied.*

*I bristled, following until we came upon the docks facing Nivis's sacred island in the distance. I opened a cast to my caeluma, his warmth melting into me from where he munched on a bucket of oats outside the Crystal Castle.*

*"Fifteen hundred years is too long," Lelyth murmured, her bright eyes staring across the azure sea that separated us from the green island. She twisted a shimmering band around her finger, its strange material casting little rainbows on her white tunic.*

*"Attalus said the Aeterna could do it," I argued, uncertain why I was the only Bellator she'd brought along to have this conversation after the eight of us had agreed...*

*"Attalus has been wrong before," Lelyth said quietly, still staring at the land mass ahead. "And is that what you want, Enya? To extend our lives so considerably? I'm not sure I do."*

*I shook my head. Of course, I didn't want this... Ordell had also questioned it... "No, but I'll do what has to be done to fight if they return after this—"*

*"I believe Olienna's plan is well-intentioned," Lelyth cut in,*

turning toward me, "But will we even be the same people then? People change over time, Enya. Humans, and even elves, are not meant to live forever. Will we all stay the course? Or will that much time erode our good intentions? I'm not convinced."

She shook her head and turned back to the sea, her eyes steeling in determination.

"What choice do we have?" I asked.

"There is always a choice, Enya. Our ancestors escaped their wrath and found refuge here, taking their power as they did. We know they will return again. When this fight is over, I think our fight is over."

I went still. "I am not going to sit by and let this happen—"

"I'm not suggesting that," Lelyth snapped. "Of course, we fight. I'm not a coward. But I am suggesting we sacrifice now to save the future generations. To prepare them as best as we can. We're not meant to live forever."

"The Bellator powers are too slippery," I murmured, shaking my head. "You make two dangerous assumptions. One, that our descendants will even survive after this war..."

I shook my head. "And two, that the ones that do survive won't be wretched assholes."

Lelyth frowned, her lips pursing.

"You should have more faith," she murmured, "And who says the power needs to remain in our bodies?"

Lelyth's eyes softened as they dropped to her hands. She opened and then closed her pale fingers over her palms. She then sent a wave of something soft, knocking on the wall I'd thrown up before all the Bellators. A wall to block their emotions, now that the bond of the Bellators was in place. She knocked at it, softly, politely. I lowered it enough to feel a wave of unease, of fear, of dread. Lelyth was scared.

"There is a way," she began.

Vulcan's fingers snapped in my face as I blinked against the darkness of the cool ice chamber. I'd gotten little sleep the past few days. Anxious claws had sunk into me, as I failed over and over again at opening the small stone containing the Advetis Bone. I had one day left.

"You're late." His voice held that familiar edge of annoyance.

I groaned in response.

"What are you talking about?" I mumbled, pulling the fur over my face. He yanked it back down and answered, "I'll meet you in the clearing outside the sparring ring."

Godsdamnit. Were we really going back to these early morning exercises after everything that had transpired?

I groaned as I slumped off my cot and tugged on my boots and fur-lined coat. The air was cooler than usual, even with embers of the night fire still glowing softly in the center of the icy chamber.

I trudged into the darkness, taking my sweet time, fully aware of the irritation it would cause Vulcan. But today, of all days...

Icy avenues glowed in a soft orange light from the various torches lining the village. I hopped over the small fence leading to the sparring ring, bracing myself for Vulcan's glare when I pulled up short, my boots slipping on melted ice. My breath hollowed out at the sight.

# CHAPTER THIRTY-FIVE

*The Messenger and the ruling gods were never heard from again. The People of the Stars and humans left their home, traveling to a new land, where they were welcomed by a world full of power and different races.*
    —*Fabia's Fables, "People of the Stars."*

"S urprise!" Vienah squealed, standing at the front of the small group and holding what looked to be a small pie, dotted with a simple decoration of dried berries on the top. A name day pastry.

"Happy Birthday, Lyvia," Ronan said, arms splayed out wide, grinning ear to ear. "You didn't think I'd forget, did you?"

My heart squeezed as I took in the little group, beads of liquid forming in the corners of my eyes. Of all places, of all the people...

Vulcan's eyes softened, and he offered me a half-smile, the most I'd ever get from him.

Nerissa rolled her eyes at Ronan, but a shadow of a grin hovered over her lips. She gave me a small nod. "He insisted."

"And that you skip your morning centering exercises," Vulcan growled, throwing a glare at Ronan.

"I baked the pastry," Vienah noted, stepping forward and holding out the small pie. "It's not exactly what you'd find in Sultira, but it's—"

"It's perfect," I cut in, eyes watering as Vienah placed the pie in my hands. "Thank you. This... This means a lot." My smile was genuine as I took in the four of them before Ronan squeezed my shoulder, and I thoroughly devoured my pie.

My smile had yet to disappear as Vienah and I made our way deeper into the village later that morning. The celebration of Maadon was well underway. Elders stood outside the icy buildings, adding scenes from the past year to the intricate carvings with small picks.

Large roasts had been carried in by the massive, tusked beasts that the Rhashtai had domesticated. A savory, salty scent wafted through the wide lanes of the village.

We returned to find Astraeus murmuring something to the guard outside of my ice chamber. A throaty laugh escaped his lips, and I caught a wide grin on Astraeus's face.

"What are you doing here?" I asked, eyeing the guard as he made his way down the road, still chuckling beneath his breath.

"Telling dirty jokes," he drawled, winking at me. "Does the birthday girl want to hear one?"

Pink tinged my cheeks, deepening as I bristled. "No."

"I'm offended I didn't get an invite." He placed a hand on his chest.

"What do you want, Astrae—" I began before I was cut off, the breath sucked from my lungs and replaced with a wild wind as strange, flat gray clouds cleared beneath my hooves.

My heart plummeted as Tiberius's view filled the space behind my eyes. Thousands of ships spread across a wide strip of blue.

*Where is this?* I asked in a panic.

*Atrulean Sea,* he answered, his mind's voice hoarse and weary. *Sailing south.*

The space between my shoulder blades burned as he beat his massive wings against an updraft, and he soared back into the clouds. I gasped as he cut off the cast. Vienah's hands were at my shoulders, and my back pressed against something hard and warm...

I blanched, wiggling out of Astraeus's arms and gaining my feet. Had I collapsed?

"Ships," I said, breathless. "Heading south. It has to be Daimos."

"Did Tiberius say anything else?" Vienah asked. Her face was pale, and her brown eyes were wide with concern. "When will they get there? We have to warn them!"

I shook my head. "He could barely hold the cast. He's weak. He's been flying too long."

Concern squeezed the center of my chest as if I could still feel Tiberius's phantom wings. Exhausted. He was utterly exhausted.

"Get the others," I said quietly. "We have plans to make."

HOURS LATER, hundreds of Rhashtai, bedecked in ornamental bones and beads, gathered in the icy amphitheater at the center of the village. Xenelpha stood at the bottom of the arena, arms wide as she quieted the excited crowd with a single sweep of her large staff. A hush fell, and the matron began to speak.

I glanced to where Lord Astraeus sat with what remained of his crew inland. His dark beard had been cropped short, and his hair cleaned, braided back, and adorned with a new set of beads. Bones, I realized, as I examined the white bits in his hair from a distance. He caught my gaze and grinned. I snapped my attention back to Xenelpha, whose eyes found mine in the crowd.

"Merry Maadon," she began, holding her arms wide, the talons strapped to her hands splayed out in a fearsome image. "A day when light finally gives way to darkness. It is a day of change. A day of *balance*. A day to remind us that light is nothing without the dark."

My mind drifted as Xenelpha continued her story, earning gasps of awe as the various mages in her counsel began displaying shows of light and wind and water as she told her story. I ran through the plans in my head.

Six amatohks sat saddled and ready to be mounted near the western edge of the village. Nerissa, Ronan, and Astraeus would take three while sending the others south. Vulcan would come with me to the tomb...

"Ice calls to water as magma calls to stone. To change, to *truly transform*, takes sacrifice. Takes courage. Water becomes trapped. Stone weakens. We must remember who we are to begin with, that our essence may be nudged, one sacrificial bit at a time, before evolution takes place. What will you let go of this Maadon to become who you were meant to be?" Xenelpha's eyes landed on my face.

"For death," she continued, letting the word dangle in the chamber, "is but a passage. A gate to the Beyond. Yet the dead suffer, trapped, in the world built by the *Ehp'uch*, who claim *god* as their title, holding them captive, waiting to suck the lifeblood of the dead, their essence. Protected only by the Lord of Death."

Xenelpha's eyes remained pinned on me.

"Our people descended from the line of Faron. And it is he whom we protect. It is his story that's written in the crypt below the lake. Faron the Cunning, wisest of the Bellators. He's been preparing us for their return. For he knew he'd only be able to show us in his death..."

I scanned the various skulls peering at Xenelpha when my eyes snagged on a flash of silver. My heart stuttered as I studied the swirl of silver in the distance, peering at me beneath an ivory skull of a small amatohk. The dune runner's wide eye sockets cast a dark shadow over the skin beneath, the glowing silver shining in their depths.

The eyes locked on me, and I realized I had stood, Honor unsheathed and in my palm. The Obscura slithered down my forearms, ready for an attack. Silence filled the chamber as hundreds of eyes landed on me.

"*Impostor*." Xenelpha's voice echoed like the boom of an air cannon.

Four Bone Warriors rushed through the crowd, leaping over rows of bewildered families as the man with silver eyes was tackled to the icy floor, warriors pinning his arms beneath them. Vulcan was at my side in an instant, tense as he watched the scene unfold.

"He was at the Eye of the Wood," he said quietly.

I shook my head. "Not him. *It*," I clarified. "It's been watching me since you sprang me from Mount Telum last year."

Ronan stepped next to him, eyes wide, and opened his mouth when the blaring of horns ripped through the domed ice chamber. The people of Rhashtai stilled as the horn sounded once more. The last note echoed through the silent chamber like the bay of an ancient beast.

My pulse pounded against my palms as the Obscura rushed to my veins, mimicking its beat. Xenelpha's face whipped to the back of the chamber, where a warrior rushed down the slick stairs, sliding to a stop at the bottom.

"*Asginas* and Nivis warriors," he warned.

Xenelpha's face paled beneath her massive mask, and she shouted commands. Chaos erupted in the vast chamber as the massive sections of the ceiling began lifting from the sides, closing the roof of the amphitheater.

Lord Astraeus moved to my side, his lips near my ear as he whispered, "We should go now."

I caught Nerissa's gaze and the slight dip of her chin before I eyed Ronan and Vulcan. They were with me. My call.

My mind spun between our options. Get out now and take the Advetis Bone or stay and help Rhashtai. And suddenly, I was back at the Lake of Light, Bayne's brilliant green eyes boring into me as I weighed a similar decision.

One that cost me my brother's life. My father's life. And one that spared many others, as I thought of the families escaping the tribute's ship. Of Evony leaping off the side.

"Nerissa," I said, sheathing Honor and turning toward our small group. "Take Carina and head to the front lines. You take the Nivis soldiers."

A fierce nod was the only response I got before she sprinted up the steps.

"Kresida, stay with Vienah and guard her while she puts out any flames that rise in the village."

"Astraeus, you and your men are under Ronan's orders to the west. Our plans before dawn don't change, but we'll do what we can while we're still here."

Nods all around except for Astraeus, whose eyes narrowed on me. "We should leave now while they're—"

I lifted a hand. "We won't leave them undefended."

I tugged back on that invisible strand of air connecting us, and Astraeus pursed his lips before turning and barking orders at his men.

"Vulcan, with me."

We set off at a trot, following the group of warriors that continued to shout "*Asginas!*"

*Ashen.*

# CHAPTER THIRTY-SIX

*I'm worried about Bayne's fixation on his growing power.*
*—Journal of Isla Jasira*

As we ran, I began to dig. I shoveled my way down, deep beneath the chasm of darkness that had so easily, so quickly filled my entire being when the Obscura had taken over. Isla's warning echoed in my ears months later. *No one can handle this much power.* But I dug deeper anyway, elbowing my way past that darkness and listening for that quiet tune that always shrank beneath the shadows.

The warmth of Bayne's amplifier bounced on my chest beneath my tunic as we hurried through the snowy woods. Shouts of terror ripped through the night as sounds of battle echoed through the icy air. Swords clashed with the armor of the Bone Warriors, and I caught sight of silver suits in the distance as Nivis soldiers sprang from their hiding places and attacked the village.

Wild screams rang from the east as a thunderous herd of ashen plowed through the trees. Vulcan closed in to my left, and I reeled in the darkness that pounded against my palms.

I had to try.

A small group of ashen broke free from the herd as they trampled saplings in their wake and veered toward us, their elongated nails and teeth slashing at anything within arm's reach.

Quiet. It was so quiet in my mind as I strained to hear the Transcindiel. I latched myself to the amplifier on my chest, thinking of Tiberius, as I commanded the darkness to silence itself. A blade rang beside me, followed by a soft warning from Vulcan as we ran toward the onslaught.

*Where are you?* I whispered into my mind.

"Lyvia!"

Vulcan's shout pulled me from my trance, and I skidded to a halt as an ashen pulled ahead and reached for me. I ducked low, letting the hard, cold body of the ashen trip over me in time for Vulcan to take off its head.

"Now isn't the time to experiment!" he shouted.

Xenelpha's words from the Maadon ceremony crouched in my mind. *To change, to truly transform, takes sacrifice.... that our essence may be nudged, one sacrificial bit at a time, before evolution takes place.*

One sacrificial bit at a time. I'd been forcing too much change into the ashen. I'd been focused on its body, the physical change.

Marian's words from months ago on board the *Evecta* whispered in my mind like a chilling clue. We'd been in her room below deck, examining Oslo's severed hand.

*Perhaps,* she had signed, *the part that makes them human or elf has died...*

But it wasn't *dead.* The soul, whatever remained behind,

had merely been *changed*. It had been nudged toward corruption, the body following its vile intention. I needed to focus the power on that single, critical part of what made us human and elf.

The soul.

*Remember who you are.*

The haunted faces of Kayj watched from my memories as I shouted the furious demand into my inner self.

A tiny, barely perceptible string of notes flitted up from the chasm my powers called home. I reached for it as I held on to the warmth of the amplifier on my chest, linking the two and throwing my palms to the next set of milky white hands reaching for me, directing it to that crumpled, corrupted bit of soul sitting at its center.

A blast of beautiful, glittering golden light lit up the night as the Transcindiel shot toward the face of nightmares. Wild, snapping jaws went slack as the golden rays spun, encasing the creature in a glittering web. Its pale eyes widened before it fell a mere foot from me, its limp body slumping to the ground.

My knees barked in pain, hitting the icy ground as the expenditure of power gripped me with claws of exhaustion.

My lungs burned as shaky breath tried to escape. I was utterly spent. *To change, to truly transform, takes sacrifice.* The amplifier burned against my chest like a living flame as my eyes scanned the dark-skinned body in front of me. Her back softly rose and fell.

It *worked*.

Despite my fatigue, a newfound determination emerged, fueled by the glimmer of hope. The Transcindiel sang within me, elated by the chance to undo the corruption commanded by Dark King Daimos.

Vulcan leaped over the body and into the onslaught of ashen that followed. I moved to kneel next to the body when the zing of an airborne spear flew past my head, finding its mark in the face of an ashen reaching for my neck.

Xenelpha's snarl followed as her amatohk leaped, its massive, clawed paws landing on another ashen's chest as she ripped the spear from its face.

"You can't save them all tonight!" she called from beneath her mask. "Decide now. Save a few of the damned or hundreds of my people."

My jaw went slack as I processed her words. The chaos of the attack seemed to slow as the truth in them hit me like a punch to the gut. I couldn't save them all tonight. How many could I save before my power guttered out completely? Until I used up the entire amplifier Bayne had so carefully crafted for me? I could feel it already, singeing the undershirt beneath my tunic. It took too much energy to lift my gaze to the matron who continued her butchering.

The amalgamation of events that occurred over the past several weeks spun through my mind. Choices... Changes... *Who will I be?*

My hands fell to my side as I realized she was right. The irony of the two powers was not lost on me. Why the two had such a difficult time coexisting within one body. A power to destroy and a power to create. Transcindiel didn't just transform. It could *create*, could save. And it was forced to exist, side by side with shadows of pure death.

That beautiful, golden flicker of hope that had sparked within the chasm of darkness trembled against the choice Xenelpha so clearly laid out. Her words from a week ago echoed in the emptiness filling my chest, the void that had begun to spread in my soul all those months ago when I began my slaughter.

*Choices shape us.*
*Decide who you want to be.*

A child's scream ripped through the night, mingling with the chorus of snarls that rose from the village, followed by the answering roar of amatohks and the warriors they carried.

"Decide, Lyvia!" Vulcan screamed at me. His wild, hazel eyes found mine as his dagger plunged into the neck of an ashen flying through the trees.

*My soul was the sacrifice.*

My heart stilled at the realization. To do what needed to be done, to save the Realm of Vael. These choices would hover, haunting my existence until my last breath.

"Take me to the horde," I shouted to Xenelpha, the words suffocating the little flame of hope that had burst into life mere moments before. I would make this choice, and I understood... I *accepted* the damage it would do to my soul if it meant saving the others.

She reached a bone-covered glove to me and hauled me atop her amatohk. Vulcan ripped through two ashen before he leaped onto the back of the dune runner and squeezed in behind me, careful not to rub against the sharp, spine-like scales.

"Take me as far from the village as you can," I said into Xenelpha's neck as we flew through the village. The words caught in my throat at the danger I'd be putting the rest of them in. The blood that still coated my hands after that fateful day in Odessa and the damning piece of steel that stuck out of the field of ash... Oslo...

"Find Nerissa," I said to Vulcan, his body shifting as he nodded in response.

A growing pressure of shadows built beneath my skin as an air-splitting screech echoed through to the west, followed by a blast of the whitest light. I sent a silent prayer up to Aelius for Nerissa as his power flowed through her on the battlefield.

Vulcan leaped off the dune runner mid-stride in search of my fellow Bellator.

Xenelpha cursed as a silver arrow bounced off the shining scales of her amatohk. I ducked, making myself as small as possible without slicing my chest and face on the scales. The dune runner snarled in response, and we broke free of the forest where hundreds of ashen crossed our abandoned camp across the frozen lake.

The amatohk's stride lengthened as he stretched his massive paws over the ice and let himself glide in between steps, quickening our flight. We neared the edge of the lake when a huge white form hurtled toward us from the side, echoing a booming roar across the distance it quickly closed.

Silver, fortissa chains wrapped around the bear's monstrous chest as he slammed into the side of the amatohk. A small whimper escaped its reptilian-like maw, and Xenelpha's scream of fury reverberated off the ice. My head slammed into the bank of the lake, scraping against the icy snow. Warm liquid pooled down the side of my cheek as I struggled to stand.

The bear bellowed as he stood on his hind legs before hurtling himself at Xenelpha and her mount. It ripped into the amatohk's ice-like hide, slicing through it with massive claws.

Xenelpha's magic erupted from her as she called the wind, throwing large chunks of ice and slamming them into the bear's head.

"Go!" she snarled at me.

I winced as I stood, slipping on the wet ice. Gods, I was so tired. My limbs dragged as if moving through tar. I risked a glance behind me as I let the Obscura race to my palms, the only thing about me that felt normal, aiming them ahead of me toward the oncoming ashen.

A dark silhouette of a soldier loomed above the massive

bear. A rider. Xenelpha stilled for a moment before she began to quake, drawing in as much power as she could.

I snapped my attention back to the danger ahead of me as I summoned the darkness, doing everything I could to hold my arms out in front of me and let it fly. A wave of euphoria accompanied the release as the Obscura ripped free. My breathing slowed as I obliterated the undead army tens at a time, a small amount of horror seeping into my chest.

Yet a sickening sense of satisfaction formed as the white-blue plains, illuminated by Renova on the horizon, turned black with ash. Despite my exhaustion, I had no need of the amplifier for this. This darkness was more a part of me than the power of transformation. And what did that say about me?

My thoughts drifted as their numbers dwindled, but I kept hold of my mind this time. The darkness yanked at the reins like an unruly stallion, but I held firm, my control never faltering. Never again would I take a life I didn't intend to take.

Nerissa appeared as the numbers died down. I closed off my fists, halting the flow of the darkness, and it rumbled slowly back into that chasm. A small remaining horde rushed toward us, and a brilliant white light shot free from Nerissa, the white fire catching them as they slowed, still staggering, swiftly burning alive.

She gave me a slight nod. Swords clashed in the distant village. My eyes snagged on a small, unmoving form. Xenelpha.

A smudge of violet spread across the frozen lake as Ganmira rose in the west. I scanned the snowy plains and the dark trees in the distance. No sign of the massive bear or its rider.

I shivered against the cool breeze floating over the plains as I knelt in the dark, wet snow next to Xenelpha. Little gasps of air escaped her chest in hollow, shaky breaths. I reached for the bone-covered hand that rested on a spear protruding from her chest. Dark eyes found mine from the shadows of her large mask as her fingers curled around mine. I reached to remove the spear when the mask shook side to side.

"No," she gurgled, her voice wet against the blood coating her throat.

I slumped to the ground next to her as I gently removed the skull from her face.

"Thank you," she rasped. "For making the choice. This will not be the hardest one to make, Shadow Shifter."

The dried blood on my temple cracked as my brows pinched.

"You must take it now," she continued. "I know you planned to. Kai will not let you leave with it. He'd rather see it destroyed."

"I don't understand," I croaked, my voice coming out harsher, drier than I'd expected.

"Faron was cunning, wise. I hoped you'd figure it out before they came."

*Before they came...* "What do you—"

"Take it. Unlock it. You'll need this," she breathed, holding up her left fist in the darkness, allowing her eyes to close.

"I'm sorry," I whispered into the darkness.

Nerissa appeared by my side.

"Whatever for?" A soft smile formed on Xenelpha's lips that sent a familiar burning sensation to my eyes.

Nerissa's boots scraped against the icy bank. Her form lowered, kneeling on the other side of the dying matron.

"It was an honor to have known you both, as briefly as I did," Xenelpha murmured. "Life. Death. Change and rebirth. Powers reforged with new masters."

"Xenelpha," I whispered. "Who is the Impostor?"

Fear flashed in her eyes before they hardened into disgust.

"He... *It*... is a world walker. It watches through silver eyes, jumping between bodies. A spy... The Messenger for the Ehp'uch, the *Embodied*..."

The blood in my veins stilled as the word hovered in the air above Xenelpha's lips. An eerie sense of awareness swept through me as the Transcindiel and Obscura wrapped around each other.

"The caeluma are the key. They didn't expect them... They will find you..."

I opened my mouth to ask more when Xenelpha's cough became shallow, her breathing more ragged as her eyes drifted to the blue-black night sky. The Obscura, despite having settled deep within that chasm, uncoiled and turned its attention to the woman lying before me.

Death beckoned, I realized, and I placed a cold hand on her eyes, pulling the lids down. As I did so, a whisper of darkness escaped my fingers. I slid it into her being and laid a calming hand on her life force as it flickered out.

Nerissa's indrawn breath pulled me from the hollowness that remained, and I found her gazing at me, a tender curiosity written across her face. I took Xenelpha's cold fist and pried her fingers open to take what she'd freely given.

The key to the burial chamber.

# CHAPTER THIRTY-SEVEN

*I am so angry. I miss Lyv. And I could kill Bayne.*
—*Journal of Isla Jasira*

T he song of battle echoed through the night as we raced through the trees, dodging the silver-armored men and warriors clad in bone that crashed among them. The bellow of white bears plowed through the night as I leaped over a fallen bench and ducked behind a building.

"They can handle Nivis. Half the bears are down, and I spotted a pack of dune runners with their riders coming south when I came to find you," Nerissa breathed next to me. "Are you sure you can get us in?"

I nodded. "Yes, but I'm sure they have it guarded tonight. Especially after the Impostor's arrival." I turned to face her, my voice becoming firm. "We leave them alive."

Nerissa's eyes were vivid. The flashes of fires among the

trees danced in her green irises as her lips tilted upward for a moment in eagerness before she muttered, "Let's go get it."

The cries in the village above reduced to mumbled thumping and the occasional thud when we entered the underground network of ice tunnels leading to the amphitheater and Faron's burial chamber.

Nerissa silenced the first two guards with a pinch on the neck, not making a sound, even as she slid them to the ground. We sprinted noiselessly down the long tunnel before running into four more standing guard in front of the large, carved stone door.

Shouts erupted as two hurtled toward us, their bone spears positioned overhead as they sprinted down the tunnel. With preternatural speed, Nerissa flew past me, dodging the first thrust and sending the staff of the spear careening into the nose of a guard. He fell with a thud as she slammed the base of the staff into the back of another's head.

I leaped over his body, with Nerissa already engaging the two nearest the door. A third went down by the time I reached them.

The last remaining guard wore the skull of an amatohk and held two sharpened femurs in both hands. He swung the bones like swords, and Nerissa met them with a single curved blade, jumping out of reach as she danced around the warrior like a wolf circling a bear.

He leaped as she drew him out, spinning farther from the stone door. Her bright eyes flashed at me as she neared, and I waited for the opening I knew she'd make. She feigned a stumble back, allowing the warrior to believe he gained ground, and she ducked at his next attack, slamming her leg into the back of his knees.

I flew past them, leaped over the large form, and skidded to a slippery stop in front of the slate door. Key in hand, I slammed the diamond tip into the center of the door and murmured the memorized spell beneath my breath. The door slid open with a hiss.

Nerissa's snarl reached my ears as the curved blade flew from her hand. Large, armored claws gripped Nerissa's muscled shoulders as his skulled head slammed into her face. Blood spewed from her nose, dotting the ivory skull with a crimson spray as she landed a knee to his groin. His thick hand clenched Nerissa's neck.

My heart picked up a furious beat as a tiny whimper escaped Nerissa's lips, and his muscled hand began to squeeze. Anger and fear pulsed through my veins as I sprinted from the open burial chamber to where he held her against the icy wall, closing the gap within a heartbeat. I speared a tendril of darkness toward the guard. The Obscura snuffed out the scream that rose in his throat as I obliterated the warrior and his bone armor.

Nerissa's limp body fell into the pile of ash left behind, and I placed two shaking fingers to her neck. A weak, subtle pulse thumped beneath them, and I breathed a sigh. I gripped her under the shoulders as I slid her down the hall and into Faron's chamber.

I snatched the round stone holding the Advetis Bone as shouts arose from down the hall.

*Fuck.* Reinforcements were coming.

I scrambled to get my arms around Nerissa.

Shouts in Rhashtai rose in echoes, and I readied my darkness, waiting for the onslaught. A shadow moved around the last corner of the hall, and my heart stuttered as Vulcan's form rounded the curve and flew to the entrance to the chamber.

"We need to go!" he shouted. His face and arms were covered in blood.

"Nerissa is down!"

His jaw clenched as he slid to a stop and knelt beside her, lifting her eyelids.

"I can carry her," he murmured. "Nivis retreated, and they've found Xenelpha. Kai is on his way with at least fifty Bone Warriors."

He swiftly tossed her over his shoulder, and we made for the exit when Kai's dark form appeared in the doorway. His teeth flashed in a malevolent grin beneath the skull he wore as his hands gripped the smooth edges of the door.

Vulcan's wide eyes found mine in the dimming light from the tunnel as the door swung shut. The deafening boom was nothing compared to the pounding of my heart that followed.

*Trapped.*

I blinked against the darkness. Pitch black.

*I am not afraid of the dark*, I chanted in my mind, but the blackness of this room was suffocating, and the building pressure of claustrophobia pushed on me from all sides.

"Breathe," Vulcan said from across the chamber. "How did you get in the first time?"

The primitive part of my existence panicked. My breath refused to fully escape my lungs as my lips greedily sucked in more air. How much did we even have left in here?

A firm hand gripped my arm.

"In," he said, "and out. Just like before dawn."

Vulcan's voice was quiet yet held an air of authority. And I listened, closing my eyes and imagining we were at the prow of the *Evecta*, with smooth waves of the Juniper lapping below the hull, the early rays of Aelius painting the horizon in soft pink. A long, shaky breath escaped my lips, and he dropped his hands.

"How did you get in before?"

"Stairs in the back," I said, my voice sounding faraway. "But they lead to the bottom of the lake. There's no way we'll be able to get out. Even if we get the door open, we'll drown."

Vulcan's hand returned to my arm, and he pulled us to the back of the chamber, where we began the slow ascent to the top of the winding, stone staircase.

"We might be able to if we can wake Nerissa. She might be able to split the water long enough for us to swim to the surface."

My breathing became ragged as the thought of trying to swim beneath the frozen lake settled in my gut, and I shook my head.

"It's frozen. Even if we can get through the door, we'll be stuck beneath the ice..."

"If you believe it's impossible, it will be," he snarled. "We will survive this. Nerissa will melt an opening for us."

Oh, gods. *This was the plan?!*

Vulcan stopped ahead of me as he slid Nerissa to the ground of the small landing at the top of the stairs. My hand edged along the round opening, feeling for any type of latch.

"Here," he murmured. "Wake up, Nerissa." He softly slapped her cheek. "Lyvia, try the bond."

My head shook. "I've never felt her. The wall she has up is..."

*Impenetrable* hung on my lips, but I realized I'd never really tried to tear it down. I hadn't dared for fear of the wrath it would unleash.

"We don't have another option right now."

My knees hit the stone with more force than I intended as I knelt beside her, taking her calloused hand in mine.

"Nerissa," I whispered. "I'm coming in."

Despite the darkness, I closed my eyes and let my mind drift through the memories of the threads I swam through. Twice now, I'd gotten to glimpse the mysterious connections that spun through the universe. One of those six, wave-like ribbons in my universe was Nerissa. The bonds of the Bellators.

I took a breath as I remembered the intricate web, feeling my way through the delicate threads. I reached out with my mind's eye as I came across the one. One was more guarded than any of the others, with an invisible fortress hewn from pain, fear, and regret. I pressed my consciousness against the wall, a silent, soft request, and waited.

Seconds stretched into infinity.

"Lyvia," Vulcan warned in the distant darkness.

*Come on, Nerissa.*

Nothing.

I leaned into the wall, sending a wave of emotion toward it. *Trust. Friendship. Safety. Open,* I silently commanded.

A crack formed, and I shoved myself through it, sending a wave of warmth along with it. Nerissa's gasp filled the small space at the top of the staircase, and she coughed against the dry air of the tomb.

She thrashed against Vulcan's grip, who quickly relayed our current situation to her.

"Can you do it if you tap into my amplifier?"

"Doesn't seem like I have much of a choice, does it?" she snapped. "Fuck. *Fuck!*" she breathed, her voice hoarse and shaky. "Okay, we'll have maybe a second once the door is open, but there's not much air left in this chamber, so take a deep breath. I'll send the rest of it into the lake. I've never used the Soleia power underwater before, so I have no idea what to expect. You may need to break through the ice."

My stomach dropped, and I looked blindly at Vulcan.

"Try not to boil us alive," was his only response.

I had the inexplicable urge to laugh. Was Vulcan being sarcastic? Surely, this meant the end was near if he was joking.

"Shut up," Nerissa snapped. She took a few deep breaths, steeling herself for the power required to get us out of here.

"Do it," she finally said, her quiet voice hardened with determination.

Nerissa pulled me to the far side of the landing, away from where the door would swing inward, as Vulcan chiseled away at the stone lid. A strained groan whined from above, and Vulcan's chiseling paused.

"Get ready—"

The amplifier on my chest burned as Nerissa reached for it. The stone lid slammed against the wall in a deafening bang, followed by a surge of lake water.

As quick as the water charged in, a rush of air whipped upward from below the stairs, shooting a tunnel of solid wind straight into the bottom of the lake as Nerissa screamed. I bent my leg as Vulcan's hands shoved me into the opening.

Nerissa moved beside me in the strange wind tunnel, as water quickly filled the space between the opening of the burial chamber and our feet. The three of us kicked against the upward swell of water. The massive sack of air floated upward, like a giant bubble. Frigid water engulfed us as the air outpaced us high above, floating beneath a wall of ice.

We neared the surface, the ice so thick that only a soft, dark hue of light escaped its crystals into the water below. Nerissa tensed as her hands landed on the surface, and her white flames fought against the water. Small bubbles formed on either side of her hands, but the wall of ice didn't budge. She shot a panicked look at me before gritting her teeth and sending more power into her palms. The water warmed around us.

Vulcan pulled me farther away from her as her hands melted into the ice, making two small indents in the thick wall. Nerissa's brows furrowed. Her brown hair glowed golden as it floated in the water, illuminated by her brilliant white light. Her eyes shuddered a moment, and she swayed beneath the surface. The white light beneath her palms flickered, and her eyes closed.

No. *No.*

Vulcan left my side, grabbing hold of her with one arm and pounding against the thinned ice with the other.

Oh, gods. We were going to die.

Devastation gripped me as Vulcan pounded against the ice in a panic, somehow still treading water with Nerissa and holding his breath.

My lungs burned as the last bit of oxygen traveled through my veins, and a sad awareness swept through me. My thoughts drifted to my friends, my found family. I would never see them again.

And Tiberius... My caeluma. He was a part of me, a part of my soul. I had the briefest desire to cast to him, but I couldn't do that. I couldn't let him see me die. He would be so lonely. Would he find other caeluma? Choose another Bellator?

*You didn't find them*, a voice seemed to whisper. *They found you. Remember.*

A soft, not-so-distant darkness beckoned me once again. Death. Would it be so terrible to go now? Maybe I'd see my father again...

*The dead are trapped*, the voice said. *Remember. See.*

Free them.

I had to be here to free them.

The caeluma found us. *They are the key. They can manifest our powers.*

My eyes shot open as Vulcan's fluttered closed beneath the surface. He was fading, barely hanging on, yet his arms still gripped Nerissa as his legs kicked and his fist beat weakly at the ice.

Aquila.

Bayne said Aquila lacked certain abilities to be a caeluma. He lacked *their power*. I kicked, realizing I'd begun to sink, and threw my mind out to the seahawk. A panicked sense of urgency responded.

*Hurry*, I urged him, with every desperate wave of emotion I could muster. A dark form materialized above the surface of the ice. I threw every last bit of energy I had left into the depths of my powers, grabbing hold of the delicate song, latching it to the amplifier on my neck.

Threads danced in my mind's eye, the golden connections that hung suspended in midair. I latched the Transcindiel power to the bond connecting me to Nerissa and Aquila, my energy draining by the second.

A distant shriek echoed from above as the dark shadow disappeared in a tunnel of golden light, breaking free a moment later, larger. The shadow of massive wings beat against the night across the surface before a wave of white flames licked along the other side of the ice.

# CHAPTER THIRTY-EIGHT

*Come to the Crystal Castle. See light where there was dark-*
*ness. She freed the Itherians. Be a part of this.*
*—Correspondence from Ordell to Enya. Date preceding*
*Sultiran Calendrical System.*

The soft lapping of water drew me from sleep, and I inhaled a deep breath of cedar. My head fell to the side and landed on soft, cottony sheets. I tugged the furs higher and reached for Bayne as my aching arm slid across the bed.

My hand found only cold, abandoned space, and I tugged it back in, huddling against the draft that snaked its way into the captain's quarters.

I blinked my eyes open, frowning at the wall of weapons before me. Axes, intricate bows, spears, curved blades. What the...

Astraeus.

I was in Lord Astraeus's captain's quarters. The events of the last several weeks raced back into view as I sat up, and nausea slammed into me. I leaned over its edge and hurled into a small bowl of stew that had been left for me.

*I was alive.* And weak, I realized, as I slowly sat up. I tugged an oversized tunic off my chest, disgusted as I recognized the pirate lord's shirt. Every part of me reeled at the thought.

My fingers grazed an oval burn blistered on my chest. *My amplifier had done this.* I sucked in a quick breath and scanned the black wooden desk where my things sat. I tiptoed to the amplifier that sat on top of the round stone containing Faron's Bellator power next to a stack of books. A small gasp escaped my lips as I lifted the pendant, still warm to the touch, and ran a thumb over the surface.

A delicate etching of ferns and flowers twisted around each other, adorning the once smooth amber in an elaborate design.

Bayne must have worked a spell into the amplifier to keep it from being destroyed. As I tapped into its power, the spell directed the resulting damage to follow a design on its surface. I gazed with wonder at the pendant and popped it open. The remains of the small, ancient creature hadn't been disturbed. Even with all the power it took to...

*Aquila.*

*Nerissa and Vulcan.*

I scrambled as I tugged on my leathers and threw on my own bloodstained shirt. Fogginess clouded my head as I stumbled toward the door. I blew out a breath as I stepped from Lord Astraeus's quarters and into the bright light of midday on board the *Hydra*.

Vulcan's scarred face was free of the blood that coated it before our trip through the lake. His hazel eyes found mine and softened, with the smallest hint of a smile forming on his lips. I opened my mouth as I moved toward him when a thin form rushed at me, wrapping her arms around my shoulders and squeezing the breath from me.

"Lyvia!" Vienah cried against my shoulder.

"I'm so glad you're all right," I said, my voice hoarse. "Where is—"

A deafening screech echoed above as Aquila's massive shadow swooped behind the mainsail, and he landed with a thud in the middle of the deck. The few remaining in Lord Astraeus's crew stumbled back at the sight of the giant bird. Who was now...enormous. His wingspan rivaled Tiberius's, and his body was large enough to carry one, if not more riders.

*Caeluma.*

His keen eyes surveyed me, and he cocked his head, sending a wave of gratitude and warmth. I placed a hand upon my chest as he bowed. A squeezing sensation built in my heart, and I blinked away a tear.

"Thank you, Aquila."

The bird straightened, his form towering over me and casting a net of shadow as he ruffled his coppery feathers.

"Is Nerissa okay?"

A wave of reassurance, hedged with concern, rippled, and he turned his head toward the crew chambers below deck.

I moved to make my way below deck when Carina strode toward me with an air of confidence I'd yet to see in her.

"Bonder," she said, adjusting her cracked spectacles. Carina stood with her chin high, and her Ravindra eyes narrowed on me. A nasty cut ran down the side of her face and across the side of her upper lip, making her appear anything but timid. The shadows of battle lingered in the traces of darkness below her eyes. Gone was the meek, mousy princess we'd left Lotrennia with.

"Your call to protect the innocent," Carina continued.

"Your oath with Astraeus. Does it extend to the innocent in Lotrennia?"

I blinked. "Yes. Of course."

She peered at me, her keen eyes studying me as if struggling with some internal decision.

"I am under orders to return the bone to my mother. As are you," she said, her eyes still hard on my own. "Do you remember the terms of her deal?"

My lips pursed as I replayed the words of Queen Antares in my head. She'd bring our fleet back to Sultira when I gave her the bone.

"They've wed," she continued. "If what Tiberius showed you was true, Bayne is king, which means fifteen thousand Lotrennians will follow you to Sultira. But only if you return to our land with the bone."

My stomach pitched. I wouldn't give Queen Antares this power. We'd find another way to dethrone Saros and return to Sultira. I couldn't let any Bellator power fall into her hands.

"Are you willing to let that go? The aid and power of the elves? Even if it means the continued sacrifice of Sultira's people while you wait to dethrone him?"

Fresh nausea churned in my gut. "She's not getting this bone, or any other bone of power," I said quietly.

Carina's eyes bounced between mine as she took a step closer. "Leaders are forced to make difficult choices. My mother has made many that have left her..."

She paused, glancing at Aquila's large form behind me. "Scarred. And changed. She wasn't always like this."

Her eyes drifted toward the sea beyond us and its vibrant waters before shaking her head. "I haven't sworn the air oath to my mother. She reserves that right for people she deems more valuable." Carina crossed her arms as she surveyed me.

"But I'd swear one to you, if your offer of an alliance still stands."

"An air oath?"

"The same words Astraeus swore to you," she confirmed. "That you receive my counsel. That you use your powers to *unify* the lands of Vael."

I blinked and nodded, taken aback by her sudden offer.

"I'll find you later," she murmured and moved to join Kresida at the back of the ship.

"Nerissa's below," Vulcan muttered as he approached, his voice dry and throaty as if he'd hurled a gallon of lake water.

"How long has it been?"

"A day and a half," he murmured as his blonde eyebrows furrowed.

We entered a small, private room below deck where Nerissa's form lay peacefully under a thick, black fur. Ronan straddled the sole chair, hunched over the back of it as he watched her.

"Has she awoken yet?" I asked quietly as I entered.

I stepped around the chair and knelt beside her cot. Ronan wiped the crumbs from his eyes, rubbing the space between them. He shook his head, light curls dull and splattered with mud and dried blood.

"Have you slept?"

Ronan turned toward me and raised his eyebrows. Of course not.

"I can take over," I said, concern squeezing at my chest. I reached out to the wall I had so forcefully broken through. My consciousness reeled back as a current of flame lashed at it. Despite the guard, my chest eased. She was still there.

"Pretty sure you're needed elsewhere," he muttered, turning back to Nerissa. "I'm not leaving."

My brows pinched in question.

"Astraeus," Vulcan answered.

I scoffed, shaking my head. "He can wait," I growled, nodding to Vulcan and pulling a chair up next to Ronan. "I'm staying."

Ronan's lips twitched.

A TUG of air pulled me from my slumber. I blinked at Nerissa, still asleep, as I sat up. Ronan lay passed out on the floor. A shade of amusement rose as I remembered the last time he offered to sleep on the floor. Such different circumstances. And instead of dredging up the stinging ache of betrayal, the memory brought a swell of gratitude along with it for his friendship. His love for Nerissa was so clearly written in his actions that I wondered how anyone, Nerissa and I included, ever missed it in the first place.

Another tug of air, this time wrapping itself around my braid.

What the hell—

A wave of irritation washed over me as I realized Lord Astraeus was pulling on the air oath connecting us.

A third tug.

I might murder him.

Another.

I stood, ready to make my way upstairs, when it happened again. This time, I grabbed hold of the air and *yanked*. Smug satisfaction bloomed in my chest as a choked cough came from above deck.

"What in Tynan's Hell is wrong with you?" I snapped as I found him smirking above deck.

He was back in his deep blue coat, hair cleaned and

braided, his beard neatly trimmed. He flashed a white smile and arched a dark brow.

"Milady." He sketched a bow. "Is that any way to speak to your captain?"

My stomach twisted. "You'll never be my captain."

His dark eyes narrowed as he stepped closer. "We'll see about that," he whispered. "I've called you to—"

"First of all," I stopped him, placing a hand on his chest and shoving him back. "Don't do that."

"Do what?" he said, the sides of his lips kicking up into a smirk once more.

"You know what," I snapped, and a glint entered his dark eyes as he tugged once more, flipping my braid over my shoulder.

My fingernails dug into my palms as I resisted the urge to claw his face off. "I swear to the gods, if you do that one more time, I will—"

"You will what?" he asked, cocking his head. "This was your idea, you know."

I opened my mouth to respond when Raek stepped to his side, eyes darting between us.

"Fish stew?" he said, holding a steaming bowl toward me.

I paused mid-breath and stared at the hand he outstretched. A savory blend of spices wafted from the hearty helping. I swallowed the growing amount of spit that formed in my mouth. Oh, gods. That *smell*.

"Err... Yes. Thank you, Raek."

I swallowed once more, taking the bowl from him as he stepped away. I lifted the stew to my lips and stifled the groan that threatened to escape.

I blinked my eyes open, not realizing I'd closed them after a couple mouthfuls. When was the last time I'd eaten?

Turning back to Lord Astraeus, I scowled, noting the look

of satisfaction that accompanied the insufferable smirk still plastered on his face. His teeth slid over his lower lip, stretching the scar, as he watched me shovel the rest of the stew down. I shoved the empty bowl into his hands.

"Raek is a good cook."

"Bit salty if I'm being honest," I murmured.

"Liar." He chuckled, the sound sending an involuntary set of bumps down my arm.

He handed me a waterskin, and I slugged it down before straightening my shoulders.

"Where were we?" he asked, crossing his arms.

"Right." I lifted a finger. "I need our coordinates, Astraeus. Others will be joining us soon."

"Tiberius, I assume?"

"Who told you that?"

He waved a hand and walked across the deck. I bristled before scooting after him to keep up with his long stride.

Tiberius. I took a quick survey of my energy and opened the connection to my caeluma. My heart warmed at the touch of his consciousness, despite the chill air that swirled around him. Still airborne then.

"We are about fifty miles east of Sultira, heading south."

My stomach pitched. *South?* I opened my mouth.

"You were the one who said Nivis is heading toward Sultira, right? We can't go west. We need to sail south."

"We need to get to Lotrennia—"

The pirate lord shrugged, and his lips kicked up in a cocky grin I longed to slap right off. He hopped up the steps to the quarterdeck, where he gave a nod to one of his men who handed him the helm. Astraeus's palms rested casually on the smooth wood as he turned back to me. His dark eyes sparked as he paused, staring at me curiously.

"What?"

"Are you talking to him right now?"

I blinked.

*Got what you need?*

*Yes. See you in a day.*

I threw my love down the bond before cutting the cast.

"I'm not sure what you mean," I said back to Astraeus.

"You're a terrible liar, Bonscaíh."

I threw him a vulgar gesture, and his intolerable grin widened.

"What is it like?" he asked quietly.

"It's like none of your damned business." I turned, stalking down the quarterdeck and headed toward Astraeus's quarters to remove the rest of my belongings.

One day.

Tiberius would be here in one day. A smile tugged at my lips. Too long. It had been far too long.

# CHAPTER THIRTY-NINE

*It must be organic. I cannot funnel power into that which holds no life.*

*—Correspondence from Lelyth to Enya. Date preceding Sultiran Calendrical System.*

N erissa's dark silhouette stood out against the deep blue of the sea in the early hours of the morning. The salty breeze pulled away the whisper of lilac wind still lingering in my nostrils. Carina had sworn the air oath the night before, Astraeus performing the spell while Kresida watched carefully.

I paused at the top of the stairs, catching sight of Nerissa and Aquila at the prow of the *Hydra*. I held my hand out to halt Vulcan, who came up behind me. Nerissa's face didn't leave Aquila's as I approached the two, who seemed to be truly communicating, speaking mind-to-mind, for the first time in the hundred-plus years she'd been alive.

I stepped up to the two, sending a wave of warmth to them both. Aquila ruffled his large feathers in return but kept his eyes on Nerissa. I glanced at the elf and stifled a gasp, noting the long streaks of silver sliding down her cheeks.

I reached a tentative hand to hers and clasped it within my own. She didn't look up, but she gripped it back, squeezing tightly. I let her hold it, silently waiting for her to drop it when she was ready. After several minutes, her hand slackened, and she turned to me.

"Aquila was there," she said, her voice soft against the lapping surf. "He was Kyson's caeluma over a thousand years ago."

My jaw slackened as I turned to the great bird and I opened my mouth.

Nerissa shook her head. "He doesn't remember most of it. The blast that broke the Vael... It changed him, shattered most of his memories. He's known enough to stay close to our bloodline. It's all he's needed, really."

She turned back to Aquila, a softness appearing on her features I'd never seen before.

"Well then," I said, smiling up at the giant hawk, "welcome back, Aquila." A surge of joy washed over me, and I bowed deeply before backing away to join Vulcan at the stern.

Vienah's arm wrapped around my shoulder as we stood at the prow of the ship, a broad smile plastered on my face as a black form took shape in the clear skies in the distance.

"They made it," she said, giving my shoulder a squeeze.

My heart sang in response.

Three months. Far, far too long. Never again would I let it

go this long. And Bayne... There was so much we needed to discuss. I needed to see him.

*Took you long enough,* I teased Tiberius as his massive wings became visible. The agrippa scoffed into my mind.

*If you were carrying two on your back, you wouldn't be moving as fast as usual, either.*

My grin widened as butterflies flapped in my stomach. My heart squeezed, the anticipation of seeing any of my friends enough for a burning sensation to form in the corners of my eyes.

Aquila's massive form rose into the skies as he flew to greet Tiberius. An elated whinny filled the air as Tiberius took in Aquila's changed form, and the massive hawk soared in circles around him.

Tiberius banked, circling around the back of the *Hydra*, and slowed his flight as he came in for a running landing. I sprinted around the foremast and skidded to a stop as Tiberius thundered down the deck.

Ti's velvety wings stretched high above his head as he gained his footing and finally stopped. They flapped as they fell to his sides. Drystan's weary blue eyes met mine as he slid off Ti with shaky legs and reached a hand up to help Marian off his back.

A lump formed in my throat as I took a step toward the three newcomers. Safe. Marian and Drystan were now safe. A wave of relief at seeing my friends warred with a surge of shock at not finding Bayne among them. I stared at Ti's dark eyes for a moment before I noticed the long, recently healed slice down the center of his chest.

*What's happened?*
*We need to talk.*

The winter wine Raek procured from Astraeus's private stash did little to quell the unease crawling over my body.

"So, the dark king has begun his conquest," Lord Astraeus mused, swirling the dark wine in a silver goblet. He reclined in his chair, ankles crossed, and black leather boots propped on the edge of the table.

"His forces must be stretched thin if he's dispatched three legions of Nivis soldiers and multiple hordes of ashen. Death Dunes, Sultira, Lotrennia..." Carina's brows furrowed as she studied the large map draped across the table in the room below deck.

"We don't really know much about his forces, other than the ashen you saw on Kayj," Ronan interjected, nodding toward the crew members of the *Evecta*.

Marian looked toward me with hesitant eyes, but I couldn't meet them.

"We have a general sense of ashen numbers, but not a full look," Nerissa answered.

"We have a solution for the ashen, don't we?" Raek cut in, his sea green eyes shooting toward me and Nerissa.

I signed a quick translation for Drystan, though he probably didn't need it with his ability to read lips. Astraeus, surprisingly, was the only pirate on board the *Hydra* who knew the language.

"Have you made a successful transformation?" Drystan responded with quiet shock.

My chin dipped in confirmation, thinking of the ashen I'd changed in Rhashtai during the attack. Had they even survived the battle?

"Once," I replied. "It took twice the energy as killing thousands of them, though."

"Either way, we have two weapons. Three, if you count the

king," Kresida interjected, my stomach pitching at the title she used to refer to Bayne. "They can destroy them by the dozens."

"I don't think we rule out Lyvia's ability to save them just yet," Carina countered.

"What of the king and queen and their elven forces?" Vien-ah's tentative question filled the void. Her recently learned hand movements were slow and tentative. "Will the rest of the Rising forces return to Sultira?"

Drystan heaved a sigh before taking a swig of wine. "The queen swore to Bayne she'd send our forces back to Sultira by the end of the year. We were allowed to leave to communicate the message."

"What about the bone?" Carina asked, eyes wide.

"She's agreed to send them and the elven forces without it," Drystan signed, his brows pinched.

"Why would she do that?" I asked, forcing the tremors from my hands.

Drystan's eyes dropped to his copper hands. "A trade..."

Vulcan paused his dagger above the whetting stone.

"For what?" Nerissa's words were broken against her whisper.

Drystan scratched at the stubble on his chin as he shot a cautionary glance toward me. "A soulbinding with Bayne," Drystan answered, his moon-blue eyes heavy with pity as he signed the words.

Silence cleaved the room. My blood stilled in my veins as my heart took a moment to continue its necessary rhythm. Nerissa had gone rigid. Even Astraeus's arrogant demeanor shifted into something more lethal.

*Khato thought that if I saw the soulbinding thread, Bayne would bind himself to me, and it would prevent Antares from getting her claws in him.* My inner voice wavered as I spoke to Ti.

*But he didn't believe you*, Ti replied, grief and anger weeping down our mental connection.

"I don't believe it." Nerissa's head shook with her reply.

"It's true," I breathed, all too aware the eyes in the room hadn't left my face.

"How would you know that?" Nerissa snapped, turning toward me, but I could no longer speak.

My breath lodged in my throat.

"Khato suspected a soulbinding thread existed between Lyv and Bayne. If it did, she would have felt it break..." Drystan answered, eyes pinching in apology for confirming what I already knew.

Numbness stretched its claws through me, and my vision started to tunnel. But instead of the usual panic that arrived, the slow, freezing burn of fury spread. Bayne was soulbound.

It didn't matter that we were human and elfkind. Fuck the rules and whatever shitty gods made them up. I'd felt it all along, and whatever magic the twin eclipse released upon the world during the Sending, it unlocked some door between us as Bellators *and* as a pair.

And he didn't fucking believe me because I was a naïve human. His doubt cost him his soul.

My heart picked up its pace, pushing against the taut skin along the scar on my neck. Powers rose beneath my skin. The Obscura bucked beneath my palms with its usual demand, the darkness writhing in raven swirls along my arms and hands. I blinked slowly, as a warm, golden power twined alongside it, the song of the Transcindiel rising in my mind's ear in powerful, outraged beats.

Tiberius's emotions flooded down our connection, a rage dwarfing his own slice of betrayal. *You cannot be forced into a soulbinding. Those compatible for it must make the choice*, he barked into my mind, fueling my powers and my emotions.

A crack ripped through my chest, as if a hammer had driven a nail through the thin layer of ice freezing over my soul, cooling it from the simmering darkness beneath.

*Why would he do this?*

Nerissa voiced the question aloud.

"Bayne wed the queen to keep the people of Lotrennia from choosing between the two of them, to prevent a civil war. He would do anything for his kingdom," Vulcan murmured, his hazel eyes focused on the dagger in his lap. "And there is only one reason to soulbind with someone who's not a love match."

"Power," Nerissa breathed. "That was the trade. An oath, only breakable upon death... His soul for more power."

*Power.* Had he done this because of his vision in the Waters of Ascendiel?

Drystan's blue eyes caught mine, his knowing, sympathetic gaze fueling the growing beast of fury soon to slip its leash. Nerissa shifted, and a sliver of rage pulsed through the cracks in her bond's barrier.

*Breakable upon death...* I mused to Tiberius. *When you created the whip in Lotrennia during your training with the queen... When the Obscura and Transcindiel powers merged, you created a weapon of death. That blast, when you cut the air between you and Antares... You severed the air oath, didn't you?*

Tiberius's affirming stomp banged from above. The eyes in the room looked up at the sound before landing on me. The scar on Astraeus's lower lip whitened as his lips drew a thin line.

*If you were able to cut the air oath, we might be able to sever a soulbinding.*

*Yes, but does he even want it broken?* Ti challenged. *And at what cost? Soulbinding bonds are the strongest of all magical bonds. If cutting a mere air oath left a mark on all of us...*

My hand drifted to the straight, fresh scar running down the center of my chest. A perfect match to Tiberius's.

*Antares has a matching injury?* I asked.

*Yes.*

Mumbled talking continued in the room below deck, and my mind slowed as my thoughts narrowed to a focused sort of precision.

*It could kill them,* my mind's voice shook. *Breaking their bond could kill Bayne. Antares knows we'd figure that out. And she thinks because of the risk, we wouldn't try to break it.*

*She could be baiting us with their bond. She wants your powers. She wants me,* Ti's words rang with finality.

*She will not have you.*

A drip of sweat slid down my neck and between my breasts, following the long scar, where it stopped. Distantly, the conversation in the room grew. The little bead of sweat tickled my chest, and the air below deck stuck to my throat, thick and stifling as I focused on filling and emptying my lungs.

My world had become a treacherous sea I struggled to stay afloat in. Every moment I broke through the surface, a storm crashed against my face and a hand shoved me back down. Yet each time, I dared another breath, another surge through the waves for one thing. The ones I loved. I loved Tiberius. And Bayne... Could he have really done this for power? I still loved him, despite the growing cracks in our relationship, didn't I? She *dared* take them from me?

*You need to get above deck, Lyvia. You need an outlet.*

Darkness and golden light joined hands in dance beneath my skin. Winding and twirling together, as if in some strange, foreign waltz, my human mind couldn't understand.

*Get above deck. NOW!*

Somewhere, people argued. There was panic. And shouting. A rough hand gripped my forearm, tugging me up. I didn't see them. I only sensed that growing waltz of death and darkness, transformation and rebirth, swarming inside.

Another hand on my shoulder, shaking it...

The Obscura and Transcindiel paused briefly in their dance, as if noticing a stranger walk through the door. I blinked as Astraeus's dark eyes flashed before my own.

"You need to get the hell off my ship," he breathed, his face inches from my own. "Up. Now."

My powers ignored his command, returning to their frenzy, and then, I felt it. A building pressure, bigger than anything I'd ever experienced. Bile rose to my throat as I realized I was about to explode.

Calloused fingers, covered in thick rings laced through mine, pressing a scarred palm to the eight-pointed star on my own. A spark, and that pressure eased enough for Astraeus to haul me up the stairs, clearing the way and ordering his men below deck. Tiberius stomped toward me, and Astraeus gripped me behind the thigh and below the knee, hoisting me onto Ti's back.

We launched into the night sky, suddenly blanketed with thick, dark clouds. Tiberius pumped his massive wings, soaring higher and higher as the air around us thinned. I threw my hands above my head and erupted.

# CHAPTER FORTY

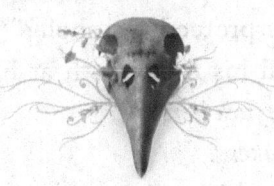

*We should use bones.*
   —*Correspondence from Enya to Lelyth. Date preceding*
*Sultiran Calendrical System.*

Aquila's talons thumped as they hit the rail of the ship. My neck ached as I stretched against Tiberius's broad, velvety side. I blinked my eyes open against the darkness. A thick layer of clouds spread across the sky, shielding us from our moons' light.

We lay at the stern, Tiberius with his legs tucked beneath him and a large black wing draped over me. He lifted his head at Aquila's landing. The two of them stared at each other for several moments before movement from the quarterdeck caught my eye.

*Can you speak to Aquila? Like you and I do?*

*Kind of. It's somewhere between words and casting. It's difficult to explain, but yes, I can communicate with him now.*

I groaned as I gingerly sat up and rubbed my face. A dull, throbbing had begun behind my eyes. *What happened?*

*You'll find out*, Tiberius's large head bobbed as Nerissa prowled across the deck.

"Can I talk to her now?" she snapped at Tiberius. "Or are you still being an overprotective asshole?"

Tiberius snapped his front teeth at her as he pinned his ears. *Tell Nerissa to go fuck herself.*

*What? For gods' sakes...*

I shook off Ti's thick wing and stood. Nausea rushed upward as blood drained from my face, my vision swimming as I swayed. Nerissa's hands caught my arms, and she swung me to the edge of the ship, where I emptied the contents of my stomach.

After several minutes of retching, I wiped my mouth on my shirt and turned toward Nerissa and waited, leaning against the rail. She handed me a waterskin. Black circles lined her green eyes.

"You," she began, pausing as she scanned my face, "had a bit of an incident."

I raised my eyebrows. "An incident?"

Nerissa swallowed before frowning, "I'm not sure how to explain it, other than your powers sort of... exploded out of you. Tiberius got you above Vienah's cloud cover, which would have been fine except it wasn't just the Obscura that you released."

*Vienah...* I sent up a silent prayer of thanks for the water witch and her influence on the weather. It was dark last night, but not so dark that a huge display of power would have been missed by ships within hawk sight. The dark clouds would have camouflaged the darkness perfectly in the night sky, but that glowing Transcindiel power...and what they were doing *together...*

I threw a wary glance at Nerissa, who watched me piece it together.

"Your powers seem to be getting along now. It looked like a lightning storm from here. More gold than the true white of lightning, but with the clouds, it was disguised enough."

"Was anyone hurt?"

Nerissa shook her head. "None on deck."

"How long were we up there?"

"Four hours," she said, glancing at my forearms.

I followed her gaze. The darkness had subsided, but the two powers coiled together deep in their chasm.

My stomach pitched. I hadn't had a lapse of control like this since Odessa. The cause of it all slapped me in the face, and the emptiness of betrayal and devastation hollowed out my chest. My lip quivered, and I looked away from Nerissa. She pulled her gaze away and leaned against the rail.

"I cannot talk about it," she breathed. "As I know you can't. So, for right now, we don't."

A single tear formed in the corner of my eye. It hung there for a moment, creating a pool of warm liquid.

Bayne was soulbound to a monster. He was a hawk, tethered and unable to fly. But he'd *chosen* this. Could I free him? What would the cost be?

Nerissa's steely gaze was hard against the deep blue horizon, and I thought perhaps I began to understand her. It was far easier to keep your feelings, your most vulnerable self, locked up tight and safe within your heart than it was to be this exposed, this broken and betrayed, this devastated.

Anger. Wrath. Fury. It was easier to let these out. The protectors, the defenders of what lay so deeply hidden. They were shields, guardians of the soft, raw, and delicate parts inside us. But I needed them all. My powers needed them, needed access to all of me to work.

I blinked, allowing that single tear to slide down my cheek, cooling as it went, and I slowly closed the gap in my heart, shutting it tightly, allowing those shields to stand guard until my powers demanded a taste.

"Astraeus asked us to reconvene at dawn. There's still much to discuss," she said quietly.

"I'm getting really fucking tired of being on his ship," I murmured before pushing off the ledge.

"WHERE WERE WE?" Astraeus drawled around the rolled enderleaf between his lips.

My blood pressure surged as he threw me a wink..

Drystan leaned over the map, pointing to Lotrennia. "The Rising fighters have agreed to help push Daimos's forces out of northern Lotrennia before they return to Sultira. They left soon before we departed. And then there are the deaths." He turned toward me and paused, raising his dark eyebrows in question.

My chin dipped in confirmation to continue.

"I've sworn the oath," Astraeus growled from across the table. "We may as well speak freely." His dark eyes scanned the group, a note of deadly authority riding his tone. His eyes met mine and softened with the slightest bit of humor.

I threw every bit of irritation into my returning glare. *Don't you fucking dare.*

His lip twitched, and I yanked my gaze away before he was further tempted into tugging on that small bit of air connecting us.

"If we are speaking freely," Nerissa snapped, straightening as she looked the pirate lord in the eyes, "then tell us about those red cuffs and the cannonballs you used in the gulf."

Raek, who'd been standing in the corner and leaning

against the wall, straightened, shifting his position as he eyed the pirate lord. Astraeus merely scratched his short beard as he eyed Nerissa with indifference.

"What is there to say? The rubellines negate magic, cut it off at the source. It's a simple spell. A larger rubelline has a larger effect, nullifying the magic within a space, depending on size."

"How did you come about it?" Ronan asked.

"The Lords of Marisarma are treasure hunters," Astraeus murmured. "My crew discovered the stone used to create the rubelline long ago. We didn't learn of its use until an unfortunate accident."

"How many rubellines do you have?" Nerissa cut in. "This isn't just a defense. This is a weapon."

"A weapon vital in the wars to come, yes," Astraeus murmured, his dark eyes brightening. "I have two fewer cuffs and two fewer cannonballs than I did a month ago."

He lowered his dark eyes pointedly to my jacket pocket, where I kept the cuffs I'd taken from him. "Alas, we aren't here to discuss rubellines," he said, jerking his chin toward Drystan and raising his eyebrows.

Drystan rubbed the space between his eyes before continuing. "The fire pox isn't the only illness. Resurgences of a myriad of maladies have swept across Lotrennia. All accompanied by strange injuries."

Vulcan shifted next to me. "All over Lotrennia? Survivors?"

"No." Drystan's usual bright eyes dipped. "It's quick. The only connection we've identified is that the first group, the ones that died at the Awakening, were all covered in the same nebulis powder. But the others seem widespread enough that the powder seems to have had nothing to do with it."

*Powder...* A memory pricked my mind.

"This, on top of the ashen released on the northern

shores," Drystan continued, his hand movements slowing with fatigue. "Lotrennia is vulnerable."

Silence hung in the room like a veil in a windless night. I fingered the amber pendant on my neck, tracing the intricate designs on the amplifier with my thumb as I replayed his words.

There was too much happening in the world. Too many places to be at once, too many powers to use, levers to flip, favors to call in.

*Choices*, Xenelpha had stressed. It was all about choices.

"We're too far from Lotrennia to lend aid right now," I said slowly, my eyes locked on the map in front of us. "We aren't prepared to intercept Daimos's forces north of Sultira and continue to Lotrennia. We'd need more time for that."

I stood and leaned over the map of Vael. "But we have new weapons at our disposal," I murmured, thinking of the alliance with Astraeus and the rubellines. "If we could reconvene with the Rising forces in Sultira while Saros has eyes in the north..." I paused, glancing at Ronan, whose sapphire eyes brightened.

"We take Aedrialis while Saros is distracted," he finished for me.

"And then send aid north before determining when to return to Lotrennia." The words caught in my throat. The guilt of leaving Bayne, Isla, and Vander in Lotrennia.

We'd return. And when we did, we'd do it with a force. I paused, looking expectantly at Carina as I wiped the sweat from my neck. Her spectacles had slid down her nose as she shrugged her shoulders. The room was notably warmer than it was when we began the discussion.

"Nothing to add from the Heir of Lotrennia?" Astraeus asked, cocking his head to the side as he examined the young elf.

A small laugh escaped her lips. "Heir of Lotrennia? I'm no more an heir to the throne than you are king of Votruvia."

The knot in my gut tightened at her words, at their implication. Nerissa's knee pressed into mine. I sensed several sets of eyes on me, but kept mine pinned on Carina's face, now bearing the look of indifference.

"He is king. They are soulbound. She'll bear a new heir."

I swallowed, a surge of emotion clogging my throat.

*We are not the same.*

Bayne's words from all those months ago now echoed in my mind like a stinging warning. It had always been out of the question for us.

"When we were in Odessa, you said there were other Rising camps," Lord Astraeus cut in, finally sitting up, his boots landing on the wooden floor with a loud thump as he leaned his elbows upon his knees. "Do you have any idea where they'd be now?"

I released a sigh, grateful for the change in subject, and threw the pirate a cautious glance, but he kept his eyes averted.

Ronan gave a rough shake of his head. "Queen Antares suggested south, but who knows if that holds true."

Astraeus stood and leaned over the map, tapping the table with the various rings on his fingers. "We'll have to scout then. Good thing we have *two* fliers now."

The color leached from Nerissa's face as Astraeus turned his gaze toward us, raising his eyebrows.

A THIN HAND gripped my own as I made my way above deck. I whirled, coming face-to-face with Marian for the first time since Lotrennia.

"You've avoided me," she signed, her tired eyes fierce. Her hair seemed to have gotten grayer, little bits fraying from the bun she wore at the nape of her neck, still windblown from their journey.

"You're one to talk." I frowned, not realizing my blunder until the words had escaped my lips. My stomach pitched, and I opened my mouth to apologize, but her lips tilted upward.

"I know what you meant," she signed back. "Can we talk?"

Talk. About Oslo? I wasn't sure I could. The pit in my stomach grew as I added names, known and unknown, to the list of people whose deaths were on my hands.

"I don't blame you," she continued, without my answer.

I eyed her doubtfully.

She nodded, signing, "I *did* blame you. I hated you. But it was unfair. I know it killed you." She tapped her chest. "In here. I know it destroyed you inside."

My chest cracked. Warm tears threatened to form, and I snapped the little sliver in my heart shut.

"I am so sorry," I said without emotion, keeping my voice level. I'd said it a thousand times.

Streaks of silver lined Marian's eyes as she stared at me through her tears. She swallowed.

"I loved him," she signed slowly. "He saved me when my husband died, years ago. He tried to save him, too. He gave up everything to get me to safety."

"Tell me everything," I said, gripping her hand.

# CHAPTER FORTY-ONE

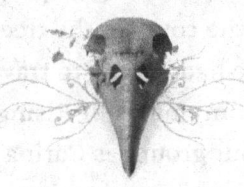

*Kyson will not bend. There will only be six Bellators Bones.*
*—Correspondence from Enya to Lelyth. Date preceding*
*Sultiran Calendrical System.*

Autumn wind filled my lungs like the first breath of air after the plunge. I melted against Tiberius's inky coat, soaking in his warmth as the wind picked up and we flew over western Sultira. We'd sailed south for the last six weeks, plotting, planning, and scouting.

Small towns dotted the coast before miles of farmland surrounding the Red River, flowing west from the Lake of Light. A smudge of gold stretched to the south as the Harena Desert unfolded in the distance.

My mind drifted to the foothills lining the eastern edge of the Lumerians and Enya's resting place. It'd been over a year since the discovery, since my life changed entirely. Over a year since my first trip on the *Evecta*. Since Bayne. Since... everything.

Golden fields yawned open below us, and Drystan pointed from behind me to a small grouping of trees in the distance, where Nerissa, white knuckling Aquila's feathers, landed. Marian stepped from the cover of the trees, hurrying to mount the massive hawk. She had agreed to travel to Krestwood for a few days to listen for any news of Rising forces. She was the least conspicuous of our group, as Carina pointed out. Most of us were either elves, pirates, or adorning wanted posters.

We banked and soared back to the *Hydra*, where Marian revealed all that she learned.

MY KNUCKLES RAPPED against the door to the captain's chambers, muffled voices and a scrambled thump sounding in response. The door swung open, as did my mouth.

Lord Astraeus's dark auburn hair was free of its braids and...disheveled. He'd slung on his sea blue coat, leaving the buttons undone. His tanned chest was bare and covered in scars, the snaking black ink that began at the strong column of his throat twisting its way down his shoulders before retreating behind his coat.

Two long slices ran vertically down both pectoral muscles, which appeared, to my greatest displeasure, cut from stone. The Marisarma *M* sat in the center of his chest, the large, gruesome brand leaving the skin raised and pebbled. Something about the damage pricked my consciousness, but I had no time to dwell on it as my eyes drifted lower to the knotted muscles rippling down his abdomen to the lines on his hips that led to the...

Oh gods. His leathers were undone.

My eyes snapped to where a lazy, satisfied grin formed on his lips.

His lips. Which I realized now curved against their fullness, looking unbelievably soft...

"Bonscaíh," he purred.

My gaze fell to the strawberry blonde perched on his bed, furs wrapping snuggly around her chest and waist.

The color leached from Vienah's face as her eyes shot to mine.

Mortified. We both were. I ground my teeth, irritated at the embarrassment he put her in, even if her presence here was... *unexpected*. Astraeus pulled the door halfway shut, though I could still see past his shoulder.

"I'm sorry. You shouldn't have answered if y-you," I stammered, looking back toward Vienah, whose face turned the color of my name day pie. My fingers fumbled with themselves until I wiped the sweat from the back of my neck.

"Had company," I finished, schooling my features as I looked back at Astraeus.

"Apology accepted," he crooned, grin widening as he leaned against the doorframe. "What can I do for you?" he asked, throwing Vienah a look that sent a tiny betrayal of heat shooting down my abdomen.

"Marian. She's back," I replied quickly, needing to put as much space between myself and the pirate as possible. I turned to leave when a hand gripped my forearm. I whirled toward him, outrage fueling the fire that replaced the whisper of feeling I'd had a moment ago. I yanked my arm, and his grip tightened.

His dark eyes sparked in curiosity as they slid along my forearm, watching my powers swirl beneath my skin, at the Transcindiel glow gilding the darkness.

"Take your hands off me," I hissed, allowing the spark of embers to light up the darkness of my own eyes.

He pursed his lips in a way that showed a hint of a smile as he dropped my arm and backed away. "I'll find you later," he murmured.

I whipped my arm back and stalked across the deck.

"WHAT WERE HIS *EXACT* WORDS?" Astraeus's insufferable, swaggering demeanor only worsened after his afternoon with Vienah.

An entire. Fucking. Afternoon.

"He said the rebels are at Demon's Door," Marian answered, irritation cutting through her normally relaxed nature.

*Demon's Door.* My mind replayed the lessons I'd received detailing Sultira's lethal prison.

Astraeus stared at the map on the large table we sat around for several long moments before his lips tilted upward in a triumphant smile.

"The rebels are *at* Demon's Door," Astraeus repeated, stressing the signed word. "They aren't being held captive there. They've *taken* the prison." He grinned, raising his eyebrows and giving Ronan an appreciative nod.

Marian blinked, processing his words.

"That took some balls," Astraeus praised.

A spark lit in Ronan's sapphire eyes, and he flashed a wide grin.

"How long until we arrive?" Kresida asked, the elven War Slayer leaning over the map to get a better look at the location marking Demon's Door.

"If the princess lends us a bit of wind," Astraeus said, eyes sliding to Carina, "less than a week."

"LYVIA," Vienah murmured as we shuffled out of the room. "Can we talk?"

"Of course," I mumbled, slowing and matching her pace, unsure why my stomach twisted.

"I just," she began as the evening sun cast deep orange ripples to the west, "wanted to talk to you about...earlier."

I offered a sympathetic smile. "Vienah, I don't care who you sleep with." I stopped at the edge of the ship and leaned over the rail. A spray of spindrift wafted from below, and I let out a soft sigh. "Be careful, though," I said, turning to her.

Vienah leaned over the rail next to me. "I know, I know. He's so..." She shook her head, sucking her lips between her teeth to suppress a smile.

*Oh gods.* "When did it start?"

"A couple weeks ago. We've been keeping it quiet... Didn't want to make the others uncomfortable. But gods, today... Today we couldn't stay away from each other. He is..."

I stole a glance as her tongue slid over her lower lip and quickly pulled my gaze away.

"Well, if he's a good fuck, then who am I to say anything?" I shrugged.

Vienah turned toward me, her expression sobering.

"He's unbelievable. I can't stay away. I'm a moth to a flame. He's unmatched"—she raised her eyebrows and shook her head—"in every possible way." Vienah held her hands apart and slowly pulled them away as if she were measuring...

I whipped my gaze away, shaking my head profusely. "Nope. No, no. I don't need that information," I said, avoiding her eyes. "Just be careful, yeah?" I stared at Astraeus's men bustling about the center deck.

Raek caught my gaze and glanced at Vienah, rolling his eyes with a soft shake of his head. He'd been rather grouchy this evening, and though I was unsure why, my emotions echoed his.

I turned my gaze east, to where a pod of pink creatures leaped through the waves in a dazzling pattern. I calmed my breathing and refocused my thoughts as I watched them. They chased one another to the edge of the horizon, their course unpredictable, yet they launched past one another in confident pursuit. Did they know where they were going? Or did their unwavering faith in each other simply lead them to an unknown destination?

I forced my jaw to relax, breathing in a salty gust of spindrift as the *Hydra* surged through a swell. I reflected on bonds I'd formed, on the warriors sailing with me and the ones we'd left behind. A reluctant admission emerged as the cool mist hit my face. My faith had wavered, these past few months. Some bonds began to crack, others bending and changing while new ones were formed. But despite the continuous evolution of my own pod, *I knew where I was going.*

# CHAPTER FORTY-TWO

*I will follow you. Beyond the Crimson Sea and what awaits*
*us in the dark.*
*—Correspondence from Ordell to Enya. Date preceding*
*Sultiran Calendrical System.*

The long, gray fortress of Demon's Door slid into view as we rounded the peninsula. Over a mile wide, the six-level prison held Sultira's most dangerous criminals, reserving the cells at the bottom of Mount Telum for prisoners of a more secretive value. Large, sharpened ivory tusks of some ancient beast lined the battlements like the gaping maw of massive fangs.

Sentinels stood at several posts above and below the prison, eyes on the *Hydra* as it approached in the distance. The slight breeze carried the soft floral scent of purple lapis trees off its coast.

*Ready to make an entrance?*

*Let's make them shit themselves,* Tiberius replied with a smile in his voice and an edge of anticipation.

I allowed myself a sliver of a smirk. Aquila leveled out next to us, and Ronan grinned widely as he took in the Rising's men stationed at the prison. Seated in front of him on Aquila's long back, Nerissa shot a look at me and Drystan before nodding.

My heart sang as Tiberius and I stretched our shadows into a large, sail-like shield, the Obscura bending to the Transcindiel's guidance as it transformed the darkness. We descended, aiming straight for the courtyard on the other side of the prison. Shouts rang from guards as we approached. We came in hot and tight, close enough that several sentries had to duck as we barely eclipsed the upper battlements, the caelumas' massive shadows like black clouds flying overhead. While arrows were poised, none were released as we landed.

Tiberius's hooves thundered down the gravel road, and as he flared his wings, slowing his speed, he allowed a small bit of gold and black power to escape into a cloud of shimmering darkness. Aelius's brilliant white light sparked from Aquila's wings, and he dropped down in the center.

I shot a look at Nerissa, whose palms held a little ball of swirling, white light as she dismounted and stood next to Ronan. Though Nerissa's face was a mask of neutral boredom, her skin paled from our entrance.

Drystan hopped off Tiberius with ease, my dear friend accustomed to being airborne by now. I swung my legs over Ti's broad back before hopping down. The massive, steel-plated domed doors clicked and slowly opened.

A middle-aged man with dark skin and a wicked scar along his neck stepped from the large archway and slowly clapped his gloved hands.

"Impressive, Commander," he said as he stalked forward.

Ronan tensed before straightening and striding up to the man.

"Good to see you, Lieutenant." Ronan clasped hands with the man, who eyed the rest of us with a kernel of distrust.

I did my best to match Nerissa's unimpressed look as we entered the Demon's Door.

"MOST OF THE cells are used as barracks, but we maintain the lowest level as a functioning prison," Lieutenant Einar said as he walked us through the prison's dark halls.

"What did you do with their previous occupants?" Drystan asked, Ronan interpreting for him.

Einar scoffed. "Seeing as half of them were Rising fighters, they're still here, only now they're well-fed and not tortured. The others, we took care of. No need to feed more mouths than necessary."

I blinked, the unease that arrived in the face of such brutality curiously absent.

"How many do you have stationed here?" Ronan asked, surveying the barracks and earning glances of admiration as we passed various groups of soldiers.

"Six thousand here in the prison and another five thousand at Khasimir," he murmured.

Ronan nodded his appreciation.

"But Saros has a force of about ten thousand occupying the Rellenor Fields. We've been trying to find a way around them for weeks," Einar continued.

We stopped as we reached the inner courtyard, where groups of men sparred in designated areas.

"Why not take Skyscape Pass?" Drystan asked, as he surveyed the warriors. A gust of autumn air whipped through the space, sending his shoulder-length hair flying across his face.

I interpreted for Einar.

He pursed his lips, shaking his head. "Skyscape Pass isn't safe right now. We've sent several scouting parties, and none have returned."

"Skyscape Pass isn't wide enough to house an entire host of soldiers unless they are passing through," Drystan replied, his brows furrowing. "What could have taken them out?"

Einar shook his head. "We're not sure. The men think it's haunted."

The Stone Witch's hiss slithered down my spine in a phantom whisper.

"What do the women think?" Nerissa asked, scanning the courtyard.

Einar blinked. She turned, her posture domineering as she looked down her nose at him.

"The families of the Rising soldiers are camped north of here in a small village we've taken control of."

"And the fighters?" she asked, pointedly.

Ronan cut her a cautious glance.

"We've no female fighters," Einar murmured. He shouted at a handful of men gawking at the four of us to get back to work.

Ronan cleared his throat. "Alright. The *Hydra* should be docking any minute. Lord Astraeus and his crew will keep their quarters on board. No need to spare barracks for them. Do you have space available for the rest of us here?"

Einar grumbled his agreement. "Aye, Commander. The prison is yours."

A nod from Ronan. Movement from the sparring yard caught my eye as a fight broke out.

"Lake scum!" a man shouted.

Einar let out a low swear as he mumbled his apologies and stalked toward two brawling men.

The larger of the two, a young man with light brown skin, threw his fist into the older man's jaw, sending droplets of blood flying from his lips. The older barreled into the younger, flipping him on his back. His head cracked against the stone pillar as he went down, and my pulse leaped as I caught a glimpse of the young man's face.

Einar shouted profanities at the two as he raced toward them, but my powers were faster. Twin ribbons of shadows shot from my palm as I let the Transcindiel power transform the Obscura into something lethal, yet tangible. The darkness stretched forward and wrapped tightly around the older man, pinning him against the pillar, suspended in midair.

Einar stopped short, whipping his head in my direction, face strewn with horror and disbelief as I held the soldier. Ezrich Hunt's face drained of color as he scrambled to his feet, eyeing the soldier in my bounds before he looked back at me with wide eyes.

Ronan nudged me in the ribs. "Easy. We don't want to scare them away."

I eased my grip on the soldier before dropping him to the ground. He shrugged out of the black ribbons as they coiled into my palms.

"I see they're getting along *very* nicely," Nerissa murmured, a smile forming on her lips.

I nodded. The two powers within me hadn't simply found the space to exist together in the chasm, but melded together, enough that I could influence the nature of the Obscura. Turn it into something tangible, and still deadly.

The Transcindiel required sacrifice. Less, if I merely nudged the essence of its focus. Khato said the two needed a binding agent. They were as oil and water. Tiberius and I still weren't entirely sure what that was, but some strange force surfaced at their pairing.

Whatever it was, we had enough of it in us. Maybe someday we'd figure out what that meant. For now, the ability to transform the raw power of death into something tangible was a weapon itself.

A flash of blue pulled my gaze across the courtyard, where Astraeus strode in with a small group of men. Hand on the hilt of his curved blade, he smirked as we made eye contact, as if in appreciation of my display. I threw him a vulgar gesture before turning back to the young man.

"Hi, Ezrich," I said, offering a small smile as Bear's son cautiously approached. I scanned the courtyard, a thimble of hope igniting in my chest at the thought of being reunited with his father or sister.

"Lyvia," he said, eyeing me up and down and shooting a cautious glance at Nerissa. "You're here. I heard the rumors... That it was you...but..."

I frowned, allowing the blaze in my irises to cool. "Didn't Bear explain what happened in Odessa?"

Ezrich frowned as he shook his head. "I haven't seen Dad since he left Rivaner for Odessa."

*Shit.* Where was Bear? And why hadn't he made it back to Rivaner to find Ezrich and Evony?

"What about Evony? Where is she?" I asked, reining in my fear.

Ezrich paled.

"He told me he sent her to safety, to Mum's cave. But when I went looking, she was gone. Cottage was burned to the ground. No sign of her."

Ezrich's voice broke toward the end, and my throat bobbed.

"Okay, we'll talk more soon," I said, nodding toward the approaching Einar.

Ezrich followed my gaze and hurried to his commanding officer.

"I'm going to the village to speak to the women there. Care to join me?" Nerissa asked as the peaceful fisherman from the Lake of Light moved into position with another partner and a short sword.

I shook my head. "No," I answered, "I'm going to Skyscape Pass."

# CHAPTER FORTY-THREE

*I've never trained harder. My powers have grown, and I'm
ashamed to admit, it scares me.*
—*Journal of Isla Jasira.*

The southern range of Lumerians squatted in gray
clusters against the dim horizon, the foothills bare by
comparison to those near Aedrialis. Rocks and
shrubs provided little shelter for the various packs of coyotes
and thin deer trudging through the hills.

Our flight took a few hours before we neared the split in
the cliffs that cut through the Lumerian mountain range.
Skyscape Pass was wide enough for a caravan to traverse, but
rocky in parts and known to flood. The Rising forces needed
this route to march to Aedrialis if they were to avoid Saros's
forces camped at the Rellenor Fields. Whatever threat hid in
these rocks needed to be dealt with.

Vienah's clouds dissolved into wisps as we flew farther

from her magic, but the sun had set, night gracing us with its cover. Tiberius landed on a wide strip of a bordering peak. He clomped to the edge of the cliff overlooking Skyscape Pass. Small cave openings and holes dotted the walls of the rocky cliff on either side, stretching sixty miles from one end to the other.

We flew most of the night, making two rounds on the entire stretch of the pass before returning to the small landing we came across, spying nothing out of order.

*Maybe we need to go down there,* Ti said after chomping through an apple I brought along for him. White foam lined his black lips as he chewed sloppily, letting bits of it drop to the ground. I stared at him for a moment, allowing my amusement to pass through our bond.

*I'm still a horse,* he quipped. *I don't have human lips.*

*Thank the gods for that.* I laughed, rolling my eyes. I tripped forward as his giant head nudged me from behind.

*There seems to be no threat from above, but something feels off out here...*

We flew to the center of the pass, and as Tiberius thundered down the rocky road, an arrow whizzed past us. He slammed on his hooves, reeling backward as I did my best not to fly from his back, a second arrow whipping past my face.

I threw my palms to the side, an orb of transparent darkness materializing around us. I squinted in the night, the darkness of the shield making it difficult to see through. I stretched it, widening its diameter, as small shadows dropped from holes in the walls of the rocky pass.

*Get ready, agrippa,* I murmured, as the dark shadows circled us, hundreds of them now closing in. I rallied my powers, ready to strike as a small voice called out from behind the line of creatures.

"Lyvia?"

My heart stopped. Mumbling gurgled from the strange creatures as they parted for the girl as she approached.

*What the fuck is Evony doing here?*

I dropped the shield, my powers siphoning back into the chasm as I stared at the creatures whose beady black eyes reflected Renova's blue light seeping in from miles above.

Those creatures... I'd seen one before.

I tensed, waiting for the intrusive grinding voice of the Stone Witch as I prepared to get Evony the hell out of there, taking out as many of these wretched creatures as I could. The black, membranous wings of the pig-nosed beasts hung limp at their sides, but they were dexterous little things, many of them swinging down from the sides of the cliff on makeshift ropes of aged vines.

The short, humanoid creatures bared sharp, yellowed canines at me as they approached, carrying small weapons of their own. Jagged rocks, broken shears, makeshift spears... Anything, it seemed, they could get their hands on.

I flexed my hands, ready to release the Obscura as soon as I got a clear view of Evony.

*We need something precise, so we don't hit her,* Tiberius's voice commanded.

I dismounted, letting the darkness pool in my palms in a small black cloud. I nodded, facing the direction of Evony's voice, waiting to get a clear view. Ti's tail swished as he turned to face the creatures circling us.

*Arrows,* I murmured back.

Evony escaped the tribute ship just to end up in the hands of the Stone Witch. A fierce, protective force of energy seemed to fuel the power pushing against my palms.

"Lyvia!" she called again.

I followed the voice as movement caught my eye. I urged the Transcindiel to join hands with the Obscura, transforming the swirling cloud of darkness into four lethal arrows. I flipped my palms, floating them into the air, poised at the creatures shuffling about.

Evony's hand shot up in the distance, and I slowed my breathing, ready to release, when the creatures parted for her.

"Oh, gods! Lyvia, is that you?"

The arrows of darkness quivered a moment, tugging on their leash. My heart stuttered in its hammering.

Evony shoved through the crowd and called to the creatures, "Stand down! She's a friend!"

*What in Tynan's Hell...*

Ti's responding snort echoed my disbelief.

The small beasts looked up at her in irritation but obeyed. They clamped their mouths shut and stayed their weapons.

Evony's bright blue eyes shone in the light of Renova, widening with disbelief as she choked out a sob and raced for me. I reined in the darkness, the Obscura mumbling its disappointment as I forced it back down.

Evony slammed into my chest, knocking the wind from me as she wrapped her arms around my waist and wept into my shoulder. I released my breath, taking her in my arms and squeezing as hard as I could.

I ran a hand over the back of her head before pulling her face away and giving it a good scan. Evony's long, curly brown hair had been plaited in tight, coiling braids that hung past her shoulders. A few scratches lined her cheeks.

"Where is she?" I asked, doing my best to hide the panic in my voice.

Evony blinked. "Who?"

Hundreds of beasts continued to gather in the pass. They filled the space between us and both cliffs, many still hanging down from branches or ropes.

"The Stone Witch," I breathed, still uncertain of our safety.

Evony frowned at me, following my gaze.

Silence rippled through the pass at my words. A scrape and thud muffled to our left, and the vibration of Tiberius's massive hooves hit the ground as he flanked me.

"She's okay," Evony said to the one-legged creature whose knit trousers had seen better days. "She's safe. I know her."

The creature narrowed its beady eyes at me.

"Gork," I murmured, remembering the name the Stone Witch had used last year in Crown Peak.

The creature mumbled something in its own language before looking at Evony. His malevolence dissipated as he turned his attention to the girl.

"Gork," Evony said, turning to him. "Is that your name?"

He nodded his response before turning away and barking a command at the others, who retreated up the cliffside. He stopped, turning and motioning us to follow.

"Come with me," Evony said, gripping my hand.

WE SAT IN A SMALL, damp cave. I'd sent Tiberius back to Demon's Door to communicate who and what we'd found at Skyscape Pass with Aquila. He would return with Vienah the next morning.

A makeshift cot sat in the corner, with mountain goat fur draped over the edge and a small sack of straw for the pillow at its top. And though Evony seemed at ease, even pouring a minty tea into a cup carved from birch bark, I couldn't shake that sense of *otherness*.

"Dad's face started showing up on wanted posters shortly after he left for Odessa," she said, sipping out of her own bark cup. "I was already up at Mum's haven when the soldiers came, but I'd run down to the house on occasion to grab more supplies. They must've been staked out for some time because they caught me on my trek down one day."

My stomach churned. "But Dad had built in a couple of traps along the path, ones I knew to avoid. Problem was, they'd seen where I went in. So, I had to leave."

"And you went deeper into the mountains?" I asked, noting how her warm, light brown skin seemed pale in the light of the flames.

Evony nodded and popped a couple of dried berries into her mouth. "Mhmm," she murmured, matter-of-factly. "And then I ran into the Ganels."

I blinked. "The what?"

She shrugged, nodding at the beastly creatures that shared the network of caves beneath the mountain.

"*Ganels*. Angels, in old Votruvian. Mum spoke it, and I know a fair bit. Anyways," she said, now grabbing a chunk of mountain goat meat and shoving it into her mouth. "They don't speak the common tongue, but they can understand it. I have no idea who the Stone Witch is... There's been no one else since I joined them."

Relief escaped my lips in a sigh, still unsure whether the Stone Witch was a true enemy or not, given the magic used to escape Kayj last year and whatever she did during the Battle of Odessa.

I shook my head, baffled as I digested what she'd said. Angels would have been the last name I'd have given the creatures bustling about the tunnels.

"Gork," she mused, staring at the wall. "I've been calling him Stefan."

"Stefan?"

She swallowed a large mouthful of meat before nodding. "Yeah. Like Stumpy Stephan from *Fabia's Fables*. You know, the boy who lost his leg because he didn't—"

I snorted and held a hand up, nodding. "Yeah, my father used to read them to me as well." My lips tugged up in a small smile as I shook my head.

"Anyways, I found them, or rather they found me after a few weeks of wandering. There are miles of tunnels and caves in the Lumerians. They were kind, so we decided to stick together. We made it to this pass about a month ago. A band of soldiers arrived... I thought they were Rising soldiers. And I went to ask about my dad and Ez... Ezrich was supposed to meet me in Mum's cave, but the kingsguards came too soon. I have no idea where he is."

I opened my mouth, but Evony grew quiet, setting her cup down, a shadow forming beneath her eyes. "I went down to meet the soldiers, to see if I could get a message out to either Dad or Ez, and..."

Her voice quivered, and she swallowed, her nails biting into the skin on her arms as she wrapped them around herself. Pools of liquid formed at the corners of her eyes.

"And what, Evony?" I asked, my tone quiet and soft, trying my best to keep the edge of fury from seeping into it.

She blinked, sending a small tear rolling down her cheeks. She rocked and shook her head. "Well, I don't know if they were Rising soldiers or a group of bandits, but they took everything I had, and then they..."

Her voice broke, and she bent forward, as if coiling within herself. The blood in my veins stilled as my powers rumbled. They surged forward, ready to rage against my palms, but I reined them in with quiet wrath.

Evony wiped her face and took a shuddering breath.

"Nothing happened," she said at last. "Stefan—*Gork*, I mean—and the rest took care of them before they could get what they wanted. Another group of them came through a few weeks later, and the Ganels killed them all. I didn't even know they'd shown up until I found them all slaughtered. I burned their bodies." She finally looked up and pinched her brows, tilting her head at me.

I swallowed a dry lump.

"Your eyes..." she whispered, glancing between them.

"I have a lot to share, too," I murmured, looking away. "But before I do," I said, taking her hands in mine, "Nothing that has happened has been your fault. None of it. You are strong. You are brave. You are smart. You are safe now. *I will keep you safe.*"

My heart squeezed for her. Morwyn's scream often pierced my dreams, accompanied by the look on Evony's face as her mother was cut down before her eyes. "Evony, you've endured more than any fifteen-year-old girl should ever have to."

A small smile formed on Evony's lips as she squeezed my hand back. "Sixteen now," she corrected.

I did my best to return her smile. "Well then," I said, "I suppose I have a belated name day surprise for you then."

# CHAPTER FORTY-FOUR

*Death comes for the snake and its books. Hurry.*
   *—Correspondence from White Hawk to Sea Spear. 50th of Summer, 071.3E.*

zrich and Evony's reunion should have brought tears to my eyes. But that delicate, soft part of me crouched beneath a wall of steel-lined shields. There was no choice. To fight for what mattered, to bear the scars of the decisions I made, those I'd yet to make, there was no room for it.

I left the brother and sister embracing in the courtyard, with Tiberius standing guard over Evony only a few strides away, before storming into the makeshift war room at the prison.

Lieutenant Einar threw me a disgusted glare as I swung the doors open, interrupting the six men who sat around the table, deep in discussion.

Ronan's eyes shot to mine. His light brows pinched in reproach. "How can we help you, Lyvia?"

I slid my gaze back to Einar, ignoring Astraeus entirely, who sat in the corner, one ankle crossed over the other. I could feel his insufferable smirk from across the room as he took in my disheveled look.

I'd spent one more night on the cliffs with Evony, attempting to communicate with Gork, who seemed to be the leader of the little army of beasts. From what I could glean, the Stone Witch was gone, and with my assurance Evony would remain safe, Gork would allow the Rising forces to pass through.

My eyes locked on Einar. "Who was the commanding officer of the first scouting party sent to Skyscape Pass?"

He glanced at Ronan before turning back to me. "Their captain was with them, he reported to Tertius."

"Where would I find Tertius?"

Einar stood, frowning at me. "And why would you need that information?"

I cocked my head. "Your men are dead, and your captain is to blame, as he allowed them to steal from and attempt to take advantage of a young girl. A sixteen-year-old *girl*. I'd have a word with his superior."

Einar's throat bobbed as Ronan swore, letting out an aggravated sigh.

"I don't trust her speaking to any of my men without supervision. She's dangerous." Einar jabbed a thick finger at me from across the room as a smile played on my lips.

Yes, I was dangerous. Dangerous when I was angry. And my blood *raged*.

Ronan sighed. "For fuck's sake." He scanned the map in front of him, eyeing all the little pieces representing Rising and

Sultiran forces, scattered across the battlements like pieces of a mehena board.

My eyes drifted to the fifty pawns in the southern part of the Crimson Sea.

"I'll accompany her," Astraeus crooned from the corner.

My jaw ached as my molars scraped against each other.

"I'll find Vulcan or Nis," I said to Ronan.

"Vulcan and Nerissa are in the village training a fearsome group of ladies," Astraeus purred from behind as he sauntered over.

Ronan's brows pinched, as if in apology. You've got to be fucking kidding me.

I left without a word. Astraeus kept pace with me at an annoying level of ease until I threw open the doors to the mess room, where a group of commanding officers sat at small tables.

Astraeus crossed his arms, leaning against the wall as I strode to the center of the room, letting my eyes simmer and darkness flood my veins.

"Tertius?" I called to the group.

While nobody said a word, several eyes shot to a portly man to my left. I sent a ribbon of darkness spearing through the room, a thick, black snake with golden eyes forming as it coiled around him, squeezing tightly.

"*Your men are dead,*" I seethed as silence cleaved the room. "The captain leading your men sent to Skyscape Pass decided their fate when he allowed ill-begotten behavior to take place."

I envisioned those terrifying moments in the festival tents at the Sun Dance celebration all those years ago as I let the snake tighten, my power a steady stream. The commanding officer's face reddened. A gasp sounded from behind, followed by a quiet snicker as Carina and Kresida arrived.

"Let me make this very clear," I said, turning to the rest of the commanding officers in the mess room. "Theft. Pillaging. *Rape...*" I let the last word dangle in the air, my eyes glowing a fierce shade of orange. "Will not be tolerated. You burn... You pillage... You hurt a single civilian in this war, in our march to Aedrialis, and I will turn you all to ash."

A SIGH ESCAPED my lips as I inhaled the leather, cedar, and grassy scent of hay. The stables were quiet when I stepped inside to inspect the herd of agrippa war horses. Eighty or so grazed on dying grass in the neighboring fields, makeshift pastures lined with branch fences. Another fifty were stalled. The unruly ones, I noted, as I strode down the aisle, most of them stomping, flattening their ears or snapping their teeth through the bars.

A handful of stallions, but mostly mares. Fierce and fearsome. I stopped at a particularly angry one, who charged the door as I stood near its bars. Part agrippa, part mountain horse, I realized, scanning her grey coat and the dappled spots on her flank. The whites of her eyes flashed through her dark gray forelock as she stared me down, the intent in her gaze more promise than threat. I allowed the burning orange to flash in my own...

*I dare you.*

She charged once more, fearless and wild.

A long whip sat next to her stall, and the burning in my eyes flashed. I picked it up, eyes sliding to the mare. Her rage simmered. I sent a kernel of Obscura into my hand and let the darkness devour the whip, falling into a little pile of ash on the stone floor.

I reached for the rope halter and lead before sliding the stall door open. The mare's eyes widened, and she tensed, ready to charge. I willed my heart to calm, the long-forgotten thrill of training a fire-spirited agrippa returning to my veins. I held my ground as I slowly lifted my free hand to her, closing a fist. She blinked, remaining where she was, tense and angry.

I waited.

*Ten bloody minutes.*

My arm began to shake, my shoulder burning until finally, *finally* the pigheaded mare took a tentative step forward and reached a velvety nose to my outstretched fist, close enough for her whisker to brush my knuckle. I dropped my arm and waited a moment as she heaved a sigh and began to lick and chew, shaking her head.

I stepped back, slowly sliding the stall door shut as I blew a sigh of my own. I jumped, turning to find Vulcan at the entrance of the stables.

"*Aelius save me*, Vulcan," I breathed. "Elves and your fucking stealth. I nearly turned you to a pile of ash."

Vulcan's lips twitched. "These agrippa need work," he murmured as I stepped toward him.

"That's an understatement," I scoffed.

"Lieutenant Einar says most of the forces here are either criminals or survivors from tribute towns. They hate Sultiran soldiers and anything that represents them, including the agrippa."

My jaw tightened as I thought of the whip. "One of the many things that will need to change before we march on Aedrialis," I murmured.

"Indeed," Vulcan agreed.

His eyes slid to me, and I waited for him to chastise me for my actions from an hour ago. Word must have gotten out by now.

"I'll be in the sparring ring when you're ready," he said before peeling away.

I LEAPED BACKWARD, slapping Vulcan's forearm away, my boots sliding on the muddy ground as he threw a second jab, catching me in the ribs. I chucked my knee up as he advanced, knocking it aside with his thigh as he caught me in the ribs once more before throwing me to the ground.

Fast. They were so *fucking* fast. I would never be able to match their speed. Vulcan pressed an ink-covered forearm against my throat, pushing the air out, before I finally tapped his shoulder twice. The ribbons of scars and splotchy ink that lined his face were healed and opaque.

"I'm sorry," I said quietly.

His brows pinched for a moment. "For?"

I looked pointedly at the side of his ruined face.

Vulcan rolled his eyes. "You apologize too much. I've had worse injuries," he murmured, standing and offering me a hand.

I reached for it, popping up to my feet and rubbing my ribs. "Astraeus is an asshole. So is Raek," I said, adjusting my stance to prepare for his next advance.

"Raek was following orders," Vulcan murmured, as he slid his foot against the mud, getting the best grip he could.

"You're defending him after what he did on the *Hydra*?" I asked.

Vulcan leaped to the side. I scooted around him, following the dance steps that had become as natural to me as riding.

"You would have done the same if someone had attacked Bayne the way I went at Astraeus," he said as I parried his blows, flying around the muddy ring.

I blinked.

"Oh, my gods," I panted. "You're right. I didn't really notice it before, but...the way he looks at him."

Vulcan nodded. My stomach twisted as a question formed in my mind. *Would I have done the same?* I hadn't really examined my own feelings, to come to terms with the thread that had slowly begun to unravel...

"Astraeus doesn't feel the same," I said, pulling away from my thoughts and dodging a few more attacks.

Vulcan shook his head and arched back in an unnatural angle as I spun into a kick I was certain would land at his ribs. I tripped, the momentum of my miss sending me slipping into the mud, before I caught my balance and got my feet under me. Vulcan opened his mouth as Ronan's voice boomed from the prison.

"Cantor!" he bellowed, his voice ripe with a level of rage and authority I'd yet to hear from the ex-queensguard.

"Good luck," Vulcan murmured as he reached for his jacket hung on a nearby post.

I schooled my features before turning to Ronan, whose face was as red as the crimson border of the white cloak he used to don.

"What in Tynan's Hell is wrong with you?" he seethed as he hopped over the fence and strode over to me.

I pulled my gaze to my bloody and muddy hands as I unwrapped the strips of wet fabric, balling them up and sticking them in my pocket.

"I'm sure I have no idea what you're talking about, *Merik*," I said in the most innocent voice I could muster.

"Lyvia," he said, leveling a deadly stare, his sapphire eyes gleaming with wrath. "You threatened fifty of my commanding officers. *They are on our side.*"

"If they are your commanding officers," I said, keeping my voice soft and sweet, "then *you* get them in line, Commander."

"I was in a strategic briefing! You don't think I'm going to address shit behavior like that? You didn't even give me a chance. Leash your anger or get the fuck out of this prison. Stop acting like an animal."

I resisted the urge to bristle. "Speaking of animals," I said, glancing at the stables. "We need to talk about their treatment of the agrippa."

Ronan looked up to the sky as he groaned. "Burning Aelius, Lyvia. For fuck's sake—"

"They've been mistreated, Ronan," I cut in, unable to keep my temper from slipping. "You want this battalion of criminals and country folk to ride to battle on the most fearsome equines in the Realm of Vael. They need to be trained. All of them."

Ronan threw his arms to the side in defeat. "Fine, fine. Train the damn horses. Do whatever you need to do to keep that temper in check."

I blinked at him. "I'm not talking about training the *horses*," I snapped.

Ronan rolled his eyes. "Fine. We'll work on that. We'll work on the men. I've got enough shit to sort through to prepare us to march through Skyscape Pass if we're going to try to leave in two weeks. Keep your temper and your powers in check, Lyvia. Or you're staying on the *Hydra* from now on."

"Like hell I am!" I fumed as Ronan left without another word.

# CHAPTER FORTY-FIVE

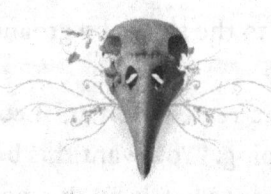

*Lord Haro of Marisarma attacked our ships at the dawn of summer. The rest have not been heard from.*
  —*Correspondence from Sea Spear to White Hawk. 50th of Autumn, 071.3E.*

As my rage simmered in the coming days, I funneled it down, deep down, into the chasm where my powers slept, fueling them as we prepared to march toward Aedrialis.

The round stone containing Faron's Bellator Bone sat infuriatingly quiet on my cot in the corner of the small cell I shared with Evony. Nerissa had personally taken to her training and had her in the courtyard sparring with Vulcan daily.

Vienah sat across from me, her dark leggings peeking from beneath her travel dress. Carina adjusted her spectacles as she leaned forward on the chair next to us and moved the round stone to peer at its top.

The membranous wings etched across the top arched around the edges. In its center, a small, hand-sized indentation spiraled. The bone flitted quietly, the power inside waiting and watching as the three of us failed once again to unlock it.

"The riddle on the entrance to the tomb could mean a lot of things. What else did Xenelpha say to you?" Carina finally asked.

I pressed my palms into my eyes, closing them against the growing ache that had begun.

"She said a lot of things," I muttered. "But when she talked about opening the stone, she stressed *'who was I?'*"

"Did she ask you any other questions?" Vienah asked, tucking a strand of strawberry blonde hair behind her ear. Her head tilted curiously as she stared at the stone container.

"About a hundred," I said, about ready to hurl the damn stone out the tiny window. Soft light filtered in the small cell in Demon's Door. "I'm sorry," I added quickly, throwing an apologetic look her way. "I'm just really stuck."

"Think," Carina added cautiously, adjusting her spectacles.

"She asked where would I go? Would I bring destruction or hope?"

A knock rapped at the door, and Drystan's copper face peered in.

"Sorry, I'm late," he signed, shuffling inside. He stretched his arms and cracked his neck as he pulled over another chair.

"It's okay. We're getting nowhere," I muttered, signing the words.

"What does it feel like?" he asked, his crystal, almond eyes thoughtful.

Carina cocked her head at my friend.

"She could feel the others," he explained, turning toward me. "You told us it sounds like wings. But what does it *feel* like?"

My brows pinched as I turned back to the stone and waited for that soft little pull. A small breeze seemed to flit from the wings of whatever power rested inside its stone chamber. I let it drift to me, and I pushed a little Transcindiel power into the feeling as it floated through the room.

"The wind," I finally replied.

My eyes landed on Drystan as they blinked open. The wind fluttered through his long ebony hair, and my heart stopped.

Drystan's almond-shaped eyes, his copper skin, somewhat darker than what was seen in Aedrialis, but warmer than the brown skin in other parts of Sultira. I replayed the old elven words etched on the lid of Faron's tomb.

*Life is nothing without it.*

*As small as a thought; as strong as the tides.*

*As quiet as whispers; as loud as thunder.*

*It exists in the light and the dark...*

"Destruction or hope," I breathed, my heart picking up its beat. "Xenelpha said, 'Will you bring *demin* or *m'ando?*'"

My eyes snapped to the hand-sized, indented section of the round stone. Could it be possible?

"I'll bring it m'ando... *hope,*" I signed the word, my eyes boring into Drystan.

His raven brows pinched as his eyes narrowed on me.

"*Drystan Amando.* Drystan, it's *you.* This is your power."

His head began to shake as Vienah and Carina eyed me with uncertainty.

"This is it," I said, my words and hand signals firm with conviction. "Drystan, you have always been my hope. Our years in study... As friends... Last year, when we found Enya's chamber... When you came for me in Kayj... You bring hope to everyone. And your surname, *Amando...*"

A smile formed on my lips as I continued. "*M'ando* is hope in Rhashtai. *You* are Rhashtai. This power is yours."

344

Drystan's throat bobbed as he continued to shake his head. Drystan had been orphaned in Krestwood. He'd never known his family.

"Prove me wrong," I said, the grin widening on my lips. "I've been talking to this damn stone, and it has been *laughing* at me. You need to *sign* it. Here."

I motioned to the smooth indentation as I shoved the stone in Drystan's shaking hands. His eyes slid down, examining the space.

"I am not a Bellator. I'm—" he finally replied, dragging his gaze back to mine. Doubt and fear hovered over him.

I reached forward and clasped his hand in mine. "You are *hope*, Drys."

His hand hovered over the space for a moment before he signed the word for *hope* into the indentation. How the Bellators of old knew the next person to claim this power would use hands to communicate was beyond me, but I didn't care.

Vienah gasped as wind stole through the room, followed by a smooth hush like the brush of sand as the round stone dissolved in Drystan's hands. The ivory Advetis Bone purred in excitement upon finding its master.

THE SHRILL CAW of crows perched along the makeshift fence cut through the autumn wind that floated over the browning grass we stood in. Drystan's fingers wrapped tightly around the Advetis Bone, his knuckles whitening as his brows pinched in concentration, yet something vulnerable flickered in his eyes.

Drystan's eyes pinched closed, and he blew a tight breath through his lips. His muscled shoulders tensed for several seconds before he threw his head back and chucked the bone into the grass, letting out a frustrated growl. We'd been at it for hours.

"It's okay," I signed once he brought his gaze back to my own. "I get how you're feeling. The Obscura did nothing for me for days."

We still had no idea what power rested in the Advetis Bone, which significantly impacted our training sessions. What were we even trying to do? He ran his copper fingers through his long black hair and frowned at me before pulling his hands roughly away.

"It only worked for you when your life was at stake," he interjected.

I plucked the ivory bone out of the grass and handed it back to him, a thought popping into my mind.

Before I could question it, I slammed my fist into his cheek.

Drystan let out a shocked yelp, his hands flying to his face where a flood of blood rushed from his nose. Immediate regret choked out the feeling of utter stupidity, and my hands slapped over my mouth.

"I'm so sorry!" I signed and cried aloud. "I thought maybe it was a reflex thing! Like you needed to be in danger and the bone would activate!"

Crimson lines dripped down Drystan's chin as he leveled an incredulous look at me. He pinched the bridge of his nose and shook his head before letting out a soft chuckle.

"I think I'm done for today," he finally signed.

I pulled out a dirty handkerchief from my coat and reached for him, but he waved me away, giving me a cautious, friendly smile instead, before returning to the prison.

THOUGH NO MORE OF Drystan's training sessions with the Advetis Bone ended with bloody noses, the results remained the same, and after a while, his soft reluctance grew into deep doubt.

The eve before our trek to Skyscape Pass, I found myself on the back of the testy mare. I'd been able to slide a rope halter on her head and tied her lead into makeshift reins.

Tiberius had some influence over the agrippa. They all seemed to defer to him, to recognize him as herd leader. But this one. She was fierce. Unbridled. A storm of her own... A *tempest*.

Though she was thinner than Tiberius before his transformation, she was tall. My legs dangled over her sides as she stood ramrod straight in the field, head high, and ears back. I relaxed every muscle in my lower body, feeding her as much calm energy as I could muster, despite the growing tempest within my own being.

I slid my hand through her mane as I gripped her leather lead and let my legs drift to the edge of her sides. Her ears flattened, but she didn't buck. I rubbed the side of her neck, doing my best to soothe her, as thunder cracked from above. Tempest twitched, and then she exploded.

Her neck arched as she threw her back legs up with a force to be reckoned with. My legs squeezed around her sides to keep my seat. She threw two more, and I tugged one side of her lead to the right, pulling her head along with it before yanking it back tightly. She yielded for a heartbeat before she realized what I'd done. She ripped the lead back, straightening out and took off down the field.

*For fuck's sake.*

My thighs burned as she flew down the brown field. Drops of rain slickened the ground while she threw in bucks along the way. I clung to her as she turned sideways, crow-hopping like a psychotic idiot.

*Get off her,* Tiberius commanded.

*Stay out of it,* I snapped.

*She's a lost cause,* he said.

*You are distracting me!*

Thunder clapped again, and I used the distraction to grab hold of her head with the lead. I kept talking to her, soothing her through ragged breath, finally gaining enough control to turn her back to the direction of the prison. Ti's wave of concern reached me before his shadow passed overhead.

We neared the stables, and she didn't slow. I dug my right boot into her side, sliding it back as I pulled with the right rein.

Fuck, we had to slow down.

Tempest eyed the building as we neared, seeming to realize it too late, and slammed on her hooves, sending her rear end slipping beneath her as she tumbled to the ground.

My head slammed into the mud, right leg barking in pain as she landed on top of me for a heartbeat before leaping to her feet and trotting off.

I blinked against the stars forming in my vision and groaned as I rolled to my side. Thunder cracked again, followed by an intense downpour. Tempest crept toward me, her velvety snout blowing a puff of air against my head. Footsteps approached, and she backed away.

A hand reached down, hauling me to my feet. My vision tunneled, and I swayed, another hand gripping my other arm, steadying me. I scowled as I turned to find Astraeus's smirk too close for my liking.

"That was fun to watch," he murmured, his dark eyes changing from two to four and back to two again.

Bile rose to my throat as I tried to pull out of his arms, but he held firm. I opened my mouth to say something rude when nausea seized me, and I emptied the contents of my stomach across the front of his sea blue coat.

"Oh gods, Lyvia!" Vienah called from nearby.

Mumbled talking sounded before I yielded to the beckoning darkness.

# CHAPTER FORTY-SIX

*The power is a drug, and the queen is addicted. It is tied to our bond, and I'm learning to control it.*
    —*Hidden correspondence from Bayne to Khato.*

T he whir of a tea kettle brought me back to consciousness, and I blinked my eyes open as Marian's forest green dress swished past. Cedar swarmed my senses, and I stiffened. I was back on the *Hydra*.

"How is your head?" Marian signed as she approached.

I closed my eyes, pinching the bridge of my nose as I did so, the head in question absolutely pounding.

"Why am I on the *Hydra*?" I asked, doing my best to keep the bile in my stomach down.

"Prison's been attacked," Marian signed back.

The world spun as I sat up.

"What do you mean? When?" I asked, frantic. This could

*not* happen again. The bloody fields of Odessa hovered like a wraith in my mind.

"It's under control," she signed back, placing her hands on my shoulders and easing me back down. "Aquila spotted them through the clouds. Minimal casualties."

Shit. *Shit.*

"We need to get to Skyscape Pass *now*," I said, realizing Marian was right and that I needed to keep horizontal, for now.

She nodded as she poured a mug of tea. "They are on their way," she signed before handing it to me.

I opened my mouth, and she let out an exasperated sigh.

"We're sailing around the south of the continent to reconvene with the rest of Lord Astraeus's forces and meet up with the Rising in Khasimir. Vulcan, Vienah, and Evony are here. Well, Evony's somewhere. Probably out for a ride on your caeluma. That girl," she signed, shaking her head. "Adolescent and pigheaded."

Marian rolled her eyes as she moved to the corner of the room where a washbasin sat. I leaned back, heaving a disgusted sigh.

"You are concussed," she signed, turning toward me once more. "Don't think about taking Tiberius for a ride. You'll tumble right off."

By the next evening, I was steady enough to wander above deck to find a group of men huddled together, many kneeling on the ground as they tossed three six-sided dice to the ground. The various celestial symbols on their sides somersaulted before landing, causing a chorus of hollers to rip through the crowd.

The loser stood and shook his shoulders out, cracking his neck as he raised his fists and turned to face a hulking form standing to the side. Vulcan, I realized, as his brows narrowed in anticipation and a hint of a smile tugged at his lips.

They sparred for less than a minute before Vulcan pinned Astraeus's man to the deck. The pirates howled in laughter, cheering in delight as they exchanged wagered goods.

I crossed my arms as I approached, doing my best to blend into the men in the back and stay unnoticed. Vienah moved to my side, grinning as she watched.

"It's called Goddess Gift," she whispered, nodding to the game. Her grin widened as she took in Astraeus, crouched at the center, grinning from ear to ear.

To my greatest displeasure, Astraeus's dark gaze found me. Vienah blossomed as his eyes skipped to her, and she straightened, striding forward as his men parted and finding a seat on his knee.

"Join us," he called, raising his dark brows at me.

I pulled my gaze away and looked pointedly at Vulcan before arching a brow.

"When you all are done measuring the lengths of your *swords*," I called, glancing back at Astraeus, "I'd have a word with you."

Astraeus's grin widened, and the enderleaf smoke between his lips dipped. His white teeth flashed in the lantern light as Tiberius's hooves pounded down the deck.

I whirled toward Ti and gaped as Evony slid off his back, beaming ear to ear. The game picked up again behind us.

"You were out flying?" I asked, incredulous.

"The night is the best!" Evony exclaimed. "The stars are incredible. Being so close, I feel like they are mine."

I stared for a moment before whirling toward Tiberius.

*You've been taking her out at night?*

Tiberius snorted.

*Are you kidding me? I told her I'd keep her safe!*

Tiberius pinned his ears as he snaked his head toward me. *Are you implying I'd let her fall?*

My molars scraped. *I didn't mean it like that...*

*She's been underground for months.*

I swallowed, turning to Evony, whose eyes hopped between the two of us.

"Are you seriously talking about me in your heads?" she asked, her voice pitching in outrage.

"I'm sorry," I said. "I don't mean to hover. I just—"

"You're not my mum, Lyvia," Evony said, her temper rising rather quickly.

I blinked. "I'm not trying to be. I'm trying to keep you safe—"

She bristled before rolling her eyes and storming below deck. My mouth fell open, and Ti blew out a low snort that sounded dangerously close to a laugh.

Evony was a *teenager*. Was that the otherness I sensed from her? Was *I* like that at her age? Gods, what I'd give for a swig of ridecus right now...

"*Dathuil,*" Astraeus purred as he sauntered up to us, a woody wave of enderleaf smoke wafting with his voice.

I blinked.

"Your word," he said, smirking as he flicked the joint over the edge of the ship.

I bristled, my irritation growing by the second. "What?"

"Dathuil. Handsome... Dashing... Charming. In old Votruvian." He cocked his head as he looked down at me. "You asked for a word."

I blew out an exasperated sigh, doing my best to quell the rising annoyance.

"Evony and I will leave in the morning. They need us at Skyscape to pass through safely."

We'd talked it through already. Evony agreed her little friends would feel more comfortable letting the group through if we accompanied them.

"No, you won't," Astraeus said, authority rumbling through his tone. "That would be foolish. You'd risk exposing yourselves over the Rellenor Fields, where we know Saros's forces are stationed."

I straightened my shoulders, doing my best to paint Nerissa's look of superiority on my face, to look down my nose at him despite needing to crane my neck to meet his gaze.

"Then we'll take Vienah with us for cloud cover," I said, matching his tone.

"Vienah's going nowhere," Astraeus growled, his voice lowering.

"Vienah will go wherever the hell she wants," I snapped.

"What's going on?" Vienah asked as she approached behind Astraeus.

Something flickered in Astraeus's eyes at the sound, and muscle feathered in his jaw.

"I was just telling Astraeus that we plan on leaving tomorrow morning to accompany the Rising through Skyscape Pass."

Vienah's eyes softened on mine, and her strawberry blonde brows tilted up. She glanced at Astraeus, who slid a hand around her waist, before agreeing with the pirate lord that it made most sense to stay on board.

My anger strained against its leash. I leaped on Tiberius's back and shot into the night sky. Astraeus's gaze lingered as we disappeared into the black, moonless night.

BETWEEN EVONY'S ADOLESCENT CHEEK, Vienah's unending need to ravage the pirate lord, Vulcan's unexpected geniality toward the *Hydra's* crew, and Astraeus's incessant arrogance, my mood improved very little over the next weeks. My powers simmered deep below.

*Patience.*

Tiberius echoed the prayer as we trained daily. We would slay one monster at a time. And when we returned to Lotrennia, we'd bring the full force of the Bellator powers with us.

I tunneled my focus into my training sessions with Vulcan, passing them on to Evony when she would listen. Astraeus's wind, a musky combination of leather and cedar, quickened our travel to an impressive level. The dull shores of late autumn Sultira were now in sight.

*My* EYES *blinked open to darkness. The door to the cabin swung open, and the captain's dark figure filled the space, the soft blue of midnight illuminating his silhouette. An intoxicating breeze followed as he stalked forward, raucous laughter and music beckoning beyond the open door.*

*The space between us went taut. My heart thumped wildly in my chest as a longing snaked its way down my lower abdomen, heat quickly pooling between my legs. We only had a few precious minutes of time together. And we'd waited so long. Too long.*

*He crossed the space in two strides, and his rough hands slid into my unkempt hair, his fingers twining and twisting through the strands as his smooth lips crushed against mine. My arms wrapped around his neck as his lips slid to that space beneath my ear. He nipped at my lobe before his teeth slid to my neck, my blood pulsing beneath the skin where his tongue touched.*

*More.*

*More of this, my body, my mind, my soul screamed at me. My hands slid down his chest, too quick to register anything but the feel of his skin and the goal of reaching his pants.*

*A howl of laughter bellowed from outside the door.*

*Hurry, I urged him, please.*

*We moved, and my backside thumped into something hard. A bed, a desk, I wasn't sure, because my hands found the warm, hard length of him. His thick, bulging cock tightened as I palmed him above his leathers, and he let out a groan, the sound pure, primal desire. I smiled against his lips, teeth grazing against his own.*

*My fingers loosened the ties, and he was free. And damn was he perfect.*

*"How do you want it?" he murmured against me.*

*I melted at the sound of his voice, an octave lower than I'd ever heard it.*

*"Fuck me," I rasped, my words a desperate whisper.*

*His lips curved into a wicked grin. He flipped me around, hands at my hips, sliding to my own leathers. Another burst of shouting and laughter echoed from beyond.*

*"Please," I breathed into the darkness.*

*My hands slapped against the cool desk as he yanked my leathers halfway down my thighs, the laces ripping free. His hand slid up my shirt with swift ease before he cupped my breast, as claiming as the teeth sliding across my neck. His other hand slipped between my legs, and he let out a soft string of curses as his fingers brushed against my soaked center.*

*And then he was in me.*

*He wasted no time. He thrust himself, filling me to his hilt, the stretch a delicious burn. He hit that inner wall, and I bent forward over the desk, the cool wood smooth against my cheek. I slid against it. Over, and over, and over again as he moved inside of me. He gripped my hip with one hand as he drove home, the other sliding up my back beneath my shirt. He moved perfectly within me, burning and pulsing combined in a mad array of pleasure.*

*"Fuck me," I moaned.*

*He went deeper.*

*His hand left my hip and slid to the front of me, his fingers meeting the drenched bud of nerves at my center as he slammed in from behind. My breathing hitched. Two rising, pulsating sensations collided as stars exploded behind my eyes in waves of pleasure. I convulsed, my body a distant, uncontrollable thing as warmth flooded through me and a whimper of pleasure escaped my lips.*

*He growled in response, as if the sound itself was his undoing, before withdrawing to the tip and slamming back in. The movement came faster the next time, and he roared into the darkness of the cabin, the entire ship shaking with his completion.*

*His scarred chest was on my back as he slumped over, hands sliding along the smooth desk and under my own. I interlaced my fingers with his as his breath tickled my ear, his lips leaving little prints of kisses along my neck. My finger rubbed against the cool metal of his rings...*

*Rings...*

*Since when had—*

Pain ripped through my forehead as it slammed against the beam of wood that jutted off the ceiling of my bunk on the *Hydra*. I pinched my eyes shut as my head fell back onto the mattress.

*A dream.*

I wiped my soaked fingers on my leathers, which were in fact unlaced, as I realized what had happened. And *who*, exactly, I'd been dreaming about while I...

I searched the dim room in a panic. Mortification sliced through me as I poked my head over the bunk to peer down at the slim mattress below mine. Evony's chest gently rose and fell, her breathing heavy. Thank the gods, she was asleep. I was certain I'd die from embarrassment. I eyed the small window and sent a silent prayer of thanks to Ganmira as the tip of her crescent shape illuminated the opposite wall.

I had to get the hell off this ship. I sent a tendril of power into my bond with Tiberius and sensed his response.

I crept from our small room and up the stairs, a cool breeze slipping past the barrier around the ship. My hands found the wide edge of the rail, and I closed my eyes as I waited for Tiberius.

A door clicked, and I whipped my head around to find Astraeus standing in the doorway of the captain's quarters, rage simmering in his dark irises. Shame snaked its way through my chest at the sight of him, equally disheveled and flustered despite his fury. A small part of me sagged in relief at his lack of elf senses, certain Bayne would have scented me a mile away.

He bared his teeth as he reached the edge of the quarter-deck and flung his feet over the side, not bothering with the stairs as he stormed toward me, a ringed finger pointed at me in accusation.

"*YOU!*" he whisper-screamed at me. "Stay the *fuck* out of my head—"

Oh gods... What the fuck had just happened? *Had he shared the dream with me?*

He was feet away, his cheeks red in either anger or equal embarrassment. Humiliating dread raced through me as he closed the gap, and I spun toward the rail, planting my hands and vaulting over its edge.

# CHAPTER FORTY-SEVEN

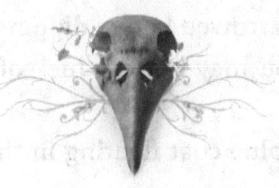

*The snake has been caged, though it took a great deal of his power. The king is weak.*
    *—Correspondence from General Calvus. 61$^{st}$ of Autumn, 071.3E.*

lthough Tiberius had rescued me from the wild swells of the Thandal Sea, our midnight escape from the *Hydra* did little to prevent me from drowning in my own mortification.

Back in his freshly laundered sea blue coat, Astraeus stalked to where I stood the next morning, cornering me with an icy gaze.

"I'll say this once. I don't take kindly to people prying their way into my mind," he seethed, his eyes darkening in threat.

The phantom intrusion of the Stone Witch's cackle pricked against my mind, an eerie reminder of her power. *I was not her.*

I opened my mouth to protest.

His voice lowered further. "From now on, you stay the fuck away. We interact only when needed. You do it again, I'll find a way to end you. Air oath be damned."

I bared my teeth at his threat. "I had nothing to do with that dream. I abhorred it as much as you did. Probably more."

His dark eyes narrowed before dipping to my lips. "I doubt that very much. You may get the fuck off my ship whenever you're ready."

He turned, his blue coat floating in the breeze, dismissing me.

My blood raged. "You do not give me orders, Astraeus."

He stopped for a moment, turning as if he would say more, anger rippling off his powerful shoulders as Tiberius hammered down the center of the main deck. A muscle tensed in Astraeus's jaw, and I gave him a cocky grin as I stepped past without another word.

*Ready?*

Ti snorted in reply.

Vulcan cocked a blonde brow at me in question as I approached, and I shook my head. He gave Evony a leg up onto Ti's back.

"I'll send horses for you. Expect them by tomorrow morning," I said to Vulcan as he handed me my bow and quiver. I slung them over the twin blades strapped to my back.

Vienah stepped forward in a dusty mauve travel dress.

"You're sure you're okay staying on board for another day or two?" I asked.

Vienah nodded, a hint of pink rouging her cheeks. "I'm safe here," she murmured, glancing at Astraeus's cabin before turning to me.

"Clear skies for your journey." She smiled. "I should be able to keep the clouds off for a few hours. Will that be enough?"

I nodded my thanks. "It will. Thank you."

"Be careful, Lyvia," she said. "You don't want to scare them too much."

Vulcan slid his gaze to her, his brows angling downward in his usual frown. Vienah did her best not to balk under his stare but averted her eyes and reached for my hand, giving it a squeeze in farewell.

"Careful with him," I warned her again, guilt slamming into my chest at the images my stupid mind had conjured in the middle of the night.

She rolled her eyes and smiled. "Kellan's not what you think he is." Her lashes fluttered before she floated to the pirate lord at the helm.

"She's not entirely wrong," Vulcan murmured as he finished checking the straps on my blades and quiver.

My head snapped to him.

Vulcan blinked at my reaction before returning his features to their usual scowl.

"Not that. Though Astraeus's crew is...." He paused, eyes flitting to Raek and the others bustling about. "Surprisingly honorable. I meant the soldiers. The rest of the Rising forces will be here. They know Ronan has brought you, that you're friends. You threaten them. They could lose faith in him. He doesn't lead by fear, and neither should you."

I bristled at the unexpected lecture.

"I'm not their leader," I finally said, shaking off his rough hands. "I am a weapon. And I'll make it clear what will happen should they step out of line."

Vulcan handed me a waterskin. "And I'll help you," he said, lip twitching into a hint of a grin.

My eyes softened, surprised at the sudden support.

Evony scooted to make room, and Vulcan stepped back as Tiberius stretched his massive wings before angling them back.

I grabbed a fistful of his mane as Evony wrapped her arms around my waist. That otherness I sensed since Skyscape Pass seemed to pulse as she pressed against my back. Tiberius thundered down the center aisle, and my stomach dropped as he threw a gust of air down the deck with his mighty wings, flying past the mainsail, billowing in Astraeus's wind.

As we neared Khasimir, a sea of Rising tents rose beyond the city. Ti banked and let the Obscura swirl from his wings into a cloud of shadows. I pushed a tendril of Transcindiel into the raw darkness, transforming pieces of it into tiny shimmering shards, reflecting off the autumn sun like a black rainbow cast across the sky as we arched around miles of Rising forces.

IT HAD BEEN six months since I'd last stood in a Rising's war tent, listening to Ronan argue with the other commanders, discussing attacks, counterattacks, and intelligence.

Apparently, the Rising commanders in the south were able to afford a more lavish camp living as I lounged in a velvet chaise in the corner of the large war tent, while Ronan and six others leaned over a detailed map of Aedrialis. Vulcan loomed in the corner a few feet from me, eyes intent on the planning taking place.

It was strange being back in Khasimir. The southern city held memories, most of which were too painful to drum up. Too warm, too nostalgic. Too many with Aeriden's face among them. Even stranger was the absence of the reigning lord. Jon Pavel, my father's close friend and ally, was nowhere to be found. His villa had been abandoned, and his fleet was nowhere to be seen. Lord Pavel commanded a large force of

Sultiran naval ships. While my father's value lay in his horses, Jon made himself indispensable with ships.

I wedged the tip of Honor under my fingernails, picking away the dried blood from my training session with Nerissa. Shadows danced along the facets of its golden gem in the dimming lantern light. We'd been in Khasimir for a week now, still arguing over the best course of attack.

"Before winter," Ronan urged, turning toward another commander whose name I'd already forgotten.

Einar grumbled his agreement as he scanned the map.

"And then we'll need to push north as soon as possible if the dark king is hitting Stynguard."

My stomach pitched at the sight of those ships heading toward Sultiran shores. Of the thought of ashen being unleashed upon the university city.

"What of the king's new city shield?" one of them asked.

I snapped my head toward the group.

"We won't be able to take Aedrialis until we bring that down."

"Leave the shield to me."

I turned my attention back to my fingernails as Astraeus swaggered into the war tent. I swallowed my disgust as the leaders of the Rising *bowed* to him. Astraeus's smile widened into a grin as he shook their hands. He slid his dark gaze to mine in warning before joining the others at the table.

Vienah stepped inside the tent, followed by Nerissa, Drystan, and Carina, closely guarded by Kresida. Though I didn't particularly like the War Slayer, she had become a part of our motley group, and I enjoyed watching the soldiers flinch in her presence.

I stood, joining them at the back of the tent. Vienah slid an arm around me, giving my waist a squeeze in greeting.

"How do you intend to break the city shield? A shield that

powerful... Nobody knows if it's ever been done," one of the men asked.

"My men have the means," Astraeus responded. "My fleet will attack from the east. If we can get air cannons in line from the south on the ground as well, we should be able to take it down."

"With what, exactly?"

"*Rubellines*," Ronan responded, raising an eyebrow at Astraeus. "A type of stone that can neutralize magic. You'd need a hell of a lot to take down the city shield, though. You have enough?"

Astraeus gave a firm nod as he scratched his short beard.

"We need to be strategic with the magic wielders," Kresida said, turning to Carina and motioning her toward the table where the men stood. "There are only six of you, and you can bet Saros will throw everything he's got at us when we arrive at his door. What do you think, Highness? Two of you in the air, three on the ground, and one from the east?"

Carina's brows pinched as she studied the map.

"We'll need a shield of our own. I can cover the front lines of our troops on the ground. Nerissa and Lyvia should be on the offensive, given their ability to fly. Focus on shielding your-selves and your caeluma," Carina said, turning to us. "Drystan will join me on the ground."

Drystan flitted his eyes to me. I held his gaze for a moment before raising my brows. Not *my* decision, I tried to tell him without signing. He nodded to Carina.

He'd been quiet since unlocking the stone that held the Advetis Bone. We'd told no one, and Drystan kept it hidden on his chest, unable to tap into its powers these past weeks.

"Vienah," Carina continued, sliding her gaze to the water witch, "I assume you would prefer to stay with the ships to keep them from turning into kindling?"

Vienah murmured her agreement, doing her best to hide the smile forming on her lips as her eyes shot to Astraeus.

"And should we have issues with flames on the field, you can send us rain?"

Vienah nodded her confirmation.

"Then you'll need to focus your troops on marching from the south," Carina continued, confidence riding her clear, steady voice as it carried through the tent. She stood with her shoulders back, one hand on her hip as she pointed at the map with her other. "Take half of them—"

"Let's get one thing straight, *elf*, you don't give anyone in the Rising, least of all its commanders, orders."

My temper flared at the sneering commander's interruption and tone with the Princess of Lotrennia. I opened my mouth to join in the arguing that erupted as a young messenger boy burst through the tent flaps.

"Stynguard!" he shouted, waving a wet and muddied correspondence in his hand at the commanders. "Nivis has retreated! Saros's forces march south to Aedrialis!"

# CHAPTER FORTY-EIGHT

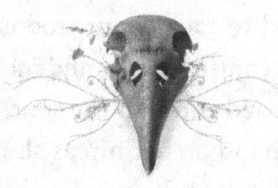

*I pray this gets to you. The king's power dwindles. Strike soon.*
*—Intercepted correspondence from Queen Galena, intended for Commander Ronan Merik of the Rising. 72$^{nd}$ of Autumn, 071.3E*

"Absolutely not," I snapped, as Evony trailed me through the muddy avenues of camp, now only a mile south of the walls of Aedrialis. "We agreed you'd keep to the back of the lines and remain with Tempest."

Though the mare wasn't up to the standards of the agrippa in our homestead in Aedrialis, she was fierce, and I was confident she wouldn't let a single person hurt her rider.

"And should I signal you, you ride back to Khasimir. *That* was the plan. That was the agreement, Evony. The only reason you are *here* with us is because you agreed to it."

"That horse is *psychotic!*" she shouted after me, reaching for my arm.

I stopped, sliding into the mud, turning to her. "I don't care if you think she's psychotic. I trust her to keep you safe, so you'll stay with her."

"I want to fight with you," Evony pleaded, a pathetic mask of desperation forcing her lips down.

"I told you I'm going to keep you safe—"

"Then what has been the point of all this?" she snapped, her temper flaring.

I swallowed, glancing around the bustling camp. "Calm down, Ev—"

"I'm serious! What has been the point of training me? You, Nerissa, Vulcan, Ezrich... Am I not good enough? I want to help. I'm *going* to help." The muscle in her jaw twitched as she dug her heels into the ground.

My powers blinked awake at my rising anger, and I did my best to leash them, resisting the smoldering glow forming in my eyes.

"I can see you're upset," I tried, forcing a gentleness into my voice.

"Oh, did your Bellator powers tell you that?" she snapped, her fists shooting to her hips as she raised her eyebrows.

"The *point* of it," I said quietly, stepping up to her, "is to keep you fucking safe. To ensure you can protect yourself. Not to blatantly put you in more danger. You are sixteen years old. I'm not allowing you to march to war."

"You're not my fucking mum."

"Morwyn would skewer me alive if she knew I sent you to war."

She opened her mouth to protest.

I held up a hand, "We're done." I stalked off as she hurled a colorful array of curses at me.

My FINGERS TUGGED the back of Nerissa's armor-enforced leather vest, tightening the laces in our dark tent.

Tiberius's hooves slammed onto the ground outside, followed by the wild flap of Aquila's wings, shuddering the walls of our tent.

"No changes," Nerissa murmured, eyeing the flaps of the tent as Aquila spoke to her.

I nodded in agreement. Our caeluma had scouted the city for the last two days. And though we knew Saros's shield was strong, we tested our magic at its barriers anyway, with no luck. Our powers bucked against it, but we'd at least been able to determine the border of the shield. When Nerissa and Aquila sent blasts of white flames against it, the light seemed to bounce off the shield, illuminating its edges.

Word had spread that Lord Pavel's ships had saved Stynguard from Dark King Daimos's forces, and Saros's soldiers now marched south. Our window to take Aedrialis shrank rapidly.

"The night before always sucks," she muttered as she began twisting two tight braids down the side of her head.

"I know," I replied, thinking of that last night on the Lake of Light with Bayne. I'd been sick with nerves, and he'd given me what I'd needed. And now, where was he? I squashed the thoughts before they could take me down a path I wasn't ready to travel.

Nerissa's Ravindra eyes slid to me as if she knew.

"We keep to the plan," she murmured. "Aedrialis. Nivis. Lotrennia."

I nodded, turning so she could do the laces on my own vest as I strapped the gauntlets over my forearms.

"Are you sure you don't want to stay with Ronan tonight?" I asked, keenly aware of how close I flew to her flames.

Nerissa straightened, cracking her neck and rolling her shoulders. "I'll see him at dawn."

Lightning cracked in the skies, its flash illuminating the shadows of the neighboring tents against the walls of our own. Nerissa frowned, sheathing her blades.

"Not good for flying," she murmured. "Maybe Vienah can get that under control."

I nodded my agreement. "Thank the gods for sending us a water witch."

My head snapped up at the swish of the tent flap. Kresida appeared a moment later, the few lit tapers shining off the wet stripe of black paint against her dark skin. Her eyes slid to Nerissa.

"Commander," she murmured, Nerissa's previous title rolling off her lips in assured confidence. Kresida held a small vial of paint and nodded to the ex-War Slayer.

Nerissa had stiffened, but her emerald eyes slid from the ebony paint to the matching wolf skull on Kresida's shoulder. I nodded to the two of them before stepping outside.

THE DEAFENING BOOM of air canons echoed below where Tiberius and I circled the gathering Rising forces in the early hours of the morning. Thousands of troops lined the fields south of Aedrialis, ready to march on the city as soon as its shield fell.

We banked, heading toward the fleet Astraeus had called to arms. My head cocked as I spied eighty ships lining the coast of Sultira, all flying the same flag, a *V* outlined with the snaking heads of the *Hydra*. The same had replaced the Marisarma flag that flew atop Astraeus's massive ship. V for Votruvia.

A blast of white light shot forth as Aquila signaled the second coordinated rubelline air cannon attack. I braced myself as forty glowing, red balls pummeled the invisible shield around Aedrialis, the wind around it rippling in a wave of magic.

*Fuck.*

My stomach dipped. The shield held.

We continued circling, and I spied Vienah in the leathers she so despised at the stern of the *Hydra*. Astraeus's blue coat flashed, and I pulled my gaze toward the forces on land. Ronan sat atop his own agrippa, a steadfast stallion I'd picked for him. He wore plain, silver armor we'd scraped up from the old keep at Khasimir.

Carina stood at the front lines alongside Kresida, with Drystan in his own armor twenty yards away. He glanced up, nodding a greeting as we passed.

Vulcan adjusted his seat behind me. Despite my protests, he and the mother hen we rode atop refused any other post I suggested for the elf.

Another flash from above and a third volley of cannons echoed from below, banging against the city's unyielding barrier.

"How many more rubellines do we have?"

"Three more volleys worth," Vulcan called as the wind whipped around us.

Ti circled behind our troops when a blur of small, dark figures caught my eye from the mountains.

"Are those—"

"Yes," Vulcan growled from behind me.

*Ti, can you—*

*Already on it.*

I glanced behind to see Aquila dive, the surrounding troops clearing the field to make room for his landing near

Ronan, no doubt to communicate the arrival of Evony's strange friends.

Tiberius picked up his speed and soared toward the creatures gathering at the mouth of a cave near the foothills. Ti's hooves hammered down as we landed a short distance away.

Gork stood at the front of the group, his peg leg clacking against the stony ground as he shuffled ahead and frantically pointed south.

I slid off Ti's back and stepped up to Gork. "What is it? Why are you here?"

Gork mumbled something in his own language, pointing again to the south.

"I don't know what you're saying." I shook my head as another flash of white light illuminated the morning sky, and the resounding canons thundered into the shield.

Gork became frantic, gesturing with his little clawed hands and pounding his makeshift spear on the ground.

"Can you draw it?" I asked, pointing to his spear. I knelt on the ground and used my finger to draw a circle with two intersecting arrows in it, not sure why the unknown symbol always seemed to come to mind.

Gork stilled as he watched me, quickly smudging my drawing with his hairy bare feet and marking up the dirt with his spear.

"Aedrialis," I said aloud, as he drew a circle with a large, spear-like structure in the middle.

"Us, yes, I see..."

He continued with little ships in the sea and dots of troops to the south. Ten arrows swooped up from below, followed by what looked to be a skull. Death.

"Troops," I breathed. "Saros's troops from the south? From Rellenor?"

Vulcan's mouth drew a thin line as I turned to him.

"Ten thousand, you think?" he asked Gork, lowering his bow.

Gork nodded grimly before turning back to his clan of beasts.

"How did they catch up so quickly? They must have had eyes on Skyscape Pass," I said, shaking my head.

Gork stopped and began shouting at us, arguing.

"You didn't let anyone else through, did you?" I said more than asked, understanding his defensiveness. "Thank you for the warning, Gork," I called after him before leaping onto Tiberius's to soar back to Aedrialis.

"If the shield's not down by now," Vulcan murmured, "we'll have to turn all our attention to the south. They'll be on us in a day."

THE ENERGY in the war tent was as restless as my powers as we stood around the same damn table, arguing over what the hell we were going to do.

"Do we know how many rubelline canons Astraeus has left?" Ronan asked the grim group.

"He's on his way, so you can ask him yourself," I muttered as I paced like a caged animal behind the line of commanders. I yanked on that bit of air connecting me to the pirate so hard it nearly knocked the wind out of me, and my breath escaped in a cough.

Nerissa's eyes glowed green against the line of paint Kresida had applied. They'd found Vulcan at some point, as the same line stretched across his face. The three War Slayers bent over the map as they murmured to each other. Carina stood on the opposite side, quiet and pensive as if working out some riddle.

The tent flaps blew open as Vienah hurried in, stepping to my side.

"I heard what happened," she said, grabbing for my hand. "Ten thousand?"

I nodded grimly as Astraeus, Raek, and four of his men stepped inside. Similar war paint donned the pirate lord's face, except five dark lines stretched down from the thick band across his forehead, as if someone had slid their hand down the front of his face. The same marked his crew.

"Astraeus!" a no-name general shouted at him. "What the hell is happening with your canons?"

Astraeus's gaze darkened as he took in the large man's sneer, but he turned to Ronan, ignoring him entirely.

"We have a problem," Astraeus said, stepping up to the table.

"No shit," Ronan replied, straightening. "The rubellines aren't working."

"The rubellines," Astraeus seethed, "are *fine*." He rubbed a hand over his short beard. "Saros's shield is just thick."

"What's our problem then?" Ronan demanded.

"Not what, but *who*," Astraeus purred, moving faster than I'd ever seen him and placing the sharp edge of his blade against Vienah's thin neck.

# CHAPTER FORTY-NINE

> *Abandon Stynguard and sail your fleet south. Rising forces knock at the gates of Aedrialis, and the shores are littered with Marisarma trash.*
>
> —*Correspondence from General Calvus to Lord Pavel.*

**B**lood leached from Vienah's face. Tremors raced through my hands as power rose from the depths.

"Lower your weapon," I breathed.

Astraeus slid his dark eyes to mine. "No."

A countdown began in my mind, and when it reached zero, there would be nothing holding the blade pressed to Vienah's exposed neck, air oath be damned. A trickle of blood slid down her ivory skin.

"Please," she begged, and my heart squeezed. "Kellan, *please.*"

"Tell them, *my dear*, about those little lightning tricks

you've kept hidden all these months," Astraeus crooned as silence cleaved the room.

My heart began a slow gallop in my chest.

"I cannot control the fire in the skies," Vienah pleaded, a small whimper escaping her lips.

"Is that so, water witch? You're more powerful than you've been letting on. Tell them about your *messages.*"

Vienah's throat bobbed as she tried to swallow against Astraeus's curved blade.

"What are you talking about?" I breathed. I couldn't pull my gaze away from the small pool of tears balancing in Vienah's brown eyes.

"Odessa... Demon's Door... And now here, on Saros's doorstep." Astraeus's tone turned deadly as he inched his face closer to Vienah, his blade perfectly still.

"I suspected something was off when that storm arrived at Demon's Door," he murmured, his face a breath from hers. "A bit unseasonal, for a lightning storm in the southern part of the kingdom, I should think. Certainly, unseasonal in the Thandal Sea."

Vienah blinked, a tear trickling down her cheek as she slid her watery gaze to me.

"Lyvia, please," she whispered, her throat dipping along the blade. "I didn't have a choice. King Saros has my family..."

My throat went dry.

I blinked once, twice, attempting to process what had happened amidst the thundering of my blood as I came face-to-face with another betrayal... *Spy,* my powers whispered beneath my skin.

Vienah had spied on the Rising, on us, on me...for months.

"Please, Lyvia," Vienah pleaded. "Father Marcus is still alive. I can help you..."

Rage squashed the growing nausea as my veins darkened, a shimmering golden glow lining them.

*Odessa.*

That evening, amidst my anger toward Bayne—when Ronan had shared his secret and Bayne's deception—I had barely registered the strange heat lightning that sparked in the night before the attack.

A message. A signal, giving away our location to Saros's forces that attacked in the night.

*Thousands* of lives were lost that day.

The pressure rising deep below began to quicken, and my fingers buzzed. Astraeus snapped his head toward me.

"Get out of the tent, Lyvia," he ordered.

I opened my mouth to respond as Ezrich hurtled into the war tent and skidded to a stop.

"Dad," he said, his voice shaking as he reached for my arm. "It's Dad, Lyvia."

My name broke off his lips, and he lifted a trembling hand to his temple.

"What do you mean? Where?"

He looked up, his dark skin pale.

"On the wall."

CRIMSON STREAKS THINNED as they dripped down the walls of Aedrialis, a stark contrast to the bright white stone illuminated by the midday sun. An excruciating, distant scream cut through the air before it crumpled into a pained moan and was lost among the shouts of the Rising soldiers. A desperate connection formed with Tiberius as I shoved my way through the soldiers, who stood shoulder to shoulder, simmering at the spiked bodies dotting the upper edges of the walls. The same pikes we used to slip into Aedrialis last year.

A message to traitors.

Ezrich shoved a path through the remaining soldiers, and my heart stopped as my eyes landed on a line of living prisoners standing at the uppermost battlements, each awaiting their gruesome sentence. Ezrich's hands bunched into fists, and numbness spread through me as I took in Bear's unmistakable large form at the front of the line, standing next to General Calvus.

My blood stilled as my powers stood at attention.

*Not Bear.*

Vulcan stepped to my side as Tiberius's dark form shot into my view.

"With me," I commanded, barely registering Vulcan's confirming growl.

Ti slowed his landing gallop, and I sprinted into the short opening ahead of me, Vulcan close behind, before leaping onto his back.

We launched into the sky, and I pushed our dark shield into place, stretching it as thin as I dared to get a better view as we flew to the edge of King Saros's impenetrable shield. Tiberius's massive wings pumped steadily as we hovered only twenty feet from where Bear stood shackled.

My heart crumpled as I took in his form. Old and new blood stained his torn, ragged clothes. The white, bubbling blisters of fresh burns lined his powerful arms, and he squinted through bruised and swollen eyelids, his face falling as it landed on me.

"Bear," I whispered, the name broken on my lips.

Something was happening to me. Rage and devastation swarmed, the Obscura seizing the emotions as the Transcindiel surged alongside some powerful force filling my being.

"We can't do anything. Saros's shield is too strong," Vulcan urged me from behind. "You've already tested it against your powers."

Blood darkened the center of the sickening contraption used to impale the bodies on the pikes lining the walls of Aedrialis. Held upright by a steel brace and pulley system, they rolled the wooden platform to the next empty pike.

"I have to try," I breathed, as I envisioned my shadows sharpening into a line of spearheads.

"We've already tried this," Vulcan urged. "Do not waste your strength. Your powers will bounce right off."

*No.*

Bear winced as he straightened, turning to General Calvus, mumbling something through the gag in his mouth. The general, a man I'd seen countless times in Mount Telum and one of Saros's most trusted advisers, pinched his brows in disgust as he looked at Bear, but gave a resigned nod to one of his men. A sneer slapped across his face as his eyes landed on me.

Bear turned very slowly to face me.

"What's happening?" I asked, more to myself.

"It's time," Vulcan murmured.

My head shook, but Bear's dark eyes remained pinned on my own without an ounce of fear in them. Instead, they held a world of memories in their depths. Was he thinking of Evony and Ezrich? Was he reliving those days of adventure on board the *Evecta* when he fought side by side with Bayne? When he saved Morwyn? Did he regret joining the Rising? Was he wishing he'd stayed behind with his family?

The guards began speaking, turning to face Rising fighters gathered below.

"Can you hear what they're saying?" I asked Vulcan.

"No," he murmured. "Not well enough through your shield."

"I have to drop it."

Without waiting for a response, Tiberius inched closer to King Saros's shield, and I dropped my own.

The guard leading Bear to the contraption called, "To grant him his final words."

My pulse stopped as I realized Bear needed to tell us something. He kept his eyes on me as they strapped him against the platform, the ropes from the pulley system lifting it upright so he was angled toward the Rising forces.

Bear's eyes softened as a single tear traveled down his broad face. A guard pulled his gag free.

Bear cried out in a hoarse, booming voice, *"Glastí!"*

My stomach pitched.

*What? What does that mean?!*

His eyes frantically searched mine as the contraption creaked, the ropes pulling the bottom of it higher so I could no longer see his face. This was happening too fast. I rallied my powers, that strange sensation twisting into something lethal, something deadly. The Transcindiel molded the Obscura into a razor-sharp spear as my hands lifted to the air and thrust it at the massive shield.

Devastation sliced through my shock, my powers raging as they bounced off, and the darkness disappeared in a cloud of shadows.

Bear's voice boomed once more. "IT'S A F—"

A scream wrenched from my throat as the platform slammed down against the side of the wall, the massive pike ramming through Bear's broad chest and cutting off his words in an excruciating cry.

Screams rose from below in violence and anguish. My

vision blurred as a flood of memories rushed in, and I was caught somewhere between grief and rage.

Sizzling bacon. The whir of a tea kettle. A booming laugh that shook the small cottage. His bravery as he stormed through the crowds and soldiers in Rivaner to get to his family. The fierceness and determination of his tenacity, his fight and resolution to avenge Morwyn on the Cliffs of Odessa. A reassuring hand on my shoulder after embedding his axe in the soldier, ready to cut me down...

*My life.* I owed Bear my life and so much more.

Tiberius remained hovering, his emotions soaring down our connection at unrivaled speed. His or mine? I didn't know. An arm slammed around my waist as I began to tip.

"SHIELD!" Vulcan bellowed, alarm spiking down my bond with Tiberius.

I snapped my head up as an arrow zinged through the air, its tip a gray whir against the white and red walls.

I tunneled intention into my powers, the shield a breath away from forming, as Vulcan's arm ripped my chest back and his body formed its own shield against mine. He let out a pained grunt as the arrow ripped through his shoulder, the tip of it slicing against my forearm.

Tiberius dipped as my shield finally snapped into place, and he soared away from the walls of Aedrialis and back to camp. Guilt dug its claws into my chest and sent the spreading numbness scattering before slamming me back into reality.

Vulcan's bloody arm slipped through my hands as he slumped into Nerissa's arms upon our landing, healers rushing forward. My vision tunneled as the Rising warriors worked themselves into a frenzy after witnessing the horror of Bear's execution.

Commanders swarmed me, and Carina placed a hand on my shaking arm as I slid from Ti's back. I stared at Ezrich's figure in the distance. His knees sank into the mud as he sat back on his heels, his arms heavy at his sides, and his face staring at the motionless figure of his dead father displayed on the wall.

So much was happening. I should go to Ezrich. I should see if Vulcan is okay. My stomach plunged. He'd taken an arrow for me...

A hand was on my shoulder.

"Vulcan will be fine. It's a flesh wound."

Astraeus's words bounced off my mind like water against rock, and my breath continued to escape my lips too quickly. It was my fault Vulcan had been shot... Why did I drop my shield? It was my fault Bear was dead. I couldn't get through Saros's shield...

*Glastí.* Tiberius's voice shook in my head. *He was trying to tell us something.*

"What's happened?" Drystan asked as he rushed through the crowds.

"*Glastí*," I replied and turned toward Carina. "What does it mean? Is it Elvish? He was trying to tell us something." My throat bobbed as the words escaped my lips in tremors, tears forming in the corners of my eyes.

Carina's brows tilted up and she shook her head, "I don't—"

"Fern," Astraeus breathed. His eyes were wide as they darted between mine and then to the slice on my forearm. "Glastí means *fern* in Old Votruvian."

Astraeus's mouth fell open as he dropped his hand from my shoulder and turned, his eyes tracing the air surrounding Aedrialis.

"It's a steepled *fern shield*."

# CHAPTER FIFTY

---

*Attempt to flee again, and you'll receive her hand with the finger next time.*

—Correspondence from General Calvus to Vienah. 30th of Winter, 071.3E.

---

The pirate's eyes shot to Carina and Drystan as he continued, signing the words, "The shield is thickest, widest, on its outer edges. We need to take it down from the top."

Carina blinked, realization brightening the green in her irises.

"He's right," she whispered. "Saros reinforced the sides of his shield by thinning out the top of it. We can break it from above." Her eyes slid to me and darted to Nerissa as she approached.

"Your friend may have just won us this war," Astraeus said in a low voice as Carina explained it to Nerissa.

382

I blinked as emotion swarmed my chest and that burning sensation pricked my eyes. I reined the feeling in, certain if I let it out, there would be no stopping the flood that followed.

"We obviously can't fly and fire an air cannon from above," Nerissa cut in.

"You won't need an air cannon," Astraeus said, glancing at me. "You'll need a perfect shot. The thinnest point should look something like that." He pointed a ringed finger at my chest, where my amber amplifier had fallen open, showcasing the spiraling creature inside.

"A rubelline arrow," I answered, understanding sinking in. We'd need to shoot an arrow to weaken the thinnest point and then send a blast of magic into the shield, shattering the rest of it.

"How will you see the thinnest point if the shield is invisible?" Drystan asked.

"If Aquila and I send enough power into it, we should see a ripple off its surface," Nerissa replied.

I opened my lips to respond I didn't have a good enough shot when a heart-stopping scream cut through the growing commotion of the Rising camp. It was followed by hundreds of black arrows raining down from above. Carina shouted as she stretched her own shield farther as forces continued to gather, the arrows bouncing off the invisible wall and clattering to the ground mere feet away. Drystan hurried to the front of the group, shooting his hands to either side, horror strewn across his face as he gazed at the spiked bodies.

Evony shoved through the soldiers, letting out a devastating sob. I steeled myself, leashing the powers that longed to rip free, and rushed to where Evony had fallen to her knees, sobbing and shaking.

"Evony," I breathed, grasping her shoulders as she wept. "Breathe, Ev. Breathe."

"I…" she muttered between gasps, "I can't… We have to…"

My hands found her face.

"Evony, look at me."

Her eyes, wild with wrath and pain, shot between my own and the wall.

"Look only at me," I whispered.

*Dad… We have to…* she mouthed, face pale with shock.

"With me," I whispered, turning her away from the walls.

"No," she whimpered.

I tugged her away from the city and through the crowd of gathering soldiers. "NO!" she screamed at me, ripping her arm away.

"NO! I can't hide. I can't do *nothing*. You can't keep me from this!" she shouted, throwing her arms to the surrounding army.

I swallowed the lump forming in my throat, dry from the truth in her words, a large, dark form appearing at my side.

"I told you to get back to the eastern shore unit!" Ezrich's words were sharp, laced with his own anger and pain.

"Fuck you!" she screamed at him. "You were supposed to wait for him!"

Ezrich's face crumpled for a moment.

"He stayed for *you*!" he bit out, his features hardening in grief. "He could have been safe with the elves. He stayed in Sultira because of *you*, not me. He knew I'd join the units passing through the Lake of Light!"

"Evony, you need to breathe," I said, reaching for her hand.

She whipped it away, her face soaked with tears.

"You have no idea what I need," she spat, throwing her hands toward the blood-soaked walls of Aedrialis. "What do you know of this?"

The blood in my veins stilled, my powers going eerily quiet as the events in the Crystal Castle crept to the edge of my memory, but I slid that steel door shut with practiced control. Her blue eyes, brighter through the fresh tears, scanned my own as she waited for my reply, but any words I had left for her remained lodged in my throat.

"I'm not going back there to hide," she spat. "To wait for this to happen to more people I love!" Her voice broke.

I swallowed, lifting my hands, the iridescent stars shining in the early morning light. She stared at them before taking a shuddering breath.

Shouts erupted from ahead, and Ronan ordered soldiers back to their posts, as arrows pummeled Carina and Drystan's shield.

"Okay," I whispered.

Ezrich turned, and the full force of Bear's son loomed over me as I did my best not to shrink beneath his fury.

"What do you mean, *okay*?" he seethed.

"You are not her keeper, nor am I," I snapped.

"She's sixteen," he growled, baring his teeth.

"And she's seen and lived through more than any sixteen-year-old ever should. She's sick of being treated like someone who hasn't."

I turned back to Evony. "You want to do something? Follow me."

EVONY SOMEHOW MANAGED to get a hold of her emotions as we strode from the walls of Aedrialis, as if being allowed to help, to *do something*, had granted her the ability to grab them by the reins.

Fresh devastation and betrayal fueled the gathering darkness as I funneled the unending emotions into my chasm of power, honing it into lethal vengeance in the hours that passed.

We'd met and planned at length after Astraeus had figured out Bear's message. Twilight stalked the disappearing hours of the day, our time running short. With the approaching army from the south, this was our chance to make Bear's sacrifice count for something. Evony's chance.

I sat behind her, arms around her waist, the armor covering every inch of her body clinking as she adjusted her seat. Aquila's large form flew from the north as we raced over the city, ascending into the clouds where the air thinned.

The dominating castle turrets of Mount Telum came into view as white wisps of clouds floated over the top of the fortress. Aquila and Tiberius circled once, twice...right before Nerissa sent a massive blast of wind into the clouds, scattering like birds in a storm. A blazing white light followed, lighting up the darkening sky and shooting a hundred feet below us to the tip of Mount Telum, where it rippled off the king's shield.

The shining, twisting pattern of the steepled fern barrier came into view as it shoved against Nerissa's magic. The spiral shimmered and slipped into nothing as its edges spun into its center, the thinnest point.

Aquila banked hard, taking himself and Nerissa out of range.

Evony's breath hissed as she drew her bow, aiming over a hundred feet away, on the back of a flying horse, at an invisible target.

"Get ready!" I shouted through the wind.

Evony's head bobbed, and Tiberius flung his momentum upward, arching backward and shot his hooves to the sky above us. My legs burned as they wrapped around him, and I reached around Evony's waist for his mane to keep her secure against me.

"Now!" I shouted, dropping my dark shield.

The world flipped, and Evony let out a war cry as the taut bowstring slipped through her fingers. The blazing rubelline arrow tip soared like a star as it ripped through the air, straight toward the center of the king's shield.

Tiberius righted himself in time to dive after the arrow headfirst. Evony clung to his neck as I threw one hand out, finally shoving out the powers that had built to a boiling point.

Vienah's betrayal. Bear's sacrifice. Queen Antares's scheming. Bayne's soulbinding.

Devastation and grief collided with a growing wrath and an insatiable need for revenge. Raw memories fueled the emotions that surged from my innermost being, and I latched them onto that strange force binding my two powers.

A twisting spear of black and golden power formed at the tips of my fingers, the Obscura seizing my emotions and the Transcindiel sucking every ounce of energy from my body. The spear rotated as it shot through the air, chasing after the arrow as if my powers knew their target. They caught the feather fletching midair just as the glowing rubelline tip of the arrow struck the center of Saros's shield.

Everything stilled, sound vanishing, before a deafening crack ripped through the air, and my ears hollowed out. My powers tore through the small hole the rubelline tip pierced in the shield. A tsunami of wind followed as the Obscura power devoured the shield, darkness spiraling out from its center.

Black, massive wings shot out, slowing our momentum. I sagged behind Evony as the expenditure of power hit me. Tiberius chased the rippling darkness as it ate through the invisible shield, leading us to the edge of the city. Shouts from below mingled with the eruption of cheers from the Rising soldiers beyond the city walls.

# CHAPTER FIFTY-ONE

---

*Bear.*
— *From Lyvia's list.*

---

"Lyvia!" Evony shouted as I slipped, vision tunneling as my consciousness ebbed.

Tiberius tilted, bouncing me back to the center. The dark waves of the Juniper came up on our left, and Ti banked, angling sharply toward a large ship leading the fleet.

*Take us back to the city,* I murmured.

Ti's derisive snort sent my heels weakly digging into his sides as he hurtled down the center of the *Hydra*.

Astraeus clapped softly, his rings clinking against one another, as he swaggered to where Ti stopped, panting heavily.

"Nicely done." He nodded toward Evony and Tiberius. His typical, insufferable swagger dimmed for the briefest moment as his eyes landed on me. He was at Tiberius's flank in an instant as I began to slide off his back and into his arms.

"Get off," I slurred, doing my best to shove him away. Despite the fact he'd figured out Bear's message, I hadn't forgotten his threat from weeks before to stay the fuck away.

His hands held my arms, steadying me as my knees buckled.

"*Get off!*" I snapped, giving him a weak push. I wobbled, my legs shaking before ceasing to work entirely, and he caught me around the waist.

"Raek!" he called as Marian moved to my side. Her hair was tied back, and she'd donned her own armor. She eased me to a sitting position on the deck as I rubbed the bridge of my nose, an ache pounding behind my eyes.

Gods, I'd *never* been this spent.

The *Hydra* rocked as an air cannon boomed from below deck. I glanced over the rail to see the cannonball smash into one of the gates to the city on the eastern shore, a perfect hit. My stomach twisted.

"I need to get to Mount Telum," I said to her as she surveyed me with a look of concern, taking something from Raek without looking. I had to get back. We needed to take Saros and end the fighting as soon as possible. "*This is my city.*"

"The siege will take time," she said, shoving a hot mug into my hands. "Drink."

I scowled, taking the mug and a slow, shaky sip of bitter tea.

"Thank you. I'm good now," I murmured as I handed back the mug and shoved shakily onto my feet.

"Lyvia," she scolded, signing my name with a jerky snap of her wrists.

I took a step toward Ti, ignoring her as best I could. She grabbed my arm and spun me around to face her.

"They need me!" I snapped. "No one else needs to die in this fight." My words broke in a choked rasp.

"You need to rest."

"I'm fine," I said, gritting my teeth as I reached Ti.

*She's right.*

*Shut up.*

"She's right," Astraeus echoed, approaching me, and a wave of amusement rippled off Tiberius.

"But as you might be too stubborn to listen to the people who care about you..." Astraeus stepped to my side. "Don't make me regret this," he breathed, his lips brushing my ear.

Before I could stop him, the pirate lord slid my hand into his, twining our fingers. Silver stars danced at the edge of my vision, and I gasped, a blast of energy bursting into my palm.

My eyes widened as power surged through, snapping me awake, as if he'd shoved his own magic *into* me. The power settled in my chest, the Obscura and Transcindiel coming fully awake and standing at attention. I blinked as the buzzing sensation subsided, the fatigue vanishing entirely. My eyes settled on the deep blue sky beyond the *Hydra's* sails, stars peeking through the horizon, as if they'd decided to rise early today.

My gaze slid back to Astraeus, whose hand had gone slack in mine, his dark eyes widening beneath the lines of paint as his mouth fell open. He held my gaze for a moment before blinking and wiping the mask of shock from his face. He slowly backed away, barking orders to his crew.

*What in Tynan's Hell was that?* Ti asked.

*I don't care,* I responded. *Let's take our city back.*

A CHOKING gray smoke wafted up the streets of Aedrialis as we soared over the Ripped River and beneath the looming Arches of Cascada. Evony was still in front and picking off the sentries on the higher buildings as we raced toward Mount Telum, Saros's castle.

The tang of blood mingled with smoke as the clang of armor and cries of battle echoed below. Aquila let out his own shriek in the distance as he flipped, dodging a set of arrows along the white walls that he and Nerissa cleared of Sultiran soldiers. Rising forces burst through the burning gates of the city, lit by Soleia flames.

"Ezrich!" Evony cried out, her words lost in the wind above the chaos.

Her brother wielded a lethal-looking axe in one hand and a short-blade in the other as he led a small party of soldiers up the battlements where the spiked traitors hung on display.

Blood rained down the stone line of stairs as his axe sank into the necks of the soldiers who got in his way. The blade in his left hand moved with a practiced sort of precision as a frantic, raw kind of fury directed the axe in his right. The whites of his eyes flashed against the blood on his dark face as we soared past.

He chased revenge.

We all did.

Ti descended until we soared over the main avenue. A small force of Rising fighters raced through the streets, cutting through the Sultiran posts stationed near the inner city. I caught the glimmer of Drystan's shield against the torches lining the road as he raced ahead, sending blasts of wind through the avenue with his arms out, steering Tempest with his legs.

I let a brief moment of appreciation pass through my thoughts as Tiberius swooped down, only ten feet above them, and we surged ahead. A group of soldiers lunged from behind an alley, and Evony's arrows ripped through the few on the left while I sent death swarming to the group on the right.

Ti plunged forward, and we banked left, scanning the blood-soaked streets below for any sign of the breaching force heading to Mount Telum. A blast of wind buckled against the looming fortress, and my eyes snagged on the back of Carina's long braid. Kresida rode next to her, with the War Slayer's arrow finding every target. Carina threw her hands forward, releasing a blast of wind with such power, it knocked aside the wagons and carriages parked on the avenue.

Ronan's light hair, streaked with mud and blood, bounced as his stallion galloped down the street. Tiberius soared over them to cheers of triumph from the group. A line of soldiers stood several feet in front of thirty priests, evenly spaced around the white fortress and bedecked in robes of gray. They slowly raised their hands as we came into view.

"Shields!" I bellowed to the group behind, throwing up my own, as the mages lifted their hands and bits of light danced between them.

Ti staggered in the air, his wings pumping as the massive blast of wind slammed into my dark shield. Buildings crashed to the ground with the boom of thunder as the force of the mages' magic hit the surrounding area. I tightened my grip around Evony as I threw a blast of shadows in their direction. The darkness slammed into a shield, and Evony reached into her quiver as we rounded the neighboring buildings.

Evony's second rubelline arrow blazed like a flame as it aimed straight at the mage in the center before she let it fly. I readied my powers to chase after the flying fletching as Carina's scream ripped through the air from below.

Her agrippa bounded down the street, and she lifted her hands, massive chunks of stone from the demolished buildings rising in the air as she held them there, before thrusting her hands toward the base of Mount Telum.

Cries echoed from the soldiers and mages surrounding the

fortress as massive chunks of stone hurtled toward its base. Kresida and Ronan pushed their mounts past Carina as she dropped her hands, sagging. The rest of them cut through the remaining Sultiran forces that weren't already scattering.

I slid off Ti's back as his hooves neared the veranda of the castle, running to keep from stumbling.

*Keep her safe!*

His hooves touched down momentarily as his wings beat and sent gusts of smoke and stale autumn air flying up. He soared back toward the walls with a fresh arrow already nocked in Evony's hands.

SCREAMS ECHOED through the arched halls of Mount Telum, the stench of blood, vomit and smoke heavy and oppressive. I raced through the halls, shoving past soldiers in black and various mismatched armor, keeping sight of Kresida, steps ahead of me.

Bear's bloody, shredded body remained burned in my mind. His agonizing cry rang in my ears like a blaring canon blast. The horror of witnessing his death, his sacrifice, hung like an ominous thunderhead. The kind that looms in the skies, somehow making them larger. The kind that stands as a warning of what is to come. A warning to all who stand in its path before a violent blend of fire and ice obliterate it all in a cascade of rage.

A rage fueling my hunt.

*Saros.*

My powers writhed beneath my skin, screaming their own cries of war. Whatever magic Astraeus had used on his ship had done more than refill my reserves. It had connected something incomplete.

"Which way?" Kresida's voice was clear, her breath irritatingly even as we reached the fork in the eighth set of stairs.

My lungs burned as much as my thighs as I raised an arm, pointing to the spiral staircase leading to Saros's tower. I'd never been to the king's tower, but I knew it lay beneath the center and highest turret of Mount Telum. Kresida's head bobbed in confirmation, the whites of her eyes stark against dark irises.

We sprinted up the marble steps, the last of daylight diminishing as we ascended, and the ornate oval windows disappeared, replaced by delicate candlelit sconces adorning the stone walls. Kresida slowed, her fist rising as her elf ears picked up noise from above I couldn't hear. She unfurled four fingers as the slightest clinking of armored boots descended the stairs from above.

My heart raced as I forced my breathing to slow. Kresida flipped the twin blades in her hands before crouching low, the look of a pure predator, ready to unleash itself on unsuspecting prey. The silver tip of a longsword peaked past the curve, candlelight glinting off its edge as it came into view.

The War Slayer's blades moved faster than I could register as she disarmed the kingsguard who had led the descent before slicing through his exposed neck. Black armor crashed to the steps, and I leaped to the side as his body fell. Three more followed in a matter of seconds. I kept my eyes forward as the soldiers gasped for air, blood choking their cries. A calm, unfeeling wave swept over me as I stepped over their dying bodies and into their blood, continuing our hike up the tower.

The stairwell opened into a tall hall where two more charged us from where they stood outside an elaborately painted set of iron doors marked by a large sideways figure eight, our moons in their center, topped by the sun. Kresida sprinted forward, prepared to take them down, but my magic was faster. It speared forward in two ribbons of black, engulfing the two and devouring them within a second. Their armor crashed to the floor as ash replaced flesh.

"I guess that works too," she murmured, surging to the doors. She reached for the handle and cursed as she whipped her hand back, a fresh line of red blisters forming on her light brown palm.

Locked with magic? I cursed myself for not waiting for Carina or Nerissa. My hand hovered over the shining metal, the Obscura restless beneath my palm as if noting there was nothing it could do. My shadows could only destroy organic material. But the Transcindiel...

"Stay back," I murmured, leashing the darkness within me and matching the Transcindiel's war song with my mind's voice. The golden wisp of magic slithered up to meet me, and I latched it to the amplifier around my neck before pushing it into the doors.

My mind formed a solid oak. A towering, domineering tree. I sent an axe crashing down at its base. Again. And again. Until the creek of snapping wood groaned in the silence of my mind. I waited for the resounding crash, for the doors to transform from iron to oak, so I could spear that darkness toward them, so I could turn them to ash.

The familiar burn of the amplifier bit at my chest, the sickening smell of sizzling flesh filling the hall. I resisted the urge to rip the pendant off, to fling it across the hall. The doors seemed to buck against me, resisting the magic.

"Try something else," Kresida breathed. "However, you're trying to change it, it's too much. Too different."

I closed my eyes, trying to ignore the smoke wafting from beneath my armored vest. Too different... Xenelpha's words returned to my mind.

*Ice calls to water as magma calls to stone.*

What did iron call to?

The tall oak in my mind's eye disappeared, replaced by the easy current of the Ripped River. I envisioned the metal doors before me melting into a blazing, silver stream. I spooled the image with that golden light, sending a blast of magic into the doors.

Golden light erupted. Kresida's arm flew up to shield her eyes. I blinked, a fresh wave of nausea rolling over me as an overwhelming, metallic scent shoved up my nostrils. The silver iron glowed orange before turning a bright crimson as it lique-fied and slid to the floor in a wave.

*Blood.*

We raced through the shallow pool, sloshing through the hall and into the chamber.

Shouts echoed through the room as kingsguards raised their swords. Saros stood at the center, the moons' light filtering in from the large window gilding his frame like a false angel. He held his domineering staff in one hand and a long blade in the other.

# CHAPTER FIFTY-TWO

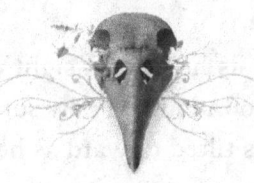

*Aeriden.*
    —*From Lyvia's list.*

ury surged into the chasm of my powers. Saros's blue eyes narrowed before his lips curled over his teeth, and he attacked with a viscous blast of wind.

But I was ready.

My magic gaped at the raw strength of the king, his power somehow greater than Carina's...than Queen Antares's... My shield held against his attack, though it buckled and pushed me back, my boots sliding toward the bloody hall we'd come from. His arms rose above his head, the wide sleeves of his robe floating down and revealing his thin, gaunt arms as he rallied more strength, more power, ready to snap through my shield. I braced myself as a strange, foreign sensation tapped against my mind.

I blinked.

So did Saros.

His momentary hesitation was enough. Wrath, devastation, and the need for revenge collided with whatever force linked my two powers as I tapped into my amplifier. Two thick ribbons of darkness snapped through the air as they slashed at King Saros's shield.

His eyes widened as he caught sight of the darkness, and he twirled his staff around him, a new sort of energy snapping into his being. His lips tilted upward as he hammered his staff against the stone floor.

A force rippled through the ground, and as it hit my shield, my ribbons dissipated. I caught my balance, reinforcing my shield, as the king launched himself at me.

He leaped forward, his staff pointed at my shield, as he rallied another blast of magic and raised his blade high above his head.

Not *his* blade.

Snowflakes and delicate flowering vines danced up the elaborate hilt of the ancient sword.

*Enya's blade.*

A snarl ripped through my lips as rage pounced. The sight of her blade in his hands snapped whatever restraining tether remained connected to my powers, and I unleashed myself.

Two sets of glowing, golden eyes blinked open as they raised their dark heads, their twisting bodies and black scales flowing from the power in my palms. Saros's eyes widened as he took in the twin snakes of darkness rising through the air.

I smiled, reveling in his shock. No, the woman whose blade he held... The elf he *murdered*... The warrior he killed for the power of death had commanded the shadows, but she'd never *transformed* them.

His eyes glazed over for a moment, awe, fear, and greed slipping into their depths. And I *lunged*. I threw everything into the serpents of death. Pain seared at my chest, and my energy drained by the second. My snakes of shadows snapped through the air as they ripped through Saros's shield and wrapped him in an armor of darkness.

His staff crashed to the floor as their tongues flicked the air and tails rattled, twisting tighter. I raised my hands from a distance and let my powers lift him into the air, the darkness shining with a hint of gold in the rising moons' light that crept in from the back window.

Emotions flooded me. Being here, back in Mount Telum, over a year after my discovery of Enya's burial site... The betrayals and deaths that followed. Morwyn. Aeriden. My father. Eira. Oslo. Xenelpha. Bear.

The Tribute. The war. The bodies in Odessa. The slaves on Kayj. It was all his fault. This man. I fed my rage to the union of Obscura and Transcindiel might that streamed from my palms in a constant flow.

Rage.

Loss.

Devastation.

Shouts of battle and the clang of weapons in the room were distant as I kept my gaze on the king. The king, who seemed to have aged *decades* over the past year. His tan, weathered skin sagged, the wrinkles forming along his cheeks deep and harsh. He looked weary as he hung suspended in midair, his gray brows pinching in disgust as he watched me.

Kresida's curse drew my attention as she spat a mouthful of blood on the shining floor. She bellowed at her opponent, the final kingsguard left in the grand tower, possibly the kingdom. Dark liquid stained his black armor, and his white cloak flew as he spun, meeting her attack with unmatched fury. Kresida crouched, ready to leap, as he paused for the briefest moment. His sapphire eyes caught mine from across the room.

*Impossible, impossible,* my heart chanted as it beat frantically for a moment before everything stopped.

My breath, my blood, my powers, my rage... My entire being came to a halt as my gaze met Cantor blue eyes staring through the slit in his helmet.

"STOP!" I screamed as Kresida lunged for my brother.

Her blade was positioned ready to slice through his armpit.

Aeriden ripped his gaze away from me as he met Kresida with a growl and a blade of his own.

"DISARM!" I bellowed at Kresida, my voice coming out strange and distant. *"Disarm only!"*

She shot me a look that would have wilted me a year ago, but I held my gaze on her, eyes hard. She snarled as she finally swung her leg out behind Aeriden and knocked the longsword from his hands with a swipe of her blade. She grabbed hold of his other arm, twisting it before he let out a grunt, yielding to the elf towering above him.

"Lyvi—" he began as he craned his neck to look up at me.

Kresida shot a look at me before removing his helmet, and it took everything in me not to crash to my knees and weep.

Aeriden. *Aer.*

Aeriden was alive. He wasn't dead. He was here, in Sultira. He was here. He was...protecting the king... He was a *kingsguard*... And in his eyes... That was... *Oh gods...*

That was *horror.*

Fear and disgust, even, at who, or *what*, he saw standing before him.

My thoughts spun in the wild flurry of impossibilities as my heart cracked at the look he gave me. What did he see in me now? A monster?

A soft chuckle rasped from Saros's lips. I snapped my attention to the king, hanging in the serpents of darkness, my magic remarkably still flowing, cutting through my shock. The heart-shaped heads of the snakes sent me back years to a certain solstice festival... Aeriden's fear...

The Transcindiel reacted to the thought, dissolving the snakes and spinning them into thick, unbreakable fortissa chains instead.

Saros's withered lips tilted in a slight grin as his eyes slid from mine to Aeriden's, and his expression turned mocking. My powers reacted without me thinking, tightening their grip, the thin fortissa chains slithering over his body.

"You've made a grave mistake, Lyvia," he gasped, his breath constricted through his closing throat.

I gazed upon the old King Saros. The man who had traded thousands of his own people, had sold them into a life of misery to the dark king in the north, and I felt only one thing. *Hate.*

*Hate* for manipulating me, for thinking he could manipulate my father.

*Hate* for arresting me. Arresting Drystan and Father Marcus.

*Hate* for sending his forces to Rivaner. For killing Morwyn.

*Hate* for allowing High Priest Helmar to conduct his sick experiments with the Obscura Bone, the power that belonged to me.

*Hate* for sending his forces to Odessa.

*Hate* for torturing Bear, for killing him.

*Hate* for what he did to Enya all those years ago.

My eyes snapped to his three-fingered hand, now hanging limp at his side.

I fed my powers that hate, urging them on, urging them to somehow burn darker and brighter at the same time. They twisted and writhed around him in hundreds of tiny chains as they spun a web of power. A growing sense of unease reached me, and though I couldn't see him through the window in the back of the room, I knew Aquila approached.

"Lyvia," Kresida warned from the corner of the room.

She had Aeriden on his knees, her fist in his black hair. Longer, shaggier than I'd ever seen it. Unruly and wild, like when we were children.

"*What are you doing?* Why are you doing this, Lyvia?" Aeriden's disgust and outrage boomed in his challenge.

"Are you going to kill me, Lady Lyvia?" the king whispered.

I stared at him as he let out another soft, vicious chuckle.

"You are not the first to want me dead. Though I think this is the closest anyone has come. Enya tried, you know."

Numbness spread through my lips as I prepared for whatever lie the king prepared to spew, whatever excuses he was about to throw my way. For however he thought he could trick me into sparing his life. But there would be no trial. Not for this monster.

"You're a murderer," I breathed, the words coming out quieter than I wished. "You sold your own people to keep the ashen off your shores. To keep your more valued citizens, your priests, your soldiers, your scholars, shielded from the atrocities in the north. You're despicable. A pathetic king, not worthy of the title."

"A king must make choices," Saros said, blood dripping from the corner of his nose.

"Lyvia..." another warning from Kresida as my powers tightened on the king, the fortissa chains twisting and constricting around his chest.

"Everyone makes choices," King Saros stressed through an airy breath. "We must all live with them until we live no longer. I've endured thousands of years with my choices. More than any one man should. But I would do anything to save my people."

My gut twisted alongside the darkness in my veins. Bayne had said something similar.

"Liar," I whispered.

"What reason do I have to lie to you, Lady Cantor?"

I paled at the title, and realization crossed the king's face in a flicker.

"And how was the Horse Lord when you saw him?" he asked quietly. "I wondered if the rumors were true of your time in the Crystal Castle. I'd ask you, but I can read it well enough on your face."

The king licked his dry lips as he studied the horror on my face. Small buds of tears formed in the corners of my eyes at the words and the accusing certainty with which he spoke.

"The nyxteria is beautiful, but it is deadly. Do you think you will ever forgive yourself? Is there anything left of the soul you've so permanently marred?" King Saros stared down at me with disdain. "We are not so different, you and I. The stone demanded Enya dive to the deepest depths of darkness before it bent to her will. It seems you have as well."

Aeriden's gaze burned against my face from across the room, but I couldn't turn to him. How could I ever face him after what I had done? I had killed our father, killed *his* father.

"Before you kill me, Lady Cantor," the king continued, coughing through the blood dripping down his nose, "consider what else Dark King Daimos brews in the north. Daimos has always sought their power. The very power that flows in your veins." Saros's blue eyes darted around my neck and my outstretched hands, now shaking against the power flowing from them.

"They will be back. They will come for them. The Bellators knew this and did *nothing*. Decided to *hide* their weapons. Selfish, rotting *cowards*, all of them. It was up to me." He gasped now, his breath turning ragged. "Up to me to find a way. And if that meant a small sacrifice of our people, to keep our kingdom safe... We needed armies. *Any* armies to defend—"

A shattered cry bellowed from the hall as Ronan stormed up the steps to the center of the large room at the same moment Nerissa's light burst through the back circular window, spraying the floor with a cascade of glass.

Nerissa ducked and rolled into the space as Ronan sprinted past me, screaming in devastation and wrath as he lifted his longsword above his head.

"NO!" I cried after him, cutting my powers off before he leaped into their path. The king barked in pain as his knees hit the floor, his weak body crumpling forward.

"Ronan!" Nerissa screamed as he shoved his blade through King Saros's chest, the ancient man's blue eyes widening as Ronan lifted him by the cuff of his robes and the hilt of his blade. The king coughed a stripe of blood across the ex-queensguard's face. Saros slid his gaze once more to mine, wan mouth open in shock as the extended life in his eyes died. A crimson line stretched into a pool on the floor.

"What have you done?" Nerissa breathed as her arms went slack, watching Ronan, who stood between us, staring down at the dead king. His blade hung loosely from his hand as blood wept from its tip. Ronan's bright eyes were dull as he raised them to meet Nerissa's and then my own.

"Ended his reign," he croaked, turning toward Aeriden and Kresida.

A look of shock passed over his numb features, registering who Kresida held at knife point. He ripped the white kingsguard cape from Aeriden's back before he slipped it over his blade, ridding it of the king's blood.

"Lyvia was doing just fine at that herself," Kresida spat, eyeing me with irritation.

I ground my teeth, allowing my powers to flare in my

palms, my eyes blazing with a rim of embers in defense. I refused to look at Aeriden, to meet his horror-stricken gaze.

"I heard what Saros said just as I arrived," Nerissa started, stepping over the body and approaching us. "About what he thinks is coming..."

"And what Xenelpha said about the return of an enemy." I bobbed my head, finishing her thought.

Nerissa's eyes slid to Aeriden before turning toward Ronan. "What of the queen? Will she be able to—"

"The queen is dead." Ronan's words were flat as he dropped the blood-soaked kingsguard cape and strode from the room without another word.

Nerissa's keen Ravindra eyes scanned Aeriden's black armor and the discarded cape.

"Lyvia, what do you—" she began.

I lifted a hand, a familiar sensation washing over me. "What is that?" I murmured, scanning the wreckage in the room.

Nerissa stilled, before she asked, "What do you feel?"

"Lyvia," Aeriden's broken whisper floated from across the room.

I stepped through the wreckage. The faintest pulsing. Not a sound. A vibration of air pushing and pulling throughout the room.

"Lyvia," Aeriden said again, his voice shaking, louder.

Push and pull. Push and pull. Here in this room. A Bellator Bone, hidden somewhere. I stepped over the large mirror that had shattered at Nerissa's entrance.

Push and pull.

"Lyvia!" Aeriden screamed at me.

I looked up to find his face tightened with grief and rage. Those features that looked so much like my father's. *His* father's.

Tears soaked his face, brightening the sapphire hue in his irises.

"Where's Dad?"

Numbness crept over me as I held his stare. The blood drained from my face as I relived those damning moments in the Crystal Castle, those moments that haunted me day and night. The moments that eclipsed my soul in a shadow of darkness.

People filed into the room. Carina. Astraeus. Vulcan.

Push and pull. Push and pull. The feeling intensified, and my powers leaned forward.

"Dead," I answered quietly, picking up the burning orange Bellator Bone from among the wreckage next to the king's staff.

# CHAPTER FIFTY-THREE

*Oslo.*
*—From Lyvia's list.*

We knelt in frigid, sodden hay. The dark space *reeked*. Bile threatened to rise in my throat as I took in the small, damp stone cell that Father Marcus had been given. His glossy eyes stared at the wall as Drystan took his frigid hands in his own, caked in blood and dirt from the day of battle.

A slice of guilt hit my chest as my mind shot to where Vienah sat six levels up, waiting to be tried. The water witch's cell was warm, clean, and dry, though, and the Rising soldiers stationed outside it were honorable. I'd chosen them myself. She'd have a cot and fresh food and water. Ronan had found and freed her family already. I bristled at the tendril of concern squeezing my chest. Had she ever been my friend?

Drystan's moon-like eyes were shadowed and dark, the

invisible scars of battle carved into his solemn countenance. The Advetis Bone fluttered nervously on his chest as he neared Father Marcus, as if upset.

One day. It had taken *one day* to take the city and kill Saros. The finality of it left me drained but not lost. I was numb, but I knew where I was going, where I had to go next. But first...

"Father Marcus, can you hear me? It's Lyvia and Drystan. We've come to help you," I whispered. I wrapped a blanket around his gaunt shoulders, one of the few I'd found in the servants' quarters that wasn't being used for treating the wounded.

He rocked back and forth, muttering foreign words beneath his breath as his eyes darted around the wall.

I cleared my throat as Drystan ran his thumbs over the top of the priest's bony hands.

"I found your journal," I continued. "It helped me with the Obscura power. It was a *bone*. That's what you were trying to tell me, right? A bone, not a stone."

Dull eyes shot to mine before darting back to the wall.

"It won't hurt you anymore," I whispered, voice beginning to shake. "I can control it. It is mine now. No one will hurt you again."

I scanned the dried blood on the floor of his cell and the various injuries that littered his arms and legs, rage returning to the chasm where my powers slept. Drystan's eyes followed mine, his throat bobbing as a small pool of liquid formed in the corners.

"Come on," I murmured, gently pulling on Father Marcus's shoulders, doing my best to ease him to his feet. "We're going up, away from this place."

My voice broke as a small puddle of tears fell onto the amplifier on my chest. Father Marcus muttered under his breath, but he took my arm.

The moment his hand touched me, he screamed and jerked himself away, eyes wild. Drystan reached for his arms, pulling him back to his feet, but he convulsed, his frail body writhing out and crashing to the floor with a pained yelp.

What had they done to him? Had *my power* done this? A sob escaped my lips as I stepped toward him and he shuffled away, pulling the sodden hay along with him.

"Lyvia," a voice echoed from down the hall, softer than I'd ever heard it. Quiet, staggered steps followed, and I lifted my head to see Vulcan doing his best to hide his wince as he made his way down the aisle. The gray fabric of his wrapped chest peeked out from beneath his shirt, and he looked pale, ragged. He'd reluctantly stayed in the war tent after taking an arrow for me, directing our forces and adding his invaluable insight into our attack.

"You shouldn't have come all the way down here," I said, wiping the snot from my face and standing.

"I brought some help," Vulcan said, jerking his head toward the stairwell without looking. My heart squeezed as Marian's face popped in the doorway, and she hurried down the aisle. Her face was tired and anxious. She reached for my hand, squeezing it.

"You're in Aedrialis," I whispered.

The color drained from her face as she signed, "Let's make this quick so I can get back."

I nodded, motioning her to where Drystan inched toward Father Marcus as if approaching a caged animal.

"I'm not sure I'll be able to help. He won't—" I began as the arrival of another sounded from the stairwell.

Lord Astraeus sauntered down the aisle wearing an insufferable smirk as he spotted me. I bristled at his appearance, barely a scratch on the man, his face free of paint and sea blue coat bright even in the dimness of the dungeon hall. My eyes shot to Vulcan, who ignored my irritation. Astraeus strode to the cell, smirk fading and dark eyes softening as he took in Father Marcus.

Marian knelt beside him, grasping his hand and placing a warm cup of tea against it. Father Marcus muttered something under his breath, but his hands stopped shaking for a moment. His eyes lifted to meet Marian's. Her gasp was almost as shocking as the sob that followed. Marian nearly dropped the cup of tea as tears formed in her eyes.

With help, Father Marcus brought the cup of tea to his lips and drank long and hard. Marian continued to stare at him for several long moments before Father Marcus closed his eyes and slumped back into Drystan's chest.

I opened my mouth to ask Marian what had happened when something foreign and urgent tugged at my mind, and I went deathly still.

"What's wrong?" Astraeus asked, the question more of a demand.

I shook my head and glowered at him. What was he doing here? Regardless of what magic he used, he'd made his thoughts about me clear enough. Alliances weren't friendships, I reminded myself.

"Lyvia?" Vulcan asked.

I pinched my eyes shut, something strange and foreign pressing on me.

"I don't know," I whispered. I blinked my eyes open and scanned the surrounding cells, searching for the source of the intrusion. A growing sense of unease snaked its way up my core, prickling the hairs on my arms as that *something* tried again to tap against my consciousness.

"If feels," I murmured, exiting Father Marcus's cell and allowing my powers to rise to the surface, "like something is here. Someone is here..."

Vulcan stepped beside me and began moving down the line of cells. I followed him, closing my eyes as that sensation struck again.

"Not here," I murmured, "lower. We need to go lower."

Astraeus moved to my other side. "Stay with the priest," he said to Vulcan with a trace of authority not missed by the elf. "Bring him up. I'll stay with Lyvia."

"The fuck you will," Vulcan growled, his usual sneer plastered on his face.

*Tap.*

I pinched my eyes shut as bickering began.

*Tap.*

"You're injured."

*Tap.*

"You're untrustworthy."

*Tap.*

"You swore to protect her, but you're injured."

*Tap.*

Vulcan went still. "How—"

"At all costs."

*Tap.* What were they talking about?

"Today, the cost is standing aside and letting another step in."

*Tap.*

My head began to ache, and the space between my eyes burned white hot.

"Lyvia—"

A hand gripped my shoulder as I swayed.

Away. I needed to get away from this feeling. It pulled me down, deep below where we stood in the stone dungeons. My feet dragged as I made my way to the staircase. My boot hit the first step leading up out of the dungeons, and the tapping turned into a vicious pounding.

"Easy," Astraeus murmured behind me.

I took another step up, a whimper fleeing my lips.

*Fuck.*

Tears slipped between the cracks in my lids as I continued to squeeze them shut. I dared another step, and blazing white pain ripped through my head. The edges of consciousness blurred in my mind.

My hand gripped Astraeus's wrist as I backed up a step, and the pounding eased to a light tap.

Down. It was forcing me down.

Another step, and that consistent tapping lightened.

We followed the damp, stone staircase down until we came to a dark hall, the last set of cells in the dungeon below Mount Telum. Astraeus lit a torch, and we wandered through the hall, checking cells that hadn't been used for what looked to be hundreds of years. I ran my fingers over the bars. Old cobwebs and dust coated every inch of the place.

"Here," Astraeus murmured. "This is the only place that's been disturbed recently." He motioned to a barely visible square on the wall of the far end of the hall.

The dust had been smudged there, and as I stepped forward, the tapping turned persistent.

"How do we get through?" I asked.

"Are you sure you want to?" Astraeus replied, his dark eyes wary as he frowned at various symbols along the floor.

The answer was no, but I kept that to myself as I ran my fingers over the ribbed edging on the wall. My powers bucked in response.

"It's definitely here," I murmured, running my fingers over the words carved into the wall.

*"The weapon rests above the cage, dormant until the return of the Hidden Hero's enemy,"* I recited, brows pinching at the riddle. I'd barely finished when Astraeus's arm wrapped

around my waist and ripped me back as rows of thick, long spikes shoved through the surface. My voice caught in my throat as I narrowly avoided being impaled.

I shoved at the pirate's arm, still locked around my waist, as if he were just as shocked. He released me, and we cautiously approached. As we did so, the iron spikes sucked back into the wall.

"*Fuck*," I breathed, my heart stammering. My mind reached into the chasm of power where the golden light and shadows slumbered, but they were tired. Whatever power Astraeus had used to refuel me left me uneasy with the pirate lord. It was intimate, somehow, as if he'd gifted a piece of himself to me. My reluctant gratitude edged against my constant irritation with him.

That persistent tapping returned, and I gritted my teeth. Okay, so we were doing this. Whatever *this* was.

I stepped back, and it turned dizzying. Left, the same. But if I stepped to the right, the tapping softened. My hand reached for the edge of the hidden door, and the tapping blazed behind my eyes. I snatched my hand back, instead trying for the wall, where it softened. I continued this game of hot and cold for several minutes until my fingers at last landed on a spoked wheel, so shallowly carved into the wall it was near invisible.

My fingers traced the edge, finding letters of the common tongue alphabet topping each spoke.

"Who is the Hidden Hero's enemy?" I whispered into the darkness. The tapping intensified, as if it could hear me.

I replayed the words of King Saros, moments before his death. *They are coming...*

Xenelpha had called them the *ehp'uch*, Rhashtai for...

My fingers found the six different letters that spelled out a word I'd heard only once. With two hands, I rotated the wheel until each letter matched up with the small divot at the top, spinning it until the combination was complete, and the wheel sank with a groan into the stone.

*Embodied.*

The hidden door hissed as it clicked. The thick stone inched forward at an angle, allowing the soft red glow of the hidden chamber to creep into the hall. A dome of iron rods, bent and curved in an elaborate cage, surrounded the Stone Witch.

# CHAPTER FIFTY-FOUR

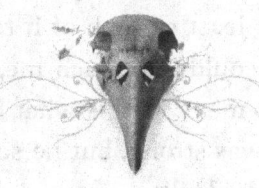

*Morwyn.*
  *—From Lyvia's list.*

Lines of blazing rubelline stone glowed red in the darkness that enveloped the lowest level of Mount Telum's dungeon.

A cage surrounded the Stone Witch as she sat covered in her own filth and reeking like rotten flesh. Half her teeth were gone, and what could be seen of her arms and face were marbled with fresh scars. That scratchy, straw-like gray hair was cut short against her scalp, and her nose had been hacked off.

The Stone Witch's violet eyes stayed fixed on me, and I felt a gentle tap once more.

"Hello, Death Digger, it's time to pay. The debt you owe grows heavier each day."

The stone-on-stone grinding of her voice was somehow

more sickening as she spoke it with half her teeth. My gut twisted at her words, and Astraeus stiffened next to me.

*Undo it for us*, she'd said, all those months ago in Odessa. *Undo his treasons.* What had he done? *Who* had done it?

I eyed the cage containing the powerful witch. Built with rubelline stone, or at least enough of it to render her powers somewhat null. She could still reach me, mind-to-mind, but she couldn't speak to me. Was this what had drained Saros of so much power? He was strong, but he seemed weaker in the tower after his shield had fallen.

"I will," I replied, still unsure what I had agreed to all those months ago. "After you tell me how to defeat Dark King Daimos."

A soft chuckle gurgled from the other side of the bars.

"What you need is me," she said, her pale, sickly gums peeking out from beneath her lips. "To help, I must be free."

"You'll help us defeat the dark king?" I asked.

"It's my right to take his soul," she hissed in the darkness, "for cursing me with the power he stole. He tricked the old king into protecting his home, for he knew I'd return to take back the throne."

"What are you talking about?" I asked softly, the pieces of a complex puzzle slowly starting to come together. "Who are you?"

"The power of the seasons remembers well. Undo it now, and I need not tell," she whispered.

A hand gripped my elbow, and I turned to face Astraeus, eyes narrowed in warning, "Don't do this, Lyvia."

"The Bonder has no choice," the Stone Witch cackled from the other side of the cage. "She has a debt to pay, sworn with her mind's voice."

Astraeus stilled before turning toward the witch.

"You swore an oath to her, mind-to-mind?" he breathed, keeping his eyes on the witch.

My throat bobbed. "I made a deal with her at Odessa. She'd warned us the ashen were coming. And I needed to access my powers. I don't know what she did, but I agreed to *undo it* for her in exchange for her help."

"How did she help you?" Astraeus's eyes were as depthless as the night as he turned them back to me. The rubelline stone brightened the red in his dark hair and cast his skin in a crimson hue.

"I..." I stuttered, searching my memories. "I...I honestly don't know. She said she'd send a sign from Aelius's brow, and then..."

Astraeus palmed one of the two rubelline daggers he always wore as he angled himself between me and the witch.

"And then the Sending occurred," he answered for me. "The moons crossed in front of the sun, creating a twin eclipse. The event that shouldn't have taken place for another two years. Yet somehow..."

The Stone Witch cackled from across the chamber.

"Clever, clever pirate lord," she whispered. "When he discovered it was gone, the good king *roared*."

"Discovered what was gone?" I asked.

"The Celestyn Bone," Astraeus answered. "She had it. And she used it to manipulate the twin eclipse last spring."

My mouth hung open.

"The Celestyn Bone can—"

"Move celestial objects," Astraeus murmured. "Break worlds."

"Where is it?" I turned back to the Stone Witch.

"Saros spent much power in binding me here. But I'm stronger than he thought, aren't I, dear?"

A sharp hammer pounded in my mind, vanishing as quickly as it arrived.

"Stop doing that," I hissed through my teeth, rubbing the space between my eyes. "I swore no air oath to you."

"No," Astraeus breathed beside me. "You bound yourself in another way. With your mind's voice. Something older, something deeper than even an air oath. There's no getting out of this. It's why she can still reach your mind, even through the rubelline cage."

*Fuck.*

Could I use my powers to cut this type of bond? What would the risk be? Would the physical blow hit my mind instead of my body, since it was sworn that way? A plunging feeling entered my chest at the thought of risking my mind...

I eyed the star-shaped divot in the center of the cage and cocked my head as I examined the lock. There was something familiar about...

Astraeus placed a white shard in my hand.

I snapped my face at him, and the corner of his lip twitched.

"You took this from Saros's tower," I snapped. "This was on top of his staff." My brows narrowed as I scanned the pirate.

"Seemed like it could be important," he murmured, his eyes still on the Stone Witch.

"Thief."

"Bonscaíh."

His eyes slid to mine before darting to my lips. I ignored the look and heaved an exasperated sigh. Well, fuck. If I tried to ignore the Stone Witch and pretend we'd never found her, she'd simply mangle my brain with whatever mental link our deal had created. And I couldn't risk damaging my mind...

"Do you need me to—" Astraeus began, his brows tilting up as he lifted a hand.

"No," I cut him off. No, I could do this without him.

I muttered the rubelline spell beneath my breath before placing the key inside the lock, twisting once as the glowing red light went dark. Soundlessly, the iron, rubelline-laced cage melted into the ground.

The Stone Witch inhaled deeply and blinked as she sat on the floor, waiting for me. Astraeus's glowing blade was at her throat a moment later, his eyes on me.

This could be a mistake...

The Stone Witch's violet eyes glowed a soft pink above Astraeus's rubelline dagger. My gaze drifted to the pirate standing guard, lingering for a moment on his scarred lower lip, before meeting his stare.

His dark eyes dipped in soft confidence as they held my gaze. "I'm with you. You are not alone," he said, his words escaping in a breath as if they'd waited there for years. The strong column of his neck bobbed as his eyes held mine, their marbled gray illuminated in the rubelline glow.

A distant memory caressed my consciousness, and I blinked, something reluctant inside me softening. I pulled my gaze back to the witch, reaching deep within my well of power and tugging on a note of Transcindiel. It lifted an ear, cocking its head at my call.

My mind drifted to the ashen as I reached out with that little strand of golden power. It floated to the Stone Witch, curving back and forth, examining the creature.

Ever so gently, it landed atop her head. I did my best not to jump as it recoiled, as if disgusted with the result of its power ages ago, but it stayed focused on her. I pushed a little harder as I reached for the amplifier around my neck, its power warming my chest.

The Stone Witch closed her eyes, nodding as I pushed more power into her. I spiraled the Transcindiel around her until she was encased in a web of golden light. The Obscura sat at attention beneath my veins, watching its twin work while preparing to unleash itself should anything go wrong.

My chest sizzled beneath the amplifier as the Transcindiel's light spun faster and faster before it suddenly retracted. I fell back as the force of the power's retreat hit me.

Long, gray hair splayed on the dark stone, surrounding the naked women. She blinked, violet eyes darker as she pushed against the floor and stood.

A gasp escaped as I took in her ethereal face, the delicately pointed ears, and the eight-pointed, luminous star shining from the center of her bare chest.

My pulse paused as realization hit me. At whom, exactly, stood before us beneath Mount Telum.

Mystic. Bellator. Queen. Prophet.

*Olienna.*

# CHAPTER FIFTY-FIVE

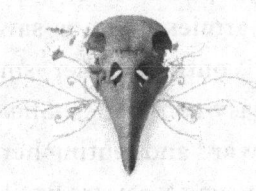

*Papa.*

—*From Lyvia's list.*

---

F ires blazed on both ends of the large chamber. The king's council room was crowded and filled with the scent of unwashed bodies and strong wine. I couldn't peel my eyes from Olienna as she stood at the head of the table, draped in a mauve traveling dress, her long gray hair rippling over her shoulders as she told her story. Not only was she the most powerful mystic alive, Olienna was possibly the most powerful being in the Realm of Vael.

Enya had tried to tell me. Had tried to show me in those visions. *Look. Watch*, she seemed to say. The Bellator had barely aged a day. A Bellator here in Sultira, all along, under Saros's nose the entire time. Trapped in the Lumerians and then caged in the dungeons of Mount Telum.

"So, the gods are coming for their powers. And Daimos has plotted their return in hopes they'll share power with him?" Carina's voice held a surprising edge of authority to it as she questioned the unseated queen of Nivis.

"When the first Bellators prepared to fight against the Embodied and their armies, Daimos saw his opportunity. As did Saros," Olienna continued, her smooth voice carrying across the room in easy confidence. She stood at the head of the table, leaning forward and tenting her feminine hands over the maps. "The war waged for years until Lelyth destroyed the doorway they used to enter this world, shattering the land between Sultira and Lotrennia."

"You were right," Nerissa murmured under her breath. "Enya didn't do it."

Nerissa had stayed close in the hours that followed Olienna's transformation, uneasy yet curious. Olienna nodded to her.

"Indeed. Lelyth had the power to move planets and other celestial objects, to break or create them. A dangerous power, but one that changed the fate of the War of Ruin. Despite what you may think, it was a war *won* by the beings on Vael. We did not lose."

"Couldn't you just give the gods their powers back? And then they'd leave us alone?" Kresida asked, the dim light glowing softly against her dark skin.

"They are not gods," Olienna said, her soft gray waves bouncing as she shook her head. "They are impostors. Beings that took this power ages ago, with the sole intent of finding and draining other worlds of it. The Bellators were only able to harness it with the help of the People of the Stars, and even then, only to defend our world."

"The People of the Stars are a myth," Carina cut in,

adjusting her glasses as she leaned forward on the table. "A people with the ability to transfer power. To literally give and take it away. There's been no evidence of their existence other than the mention of them in fairytales."

Olienna's brows pinched up as she gazed at Carina.

"Oh no, my dear Princess. They were very real. The Starlings are out there somewhere."

Something stilled inside me as I listened, the air warming, as if some cooling breeze had vanished.

"Regardless of these people," Astraeus cut in, stepping toward the ornately carved table, "What does this have to do with Daimos? What else is he planning?"

"I don't know," Olienna continued, "but whatever it is, we need to prepare the world for a second war. The second coming of the Embodied. Everyone suffers with their return."

"A weapon, maybe?" Nerissa asked.

"Perhaps," Olienna said.

Ronan spread a large map of the realm on the table, covering the smaller map of Sultira.

"Our powers," she continued, turning toward me and Nerissa, "are but a *sliver* of what the Embodied hold. And they wield it without conscience. They're not beholden to the ideals of men and elves. Good and evil, it doesn't exist in their minds. The essence of who they once were, whatever type of beings they came from, dissolved in the taking of their power. So, no, we cannot just give it back."

Olienna turned once more to Kresida, whose dark brows narrowed in response. "The War of Ruin brought winged beasts of hell, demons of other worlds you could scarcely imagine..."

My mind drifted to the carvings in the amphitheater in Rhashtai. Fire and ash, fangs and claws. "We need armies.

Armies with the powers of the Bellators." Olienna strode around the room as she spoke, her dress swishing.

"And what are those powers?" I asked the question Drystan signed from the corner, doing my best not to stare at the space on his chest where the Advetis Bone sat hidden.

A cautious reluctance had grown in his eyes since the stone container had opened, presenting him with the Advetis Bone. His attempts at harnessing the power were continually unsuccessful.

"Eight powers were taken from the Embodied. Obscura, darkness and death, as demonstrated," she said, motioning to me. "Along with the Transcindiel, which I am not sure how exactly ended up in your hands. Or rather, chose you. You're unlike its previous bearer, Ordell."

For whatever reason, her words hit like an insult. I squashed the flare of irritation.

"Soleia, split between the Ravindra twins." Olienna waved a nonchalant hand toward Nerissa, who bristled. "My own, Palaega, is the power of the mind. As many of you know," she murmured, grinning at Nerissa, "I can speak to whomever I'd like, mind-to-mind. And I have the ability to influence sleep."

"The others, we must track down. I held onto the Celestyn Bone until Saros captured me. I left it with some friends so as not to let Saros get his hands on it. Celestyn was Lelyth's power."

I blinked. Those creatures that had found Evony. *They* had a bone of power. *Gork* had it. It'd been right under our noses the entire time.

"We must find them," Olienna said, more to Ronan than the rest of us. "It is *vital* we find the Celestyn Bone. I must insist you send out a party searching for the creatures at once."

Ronan murmured his agreement before she continued.

"Advetis, Faron's power, was that of travel. He could transport himself and others across immense space in the blink of an eye," Olienna explained.

I kept my gaze locked on Olienna as she spoke, in awe of the new power and resisting the urge to look at Drystan. We'd agreed to keep the discovery of the bone quiet, unsure of our trust in Olienna.

"Ramadiel, the last I knew, was taken by Daimos. The power to heal will be vital." Olienna's eyes scanned the thick scar on my neck. *To heal...* We would need this power for Lotrennia with the deaths that had spread.

"That leaves the Aeterna power," Olienna said, glancing down at the simmering orange Bellator Bone resting at the edge of the map. It sat in the center of the intricate celestial setting atop King Saros's staff for hundreds of years.

"The power of everlasting life. We all know who held onto that for the past two thousand years." Olienna pursed her thin lips.

My mind's eye flashed to those last few moments of extended life in King Saros's eyes before death lunged, as if it'd been hovering, waiting for him for thousands of years.

"Why would we need the Aeterna power?" I asked, eyeing the strange Bellator Bone, my mind drifting to the visions Enya had shared. I shifted, uneasy with it sitting here in the center of the room.

"These wars last hundreds of years, if not thousands. We need people who will remain to see it through. So that the information gleaned is not lost among the generations that come and go."

My stomach knotted as I remembered the fleeting conversation between Enya and Lelyth. They'd disagreed.

"So, we need armies," Ronan muttered after a long silence.

"Half of the Sultiran forces are marching south from Styn-guard. The commanders from the Rellenor Fields have yet to surrender. Word will have spread by now that Saros is dead, but Lord Pavel's fleet hasn't been seen since they chased off Nivis in Stynguard. We need to find him. Our forces are scat-tered, and their allegiance is uncertain."

"We need every army of the world," Olienna continued. "Sultirans, Nivisians, Lotrennians, Votruvians, and the fleets of Marisarma."

I chewed on her words for a moment, weighing whether I should mention anything about the Rhashtai in the Death Dunes. I caught several eyes of others in the room, waiting for me to mention the deadly bone tribes. Olienna's violet gaze slid to mine for a moment before continuing her speech.

A wave of apprehension, followed by another, *anticipation*, rushed toward me, and Nerissa looked up. Aquila and Tiberius were nearby.

*I am looking forward to meeting your caelumas. Though I suspect Aquila won't remember me.*

My heart leaped into my chest as Olienna's sing-song voice trilled in my mind. Nerissa went deathly still, keeping her eyes on the queen as lightning flickered in their depths.

"High Steward," Olienna said aloud, turning toward Ronan, who blinked once and pinched his light brows. Olienna grinned. "Well, I suppose that's who you are now, correct? With Queen Galena and King Saros deceased, their little one is the sole heir of the Kingdom of Sultira. As leader of the Rising and your history as queensguard, I would assume you are now the leader of Sultira until the young prince comes of age."

Ronan's throat bobbed as his eyes shot to Nerissa.

"Indeed," he said, his voice ringing clear and confident across the large chamber as he stood and pulled the maps from the center of the table.

My lips remained shut, as did Nerissa's and Vulcan's, as I was sure they recalled exactly what Ronan had shared with us. That Galena's child was certainly not sired by King Saros.

Carina's gasp interrupted the murmured conversation that followed. She leaped up and leaned forward, placing her palms on the table to get a better look at the large, glowing orb that had been concealed beneath the map. Gold and white writhed within the orb as if something living stirred in a pool of liquid sunlight.

"What's wrong?" Ronan asked, his eyes shooting to the orb in the center.

"You've seen this before," Olienna murmured, her eyes studying the princess.

Carina nodded, disbelief showing on her face. "In the Gilded Fortress... My mother's chambers."

Nerissa stilled as we processed her words.

"Cunning Saros," Olienna mused as she stepped beside Carina and floated her hand over the glowing stone. "This is the Aelius Orb. One of what's rumored to be five."

"What is it?" I asked, leaning forward.

"Much mystery surrounds these orbs," Olienna explained. "And though we know they are powerful, the full extent of their might remains a mystery. We know they can communicate with the masters of the other orbs."

My mind spun. King Saros held an Aelius Orb, and Queen Antares held another. Had they been communicating with one another? Carina's face drained of color.

"Try it," Ronan murmured as he stared at Carina. "We've been cut off from Lotrennia for six months now."

I glanced at Nerissa, who'd gone pale.

Carina held her small hands over the orb for several moments as the room stilled. She murmured something beneath her breath, and a bright, white light flashed, as if

A.M. KAY

responding to her words. As her fingers touched the orb, the swirling light paused, and the orb turned opaque and then as clear as crystals, reflecting what looked to be an ornate room, with flowering vines lining the walls.

"*My gods,*" Carina breathed.

The room froze as we peered into the Gilded Fortress.

428

# CHAPTER FIFTY-SIX

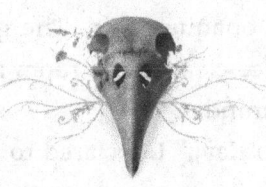

*Xenelpha.*
—*From Lyvia's list.*

"C an anyone hear me?" Carina asked.

My heart continued a thunderous beat as my breathing stopped, and I waited. Waited, and scarcely dared to hope that Bayne's face might appear in the orb, unsure of how I'd feel if it did. A servant's head bobbed into view. Her eyes were wide for a moment before she ran from the room.

"Wait!" Carina called.

The face of the queen materialized. My powers surged at the sight of her, a raging chorus echoing with their demand for release. Dark bags sat beneath her exquisite blue eyes.

"Carina?" Queen Antares questioned, her blonde brows pinched. "You're...in Mount Telum? What's happened?"

Carina opened her mouth to explain.

The queen cut her off. "It doesn't matter. Our forces sail to Kayj. The plague that's spread...the death, the decay. It's not what we thought. I must go. The king has already left. Don't use this again. We can't trust it."

My stomach pitched as Queen Antares's face disappeared, and the orb turned opaque again. The glowing, shimmering light returned. Silence cleaved the room as the queen's words echoed through my mind.

"We must sail to Kayj," I declared to no one in particular. "It's time."

"I can't send the Rising forces at a moment's notice," Ronan countered. "We're scattered. We've got a southern host to deal with, and I've no word back from those marching back from Stynguard. If I send the Rising forces, we're left with less than half to protect the city."

"Then just a few of us will go," I said, eyeing the others in the room. "The Lotrennians and any willing mages. Whoever wants to stay and guard the city can do so."

Ronan opened his mouth to respond, but Astraeus's voice cut through the room.

"The Marisarma fleet will sail with you, Lyvia," the pirate lord declared from the corner of the dark room.

My brows pinched up as I eyed Astraeus, a tentative piece of my heart softening despite the ringing doubt in my mind. I wasn't convinced he offered out of the goodness of his heart. He'd said as much himself. There wasn't an ounce of goodness in the man. He was bound to me in an alliance, bound to protect the innocent, yet something in those words beneath the dungeons... *I'm with you. You are not alone...*

"And I'll fly with you," Olienna said, a note of pride riding her tone. "We need to prepare to leave. Bellators," she said, turning to me and Nerissa. "A word in private."

The rest of the group shuffled from the room.

Once the echo of the door shutting died off, she said, "We share a bond as Bellators, a certain connection that allows us to feel one another's emotions. Based on what I've gathered since my freedom, the two of you know this but have figured out how to block it from each other."

I side-eyed Nerissa, knowing fully well she was as aware of this as I was. "This bond had nothing to do with your parents being soulbound, Nerissa. Soulbinding does not connect your emotions. That power, that connection, was passed down from Kyson."

I knew by now my emotional connection to Bayne hadn't been our soulbinding thread. It had been our bond as Bellators.

"Open yourselves up to each other, to me as well. The only way we can defeat the Embodied is by working together, and this innate, shared connection has allowed us to communicate in ways that changed the fate of the War of Ruin. We leave at first light tomorrow." Olienna's expression turned serious as she left the room.

"I don't like her," Nerissa said after a moment.

"You don't like anyone," I countered, glancing at her. The tips of her lips twitched.

"I like my brother on occasion. I tolerate Vulcan and Isla. Sometimes, I like you."

My lips kicked up in response until my thoughts drifted back to Bayne. "I suppose we should check in with Aquila and Ti. And then with the *High Steward* before we leave."

Nerissa rolled her eyes but nodded.

DESPITE DONNING SULTIRAN BLACK, I recognized the pair of Rising soldiers standing outside the late Queen Galena's quarters.

They nodded as I approached and slid open the double doors to the large living chamber.

Evening winter sun, tinged with pink and lavender, shone through the arched windows that lined the curved edge of the room and painted the marble floors like a watercolor canvas. A large bed sat in the middle, draped with used, soft pink linens and gray furs. Ronan hadn't allowed the maids to touch the room once the Death Scholars had removed his sister's body to ready it for burial.

I recognized the names of those they had brought in, but I had no desire to see them. To allow them to see me. Not after Aeriden and Father Marcus, both of whom were horrified by me, by the shadow I'd become.

My eye caught on a small bassinet on the other side of the bed, a mobile with stars and moons hanging above. I moved to leave when the smallest, softest sound cooed from the opposite corner of the room.

I looked to the source and started as I found Nerissa's tall form leaning against the wall that curved inward toward the adjoining sitting room. I joined her and peeked around the armoire to find Ronan, his light, curly hair a mess, dark bags beneath his closed eyes, reclining in a velvet chair. His curvy lips were parted as he breathed heavily, with his head bent forward. And there, in his strong arms, was a babe of only a couple months. Tiny and delicate. Fresh.

The babe was awake, his little hands reaching out of the snug blanket Ronan had wrapped around him. A soft snore rolled from Ronan's throat, and the babe responded with his own heart-melting coo. The tiny hand reached up, fingertips brushing against Ronan's stubble.

Emotions threatened to surge at the sight of the ex-queensguard and his nephew.

Loss for what might have been, those days in the Lumerians when I thought I'd been falling in love with him. And an envy I didn't exactly understand. Pain at the words Bayne spoke last year in Rivaner...

*We are not the same*, chanted often in my mind when I spiraled into a pit of self-doubt, self-hate, and led to the painful conclusion I'd come to over the past year...that I was not enough.

Self-pity gave way to rage as my thoughts flowed... Rage at Queen Antares for her manipulation, disbelief at Bayne for binding himself to her. Anger at him for not believing me, at myself for not pushing harder, for losing something I'd never had.

I watched them for several long moments, when out of nowhere, a tiny sliver of emotion drifted toward me.

*Pain... Regret.*

I blinked, doing my best to clear my head as I looked at Nerissa, whose skin glimmered with a single tear as it eased its way down her cheek.

I reached for her hand, lacing my fingers in between. She allowed the connection to stay open, and I gently pushed my own feelings back. She knew what I'd lost with Bayne. Her fingers squeezed.

"It was always him," she breathed, nodding at Ronan.

My throat bobbed as I dipped my chin in acknowledgment. She'd always love Ronan.

"We need to leave," she murmured after a moment.

I swallowed, continuing to stare at the small babe in Ronan's arms.

"You could stay," I whispered back, knowing she didn't *need* permission, but feeling as if she might need to hear it.

Nerissa blinked, a few more tears chasing the first down the side of her face. She shook her head, her loose brown hair swaying. "We need each other right now. And Bayne needs us both."

A surge of warmth swelled in my chest.

I nodded, the truth of her words steeling me. Bayne was a Bellator. He needed us as we needed him.

I replayed the words of Olienna's prophecy that Nerissa had spoken over a year ago as we climbed the foothills of the Lumerians.

*If shadowed and dark,*
*Death to the Monarch.*

OLIENNA WAS RIGHT. I was shadowed and dark, and Death came to the Monarch of Sultira. The rage that funneled deep into my core, into the chasm that housed the dark and the light, continued to spark like the warrior's eyes. And I would come for the rest of them.

"Dark King Daimos first. Then Queen Antares."

# CHAPTER FIFTY-SEVEN

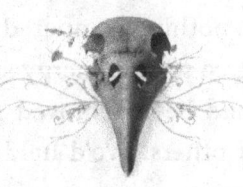

*Eira.*

　　—From Lyvia's list.

T he brindle hounds bayed as Tiberius's form cast a dark shadow over Cantor Manor on the edge of Aedrialis.

*It's strange to be back,* Ti murmured as he banked and began a speedy descent into the courtyard that separated the stables and my old home. My stomach twisted in agreement, uncertain how I really felt about being here.

*Do you think they remember you?* I asked, eyeing the group of mares in the pasture lining up at the gate, ears forward and tails high as they watched us sore over their land.

*They remember,* he said.

*But they know you're different.*

Though Ti didn't respond, I knew his loneliness. The *otherness* of being the only one of his kind.

435

Ti's hooves thundered down the lawn, still manicured despite the battle that raged through Aedrialis only two days ago. The bright green of summer had faded into brown as crisp winter winds whistled through the city.

Evony slid off Ti's back. Her balance and skill at riding him had grown, but it was nothing compared to her love for flying. She carried a wild, fierce sort of energy since taking down the shield. Bear's body had been removed from the wall, along with the hundreds of others. We'd held a private funeral for him in the royal gardens.

Though no Bellator connection linked us, I swear I could feel Evony's emotions simmering below the surface, fueling the energy buzzing off her skin. And though less obvious these days, I still sensed that otherness when she was near.

A pair of Rising guards stationed near the gated entry points nodded as I dismounted. The hounds quieted as they peeked around the corner, cautiously taking in the new arrival. I let out a soft whistle, and the bravest of the group approached, his thin tail tucked between his legs. I knelt, extending a hand, the white star shining in the frigid morning light as he dared a sniff.

"It's me, buddy," I murmured, earning a slight tail wag as I scratched behind his ear. I stood, and he bounded off to join the rest of the small pack that patrolled our land.

The wide doors to the back of the manor swung open, and Aeriden stood between them, staring as if he didn't know who I was. The small piece of my heart that had healed upon seeing him alive ripped open, the fresh scar unsealing.

I shoved that wound down as I looked up at the spitting image of my father, meeting him with my own unflinching gaze.

*Aeriden was alive.* I repeated the words again, forcing my mind to believe what my eyes saw. Dark King Daimos must have used the Transcindiel on the severed head to create something that looked close enough to my father...

Aeriden's azure eyes slid from my own to Evony before landing on Tiberius. His mouth parted as he took in my caeluma's massive form before he pursed them and stepped to the side, waiting for us to enter.

A strange sense of detachment numbed my limbs, and my body seemed to float into the brightly lit day room. *I didn't belong here.* A lady's maid I didn't recognize brought a tray of tea to the small table in the corner as Aeriden pulled a chair out for Evony.

"Aeriden," I began, my voice foreign and far away. "This is Evony Hunt from Rivaner. I knew her parents well, and I'd like to ask you—"

"That's the first thing you're going to say? It's been two days, Lyvia. Two godsdamned days. I've been waiting for you to come here to see me for two fucking days. What in Tynan's blistering hell of darkness has happened to you?"

Aeriden's eyes swept over me as if searching for the living powers slithering beneath my skin.

I ground my teeth, irritation flaring at the judgment, at the disgust in the depths of his eyes. "Look, a lot has happened. Unfortunately, I really don't have time to unpack every—"

"I came for you," Aeriden snapped, looming over me.

Despite my height for a Sultiran woman, he was so much taller than me. My stomach twisted.

"I came to find you when Dad went missing, and then they started saying all those things about you. I was supposed to return to Aedrialis, but I knew something was wrong. They said you were sighted near the Lake of Light, so I headed there. But..."

I swallowed, knowing if I hadn't left to return to Rivaner, I would have found him. And maybe we could have fought together, maybe he could have helped, and I wouldn't have ended up in Nivis...

"She left to save Rivaner," Evony hissed, her temper flaring at the accusation in Aeriden's tone, "to save me. Save my family from being taken as Tribute. As *slaves*. The Tribute that was ordered by the king you so diligently served until the very end—"

"Evony," I snapped, holding out a hand.

Aeriden's eyes darted to the star gleaming on my palm, and I brought my hand down.

"I'm sorry, Aeriden. I was looking for you, but my circumstances changed and—"

"And you what? Figured out how to summon dark magic?"

"I didn't ask for this!" I shouted, my temper boiling. I willed it to cool as the rising swell of emotions built in pressure, my powers creeping toward the surface.

Aeriden blinked as he studied my eyes before I tore them away, staring at the brightly tiled mosaic on the floor.

"I don't have time to explain everything—"

"Then don't explain it all," Aeriden urged. "Just explain what Saros meant when he asked about Dad."

Every thought eddied out of my mind at Aeriden's question. A paralyzing stillness stole through my limbs as the words formed in my mind, locked behind my lips. A heartbeat passed. And then two.

I couldn't move. Couldn't answer this.

Tiberius's massive form loomed in the doorway a moment later, his huge head snaking into the small parlor as he huffed. He bared his teeth at Aeriden, flattening his ears against his head, the message clear enough.

A flood of love and forgiveness poured from my caeluma, and I cut him a grateful glance. It was enough to patch up that crack in my heart for a few moments longer.

"I'm asking for a favor," I finally said, changing the subject. "Evony and Ezrich Hunt... They need a place to stay while I'm gone—"

"And where are you going?"

"To Kayj, Aeriden, I'm going to an island of darkness where an evil elven king plans to take over the fucking world, annihilating or enslaving every human being in the process."

Aeriden blinked and studied me, his eyes softening.

"Well, if that's true, then I'm coming with you," he said, his tone shifting into the familiar protectiveness of a brother, and for a moment, that was who he was.

I opened my mouth to respond when a knock rapped at the glass doors to the dining room.

"Milady, milord," the lady's maid said to the two of us, nodding her greeting. "Lord Kellan Astraeus of the Marisarma fleet."

An irritated groan escaped my lips as heavy booted steps thumped in the marbled foyer and Astraeus swaggered into the sitting room. A wide grin stretched across his freshly manicured face. His dark beard was cropped short, and his usual unruly, braided pirate hair was washed, half of it pulled tightly back.

"Morning, Bonscaíh," he murmured as he gave me a wink and stepped toward our small table. "*Éitilte*," he said, flashing a handsome grin at Evony.

She blushed, rolling her eyes at the sea lord, but offered a small smile. Despite what she said, she loved his nickname for her: Éitilte, *Little Flier*, in Old Votruvian.

"Lord Cantor," he finally said, offering a small bow to Aeriden, who eyed the pirate with equal annoyance.

"What do you want, Astraeus?" I asked.

"Touchy, this morning," he said before reaching out to tug on my braid.

I batted his hand away as his dark brows pinched downward.

"I came to offer Lord Cantor a place on my ship should he desire to accompany us to Kayj."

I blinked.

"You can't," I stammered. "Aeriden is still being tried in Sultiran court. He'll probably be pardoned, based on the lies Saros told him, but he needs to be here for that."

"Not if he's a member of my crew." Astraeus shrugged. "The *Hydra* and Marisarma crewmates aren't beholden to Sultiran courts. Not if the Lord of Marisarma takes them on as wards."

I scoffed, crossing my arms. "If he were to do that, then he'd forfeit his title as *Lord* Cantor, Sultira's horse lord."

Aeriden eyed the sea lord as he stood.

"Of course I'll come," he said, clapping hands with Astraeus, satisfaction stretching across his face. "And I'll face judgment when we return. I'm not giving up my title. I'll speak to the High Steward about it."

"Already done." Astraeus's smile widened as Aeriden seemed to relax.

I ground my teeth and shook my head at the men who simply made up their own godsdamned rules.

"You can't leave," I cut in. "Someone needs to watch over Evony and the herd while we're gone."

"Hello? I'm standing right in front of you. Please stop acting like I'm a child."

I blinked at the teenager, whose flushed face was inches from mine.

I opened my mouth as Astraeus held his hand up to Evony. "Drystan has offered to stay to care for the herd."

"H-he..." I stammered, realizing Drystan was likely the best person to watch over the herd after having grown up with it.

Drystan wanted to stay. He loved Sultira. He missed the Temple of the Sky, the Order of the Death Scholars. And it was safest for him here while he figured out how to harness the Advetis Bone. He wasn't ready yet. He'd said as much the night before, and I wouldn't push him. I could almost feel his fear.

My brain raced as I searched to find some way to keep my brother in Sultira. Keep him as far away as possible from Dark King Daimos.

"He'll be here in half an hour," Astraeus continued, turning to Aeriden and Evony. "If you would be so kind as to allow Evony and Drystan to watch over your home, I would be forever in your debt."

My eyes shot to the ceiling before I shook my head at the gentlemanly nature he'd adopted.

"You should pack your things," he said to Aeriden. "And perhaps, the lovely miss will show Evony to her new quarters."

The maid's cheeks flushed as she hid her smile and adjusted her skirts where she stood by the door. I resisted the urge to roll my eyes. Aeriden gave him a swift nod before motioning Evony to follow him into the house.

Alone with Astraeus, he turned to me.

"My answer is still no," he murmured. "But we'll be right behind you."

"Olienna is the most powerful mystic alive," I groaned, my words dripping in irritation. "A Bellator. We would be stupid not to use her abilities."

"I said I won't do it," he replied. "I don't trust her. I will not allow her in my mind simply to get my ships airborne. We'll be right behind you, *on the water*."

My eyes dropped to my hands. Could I really blame Astraeus for being cautious? Memories surged forward, and my stomach twisted at Isla's haunted face. The Stone Witch, or rather, *Olienna*, reached into her mind to fly the *Evecta* to Kayj to rescue me last spring.

And now I was *returning* to Kayj. Willingly.

Nightmares hovered like wraiths as images from my time on the island crouched in dark memory. The crescent scar on my breast prickled, my hair standing on end as *Cyril's tongue flicked over his lips... phantom, predatory hands ripping into my hair, beneath my dress...*

Breaths escaped my lips in quick huff as my vision tunneled. I swallowed, a growing sense of ruin and impending doom twisting in my chest as my fear of returning to the haunted island intruded on my vengeful purpose. Astraeus's eyes softened as they scanned mine.

"You're scared," he said quietly, closing the distance between us and lifting a hand, pausing as my eyes flitted to it.

Astraeus's leather and cedar scent washed over me, his presence scattering the air around us.

I shook my head, tearing my gaze away from his outstretched hand as blood rushed to my cheeks, irritation surging at my weakness.

Astraeus's brows tilted as he leaned forward. "It's okay to be scared," he murmured.

His face was inches from mine, and his scent enveloped me like a cloud.

"I'm not—"

"You are not *alone*, Lyvia. I'll stay close," he said, eyes sliding to my lips as his throat bobbed. "We'll be right behind you. On the water."

I gritted my teeth, annoyed with my lapse in control, and took a step back, needing to distance myself from the pirate lord. "Fine."

"*Fine.*"

# CHAPTER FIFTY-EIGHT

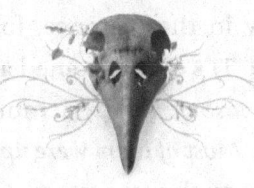

---

~~Aelius Soleia~~, *harnesser of suns. Fire and flame bow to his name.*
—*Lock Scroll, the Arx.*

---

Black clouds rose in the distance like a smudge of coal across gray linens. The winds tore at us, and though my shield held, it did nothing against the heavy, wet snow leaking from the sky. Winter had landed.

We'd flown hard and fast along the coast of Sultira for the better part of two weeks, now nearing Kayj. Flying for the Ramadiel Bone and the dark king. For vengeance.

Enya's blade pressed against my back, its hard presence like the steady hand of fate pushing me forward. Despite my numb fingers tangled in Tiberius's mane, my body was hot.

Raging. Ready.

Ready to return to the place of horrors I'd escaped months ago. I left Kayj with a rip in my soul. Broken and bleeding and hating myself for what he'd done. For what *I'd* done. I would return ready to rip through Dark King Daimos and his fragile castle. Ready to shoulder the burden required to save the ashen, to rid the realm of evil. Ready to sacrifice my soul for the damned and fight for the living.

A dark form flew in the distance, followed by a wave of apprehension. Aquila. Ti's ears flattened against his head.

*Lotrennian ships east of Kayj,* Ti murmured, relaying the message from Aquila. *Most of them were upturned.*

Alarm sparked through my system. I squinted against the blur of white and gray that made up the wintery horizon, cursing my human eyes.

"At least two hundred ships," Vulcan called into the wind. He shifted behind me as he adjusted his grip on Ti's mane, unstrapping his bow and taking aim at the warriors he could spy from above.

A confident push of determination washed over me as Olienna's Bellator connection materialized in my mind.

*Leave the ships. Head to the fortress,* her crystal voice sounded in my and Nerissa's minds, the shared channel of communication somehow less alarming than the Stone Witch's forced entry.

Daimos had created a monster with the Transcindiel power that now swirled in my veins. Turning Olienna into something she dreaded, something she hated, and twisting the spell so she couldn't speak of it to anyone, her words escaping in riddles and rhymes. She couldn't tell anyone the truth, even if she wanted to. But this bond... This *connection* with those who shared the Bellator powers was as much a part of my soul as my connection with Tiberius.

I glanced back to where seven Sultiran ships flew in a steady pyramid, like an imposing air invasion. Olienna stood in the center of the leading ship, in front of the mast, with her slender arms extended to either side, bits of light sparking off her. She seemed younger since leaving Sultira, her eyes brighter.

Her gray battle gown billowed around her high boots. The black armor lining her chest and arms sharpened her features. Her violet eyes glowed as she sent an unfathomable amount of power and wind into the sails of the small fleet, controlling each and every one of them. Tiberius and Aquila banked left as the clouds parted, and my gut sank.

Hundreds of white and gold Lotrennian ships dotted the gray-blue waters of the Juniper Sea, too many upturned and blazing. We passed into the black clouds of Kayj, where a line of War Slayers engaged with the silver-armored elves of Nivis, blades glinting against the sharp, blood-soaked rocks that bordered the shore. A loud *thunk* drummed, followed by the stinging hiss of an arrow... No... a ship's *bolt*. Panic ripped through Ti's bond.

"LEFT!" Vulcan screamed as the six-foot-long ship's bolt hurtled toward us.

Tiberius flipped, his wings going vertical as he spun midair. I clung to his neck, my shins glued to his side. I stole a glance behind in time to see a dark smudge of ships in the distance, and though I couldn't see it, I knew the *Hydra's* flag flapped high above them, less than an hour behind us.

As Tiberius righted himself, the airborne Sultiran ships crashed into the dark bay, rocketing cannonballs into Nivis's fleet. Three bolts fired from below. Tiberius's huge body dodged and dipped, avoiding each one as he allowed instincts to take over. Aquila spiraled around them in the distance before narrowing his focus on one and diving.

Nerissa's arms extended in synchrony with Aquila's wings, and a beam of white, blazing light ripped from their falling forms, exploding into the Nivis warship below. The blast echoed across the sea, drowning out any screams from the soldiers on board.

Nerissa leaned forward on Aquila's back as he climbed higher, away from the blazing debris. I pulled my gaze away as another bolt ripped through the sky. My stomach dropped as Tiberius flipped. The whiz of the iron was close enough to feel its heat. My eyes snagged on the massive black device at the prow of the warship below, where soldiers inserted another bolt. Tiberius's wrath melded with my own, and we narrowed in on the ship below.

*Let us out,* the Obscura demanded.

Tiberius tucked his wings in tight as he dove, locking onto the ship as they aimed the deadly iron tip at us. His wings ripped open as men hurried to their stations, and we sent pure, unbridled darkness raining down at them. Black shadows of mist and smoke enveloped the ship, and an eerie silence cleaved through the air as the ash sank into the waves, a stark contrast to the thunderous blast from Nerissa and Aquila.

Tiberius banked as we scanned the horizon, searching for our next target, when a massive flash of light ripped through the storm raging at the center of the island.

Brilliant, white light. The light of life and everything good. *Bayne.*

I whipped my head around, searching for Aquila and Nerissa when a wave of alarm rushed in from behind. Aquila's massive form swooped down and soared inland.

Tiberius's wings pumped wildly as we chased after Aquila and Nerissa. The storm of Kayj intensified as we flew over the battle raging on shore. Blasts of magic and clashes of swords rocked the space, and I caught sight of two Lotrennians below, surging through the surf as they raced toward their country-men. Carina, arms out with a look of pure hatred on the small elf's face, was flanked by Kresida. Her blades were out and bright with blood.

"Do you want me to drop you down—"

"No," Vulcan snapped behind me. "I'm not leaving you."

"No, you've hovered ever since we left Lotrennia," I said through breaths. "What was Astraeus talking about in the dungeons?"

Vulcan had been moodier than usual since their little spat outside of Father Marcus's cell.

"I've been guarding your back. Stop being a spoiled brat and appreciate the backup— Right!"

My breath whooshed from me as Ti banked, avoiding arrows from below.

"Astraeus said—"

"I made a promise," Vulcan cut me off.

My stomach dipped. "To what?"

"Keep you safe," he growled. A warmth squeezed at my chest despite the icy winds we flew through.

"At all costs," I finished for him, remembering the beating he took on the *Hydra*, the arrow he took above Aedrialis. Had he sworn an air oath to Bayne?

"Why?"

My breath was lost in the gust of wind that surged from the center of the island.

"As irritating as you may be," he grumbled, adjusting the position of his nocked arrow to the opposite side, "you're strong. You've survived longer than I expected. Your resilience and sacrifice could make you a great leader. And despite the annoying sound of your voice..."

I scoffed, my brows furrowing as I did my best to keep my attention on the land ahead of us.

"I've come to...appreciate you. You're perhaps what I'd imagine a sister to be."

The warmth that swarmed my chest burned to the point of pain, and I blew out a slow breath to keep tears from forming. "Vulcan, I—"

"Perhaps we can have this conversation another time," he growled, turning and loosing another arrow.

We flew over the shores. Moans of the fallen and the clanging of metal echoed from the rocks below as my attention snagged on a group of fighters toward the north. Rising fighters.

Vander's eyes locked on mine as we flew by, his ragged face tired but fierce. His lips turned up, and he thrust his blade into the sky, bellowing, "Bonder!"

Triumphant war cries erupted from the surrounding soldiers.

I snapped my attention up as we tore through a sheet of icy rain that stole my breath. The wind spun as we flew inward. Ti's wings wavered against it. Aquila flattened his head before a blast of wind caught his wing, and he flipped, slamming Nerissa to the ground. She tucked and rolled as lightning lit up the sky above us, the resulting thunder rattling my teeth.

Tiberius angled to where Nerissa fell and dove. His body shook as he aimed for the rocky ground, and my shield finally broke. I gasped as it fell away, and Ti's hooves thundered to the ground. Wings tucked in tight, he braced himself against the onslaught of wind.

"Nerissa!" I called through the storm.

She lifted an arm. Tiberius staggered against the wind, his form too tall and wide to stand against it. Vulcan leaped off his back and ran alongside him.

*Find Aquila and get back to the bay!* I called to Ti. *Take out Nivis's fleet before this storm gets any worse!*

A wave of determination was the only response I got. My

legs stumbled along the uneven ground. Tiberius didn't slow as he turned and thundered away from the storm.

A groan escaped Nerissa as she reached for my hand and popped to her feet, giving us a quick nod, her eyes bright with fire and determination. We sprinted through the thick trees, weaving in and out, doing our best to push against the wind.

*Where are you?* I reached into that strange, quiet place where Olienna's voice found me.

*We've breached the eastern port and are headed into the island,* she responded.

*Bayne is here. We're heading north, but the storm is too wild for Aquila and Tiberius,* I added.

*This isn't a storm,* Olienna replied before severing the connection.

My spine stiffened as a piercing shriek, deadly and familiar, cut through the whipping wind.

*Ashen.*

"Keep running! Don't look back!" Vulcan called as another scream ripped through the storm.

Nerissa pumped her arms as she raced through the trees. Vulcan slowed his pace to match mine, stealing a quick glance back.

Behind us then. My lungs burned, either from the wind, the running, or the smoke that spiraled alongside the dirt and debris the air kicked up. As we raced through the edge of the woods, we slowed, the wind dying. My knee crashed to the ground as our footing angled upward at the base of a hill. Vulcan's hand was on my collar, lifting me to my feet as we clambered up the rocky incline.

My breath caught as we stumbled over the edge of the hill overlooking the valley of ashen camps and the massive Onyx Tower of Kayj. My jaw slackened as I gazed at the uprooted trees and debris surrounding the flattened space in the center of the valley, where a wild, spinning wall of air shot to the sky. And through the massive tunnel of wind, two elves stood against the dark king.

A vice gripped my chest. Daimos's sickly, yellow eyes glowed in the night, his face wild with murder as he sent blast after blast of deep blue light at them.

Bayne's brilliant white light flared again. His green eyes were fixed on the dark king as he threw his shield up, blocking attack after attack. Isla's petite frame stood back-to-back with Bayne's looming form as she sent the surrounding air into the tunnel stretching to the sky, encasing the three of them in a cage of wind with unfathomable power.

I gaped at the display of magic as we stood atop the hill. At Isla, whose strength with the wind had grown to unfathomable heights. At Bayne, who threw himself at the dark king, his power stronger than I'd ever seen. A small, pathetic part of me wilted at the sight. At what distance would do to us both.

Light flashed from my left, snapping me from my reverie as Nerissa's power flared not toward the dark king, but behind us. Bayne's face jerked to where we stood, his mouth opening in shock as he took in the three of us. His green eyes blinked rapidly as they landed on me.

Isla screamed his name as that chilling screech ripped through the valley, and a horde of ashen broke through the trees, racing to where we stood. Vulcan was already halfway down the hill, cutting through the horde as Nerissa's white flame engulfed the group to the right. I turned, rallying my strength as the first elongated claws and snapping jaws reached me.

I hesitated for just a moment, my powers at odds with each other, and the creatures raced toward us. The amplifier, heavy and warm on my chest, waited for my call when Bayne's cry ripped through the air.

The Obscura took over as I whipped my head to where Bayne stood, his mouth parted as the dark king bellowed and threw a wave of magic that pierced Isla's wind tunnel. Bayne and Isla flew backward, the channel of air vanishing as they crashed against the rocky ground.

"*NO!*" Nerissa screamed as she turned toward the dark king.

Vulcan grunted behind me as Nerissa pulled her powers away from the ashen and held her hands to the side, gathering swirls of bright, white light in her palms.

My heartbeat stuttered, as if tripping, *staggering* in its desperate panic.

*Choices.*

Xenelpha's words echoed in my mind. The ashen swarmed Vulcan as cries of agony erupted from the center of the valley where Isla and Bayne fell.

Vulcan's cry rose from the bottom of the hill, and his blonde head dipped below the white limbs of the ashen. Another brother.

The dark king's attention slid to Nerissa as her hands gathered white, glowing balls of light before raising them above her head. He smiled as he reached a hand of sinister blue light in her direction.

Choices.

Everyone screamed.

*Fuck choices.*

# CHAPTER FIFTY-NINE

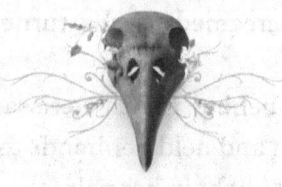

*Rinla Ramadiel, master of affliction. Of remedy and blight,*
*unmatched power and might.*
—Lock Scroll, the Arx.

The powers writhing beneath my skin stood at attention as I made my decision, throwing both hands to the side and splitting my focus.

Flesh sizzled as the pendant on my neck burned through my skin and cotton undershirt. Power tore through my palms. Golden, Transcindiel light spun wildly through my right hand as it engulfed the herd of ashen surrounding Vulcan, while pure darkness ripped through my right, spearing straight for Dark King Daimos.

Clouds formed in my vision as my mind became fuzzy and light. My powers flowed through me like a river bursting through a dam. Or was I their vessel? A ship carrying two gods. I swayed as the powers drained me. Panic crouched, ready to pounce, as hazy visions of Odessa crept into my mind. *Focus. Rein them in.*

*Lyvia!*

Someone called to me in my mind. Tiberius. Or was that Olienna? Had she come to save us?

"Lyvia!" a voice growled from behind as something large barreled into me.

I fell. And then a crack. Pain.

Something wet dripped down the side of my head, and a hand slid into mine, a spark of power shooting into me as I lay on the freezing ground.

"GET UP!" Astraeus bellowed as he hauled me to my feet.

I staggered against him, blinking against the icy rain. Blood dripped from the side of his head into his hair, wet and muddy from battle. His shoulders sagged. His features were dark from exhaustion.

His arm gripped mine, eyes scanning the crimson valley in which we stood. Piles of bleeding bodies, *elven* and *human* bodies, lay strewn on the incline of the hill. Vulcan lay unmoving among them.

My eyes drifted to Nerissa's tall frame that lay at the top, to her chest that slowly rose and fell. To the center of the valley, where three elves began to stir.

"Lyvia—" Astraeus began as clanks of armor surged from the south. The pirate lord whipped toward a small group of approaching Nivis soldiers, and I pulled out of his hold, staggering down the hill to where Bayne and Isla lay.

They were moving. They were alive, but—

A gasp escaped my lips as I neared, the evidence of what Dark King Daimos had done displayed on their bodies. I crashed to my knees as I reached Bayne, unsure where to place my hands.

"Bayne," I croaked, warm tears mixing with the freezing rain, wetting my face.

A pool of blood surrounded him. A matching pair of black eyes shadowed the brilliant Ravindra green, bordering a broken nose. What had the dark king done?

His left ankle jutted out to the side at an unnatural angle, and his wrists... Broken and twisted. His skin was pebbled in a dark red rash... And as my eyes followed his arms...

"*No*," I moaned, a vice tightening around my chest.

Those scars... Those long, deep slices down the center of his forearms. The ones he'd inflicted on himself while here on Kayj over a year ago when he tried to save Lida. Leaching himself...

Blood pooled.

"No," I said again, shaking my head. "How—" I choked.

Bayne's brilliant eyes found mine, and his face crumpled. Doubt and concern replaced the pain rippling across his features. He opened his mouth to speak, but he choked, blood spurting from his lips. His eyes shot to my neck, to the thick scar always on display, and a sinister chuckle rasped from behind me. My stomach curdled as it all came together.

I turned as Dark King Daimos stepped toward me. A grin formed on his bloodied lip, and the Ramadiel Bone on his palm glowed a deep, deadly blue. It looked different from when I'd last seen it, twisted and rotten, somehow.

"*Bayne the Unbroken*," Dark King Daimos mused. "How easily he breaks."

Another spasm of power erupted from the dark king's hands, and Bayne's body convulsed as a scream ripped through his lungs. I threw my body over his as it shook against the power.

My mind spun as the events of the past year fell into place. The Lady of Tomorrow. Her injuries. Her ailments. As if every *injury*, every *illness*, every bit of *damage* her body had ever endured over her lifetime had suddenly slammed back into her. The shock it would cause to a body, to endure it all again, all at once. No one would survive that.

My heart cracked.

I slid my gaze to where Isla lay. Her amber eyes fixed on mine, a single tear sliding down her beautiful, bronze skin. Black, hand-shaped bruises formed on her neck and her swollen, puffy lips. Dark, red lines began to form along her abdomen, dripping into small pools of blood.

"What have you done?" I breathed, my gaze slicing to the dark king's glowing eyes. The clang of Astraeus's blades in the distance was lost against the pounding of my heart.

"You've twisted it..." I choked as a sob formed in the back of my throat. "Twisted it into something..." I shook my head.

"I've *perfected* it," the dark king said, a note of triumph in his voice as he held his hands to either side, the Ramadiel Bone pulsing on his palm.

I swallowed the bile rising to my throat.

"Weaponized it." He grinned at me, the yellow of his eyes somehow glowing brighter.

"You sent it to Lotrennia... Infected people? How?" I asked, defeat hovering nearby.

"Poisoned is the correct term, Daughter of Darkness," Daimos purred. "The Lotrennians love their traditions. Though my spies were only able to poison one shipment of nebulis..."

My mind spun, horror coiling as I remembered the deaths at the Awakening... He'd poisoned the powder at the celebration...

"They had more success lacing the vats of sparkling wine that came in from the east. And though he was often reckless, Cyril did have his uses."

*Wine.*

The Lady of Tomorrow had a bottle of sparkling wine with

her. Had no one checked it for poison? I had barely noticed it... And Cyril. Oh gods, that was a grape he'd examined in his tower. A grape and the powder...

"Ah," the dark king continued, a note of surprise in his voice as his attention shifted. "I see you've at last learned of my deceit." His unnatural eyes slid to the pile of bodies on the hill.

I followed his gaze to where Aeriden caught the blade of a Nivis soldier positioned at Astraeus's back. My chest caved. *No.* I wouldn't let him take Aeriden.

"The Transcindiel does wonders, but it's not perfect. You never looked very close at the head in the ice trunk." A pale tongue slipped over his lips as if savoring the memories from the Crystal Castle.

"Their numbers are dwindling, Your Grace," a female voice crooned from across the valley.

*I knew that voice.* My head snapped to the left, and my gut sank as it landed on Selvina, memories from the Crystal Castle surging forward.

The dark king's niece strode across the field of ash, *my ash*, in a war gown of deep blue, reinforced with leather armor, a nyxteria in full bloom on her breastplate. Tendrils of her white-blonde hair blew loose from the elaborate twist of braids and sapphires. As she approached, the rain fizzled into soft, white flecks of snow.

A female slave strode behind her, her thick iron collar stark against her pale skin. The Tauruk followed closely behind, his horns gleaming white and his crimson robes trailing behind him. Flashes of my father's time here...of the torture inflicted on him by the Tauruk fueled a white-hot rage gathering within me.

A torrent of bloody images flooded my memories, my emotions spinning in my chest, and I urged the darkness and light to rise to the surface. Selvina locked her gaze on mine as she approached from a distance.

"Your return is timely, Queen of Darkness," she called, her gaze bearing into me.

I blinked. Where had I heard those words before?

"Indeed," Dark King Daimos drawled, taking a step toward me. Those glowing yellow eyes slid to my hands and back to my face, no doubt studying the blazing rim of orange that surrounded my pupils.

I reached for my bond with Tiberius, willing all the power left in that deep chasm to cast to him. To call him here, but the chasm was quiet.

*Here*, I urged into the darkness, into that space I found the threads. *I'm here. Help us.*

"Welcome, Father Killer. Tynan's Accepted... Though I'm not sure the gods will appreciate what you've stolen. You've committed treason by *harnessing* their power. Just like the Bellators. All of you," he said, glancing nonchalantly at Bayne and Nerissa. "How they will reward me when I present you to them." Daimos smiled as he held his hand with the Ramadiel Bone to me.

The dark king sent a thin tendril of dark blue power, like a living stream of water, snaking through the air to me. An overwhelming sense of panic took root, and I threw my hands up, rallying what little strength I had left to surround myself in a shield of darkness when a blast of violet light and wind slammed through the valley.

Black ash spun through the air like a cyclone of darkness, and I sensed Olienna's presence before the dark king bellowed her name.

# CHAPTER SIXTY

~~Krunas Aeterna~~, *extender of life. Immortality and power will make the worlds cower.*
—*Lock Scroll, the Arx.*

I found my feet as the ash settled. Olienna's shield held tightly in place around us. A blanket of confidence fell over me as she stepped to my side. Her violet eyes slid to mine, and I gave her a nod, despite feeling utterly spent. Her lips tilted into a smile as she narrowed her gaze on Daimos, who had fallen to his knees.

Done. He was *done*.

Olienna took another step toward the dark king, whose eyes were shut tight. His shoulders shook as his jaw went rigid.

What was he doing?

Something small and distant tugged on me.

Realization dawned as I glanced again toward Olienna. Her eyes were wild, so much like Daimos in his crazed attacks. Her smile had widened into a grin, her too-white teeth gleaming in the dim light hiding behind the clouds. A wolf on the hunt, attacking his mind.

A scream finally wrenched from Daimos's throat.

"They..." he gritted out through his teeth. "They will *annihilate* you..." A manic laugh escaped his lips. "You especially. You will pay... He is *coming* for you. He's..."

Olienna's upper lip curled into a snarl as she stepped closer. Whatever damage she inflicted caused Daimos to fall forward and wail, his hands flying to his face.

He looked up, yellow eyes bleeding as they landed on me. "Do you know what she did?" the dark king cackled. "They called her the Betrayer—"

*Betrayer...*

A weight dropped in my gut as she lifted both hands, readying her final blow. Dread pitted in my stomach... I'd been here before... Before a dying king who held vital information. Hatred and curiosity warred within me in the split second it took for Olienna to take one deep breath and let out a war cry.

"WAIT!" I screamed as she threw her hands forward with an animalistic snarl. Nothing left. I had nothing left to stop this. I reached as deep as I could go to find any last bit of power. Empty. *Empty.*

I threw my hand toward Olienna and Dark King Daimos as someone slid theirs into my other. *A spark.* Astraeus's power sizzled through my veins, where it summoned the Transcindiel and Obscura.

A wall of darkness sliced through whatever invisible line of magic Olienna used on Daimos.

The two of them snapped their heads toward us, eyes wide as they landed on Lord Astraeus. Twisted rage fell on Olienna's face, and Daimos spewed droplets of blood on freshly fallen snow as he choked out a laugh.

"You've found them!" Daimos cackled, eyes wild with greed. "And you've brought him *here?*" The dark king howled with crazed laughter.

*What?*

My mind whirred, powers wavering as Astraeus continued to keep them from falling back into that chasm. His bloodied hand had a steel grip on mine. I resisted the urge to look at him, and instead found myself staring at Olienna, whose gaze had turned murderous.

"Drop his hand, Lyvia," she commanded, her voice lethally quiet.

"Don't," Astraeus breathed, tightening his grip, a shield of his own forming around us.

*Listen to me, Lyvia,* her voice urged in my mind. *This man is not to be trusted. Drop his hand. Drop your shield.*

*I want to hear what Daimos has to say,* I responded.

*Daimos is full of lies,* she purred. *He is the reason your father is dead. He is responsible for the ashen. Your friends are dying because of him. He will kill you next.*

A wave of trust, of confidence, of *love* washed over me, and I blinked at Olienna. A soft smile formed on her lips as she inched closer. Her fingers drifted to the shield Astraeus threw up between us. My grip slackened in Astraeus's hand.

"Lyvia," he growled, squeezing, holding onto the connection his power needed to reach me.

My eyes remained locked on Olienna's. On those beautiful, violet irises. What would it be like, I wondered... To have a mother who looked at me like this? Who loved me like this?

Olienna's eyes softened, and her head nodded softly.

"Block her out," Astraeus breathed, straining to keep his shield up and his power pulsing through me. *"BLOCK HER!"*

Olienna's face snapped to him, and her lips curled into an ugly snarl as she threw her hand toward Astraeus. His cry punched through the valley as she tore through his shield, both mental and physical. He slapped something hard into my hand before he crashed to the ground, and I staggered as my own shield fell.

Olienna snapped her attention back to Dark King Daimos, his arms wide as he threw the Ramadiel power at Bayne and Nerissa, tearing screams from their lips.

"*STOP!*" I cried.

Daimos cocked his head and narrowed his eyes at Olienna through his shield.

"Will she save your Bellators, Daughter of Darkness?" Daimos asked quietly, a soft smile stretching across his bloody lips. His eyes slid from Olienna's to my own.

"She's a Bellator," I said, remembering that warm connection, that confidence and love.

Olienna's eyes slid to Bayne and Nerissa, whose bodies writhed and bled beneath the twisted Ramadiel power.

"Ah, yes. She has the power of the gods," Daimos murmured as his smile grew. "And what secrets does she hold? She's taken the life stretcher. Or did you give it to her?" he choked out before Olienna took another step toward him.

I blinked. *Life stretcher.* I snapped my head to Olienna, eyes traveling along the length of her braid, which seemed darker somehow. Were there fewer grays? Her eyes were brighter... younger.

*She'd taken the Aeterna Bone from Aedrialis.*

"And there's a Conduit with us now," Daimos continued, his bloodshot eyes slicing to Astraeus. "Has he been with you all this time?" A chuckle escaped the dark king's lips, more specks of red dotting the accumulating snow at his feet. "And you didn't know? History seems to be repeating itself, Olienna."

I glanced at Olienna, who stood with a dazed look on her

face. She licked her lips as her eyes darted to Astraeus, and back to Bayne and Nerissa in animalistic greed.

"What are you talking about?" I asked, dread seeping through my system.

"Olienna. Queen of Nivis. Prophet. Bellator. And the ultimate Betrayer," Daimos spat as he sent another blast of Ramadiel power into Bayne and Nerissa, whose screams turned to whimpering moans.

"STOP!" I wailed, tears streaming down my face. Astraeus's body lay unmoving in the wet snow.

*Tiberius! Help us!* I called in my mind.

"History *does* seem to repeat itself. The queen of the Starlings under your nose, all those years ago. And one of her sentries, now found his way to your little death digger."

I blinked, glancing down at Astraeus's bloody body and noting the rise and fall of his chest.

"Olienna has claimed two powers. And now, there are four others, here in this valley," the dark king continued. "Ripe for the taking. The *Conduit* laying at your feet."

Olienna's hands shook as her eyes swept over Bayne, Nerissa, and at last, landed on Astraeus. Daimos's bloody eyes were fixed on Olienna. He was *baiting* her. I slid my eyes to the Tauruk, who circled behind Daimos, the dark spaces in his giant, horned mask pinned on Olienna.

Movement to the left caught my eye, to where the pile of bodies lay strewn on the side of the hill, where Aeriden crouched next to Vulcan. I whipped my gaze back to the king and queen in front of me, hope sparking in my chest at the sight of my brothers.

*Here. Hurry*, I called into that well of threads before I lunged, grabbing Olienna's hand and sliding the rubelline cuff Astraeus gave me into place on her wrist. Her face went blank for a moment before igniting with rage.

Her scream echoed through the valley as I barreled forward. I unsheathed Honor as I hurtled toward the dark king, whose eyes were wide on the blazing red cuff locked on Olienna's arm. The massive form of the Tauruk rose to my left, his arms wide with a hatchet in one, his other outstretched toward me as Aquila's massive form dove from the clouds.

The Tauruk's swing was cut short as the flare of a sword caught the metal of the hatchet. Aeriden's face was a portrait of pure vengeance. He whipped his blade free, swinging to the right, but the Tauruk was fast, dodging his blade with a bellow of fury. Aeriden ducked, palming his dagger, and he shoved the tip beneath the mask into the soft part above the Tauruk's throat.

The creature roared, his massive, gloved hands reaching for the hilt when Aquila's blade-like claws wrapped around his arms and ripped him from the ground. The hawk's battle cry reverberated through the valley as he lifted the Tauruk into the air and sliced through his arms, the monster's massive body crashing to the wet, slushy ground.

Daimos's shield dropped as he whipped his head around, spearing twin blasts of Ramadiel power toward Aeriden and Aquila. Aeriden collapsed, a scream forming on his lips as a shriek of pain ripped through Aquila's giant beak before he fell from the sky.

Selvina sprinted across the field, unsheathing a thin blade and heading toward the dark king as the familiar thunder of hooves drummed from behind.

Tiberius's dark form broke through the clearing fog behind Daimos, and my heart stuttered in relief at the sight of him. The dark king spun, cutting off the Ramadiel power from his targets, and raised his hand toward Tiberius.

"NO!" I screamed, but my legs dragged as I raced toward

them, searching for any last bit of power I had left to stop what was about to happen.

The dark king raised soaked arms at Tiberius, a line of deep blue glowing bright at the tips of his fingers, as my caeluma reared onto hind legs. Daimos screamed as Tiberius's massive hooves crashed into his chest, bone crunching beneath his sternum.

He slammed his palm onto Tiberius's leg as the horse attacked. A sickening, whinny-like scream escaped Ti's mouth as the dark king shoved the Ramadiel power into him. The horse crashed to the ground and kicked the air, writhing in pain. Daimos struggled, choking through his broken sternum, but holding tight to the bone and healing himself.

I was *almost* there.

I sprinted for them, ready to rip the godsdamned Ramadiel Bone from his hand when Selvina stepped beside him.

"*Finish her!*" he choked at Selvina, who stood with her thin blade out, aimed straight at me.

I surged forward, ready to bury my dagger in her throat when she called, "*Lyviánala!*"

My hunt wavered for a moment, shock sparking through my system at the name and the sudden connection.

Lyviánala.

Queen of Darkness.

She nodded as she caught my eye, blinked once, and with preternatural accuracy, spun and sliced the tip of her blade over the top of the dark king's hand, freeing the Ramadiel Bone from his palm.

Dark King Daimos bellowed in rage, fumbling for the bone. He threw his head back as it sailed through the air, his bloody hand reaching for it, and I narrowed my focus on his exposed neck.

A murderous calm settled over me as my legs pumped.

Enya's blade pressed into my back, urging me toward the dark king, but I kept it sheathed. I wanted to *feel* this.

I leaped over Ti's bleeding body and shoved Honor's sharp tip into the dark king's pale neck. His cold skin was clammy against the rage that burned beneath mine. The warmth of his blood pooled over my hand as I held it there. His yellow eyes were wide in shock as they shot to mine. We fell to the ground, where his stumped hand thudded against my back, and I shoved again, twisting as I drove the life force from his body.

A spray of blood escaped his lips as he attempted one last breath, the air catching in his lungs and coming out in a choking gurgle. His chest convulsed once more before the yellow light in his eyes died completely.

My arms shook as I ripped Honor free and turned to find Selvina standing before me, the Ramadiel Bone resting on her palm.

# CHAPTER SIXTY-ONE

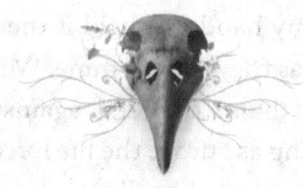

---

~~Meili Advetis~~, *traveler of worlds. Distance and time walk a fine line.*
—*Lock Scroll, the Arx.*

---

he Nivis royal met my gaze as her delicate fingers folded over the bone one by one. Her eyes drifted closed for a moment before she turned and strode toward the female slave standing at the edge of the hill.

"Selvina," I said, my voice sounding far away. I stood, ready to fight for the bone of power resting in her hands.

She ignored me and surveyed the pile of bodies on the hillside, eyeing the humans and elves now stirring and whimpering. Ashen, no more.

"*Selvina!*" I shouted, allowing the weight of the wet dagger in my hand to steel me. I needed the healing power in her hand. I needed it for my caeluma. For my friends here, for the friends I'd left in Sultira. My *family*. And I would kill for it. I slogged past Tiberius's heaving form and stopped short as the slicing whine of a blade rang behind my head. Something sharp slashed at my face and neck.

Olienna's face contorted in wrath as she unsheathed Enya's blade from my back and attacked. I ducked, the tip of the blade painting a crimson stripe against my cheek. Drips of blood pooled along the line as I leaped to the side, flipping Honor's hilt in my hand. She surged forward with the Bellator's blade, crashing it down in the ashy slush. I swept my leg behind her knees as she heaved the sword in my direction, shoving up with the butt of Honor and crashing it into her wrist. She screamed as the blade flew from her hands and slid along the edge of the hill.

Olienna spun through the air, the Aeterna Bone blessing her with the speed of her youth, and her boot crashed into my wrist. The golden gem in Honor's hilt dimmed as it flew through the air. She barreled into me, knocking me to the ground. She straddled me in the blood and frigid mud, her nails digging into my skin as her hands found their way to my neck.

"Lyvia—" Astraeus groaned from where he lay nearby.

My hands grappled with hers, slipping against the blood. My mind whirred, searching, *searching* for those lessons of defensive moves I'd learned from my friends, my family, this past year. Bayne, Ronan, Nerissa, Vulcan... They had drilled them into me, but my mind grew fuzzy. Panic broke through my carefully built-up wall. My fingers slipped between her palm and my neck, but she was so strong...

"Hand... Your hand..."

Hand.

My hand.

My hands were the only things stopping her from squeezing the last breath from my lungs. I would die.

A gentle tug on the line of air that tethered us, like it was saying, *I'm here... I'm with you... You're not alone.*

Kellan Astraeus.

But I couldn't take my hands away.

A sound escaped my lips as she squeezed harder, and that tug of wind turned into a yank. A demand. Tunnel vision darkened my sight, and I pulled one hand away, the back of it hitting the snow.

That hard, calloused hand clasped onto mine. It was familiar. It was safe. It squeezed as a spark of raw power stormed into that chasm of magic, fueling the Obscura and Transcindiel.

And my powers reared in response.

I ripped my hand out of Kellan's and clasped them around Olienna's head. Black mist and golden light collided. An iron-like mask of darkness formed around her head and face, quickly wrapping itself around her body, ripping her hands away from me. She screamed, going rigid as the cage clanged to the ground.

Air filled my lungs in quiet chokes as I rolled to the side toward Kellan, his hand still outstretched toward me. His dark eyes stuttered under his lashes before gently closing as he let go of that small bit of air connecting us.

I stared at him for a moment, my emotions paralyzed despite my powers still streaming into Olienna's cage. His chest slowly rose and fell, and I reached a tentative hand to his cheek, the back of my fingers grazing his skin. A yelp drew my attention to the slope of the hill, and I whipped my head toward Selvina.

The Nivis elf knelt in the snow, her hand hovering over the slave's ankle. My legs were heavy and foreign beneath me as I shoved against the ground, snatching Honor from the frozen slush. Selvina murmured a few words beneath her breath, and blue, *beautiful,* crystal blue light sparked around her outstretched palm, settling on the slave's foot. Power brushed against my neck and my ankle, as if the healing that had occurred there was reminded of the touch of magic igniting across the field of blood.

A cool breeze picked up as the snow stopped falling, and evening streaks of resting sun peeked through the parting clouds. I blinked as she gripped the slave's scarred hand and pulled her into an embrace.

Selvina's manicured hands slipped around the woman's pale face as she pressed her dark mouth to her lips. She pulled away, reaching behind the woman's neck, sliding a key into her thick collar, which dropped to the ground with a dull thud. The slave looked up, as if finally noticing me, and a gasp escaped my lips.

*Eira.* The slave who had given her life for me during my time at the Crystal Castle, but not quite. I staggered a step back as crystal blue eyes found mine. Eira's *sister.* And Selvina's lover, it would seem. A moan from behind me drew me back.

"Selvina," I snapped, and the royal elf finally turned toward me.

"Lyviánala Natara," she said, clasping her hands together and bowing her head.

"Heal them," I demanded, taking another step.

Selvina's eyes scanned the bodies strewn across the valley as a wave of irritation drifted toward me. I stumbled back a step, glancing around.

Selvina snapped her gaze back to mine, noting my reaction.

"*Now,*" I said again, slamming my own emotions back into her. *Obey.*

She bared her teeth before cracking her neck and stepping forward. "I don't take orders from you," the elf said as she held her hands out.

*Empty.*

No bone. I didn't need her to disrobe to know that an eight-pointed, luminous star gleamed on her chest. Selvina harnessed the Ramadiel power, and it now lived within her, marking her as a Bellator. Questions surged from the depths of my mind.

My powers continued to stream from my hand, keeping Olienna captive as I watched Selvina step toward the fallen. Glittering, crystal blue light lifted from her hands and settled on the pirate lord.

"I will need him if I am to heal the rest," she murmured, and something tight in my chest loosened.

Kellan stirred as the healing, blue light surrounded him. He groaned as he got to his feet, his dark eyes flashing to me before landing on Selvina.

*Help me*, I wanted to say, but the words caught for some reason. My throat bobbed. His gaze softened on mine as he approached Selvina with an outstretched hand.

Selvina gasped as he sent a spark of power into her, eyes widening. She stretched her hand toward the valley, and light after light shot from her palm in waves of blue and white, each landing on a broken body.

Kellan swayed as the last of them settled on the bodies at the bottom of the hill, on Vulcan and those who had suffered as ashen. The slave woman rushed forward as Selvina collapsed, her hand ripping free from the pirate lord.

My mouth parted as I stared at Kellan Astraeus.

Lord of Marisarma.

Captain of the *Hydra*.

The Starling Sentry.

The Conduit.

All of those names, I thought, not sure who I was really

looking at. His throat bobbed as he turned toward me, his lips parting.

"Lyv," Bayne's voice broke as he staggered to his feet.

I tore my gaze away from Kellan as Bayne rushed toward me.

Conflicting emotions swarmed as he reached for me. His green eyes were wide as he took in the cage of darkness I spun around Olienna. He snapped his gaze at Kellan, warning biting across his features. Bayne reached for one of my outstretched hands, cutting off the power flowing into the cage, which disappeared. Vulcan was at Olienna's back with a blade to her neck before she could move.

Bayne's bloody hands were on my face a moment later, and I felt myself jerk backward despite the wave of relief sweeping over me. Bayne's brows narrowed.

"Lyv, you shouldn't have..." he stuttered, shaking his head, unable to find the right words. His eyes continued to dart to the thick scar on my neck as if he didn't yet believe it hadn't ripped open, its healing undone. My head shook from side to side, my stomach dipping.

"You figured out what caused the deaths," I continued for him, pulling back. "It's why you didn't want me to return to Lotrennia. Because of the Ramadiel poison."

The corrupted power that Daimos sent into Lotrennia had slowly infected and killed its inhabitants, and had I been there, not knowing what it was... My hand reached for the scar on my neck. The thick, bulbous scar I would never be able to hide.

"I would have died," I finished.

His dark head bobbed in confirmation.

"I couldn't risk you returning. And I'm sorry. You..." He shook his head, tearing his eyes away as he dropped his chin to his chest.

"And I couldn't be there for the marriage, the soulbinding,"

I said, my heart steeling under the weight of his decisions. "I would have tried to stop you."

Bayne's lashes fluttered, yet a muscle in his jaw ticked as his lips drew a line.

"You needed the power," I continued, turning my head and surveying him. "Needed the unity. But now that Dark King Daimos is dead... Bayne, I can *undo* it for you." An unwavering determination slid into my words. "It could be dangerous, but—"

I paused as he looked up, pity and doubt flashing across his eyes for the briefest moment before they disappeared, replaced with a half-smile. But that pity... I wilted beneath that small part of Bayne that always seemed to find the naivety within me.

I swallowed the pain that came with it, pulling myself back to where we stood. I blinked and stepped away, scanning the valley of blood surrounding us in the evening light.

Carina had arrived, Kresida by her side, with Vander and a small group of bloodied, Rising soldiers bringing up the rear.

Nerissa knelt among the changed ashen, the gaunt elves and humans, either sitting in shock, staring out at nothing, or weeping, unsure where they were and why.

Tiberius's wave of wariness washed over me, and I caught his gaze from a distance as it landed on the back of Bayne's head. I heaved a breath before spotting Isla, still sitting on the ground, and I rushed toward her.

"Isla," I croaked, my knees crashing to the gray mix of snow and ash.

Her amber eyes were dull, deep black shadows beneath them as she stared at the forest. I scanned her body. She'd been healed, but...

"Isla," I said, gently this time, moving to put my arms around her.

She flinched at the touch, her wide eyes snapping to mine.

Fear.

And pain.

Of whatever memories reliving those injuries had brought forth. Whatever trauma she had endured for the second time. My stomach churned remembering the dark bruises that had formed on her neck and the blood. So much blood...

"Breathe," I whispered. "You are safe. You are with friends."

I repeated those words to her, the affirmations I needed to hear on the *Evecta* after surviving my own trauma. This would take time to heal. I scanned the rest of the valley, the rest of those healed, and noted the same haunted look in everyone's faces.

"Their fleet has retreated to Nivis. They're heading up the coast," Kresida said, her gaze shooting toward the Lotrennian soldiers filtering in from the woods.

"Go to them," I said.

She gave me a curt nod before trotting off.

Bayne stepped forward and clasped a hand on Carina's shoulder. His eyes scanned her bloodied body, as if seeing her for the first time. His small, bookish cousin turned warrior.

"*Sobraen,*" he said, squeezing his hand and nodding his head. "Thank you."

I paused mid-stride, staring at the two of them speaking quietly as I processed that word. *Sobraen.* An elven word. One I'd heard used twice before. Between Nerissa and Carina. And in my room at the Crystal Castle... With Eira...

"Good to see you in one piece, *Bonder,*" Vander said, pulling me into a bloody embrace.

"Van!" Aeriden cried as he stumbled down the hill.

Vander's head whipped around, finding Aeriden's bloodied smile from across the valley, mouth falling open in shock and disbelief.

*"Aeriden?"* he gasped, releasing me and stumbling toward my brother.

My lips slid into a soft smile as I looked at the bodies on the side of the hill. The ashen, cured, *transformed* back into their true nature. The Transcindiel's hopeful song echoed between the rivers of darkness that lined my arms, moving freely, shining, and ready.

# CHAPTER SIXTY-TWO

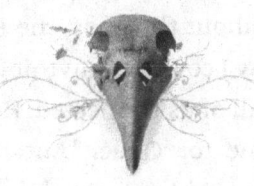

---

~~Herrah Celestyn~~, *commander of orbs. To shatter or shift, a world of power, the ultimate gift.*
—*Lock Scroll, the Arx.*

---

Thee shrieks and cries of the ashen echoed through the rocky cliffs surrounding their caged camps. Soft breath of the Juniper Sea floated in from the east, as the bright morning light painted the cliffs in golden tones. An involuntary twitch pushed me forward as Bayne's hand found its way to the center of my back.

I was relieved to be reunited, to see him safe, yet over the past months, something had wedged into the connection with Bayne that I had so desperately clung to. Choices, it seemed, shaped more than simply who we were. They shaped our connections, and something had grown between ours.

My mind turned over the emotion as if it could dissect exactly what was happening to it, the Transcindiel flitting up in encouragement as I examined the change, until I came to the sad conclusion that choices could also shape love. And though I had fallen out of love with Bayne, I still cared for him. And we needed him.

That threat... Whatever Olienna, Daimos, Saros, or Xenelpha had to say about the gods, the *Embodied*... we'd deal with it. Because I knew I could do anything with my family and my friends. We were all of us connected. Humans and elves.

And I would come for Queen Antares. The cunning elf remained behind in her golden castle, her powers mightier and her defenses greater since I left the Land of Light and Life. But I'd learned patience these last few months. And though her life was now tied to Bayne's, I'd free him and claim hers someday.

My hand drifted to the amplifier around my neck. I tugged it out of my undershirt and held it in front of us, running my fingers over the intricate designs etched on the surface. Ferns and vines twisted in an elaborate pattern, bordering a small, budding flower in its center. The nyxteria, the flower of Nivis. The lullaby my mother sang to me as a child, to *Lyviánala*.

I swallowed against emotion rising to the surface and the inevitable conclusion I'd come to. Eira had named me *sobraen*.

Cousin.

I hadn't approached Ursa, Eira's sister, yet to ask her. Or unraveled the mystery of *how*, given the impossibility of it all.

Bayne took the amplifier from me and examined it, his dark brows pinching together.

"Are you sure you've got this? You can rest first if you need to. Looks like you've been busy," he murmured, his words fueling the growing doubt.

I shuddered, my stomach pitching at the task ahead.

A soft tug of wind drew a loose strand of hair free from my cheek. It slid along my neck, and I swallowed before turning toward Kellan, who approached alongside Tiberius. The horse's big black head bobbed in greeting toward Bayne before he clomped to me and placed his velvety muzzle in my palm.

*Ready?* he asked.

*I think so.*

He sent a wave of calming reassurance that surrounded me in a blanket of warmth. My caeluma. My shared soul.

Nerissa stepped forward alongside Vulcan.

"We're ready for you below," Nerissa said, nodding at the camps.

Outside of the gates, menders stood among Rising and Lotrennian soldiers, Selvina among them. Wagons of healing supplies, including hundreds of vials of the nyxteria sleeping draft, dotted the gates.

We'd met at length last night, making plans and discussing the best way to approach this. Because when the ashen were saved, when they were transformed back into their original forms, chaos would ensue. A humanitarian crisis. Bayne ordered shipments of food from northern Lotrennia, and we'd found a third Aelius Orb in the Onyx Tower, allowing us to communicate with Sultira to ask for aid.

I took one last glance at the first of eight camps below, my throat bobbing. Could I do this? I turned to our small group. Bayne approached Vulcan, gripping his shoulder as Aquila swooped down from above. His wings sent the dusting of snow dancing around us. Though his emotions were blocked, I could see the pain etched across Bayne's face as he approached Aquila and placed a hand on the giant hawk's beak.

He'd yet to pull his mental shield down, yet to allow the true caeluma and Bellator connection to come through to ensure the queen had no access to him. My heart broke for them, for the wall that had been put up. But I'd free them if he let me. And I'd end her.

Kellan stepped toward us, his dark eyes sparkling beneath

the early morning sun, and Bayne's shoulders stiffened, turning to the pirate lord.

"After you, Bonscaíh," Kellan murmured, lifting a hand toward Tiberius.

I nodded, and Bayne went rigid.

"It means *shadow*," I explained, offering a soft smile to him.

Warning flashed in Bayne's gaze as he stared at the pirate lord. Had he heard me?

We'd argued about this little detail. And I'd only won after I showed Bayne the oval brand at the center of my chest, next to the crescent scar Cyril had left me last year. While the amplifier Bayne had gifted me worked, the fire in his power, the pure sunlight, somehow activated when I used it. And I had the scar to prove it.

I'd need Kellan's help to do a job this big. He was a living amplifier, in some ways. Everyone kept strangely quiet about Kellan's powers in the past day, as if fearful to speak to him. To even speak *of* his power. And the pirate lord didn't offer any explanation. In fact, he seemed removed, his usual swagger replaced with a cold, dangerous thing. Had it not been for the months of close contact and the air oath between us, his presence might have sent me running from the room.

My stomach twisted as I eyed the camps below, hundreds of ashen wandering mindlessly about. Could I do this? I kept turning the same question over and over in my mind. I eyed my elven friends. The superior beings, in some ways.

*We are not the same.*

If we had been, could I have saved them sooner? Would Bayne have believed in our soulbinding thread? Would fewer people have died? Would I have mastered these powers before leaving Lotrennia?

Bayne's brows pinched as he examined me, but it was Kellan's voice that sounded from my side.

"Don't for one second lower yourself, Lyvia. You are every bit their equal. Every bit as important, as incredible. I'm with you," Kellan said once again, holding out a hand.

*I'm with you...* I blinked, turning to him, and in that glimpsing second, his dark eyes held the promise of hope and memory. The tendril of air connecting us stilled for a moment as his words found their mark, and for the first time, I looked at myself through my own eyes, and no one else's.

I was imperfect. My choices shaped who I'd become, and though I was dark and shadowed... Though I'd killed out of necessity *and* out of brutality, I'd also saved. I was human, and I was strong. And though I had changed, one critical piece of me remained the same. A power that existed within me long before I harnessed either of the godlike forces now swarming inside me. The one that made it possible for the two not only to coexist, but to *thrive* together. The power that drew Enya and Ordell together in the first place.

Love.

I could accept *and* love myself for the person I was today, and I could do this. I was ready. I took the hand Kellan offered and slung my leg over Ti's back before giving a firm dip of my chin to the others.

"Let's go," I said to the group.

Kellan pulled himself up behind me and settled into place. Tawny, copper feathers lifted Vulcan and Nerissa into the skies above, and Tiberius took off at a gallop along the edge of the cliff, his black wings beating twice before his hooves touched only air.

"Rise up, Lyvia," Kellan murmured against my hair.

We soared over the camp, the rush of wind drowning out the shrieks of the pale creatures below.

*I'm ready*, I said to Ti, who relayed the message to Aquila.

The hawk soared south, to where the line of menders and soldiers stood, ready to intervene.

"Take what you need this time," Kellan said into my ear, his breath warm against my cheek. "I'll give you a taste and then take what you need. I'll pull back if it's too much."

I nodded my understanding and blinked against a tunnel of frigid wind as we swept over the northern ridge of the camp and circled back. I closed my eyes for a moment, allowing myself to dive deep into that chasm of power.

I passed through rivers of darkness and death, nodding my greeting to the Obscura. I soared deeper and deeper until the Transcindiel's lilting tune announced its presence. I grabbed hold of that tune and pulled it up with me, higher and higher until a wave of golden light had gathered around me.

Kellan's hands slid over my leather jacket and beneath my arms, lifting them to either side of me as Tiberius soared through the clear skies. I kept my palms facing down toward the ashen as we began the first sweep over the camp.

Keeping my eyes shut, I nodded, and Kellan's rough hands slid beneath my palms, and he laced his fingers between mine. My back pressed against his chest, and the tip of his nose grazed the side of my head as he took a long, slow inhale. His spark followed, and I sent that golden Transcindiel light soaring toward the ashen below, a tune of triumph and redemption eclipsing the monsters' shrieks.

Shimmers of golden light erupted below as Tiberius added his own Transcindiel power to the mix, and I blinked my eyes open. Kellan's power poured into me as we made sweep after sweep, the transformational power devouring the pirate lord's magic.

Ravenous shrieks turned to moans and cries of agony. Human cries. Elven cries. My eyes drifted closed as Tiberius took us back and forth, and I leaned into Kellan Astraeus as he kept his hands clasped around my own, our powers a healing caress to the souls below.

Time didn't exist in this place. This place of transformation, of rebirth. The wind continued to whip around us before fatigue finally stretched through me. I slumped against Kellan. His hands were around my waist as Tiberius banked hard and descended, aiming outside the gates of the camp.

"We did it," I mumbled, fighting against the claws of exhaustion.

"*You* did it," he murmured against my hair.

My feet hit the frozen ground for a mere moment before they were swept up, and Kellan cradled me in his arms. I groaned, ready to protest, when he set me down on the cliff's edge, my back against its small, rocky face. He plopped down next to me and his shoulders slumped back.

We watched silently as menders knelt next to bodies, and cries floated up from the camp. Selvina's shimmering blue Ramadiel light twined through the crowd, encircling some entirely, others sending tiny sparks to heal minor injuries.

Bayne's dark head bobbed as he moved through the camp, searching.

She was here, I'd realized, in that strange, dream-like state I'd entered moments ago above the camp.

My lips tugged up as he stopped halfway through the camp and knelt next to an emaciated, tall elf. Her dirty hair was golden and brown like the stalks of wheat. Lida's thin arms shook as she wrapped them around Bayne's neck. And those fears, those insecurities, I'd harbored all those months ago in Lotrennia. The fear of losing him... Such a small, insignificant risk amidst all that we faced. All we had yet to face, and I smiled at their reunion.

"Well damn, would you look at that." Kellan sniffed.

I shook my head, eyes still on Bayne and Lida, my grin widening.

"Getting sentimental, Astraeus?" I murmured, turning to find him staring at me.

My grin fell as my eyes landed on him. Kellan's face was pallid. His head rested against the rocky line of the cliff, dark eyes boring into mine.

Two lines of crimson dripped from his nose.

"You're bleeding," I murmured, inching closer and pulling a rag from my jacket.

His eyes followed my hand as I leaned in and paused.

The blood dripped over the soft curve of his lips, pooling between them before sliding alongside the white scar. I stared as it dropped to the cropped dark beard on his chin.

My gaze floated up to meet his.

"I will bleed for you, Bonscaíh."

# CHAPTER SIXTY-THREE

*Tynan Obscura, bringer of death. Shadows and night bend to his might.*
—Lock Scroll, the Arx.

Gentle waves lapped a lullaby outside Isla's small cabin on the *Evecta*. Honor whined as I sliced a thin strand of leather from my belt, the scent driving my thoughts to the pirate lord and his words. Why did I know his scent?

I tied the leather strand around the base of the ebony braid I'd plaited in Isla's clean hair. She sat on her cot, legs crossed and feet tucked beneath her thighs. It'd taken a day to coax her out of her bloody, sodden clothes and into a fresh set of leathers.

Wax dripped from the tip of the sole taper in the room as I tilted its flame and lit the end of a bundle of incense. The sizzling spark sent a gentle line of smoke snaking toward the ceiling. I closed my eyes and took a deep inhale of the calming peppermint.

Isla's haunted eyes remained on her hands. Her lips were drawn in a thin line. Selvina had healed her physical wounds. But the trauma of enduring it all a second time... I didn't ask her what she'd relived or if she was okay. I knew she wasn't. Just as I knew that had Dark King Daimos used the Ramadiel power on me, forced me to relive every pain inflicted on my body, I'd be far from okay.

"I'm here, Isla." I once again whispered the only words that seemed appropriate. Anything else, any questions felt prying, even the empathy in my heart seemed assumptive. She dragged her amber eyes toward me, a small bud of silver pooling beneath them.

She lifted a tentative hand to mine, and I raised my brows in question. Her throat bobbed. Her bronze skin was now free of those haunting, hand-shaped bruises. Every touch sent her reeling, spiraling back into whatever dark place had awoken inside her. Her brows pinched upward, and my hand slowly reached for hers, clasping tightly around her still-frigid fingers.

I held more than her hand in that moment. I held her heart, her friendship, the memory of the light that had disappeared from her eyes in those moments in the valley with the dark king. I held onto those memories in the Living Library and at the Awakening. I held onto strength for the both of us. For we would need it if we were to face what was to come.

She gave a weak squeeze back as a soft knock tapped on the door.

Her eyes darted behind me, and she gave a soft nod. I held on a moment longer, squeezing once more before she let go and slumped onto her bed. I draped a thick fur over her before turning to the door.

Bayne loomed in the dark hall with a taper in his hand. I

quietly closed the door as I squeezed into the small space with him. His dark brows rose in question. I pursed my lips, shaking my head, not needing to explain Isla's state. When Isla was ready for others, she'd let us know.

My hands rubbed against my face to keep my fatigue at bay. Bayne's hand gripped my forearm, and my eyes shot open. We'd yet to have more than a glimpsing moment of privacy together, and there was so much we needed to talk about. His brows narrowed as his gaze darted between my arms, something like cautious recognition flickering in his green eyes.

A twisting of shame and unease coiled its way into my chest as I followed his stare to the gilded rivers of black slithering beneath my skin, a permanent marking of my powers on full display. I wasn't sure when it had happened, when the black and gold markings on my arms stopped disappearing after the use of my powers. They were here now, and they did not leave.

He schooled his features, recovering quickly. His eyes darted back to my own. But in the span of that mere second, that momentary lapse of control, I saw it. I *felt* it. The fear. The doubt.

Bayne released his grip, tilting his head to the stairs. My stomach twisted. We had so much to talk about...so much I needed to unpack and unload. So much I needed to understand, needed to confess. Because while I cared for him, the force binding us had shifted. My feelings for him had reshaped. I made to follow when a piercing wail shot through the corridor.

My hair stood on end at the sound of Lida's torturous cry. Bayne's head snapped to the door at the end of the hall.

"Go," I breathed, wrenching the word from my lips.

Lida had been shaken, uneasy, barely willing to leave Bayne's side since her transformation. Her caramel skin had returned its normal hue, but bags sat beneath her haunted tawny eyes.

Bayne's brows pinched in apology, but I gave him a firm shake of my head. She needed him more right now.

I paused as Isla's door creaked upon pushing it open. I poked my head inside and noted the slow rise and fall of her shoulder. Her thick lashes were a dark smudge above her high cheekbones. I slowly eased the door shut when a sliver of wind gently wrapped itself around my long braid.

My heart stilled for a moment as the leather and cedar scent followed.

KELLAN's tall frame was a dark silhouette at the edge of the sea. Wind whipped off the Juniper waves, and I sucked in a sharp breath, steeling myself against its frigidness. My boots sank into inches of powdery snow that covered the sand.

"I told you not to touch my hair," I murmured as I stepped next to him, but I couldn't help the upward tug of my lips.

Kellan huffed a laugh through his nose but kept his eyes on the dark horizon and remained quiet.

"Strange to see snow on sand," I finally said, wrapping my arms around myself.

"Strange, but beautiful," he replied. "It's better than blood."

A memory tapped against my mind, and my brows furrowed, unable to place it.

"I've been thinking," he began, as he crossed his arms and turned to me.

"Congratulations," I cut in, pinching my lips between my teeth to keep from smiling.

The corner of his lips kicked up, but the smirk was half-hearted. My throat bobbed at the solemnity that had befallen him.

"I need to tell you some things, Lyvia," he continued, and his head tipped back as his gaze followed the long line of stars stretching up the sky.

"Okay," I said, tucking a stray strand of hair behind my ear.

Kellan turned back to me and rubbed a hand over his face as if he could wipe away the exhaustion.

"I know you can break the air oath," he said. "And if you wish to do so after I share this with you, I won't try to stop you, but you are someone I want to be honest with."

My brows pinched, and my chest squeezed as unease slipped into me.

"There is a reason Xenelpha held me in that cell in the Death Dunes. Why she thought I was a bigger threat," he continued. His dark eyes softened as his brows tilted up, as if long-held secrets waited cautiously beneath the surface.

I swallowed as he paused. His eyes drifted to his hands.

"You are one of the Starlings, the People of the Stars," I said for him.

Daimos had said as much. *Children of the gods*. His dark eyes sparked as they slid up to mine, and for the first time, those tiny bits of gray seemed to lighten, looking eerily similar to the stars shining above us.

As his chin dipped in confirmation, the gray flashed to silver, and I staggered back a step, fear pulsing through me.

"I'm not him," he said, holding a hand out. "I'm not an imposter. I'm not the *Messenger*." His brows pinched upward.

My powers surged as my eyes skipped between his. Those silver eyes, so similar to the Impostor, the being watching me. But Kellan... His mouth parted as his eyes searched mine.

Paralyzed, unable to move beneath his stare, I let the feeling sit, my heart banging against my ribs.

A hawk trilled nearby, and a flash of white drew my attention inland. The snowy white hawk swooped overhead and soared toward the Onyx Tower. *Nishanth*, Selvina's hawk, the one I'd seen out my window during my time at the Crystal Castle.

Kellan took a step forward, and I shook my head.

"I need to see Selvina." I tore my gaze away from the cooling silver in Kellan's eyes. His brows pinched upward as I left him on the snowy beach.

A SOFT CRACKLE popped in the fire that lined the back of the throne room of the Onyx Tower, and I breathed in the burning wood. My powers stood at attention upon entering the fortress, and my blood pumped wildly at being back in this haunted place.

Selvina's blonde-white hair was tied into an elaborate braid that rested over her shoulders as she paced in front of the dais. Her eyes frequently shot toward the man in the velvet sitting chair, his jet-black hair disheveled as he ran his hands through it, turning his sapphire eyes toward me as I approached.

There was no warmth in Aeriden's gaze. My eyes shot to Selvina, who held them without balking. How much had she told him? Had she assumed *I'd* told him what I'd done to our father? Shame and self-hatred writhed in the pit of my stomach at the thought of what she must have revealed to elicit the empty look he gave me now. I tore my gaze away as I clenched my fists, forcing them to stop shaking as I approached.

Ursa's crystal blue eyes sparkled in the light of the fire as she watched Selvina. I pulled my gaze away, finding I couldn't look at her. Not without dredging up a torrent of pain from the well of emotions I kept locked down. She looked so much like her sister Eira, like the elf who had given her life for me.

"Sacrifices had to be made," Selvina finally said, her long, blue nightgown swishing as she stopped her pacing. "And they will continue to be made."

"It didn't have to end the way it did," Aeriden gritted out. "You were all there. You could have helped her. *Helped him.*"

The musk of exhaustion that had settled on me was wiped away with a nauseating, plunging feeling.

"I *did* help her," Selvina snapped. "In more than one way." Selvina's eyes slid to the scar on my neck before returning to Aeriden. I frowned. Had *she* healed me?

"The Court of the Two Moons *pales* in comparison to the dangers of the Crystal Court," she continued, her hands bunched into fists at her sides. Selvina's white blonde brows narrowed as she spoke to Aeriden. "King Saros played the part of a good king for thousands of years. Ours was not so worried about appearances. You have *no idea* what I've had to endure. What we've *all* endured."

Selvina straightened, her face inches from Aeriden's. "She is the *Bonder*. And she would not be able to do what it takes had she not given your father the gift of mercy. He made the ultimate sacrifice. So did Eira, Ursa's sister."

Aeriden's stare landed on me, but I kept my own locked on Selvina, still unsure what role she had played in the Crystal Castle.

Selvina's eyes softened on Ursa, who blinked and slowly wiped a tear from her face.

"We've been waiting for you." Selvina stopped to place a hand on her lover's shoulder as she turned toward me again. "But you're early."

"Olienna," I frowned.

The ancient queen of Nivis currently sat in the dungeon below where we stood, two rubelline cuffs strapped to her wrists, chained to the wall. The Aeterna Bone she stole had been recovered and remained under lock and key on the *Evecta*.

"*The Sisters shield us from the Brother, and signal the coming of another,*" Selvina recited Olienna's prophecy.

"But the twin eclipse came two years early." I nodded. "And I had already harnessed the Obscura power before Odessa. Here." I flinched as Cyril's phantom touch licked up my spine.

"Yes," Selvina murmured, her lips drawing a thin line. "And then the twin eclipse occurred when you were in desperate need. How Olienna got her hands on the Celestyn Bone is beyond me, but she manipulated the moons enough for them to cross in front of the sun, triggering the spell to unlock its full well of power." Selvina crossed her arms.

"Olienna saw her opportunity. Saw you with the Transcindiel Bone in Odessa and knew if she nudged those moons across the sky, there was a chance you'd harness it."

"So, the Bellators of old somehow locked my powers? Tying them to the Sending?" I asked.

"We believe there were a number of safety measures built into separating the Bellators powers from their physical forms." Selvina nodded. "Enya's power was hidden and could only be triggered by someone of her bloodline."

My mind raced through memories, spiraling until it slammed into those moments in Enya's tomb when I'd cut my hand. And when I'd tried to pull the octahedron from that strange cage of wind between the stalactite and stalagmite, it hadn't worked at first. Only when I had reached with both hands, with my *bloody* palm... My stomach dipped. I rubbed my thumb against the small white scar at the base of my palm.

"When Dark King Daimos took control from Queen Olienna, Enya's clan, *my* clan, fled to the mountains." Ursa's crystal blue eyes locked onto me as she poured a large goblet of winter wine.

"Olienna was always power hungry, but she united the Bellators. She spent years tracking them down, preparing the world for the return of the gods whose power they belonged to.

"But what Olienna didn't know was that Lelyth, the Votruvian Bellator, had a plan of her own. She never trusted the mind-commander. And in the time it took the group to win Enya's trust, *Lelyth* won Enya's loyalty. Lelyth was a Votruvian. She had the power to move planets, to *break* planets..."

Kellan Astraeus had said as much. My mind drifted to the map I'd discovered in Enya's tomb, the continents and seas all wrong... the massive isthmus that used to exist between Sultira and Lotrennia...

Ursa nodded, reading the understanding on my face.

"Lelyth broke the continent. She destroyed what we believe to be a door, a gateway from the world they rule, to ours. But she was also Queen of the Starlings, the *People of the Stars.*" Ursa paused, cocking her head as she surveyed me. "And I think you've experienced their power...*his* power, several times now."

I swallowed against the lump forming in my throat. The thought of Lord Astraeus, of what had transpired... His secret revealed... What was his connection to those eyes that followed me? The Messenger?

"What is his power?" I asked quietly.

"It will end all or bless all. It is either our salvation or our demise," Selvina said quietly, her hand flexing as if she could feel Astraeus's touch.

I blinked. *End all or bless all...* Where had I heard that before? Selvina's next words scattered my thoughts.

"The power to give and take. It's how the original Bellators created the bones. Enya and Lelyth knew if they could store the power in an amplifier, they'd be able to hide it."

"From whom?" I whispered.

Selvina's eyes darkened. "From the Embodied. And from a young commander in the west. The Hidden Hero."

"Saros," I murmured.

"But not all the Bellators agreed on this path," Ursa continued, taking a sip of her winter wine as she rubbed the scarred place on her neck where her collar had sat. "Olienna, for one, as she was the last to find out. And—"

"Kyson," I answered, cutting her off.

Ursa nodded and cocked her head, waiting for me to continue.

"That's why there was never a Soleia Bone, right? Kyson didn't allow Lelyth to transfer his power to the bone."

"He did not," Ursa confirmed. "And it stayed hidden in his bloodline until the birth of the Ravindra twins."

"How do you know all of this?" I asked, narrowing my gaze on her. "Who are you?"

Ursa straightened, setting her goblet down.

"I am the last of the story keepers. A descendant of two Bellators, Enya and Ordell. I'm your *sobraen*."

# CHAPTER SIXTY-FOUR

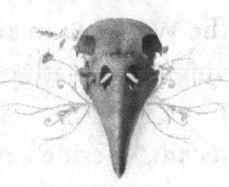

Renova and Ganmira Transcindiel, twins of the moon.
Change and rebirth may cost more than they're worth.
—Lock Scroll, the Arx.

"**M**y cousin," I croaked, as a strange and lost piece of me seemed to fit into place, answering an unspoken question asked long ago. *Who was I?*

Aeriden jerked upright, and time seemed to stop as the revelation sank into my bones. The spinning thoughts in my mind slowed, and emotions bubbled from below.

"When Enya died, her body and the Obscura Bone were secretly taken to Sultira to be hidden from the remaining monarchs of the world, from Saros and the dark king. One family, one ally in the War of Ruin, vowed to protect it. To guard its whereabouts until it was time. A family that honored Enya's caeluma with their own unique weapons. *A herd.*"

Selvina pinned her eyes on Aeriden as Usra gave him a soft nod. A small tear formed at the corner of my eye.

"The Cantor name dates to the days of the Hidden Hero in Sultira. And has had a secret line of communication with the Natara clan for over a thousand years. We believe the Lord Cantor at the time of the War of Ruin swore his allegiance to Enya. Perhaps even giving an air oath of his own to hide her body and her power."

"*For blood and for bonds,*" Aeriden murmured, running a hand through his ebony locks. His sapphire eyes softened as they slid to mine. He reached a hand to me, the gesture pulling a relieved sigh from my lips as I gripped it tightly.

"*May the sacrifice of our house never be forgotten,*" I finished for him. "The words from the Cantor Family Crest."

My mind drifted to the vision Enya had sent me last year of an ebony-haired man in black armor, kneeling before her. He'd looked at her in devastation as she gave him his final mission. Along with a vial of her blood...

"And twenty-three years ago, a baby girl was born in the mountains of Nivis, in the middle of the night," Ursa whispered, "on the first day of the year that darkness begins to outlast the light, the Autumnal Equinox."

*Maadon.*

"I was there," she continued, "I remember the night where blood soaked the snow-covered hillside of our peak. Rows and rows of nyxteria blossoms glowed in the moonslight as your mother brought you into this world. The next morning, Ganmira and Renova crossed each other, a dark shadow eclipsing the brilliance of Aelius for hours."

I stopped breathing.

"We knew you were the one. Knew you'd be the one to harness Ordell's Transcindiel power that we'd kept hidden for hundreds of years. Knew you'd find the Obscura someday. And we kept you safe, moving through the mountains. Until Daimos found us.

"Your parents had little training, and none in our clan had dared try to use the Transcindiel bone of power for a thousand years for fear of Daimos finding it, finding us. But in the chaos that ensued when he did find us, they used it together on you, transforming you from elf to human."

The truth of it crashed into my soul like lightning in the night, and I reached for my ears, their smooth, rounded curve. I closed my eyes, allowing myself to drift down into the chasm, searching for the golden light.

A warmth surrounded me as the Transcindiel power nodded in confirmation.

"Our clan was destroyed, all of them killed on sight, except for me and Eira, who they brought to the Crystal Castle to be made an example of." Ursa's eyes slid to Selvina, whose frigid nature seemed to melt.

"Ursa and Eira suffered for years. And when she was marched into the halls of the Crystal Castle by the Tauruk, I sensed our tether. That soulbinding thread," Selvina murmured, her porcelain hand pale as she squeezed Ursa's. "She told me what happened, begging for my help, but before I took over the communication, your parents had already conveyed the most important piece of information. That one small, human babe had been hidden in a wooden chest at Elpis Point. And that *Black Horse* had already come for her."

Elpis Point.

*Elp... is... Point...*

Oh, gods.

Saliva flooded my mouth. Bile rose to my throat and surged up through my lungs as I realized the intention of my father's last words to me... He'd tried to tell me about Elpis Point... Before I...

Aeriden's chair crashed to the ground as he stood, reaching for me and pulling my hair back. My stomach emptied on the dark stone floor. I wiped my chin on my sleeve before looking up to them. The two of them eyed me expectantly.

No.

I wouldn't say... I *couldn't* say it.

They were silent for several moments. Aeriden stepped back as Ursa leaned forward and put a firm hand on my shoulder.

"I know it's a lot," Ursa said quietly. "But it's not the only thing we called you here to discuss. Daimos has uncovered something. We fear he's found a new gate."

Her tone had turned dark. Her jaw clenched as raw determination entered her eyes.

"We should gather the others. And the caeluma, for this part. Speaking of caeluma..." Selvina paused. "I have a request, Bonder."

SELVINA's white hawk perched on the stone wall outside the Onyx Tower, her snowy feathers glowing a soft blue in the moonlight.

Nishanth's keen eyes tracked me as we approached, and I opened a sliver of emotion toward the bird. Aquila's trill sang from above before he swooped down and landed a few feet away. Tiberius's clomping hooves crunched in the snow behind me as he approached. Nishanth ruffled her feathers as the two caeluma surveyed her.

*She's the one*, Tiberius confirmed in my mind. *We both agree.*

And with that, I lifted an ear to the golden, lilting tune inside me and pulled a strand of Transcindiel power to the surface. My fingers spread wide as I sent the power of transformation and rebirth spearing toward the snowy hawk.

Moments later, a showering of gold and blue sparks lit up the night, forcing back the darkness that loomed off the Onyx Tower.

Selvina fell to her knees in the soft powder as Nishanth spread her massive wings, showering us in a magnificent blast of illuminated snow. The giant hawk bowed to her Bellator before sending a wave of gratitude and something like *duty* to me. I returned it with a nod before mounting my own caeluma.

ALL OF THEM, Bellator or not, human or elf, the leaders of this world, the *good* in this world, needed to see this together, I decided as the two Nivisian elves shared where we were headed.

My stomach twisted. *Drystan should be here*, I kept thinking. My friend was a Bellator. He should be here with all of us, with his brothers and sisters.

Dawn still distant, the hills of Kayj were eerily quiet as the easy beat of Nishanth, Aquila, and Tiberius's wings thumped in the distance, carrying the last of our group to the cave entrance carved into the foreboding cliff edge.

I suppressed a shudder as the sinister yellow glow pulsed from deep within the cave, only bits of it dancing against the entrance. The same yellow glow of the dark king's eyes. A sickening yellow... The yellow of disease, of pus, of dying things.

Nerissa and I flanked Bayne as we approached the entrance, followed closely by Carina and Kresida. Vulcan had remained behind with Isla. Aeriden lingered toward the back of the group, staring out at Kayj's black coastline.

Kellan slid off Tiberius's back as his hooves slammed into

the rocky footing. He stepped forward, ignoring the rest of us as he slid his gaze from Selvina, who stood at the entrance of the cave, and the chilling glow beyond. His dark brows narrowed as he surveyed the manmade gap, and his lips curved up in a snarl for the briefest moment.

Carina stepped forward, passing the rest of us, as she adjusted her glasses, frowning.

"*Vael's Lacrima*," she breathed, barely audible for the rest of us to hear.

Selvina's eyes shot to hers, scanning the small elf.

"Hopefully not," she murmured to Carina, turning toward the small group now. "For thousands of years, Kayj was merely an outpost of the Kingdom of Nivis, a small, sacred land of rocks and hills," she said, sweeping her hands out to the landscape surrounding us.

"It was a cash hold of Larimer stone," she continued, nodding toward Aeriden and the other humans gathered nearby.

A strange sort of quiet drifted toward me, as if that little bit of air connecting me to Kellan had suddenly stilled. I stole a glance at the pirate, who, even in the little blue moonslight that was left in the sky, had gone pale.

"King Saros's interest in the stone hundreds of years ago and his deal with Dark King Daimos is what brought the darkness here. Humans for stone, humans for protection, or so it went. Until the last of the Larimer was mined, and the dark king created the camps."

I couldn't tear my gaze from Kellan. His eyes were near black in the night, every trace of silver gone. His body was poised and ready for attack.

"There is no Larimer stone left in this place?" Kellan's words were clipped and hollow.

Selvina shook her head, looking to Ursa before continuing,

"But in those years of mining and digging for Larimer and gems, the slaves of Kayj stumbled upon something far more dangerous."

Bayne shifted closer to me as Selvina turned toward the entrance of the cave, motioning us forward.

"Stop." Kellan's voice was a hard, unyielding demand from behind.

My feet slowed.

Selvina turned and scowled at him, the rest of them slowly shuffling in through the cave entrance. A massive, hollowed-out space the size of Mount Telum's throne room opened to a large chasm in its center, the source of the sickening yellow glow. A stone walkway jutted through the center, a bridge connecting the two ends of the cave. And in its center was an elaborately carved archway.

My lips parted as I gazed at the sight, unease twisting my stomach. What would Drystan think of this? *He should be here.* My mind spun, continuing to drift back to my friend.

The air in the cave smelled different...like a window from distant shores had opened. Carina slowed her pace, lingering at the cave's entrance as her eyes scanned the massive space before snapping them at Kellan.

"We must figure out how to destroy this," Selvina urged, and as she stepped forward, a deafening crack echoed from the entrance of the cave.

Blades were drawn as the group whirled toward the cave opening, and yellow light flashed from the arch. Drystan's eyes were wide in shock. His silhouette was a stark contrast to the violet glow of the distant sunrise, with his black robes billowing against the wind. A terrified Evony stood next to him, her long braids trembling, as she let out a shocked yelp. Her hand was clasped in his, and she grappled at his Death Scholar robes with her other.

Drystan's crystal eyes shot to mine, and I noted the luminescent tip of a star pointing from the bit of copper skin that peeked from beneath his shirt.

My lips parted as realization hit. Drystan had harnessed the Advetis power. How did he know we were here? What was he doing here? And with Evony?

Shocked silence stretched across the cave for a heartbeat before Kellan shouted, "We need to—"

One moment, a foreign breeze stole through the archway and out of the cavern. The next, I doubled over as a spine-stiffening scream ripped through the air. Or was it my mind? The most pain-filled, gut-wrenching sound deafened me as my hands clasped over my ears, and I pinched my eyes shut. My knees barked in pain as they crashed to the stone floor.

My powers writhed deep within my chasm, but not in urgency to unleash, to defend. They awakened in a state of panic, of *raw fear*, and I barely registered the tug of wind from behind.

The screaming didn't stop. Wouldn't stop.

I moaned against the sound, my hands dropping to the floor. Wincing, I opened my eyes.

I forced my head up as the screaming continued. Selvina's slim form lay crumpled several feet from me. I scanned the cavern floor. Bodies everywhere. And that *scream*.

"*HELP!*" the woman shouted.

My stomach plunged. That was Olienna's voice.

Bayne moved. His boots slowly pressed against the floor as he staggered upright, his teeth clenched as if fighting some invisible battle. His emerald gaze found mine, dark brows angled downward, and he gave me a firm nod.

Olienna howled into our minds, a wretched, torturous, high-pitched sound that turned the insides of my stomach.

I pressed off the ground, my legs shaking as I stood, eyeing the others slowly stirring, attempting to break free of the gruesome sound.

Another deafening *crack*, and Drystan's form vanished.

My powers continued their panicky chaos as I reached for Honor. The scream peaked, the agony in Olienna's cry enough to raise the bile in my throat, when it was cut off completely.

I blinked, my grip on Honor's hilt a wet, slippery thing. Those of us in the cavern looked around, blinking through confusion when two voices echoed from beyond the elaborate archway.

"Hello, little thief," they purred.

# CHAPTER SIXTY-FIVE

---

*Sintarrak Palaega, weaver of dreams and thief of thoughts.*
*Conquer the mind, and they shall fall blind.*
*—Lock Scroll, the Arx.*

---

E very drop of blood in my body stilled. My hair stood on end as the open archway turned from nothing to a sheet of black, and two glowing blue orbs materialized in the distance.

Something deep within me stirred as the tiny orbs grew in size. The shape of two women took form as they slowly stepped into the archway, as if approaching from a long tunnel.

The women paused at the entrance, their naked bodies identical in form but polar opposites of each other. One had skin and hair as dark as the night sky. Her entire left eye was a dark space of black eternity, while her right shone blue, as bright as the moon. The other woman strode in identical form, skin paler than ashen, with hair whiter than snow. And her eyes— a white space of nothing on her right, with a shining blue iris on the left. Long, thin, pointed ears poked through their straight, waist-length hair.

The two lingered at the edge of the darkness in the arch, their blue eyes drifting to the yellow light that pulsed on the stone walkway just before them.

My power writhed below the surface, the Obscura coming to its senses, surging upward at the impending threat. But the Transcindiel...that transformative power *screamed*. It dove deeper, cowering in fear. I snaked a tendril of my consciousness down and listened. A quiet, panicky tune picked up, and the two women snapped their eyes up, their spine-stiffening gazes landing on me.

The smallest smile formed on their contrasting lips as they both cautiously slipped a foot out of the darkness onto the stone bridge. I dropped the Transcindiel and threw my entire focus into the Obscura as I raised my hands. In the split second it took to rally my power, I knew that the two creatures stepping from the Vael Lacrima were Ganmira and Renova. Two of the Embodied, back for what they thought I'd stolen from them.

*Transcindiel.* The power of the moons.

A shield formed in a hiss as the women reached two glowing hands toward me. Golden light ignited at the tips of their fingers, erupting into a flash so bright, power so great, it sucked the breath from my lungs. A gust of air whipped my head and my hands forward, as a massive shield slammed into me from behind, and another flash of brilliant white light burst forth from beside me.

Bayne's sunlight was a mere ripple among the sea storm of power coming from the twin goddesses. Were these the creatures he had seen? What he had been preparing for? Golden beams clashed with white light before devouring the Soleia magic. The Obscura pounced as Bayne was thrown back. A groan escaped his lips as he struggled to stand.

Powers chased my own. Nerissa's light scalded the air around us as Selvina speared a dark line of blue at the goddesses. Astraeus and Carina were somewhere, reinforcing our shields and sending their own blasts of wind at them, as I panted in the lilac, leather, and cedar-scented air.

*Our powers are but a* sliver *of what the Embodied hold.*

That was what Olienna had said.

Ganmira and Renova's features sharpened, their lips drawing up into soft snarls as they effortlessly blocked each attack.

My hands ached as black shadows and mist spiraled through the air. Darkness clashed with light, the Obscura an endless pit of Tynan's Hell unleashed upon them. They snarled and slashed at it, and more golden light poured from their hands.

Our powers spun in the air, and my darkness began to waver, the golden light overpowering it as two blazing red daggers soared through the storm of magic.

Kellan's first dagger found its mark in the center of the dark one's chest. Her scream ripped through the cavern, ugly and unnatural, hands closing off her magic and flying to the glowing rubelline dagger in her chest.

The white one moved quickly, almost avoiding the second dagger's edge that landed in her forearm. She bellowed in rage, the golden light disappearing as the two strange forms writhed in pain and wrath.

"Get down!"

A small part of my brain registered Kellan's command, and I dropped to the stone floor as a blast of white and blue light ripped through the wind shield and slammed into the two

Embodied, blasting them back into the darkness beyond the archway.

"Close it!" Carina screamed. "*How do we close it?!*" Her voice held a frantic edge as she poured her magic into the shield separating us from the archway.

Kellan's dark form leaped over me, and he sprinted over the bridge to the gate. His fingers traced the strange markings on the archway, his eyes frantically scanning the symbols.

Blood soaked through my leathers as my knees scraped against the stone floor. A hand gripped my shoulder. Bayne. My eyes scanned his weathered face. Blood dripped from his nose. People screamed. Smoke wafted through the vast cavern, that strange yellow light still hovering around the stone walkway and disappearing into the sheet of black in the open archway.

A vice gripped my chest. *It was still open.*

"KELLAN!" I screamed.

He snapped his face toward me as two blue orbs flashed from whatever lay beyond the arch.

Before words could form to warn him, before I could muster up the strength to shield him myself, twin ropes of golden power wrapped themselves around his arms as the hooked tip of a golden spear was thrust through the center of his chest, an agonized grunt escaping his lips.

His dark eyes locked on mine, and for a moment, everything stopped.

My breath. My blood. The noise. The smoke itself stopped its lazy wandering in the air.

Blood trickled out of his mouth as he tried to speak. Those little gray specks in his eyes were somehow brighter against the dark opening of the archway.

*Bonscaíh*, he mouthed, right as the hooked end of the spear embedded itself into his bleeding abdomen, and he was yanked through the archway and into the waiting darkness beyond.

My senses reeled as the sounds and scent of chaos seemed to flood back into the cave.

My eyes were locked on the sheet of darkness as that little tendril of wind connecting me to Astraeus weakened by the second.

Dying.

Lord Astraeus was dying. Kellan was dying.

The air oath between us began to diminish as his life force slipped away. My lips buzzed as my body began to succumb to shock, but my mind stayed focused on that black tunnel of nothing.

My hand raised toward its opening, that small bit of air twisting around my arm and out of my being as it followed the man dying at its other end. The Starling Sentry, whose power would end all or bless all.

Bonscaíh.

*Shadow*. Was that really what it meant?

I'd been given all these names. The titles spun wildly through my mind as I continued to stare at the open archway. Death Digger. Queen of Darkness. Tynan's Accepted. Bonder. Bonscaíh. Angel.

The last word dripped with irony and shame. It crashed against my intrinsic nature. Against who I knew I was in the marrow of my bones, of who I'd become. The man who'd given me that name had a firm grip on my arm as he hauled me away from the stone walkway leading to the gate.

But I was no angel.

I was *Death*.

I blinked once, a moment of clarity blossoming in the fog that had drifted into my mind as that last bit of air flitted around my fingertips.

Bayne growled as I tried to twist out of his grasp. His fingers dug into the flesh of my forearms. Thunder echoed inside the cavern, the stone floor rumbling as Tiberius stormed toward me. Without thinking, my dark shield had formed, throwing Bayne back as his fingers ripped through my skin.

My hand laced through Tiberius's mane as I launched onto his back, and we galloped toward the archway of darkness, to the *Vael Lacrima*: the Gate of the World.

*We are Death.*

Two more strides.

The stone edges of the archway disappeared as we leaped into darkness.

# CHAPTER SIXTY-SIX

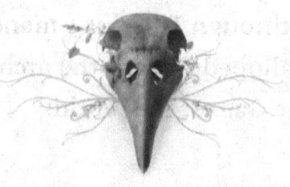

---

*Kellan.*

*—From Lyvia's list.*

---

I fell.

For how long, I didn't know.

Minutes. Hours. Centuries, perhaps.

I was alone, but I wasn't. Just like I was never really alone. Tiberius was here, but his body was gone, his mind quiet. Darkness was everywhere, a windless tunnel devouring every sound, every breath my lungs dared to make.

A single thought anchored me to my destination, my mind chanting his name repeatedly. Every memory, every touch of our wind, every breath of his scent, all of it exploding in my mind like his spark of power.

*Vael needed him,* I reminded myself.

My feet slammed onto slimy, wet ground. I stood, blinking

against the darkness in an attempt to make out my surroundings.

I took a breath.

A real breath, in my real body. I reached deep within that chasm of power before I stopped, as the eerie awareness of another's presence crept up my neck like a spider.

*I am not afraid of the dark.*

I took another breath. One... Two... And then a voice.

*"Hello, Lyvia."*

# CHAPTER SIXTY-SEVEN
## RONAN MERIK, HIGH STEWARD

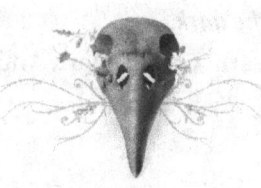

*Mount Telum. Aedrialis, Sultira.*

---

*The gates will remain closed, unlocked only upon the gathering of the eight.*
*—Unmarked Scroll. Private Library, Mount Telum.*

---

Mount Telum was chaos. The walls of Aedrialis's fortress shook, tremors reverberating throughout as soldiers and servants sprinted through rooms, bringing aid to those who had been injured during the event and cleaning up the mess it had made.

"*Vaelquake!*" people had shouted, as the deafening blast rocked from below the castle, shaking the walls of the enormous fortress and sending sculptures, priceless works of art, and chandeliers crashing to the ground.

*Owyn.*

The name pounded through my head. I'd been in the

armory on the second level when Mount Telum shook with unimaginable force.

Word from Kayj had finally reached us, Aelius's Orb pulsing brightly in the center of the table in the Grand Council room. I'd placed my hand on it, expecting to see the golden-haired, elven queen of Lotrennia when Nerissa's face peered out from the glass globe. She was in a large, dark room. Heads of various animals lined the black walls behind her, and she looked like hell. Dark circles smudged the space beneath those bright green eyes, but damn, was she beautiful.

*Please.* The word had lingered on my lips all those months ago when I'd finally told her about Galena. I'd fucked up so bad. Led her to believe at first that she was nothing to me, just a spoiled and vain young queen whom I was assigned to guard. And then when those rumors, those *sick* rumors began to circulate, Galena and I had decided it was better than them discovering the truth, so we let the repulsive gossip continue.

And I let Nis believe them too, not trusting her enough, not placing my faith in the woman I'd fought with, schemed with... The woman I'd fallen in love with. For fear it would ruin it all, put my sister in danger, put the Rising at risk. And it all went to shit anyways. I'd begged Nis's forgiveness. I'd pleaded. But Nerissa's heart was a steel chamber, her trust a vault locked deep inside. I knew that. I fucking *knew* that, even before I tracked down that soulbinding song...

Her lips, those sensuous, soft, perfect fucking lips, parted for a moment, as if surprised in seeing me, before they clamped together in a thin line, and she relayed everything that had happened on Kayj.

Daimos, dead.

Olienna, behind bars once again.

The ashen, saved, freed, and in desperate need of resources we really couldn't spare. But so many were Sultirans, were *our* people, were Owyn's people. And I'd be damned if we let them suffer a moment longer. I'd sent forty ships along with enough food and medicine to aid over a thousand refugees for two months. The revelations gave me a pounding headache days later.

*Owyn.*

I pulled my focus back. I had to get to my nephew.

My muscles warmed as I sprinted up the spiral staircase, skipping steps and dodging servants until finally I heard his cry. My heart thundered in response, adrenaline spinning through my veins as the sound registered, my body reacting the same way it did in battle.

I had known two truths when I broke down Galena's door during the siege of Mount Telum: the first, upon seeing her lifeless, frail body draped in the satin black veil, was that I would kill Saros. There would be no future where he continued to draw breath in this world.

The moment my eyes caught on the little hand poking out and gripping the matching black bundled blanket was that I belonged to the little prince. I'd be his sword. His shield. His ear. His shoulder. Anything he needed. I would kill for him. I would die for him.

And while there would be a formal ceremony pledging my fealty to the Prince of Sultira, I knew in the depths of my soul that he was my purpose. I knew I wouldn't be able to fill all roles, all those important, critical roles in his life as he prepared to lead the people of Sultira, but I'd be Uncle Ro, whether he knew it or not.

I flew past the table strewn with cryptic scrolls found in Saros's private library before swinging the door to his nursery open. I reached for him as his nursemaid hurried toward me, eyes wide as she looked around to the glass-riddled, marble floor.

"What's happened to the castle, milord?" she asked in a breath, her hands shaking as she raised a knit, black horse in front of Owyn's small face to calm him.

I paused, the new title barely registering as my eyes slid to the oval window at the opposite end of the room.

I made a soft, shushing sound as I bounced the fussing babe in my arms, my gaze fixed on the blinding, glowing red spire in the distance. I crossed the room to the window, my lips parting as my gaze landed on the nearest turret that rose opposite our tower.

"Are we safe here, milord? Should we leave?" The nursemaid's voice shook as she followed, staring at the glowing red spire.

I whirled around, palming my dagger as the door behind us swung open. Drystan's soft blue eyes were bright, and his face was wide in alarm. His black Death Scholar robes were covered in debris. Evony rushed in behind him, her face pale.

"Something's happened." Drystan's hand movements were firm.

I opened my mouth to respond when Evony rushed past him.

"He did it," she said in a rush. "He harnessed the Advetis Bone! He took us to the others!"

"Explain," I signed with one hand, bouncing Owyn as his fussing worsened.

"I felt *Lyvia*. I don't know how to explain it, other than it was the strongest pull," he began when Evony cut in.

"We were bringing the agrippa mares to the castle stables, and Drystan just grabbed his chest," she began, her blue eyes wide as she waved her hands in the air. "I touched his shoulder, and we *vanished*!"

"Something is wrong," Drystan continued. "I took us to a

cave. It had to have been Kayj. Everyone was there. Seconds after we arrived, something happened. A blast or—"

"It was like a storm," Evony blurted, shaking her head wildly. "The cave got windy, and it smelled different, and then there was this woman screaming. It was the worst sound I've ever heard... It was like she was in my head—"

"She screamed into our minds, because *I could hear her*," Drystan finished, his chest rising and falling rapidly as he looked out the window. "I don't know how, but I somehow got us back here after that. I'm worried about the others."

Drystan rubbed at his chest as his eyes focused on the glowing spire out the window.

"Is that—" Evony began.

"Drystan," I cut in, noticing the glowing tip of skin peeking through his tunic beneath his robes. "Your chest."

Drystan's head bobbed as he looked down and split his tunic. There, on his chest, sat an eight-pointed Bellator star. His copper fingers drifted over the fresh marking.

"The bone is gone," he finally signed.

"And when we returned," Evony murmured, stepping toward the window, "this happened."

"What is it?" the nursemaid asked, her voice shrill.

The four of us moved to the ornate window and gazed at the exterior of the castle we stood in. Everyone knew Mount Telum was hewn from precious white stone. King Saros IV began the construction of the castle at the start of the Second Epoch.

What the world didn't know, and what the Rising and the crew of the *Evecta* knew, was that it had been the original Saros, all along, who'd struck the deal with Dark King Daimos over a thousand years ago to get access to this precious stone. We'd never really deduced why or bothered to care.

"*It's a rubelline,*" Drystan answered. He held his hands out in front of him. His crystal blue eyes were wide in shock as he scanned his palms, attempting to access his magic and failing to do so.

The bright red glow filtered into the room, as if the walls of Mount Telum continued to grow in their strength. My eyes fell once more to the turret across the sky, to the smooth stone bricks stacked one on top of the other, the Larimer stone used to create *rubellines*.

I followed Drystan's gaze as he traced them over the walls of the castle, of the massive rubelline activated in the center of Aedrialis, Sultira's capital. A rubelline this large...

"How far do you think its power reaches?" Evony asked as she stepped forward, her eyes scanning the city below and the Juniper Sea in the distance.

What was the purpose of this? Why create a rubelline this large, construct a godsdamned castle with it? Saros had expended so much of his energy on his shields... A way to protect his kingdom. Was that what this was?

And now, in Aedrialis and perhaps farther, Mount Telum stood like a massive nullifier. King Saros had essentially wiped all magic from the Kingdom of Sultira at the start of his reign, the lost art scrubbed from our history. He'd secretly constructed his castle using a material that would nullify it, but why?

A war was coming. Weapons, Lord Astraeus had claimed. The cannon balls, the arrowheads, even the cuffs... Weapons that would be vital in a war where the magically gifted outnumbered the powerless, and Sultira was a kingdom without magic, once again.

# ACKNOWLEDGMENTS

As always, a giant, epic thank you to my husband, Michael. You are better than any book boyfriend I could read about or write. Thank you for being my biggest cheerleader, for your endless encouragement and for the countless hours you spent with the girls to give me time to write. This book wouldn't have been written without your love and support. I love you mostest.

Julia— Thank you for being the most amazing, supportive friend. I've always said your superpower is your friendship, and there is a little bit of you in the friendships and sisterhood written into this book.

Kate— Thank you for cheering me on, always being there to bounce ideas off, and for sharing in this writing and motherhood journey with me.

Emily, my incredible PA and proofreader— I can't begin to explain how grateful I am to you for your friendship, your excellent advice, your incredible organization, and your support. I'll be forever indebted to Kathryn for connecting us.

Jen, my amazing editor— Your partnership in this story has meant so much to me. Thank you for your amazing attention to detail, your encouraging comments and ideas, your excellent suggestions and for always being willing to hop on the phone with me and talk things through (even if it's just for a pep talk).

Rena, my talented cover artist— I cannot imagine anyone else working on the covers of my books. Your talent, your care for detail, your patience with my constant "what if we did this —"... I'm so grateful you've partnered with me on these books.

My alpha and beta readers (Abbe, Ana, Angela, Callie, Emily, Jacklyn, Julia, Kate, Lizzy, Marena, Natalie and Sara)— Thank you so much for taking the time to read the early drafts of this book, for your incredible feedback and ideas, and for helping me work through the sticky parts.

My street team— Thank you for taking a chance on this book and all the incredible support you've provided these past months. I still cannot believe I even have a street team. I am endlessly grateful to have connected with every one of you.

Adam and Aaron—Thank you for your incredible support of these books. So much of who I am today I owe to you both. Thank you for the countless conversations about science-fiction, fantasy, archaeology, and for just being amazing brothers.

Mom and Dad— Your support of these books and my writing has meant the world to me. Thank you for telling (literally) everyone you know about my books. Thank you for indulging in my love of horses and archaeology and always encouraging me to follow my dreams. There is no doubt in my mind that these books would not have been written if you hadn't raised me the way you did.

C & V—Thank you for inspiring me every day. I hope, some day when you're old enough, you love these stories.

My sisters— Whether we bonded through shared interests, our passions, because we were forced to sit through the same classes or live in the same dorm, through our corporate jobs or simply connected on a deeper level, thank you. I hope you all know who you are. I'd be nowhere without you, and I love you so much.

Lastly, thank you reader, for diving into this world with me. I hope you enjoyed reading this book as much as I enjoyed writing it. And I hope you're ready for more adventures in the Realm of Vael.

# ABOUT THE AUTHOR

A.M. Kay grew up in the Midwest where she spent countless hours on horseback, daydreaming about epic fantasy battles and studying archaeology. She has always had a profound love for reading and all things fantasy. She found her passion for writing in 2023 and believes it's never too late to chase your dreams.

instagram.com/authoramkay

tiktok.com/@a.m..kay

threads.com/@authoramkay

# TRIGGER WARNINGS

- Thoughts of self-hatred
- Explicit language
- Explicit sexual content (open-door romance)
- Mention/discussion of attempted rape
- PTSD
- On page gore, violence, death and threat of harm to humans and non-humans (including animals)
- Death of a parent

www.ingramcontent.com/pod-product-compliance
Lightning Source LLC
Chambersburg PA
CBHW010649100726
47901CB00012B/2490